SHANGHAIED!

"The girl died because of weightlessness. You're responsible for her death."

"It's true," the robot said, "I have caused a death. I grieve. I am grieving." The image of the face jiggled and blurred several times.

Peake finally touched Froward's arm and said, "What do you think?"

"For all I know they could be planning to gas us all to death in the passenger cabin!"

"Completely not!" the robot said unexpectedly. "I grievously regret the death of your passenger. This accident ended the he-she's probability of a long life and happiness as one of the crew."

"If you're really concerned about the safety of the passengers, return them to Earth," Froward snapped.

"It's impossible to return to Earth, even if we wished to. There is only enough fuel to go to Charon. You and the other persons must cooperate. Noncooperation will cause the deaths of persons."

CHARON'S ARK

RICK GAUGER

A Del Rey Book

BALLANTINE BOOKS • NEW YORK

A Del Rey Book
Published by Ballantine Books

Library of Congress Catalog Card Number: 87-91145

ISBN 0-345-31773-4

Manufactured in the United States of America

First Edition: August 1987

Cover Art by Don Dixon

This book is dedicated to my father,
Paul Gauger,
who read science fiction when nobody read science fiction,
and passed the love of it on to me.

Chapter One:
One of Us Is Happy

It was deep midnight over the central Pacific, and the stars clustered against the cockpit windshield. The Boeing 747-200C flew straight and steady, instruments nominal, except for one oddity: the trim indicator read full left.

The boy sitting in the captain's chair said, "I'll be honest. Nobody is ever going to pick me as most likely to succeed. In the school annual, I mean."

Copilot Froward was inclined to agree. The kid was overweight, pimply, oily-haired, and he needed a bath. Froward recognized the type: a casualty on the battlefield of puberty.

Froward wasn't doing so hot himself. His hangover had eased off, but Captain Milanovitch had warned him that he would be having a word with Froward, later. Also, he reminded himself, he hadn't noticed the trim indicator until just now. Froward had invited the kid up to the airliner's cockpit, so he felt obliged to hold up the adult end of the conversation. "You mean, only the best and brightest were picked to go on this trip?" he asked.

The kid snuffled wetly. "That's right. I don't know why they picked me. I guess it was because I was chairman of the Mesozoic Club."

"What's the Mesozoic Club?"

"It's a sort of club we have in school. Not many people belong to it. Actually, it's mainly me and a few of my friends that I went to grade school with. I liked dinosaurs. I mean I still like dinosaurs." Froward, listening through his diminishing headache, could tell that the boy was used to being laughed at on this subject.

Froward had noticed the boy in the passenger cabin. The boy

had been awake, his eyes following Froward as he passed along the darkened aisle. When he'd flown with the passenger companies, Froward sometimes talked to kids like that, kids who were too interested in their surroundings either for horseplay or sleep. When Froward was the boy's age, he'd given up dinosaurs for sex, or its pursuit.

"I like dinosaurs, too." Froward said. "I used to draw pictures of them when I was little."

"Right. Me, too. Anyway, the Mesozoic Club goes on fossil-hunting trips. Mrs. Robinelli takes us. She's our science teacher."

"That the tall lady I saw getting on the plane?"

"Yes," the boy said, snuffling. "What's this, the radar?"

"That's right. Don't you have a handkerchief?"

"No," the boy said. "Is the radar turned on so you can see other planes?"

"No, it's for spotting thunderstorms. We keep it on all the time." Froward checked the small orange and black screen out of habit. The radar was set at maximum range and showed nothing except a streak far to the west, which seemed to be moving parallel to their own course. Froward pointed it out to the boy.

"Is that another airplane?"

"It looks too big to be an aircraft," Froward said. The boy was obviously on what was, for him, his best behavior. "It's probably a cloud top or a vapor trail. What did you say your name was?"

"Charlie. Charlie Freeman." The boy sniffled again. "There, the blip is dropping behind us. Too bad this radar only looks in front of the plane. Have you ever been to Nauru?"

"I never even heard of it. Where is it?"

"It's an island in the Pacific. It's right on the equator, almost. It's where we're going. We're supposed to take another flight from Tahiti. I can't believe I'm actually going to see these places. Would you believe this is the first time I've ever been on an airplane? Isn't it weird? My mother could hardly believe it when I told her."

Peake, the flight engineer, was eavesdropping from his post behind the copilot's seat. "Let me get this straight, Charlie," he said, laughing. "This high school club you belong to. You're saying it chartered an airliner for a flight to a Pacific island? Who's paying for it, Mrs. Robinelli?"

Even in the gloom of the cockpit Froward could see the boy

trying not to give in to his enthusiasm. "No! That's what's so weird about it. The whole thing is being paid for by the government of Nauru. Did you know Nauru is the richest country in the world? Per capita, I mean?"

"No, I didn't know that," Froward said.

"I did," Peake said. "I read about it in the *National Geographic* in my dentist's office. The interior of Nauru is covered with phosphate mineral. The deposit is estimated to be worth three billion dollars, and there are only about three thousand Nauruans. They just dig it up and ship it out."

"And Nauru is paying for the trip?" Froward asked.

"It's an exchange-student thing," Charlie said. "The government of Nauru is building a museum of natural history, and we're supposed to help with the displays and stuff. After that, we're going on a 'round the world tour!"

"You're going because you're in the dinosaur club?" Peake asked.

"The Mesozoic Club," Charlie said. "I think I got to go because I'm chairman of the Mesozoic Club."

"A world tour. Why wasn't there a club like that in my high school?" Peake said.

"The only club I ever belonged to was the beer club," Froward said.

"I was president of the master baiters' society," Peake said.

Charlie guffawed and snuffled.

"So, this planeload of kids, they're the Mesozoic Club?" Peake continued.

"Oh, no," Charlie said. "I'm the only member of the Mesozoic Club on the trip. Which is too bad, since the other members would have really liked coming along. This group on the plane is honor roll students and big jocks and members of student government and all, supposed to be good at science and biology and all. B.F.D. They're too coo-ool to belong to the Mesozoic Club. That's why I said I didn't know why I got picked to go on this trip. I don't even make good grades. This radar screen looks like a video game."

Froward glanced at the small screen again. It was still clear, but occasionally a ruler-straight line flickered vertically across it.

"Like a laser beam or something," Charlie said. "I mean I

know there're no such things as laser beams, not like in the movies, I mean." He snuffled.

"That's another radar transmitter," Froward said. "Its beam is showing up on our screen."

Peake leaned over the back of the pilot's seat to see the screen. "It's odd," he said. "What other radar would there be, out here in the middle of the Pacific?"

"Maybe another plane is overtaking us in the dark," Charlie said. "What are you supposed to do when that happens?"

"That never happens," Froward said. "Each flight has its own airspace assigned to it, and each one of them stays in it."

"What if you change your mind about where you want to go?"

"If there's an emergency change of flight plan, the pilot radios the traffic controller in Hawaii and gets a new airspace assignment."

"What if you don't tell them you've changed your destination?"

"If you don't tell them, you lose your airplane driver's license and your official badge," Peake said.

The radar screen continued blank except for the flickering line, which appeared every third or fourth sweep of the 747's own beam. "I still think there's another plane catching up behind us," Charlie said.

The airliner bumped, as though it had flown through a patch of turbulence. "See, there it is," Charlie said, smirking at Peake and Froward.

Froward looked through the windshield into the dark. There was nothing to see except stars and the indistinct flash-flash, flash-flash, of the navigation lights reflecting off the window edges. "Looks like we might be getting some turbulence," he said. "I guess you'd better go back to your seat, Charlie."

"Okay," Charlie said. He struggled out of the pilot's chair and squeezed his bulk past Froward's elbow. "Thanks for letting me come up here. I really appreciate it," he said.

"Any time," Froward said, smiling briefly at him, returning to examine his dials and lights.

"So long, Charlie," Peake said.

The fat boy started moving carefully through the narrow passageway between the aircrew seats in the cockpit.

Froward flicked the switch that turned on the fasten-seatbelts sign in the passenger cabin. "Peake, do you know anything about this trim indicator? It's reading maximum left."

"That's one of the things that came up during the preflight."

"Oh," Froward said, feeling a sickly lump in his stomach. He'd been late arriving for the preflight. The latest instance of his drinking interfering with his work.

"Tell me about it."

"Milanovitch noticed it. He called one of the company technicians, we looked it over. Milanovitch decided that the indicator was off, but there was nothing wrong with the system. We got the go-ahead, and here we are."

"Hell, Peake, that's an FAA violation."

"We got the takeoff order from the chairman himself. I guess the company can't afford another flight cancellation."

The plane jounced and rolled slightly. "And Milanovitch agreed?" Froward asked.

"I guess he figured you don't get anywhere by refusing the owner of the company."

Without warning, the plane surged ahead, as though it were being pushed by a giant hand. Charlie, on his way back to the passenger cabin, had just passed the airliner's chief pilot. Arms windmilling, the fat boy was propelled straight ahead, past the stairway leading down to the main deck, into the narrow space next to the airliner's kitchen. The stewardess stood there, braced against the partition with the public address microphone in her hand. Charlie flailed into her, and they staggered together out into the passenger cabin.

The students were all awake and excited. Laughter broke out as they caught sight of the stewardess, her tight dress pulled up to her thighs, Charlie's face looking pop-eyed over her shoulder as he clung to her for balance. The stewardess regained her footing, pushed Charlie away, and pulled her dress down.

"Shame on youoo, Freeman!" one of the boys said in a loud voice. Charlie, his face scarlet, puffed down the aisle toward his seat.

"Was Captain Kirk flying the plane, Charlie?"

"Did you tell him all about your favorite video games, Charlie?"

"Sit down somewhere, Freeman; you're tipping the plane!"

"How about dinosaurs, Charlie; did you tell him about dinosaurs?"

"Charlie's a dinosaur himself—Godzilla!"

Charlie flopped into his seat and jerked his seatbelt tight.

"Ladies and gentlemen," the stewardess announced over the cabin loudspeakers. "The captain has turned on the fasten-seatbelts sign. Please bring your seats into the upright position. Please observe the no-smoking signs."

In the cockpit, Captain Milanovitch was strapping himself into his seat. "How'd that kid get in here, Jeff?" he asked Froward.

"I noticed him while I was taking my break. I asked him if he'd like to see the front office after a while, and he said yes."

"It's against company regulations to allow passengers in the cockpit."

"I didn't realize," Froward said. "We used to do it when I was working for Pan Am."

"You're not working for Pan Am anymore, Froward. This may only be TransPac Air Charters, but we don't allow passengers in the cockpit. You've read the regulations, or you should have."

"Okay, okay." Froward couldn't keep the anger out of his voice. Milanovitch was ten years younger than Froward.

"While we're on the subject, Froward, I have to tell you something. I'm going to have to report your not showing up on time for the preflight. It's the second time you've been late."

Froward's insides shrank. "Uh, look, that wasn't my fault. The preflight was started two hours earlier than scheduled, and I didn't know about it."

"You would have known about it if you'd read the bulletin board in the office—"

Froward heard himself lying abjectly. "I had a phone call. I had to go home—" He kept his hands down so Milanovitch wouldn't see them shaking.

"I'm sorry, Jeff. One of the dispatchers saw you in the airport lounge. When you finally did show up, you were so hung over you could hardly see. Look at yourself. You look like somebody's goddamn laundry bag."

"Look, George, if you report me, I'll be fired. I owe a lot of money. I got child support payments to make. I need the work."

"I don't like it any more than you do. I've covered up for you before—"

"I appreciate that—"

"I can't do it for you this time. It's irresponsible. It—"

"Who's irresponsible? You took off with a planeload of kids and a malfunctioning trim system indicator."

"I'm not going to argue with you, Froward."

Froward didn't want to argue either; he'd lost control of himself, said too much already. He could at least keep some of his phony dignity. Keep it through what was coming: unemployment again, explanations to his ex-wife. He knew someone, an old schoolmate, who was doing all right in the used car business.

The airliner dropped and recovered. Back in the passenger cabin some of the students yelped in fear. Hidden in his seat, and forgotten by his fellow students, Charlie heard a roar like muffled thunder. It seemed to come from outside the airliner. He concentrated on the noise, but was interrupted by a high, feminine voice.

"Charlie, You were up there, weren't you? Do you know what's happening?" Charlie looked up and saw Eva Wilcox peering at him through the gap between the seat backs in front of him, her wide-eyed face fringed by silky blond hair. So far as he could remember, it was the first time she had ever spoken to him.

"Yeah," he said. "The engines are on fire. We're about to crash. We're all going to die together."

"That's not true!" the girl said. The plane renewed its bouncing.

"Piss off," Charlie told her, before he could stop himself. She jerked her face out of sight. Charlie froze with trepidation, both at the motion of the airliner and what he had said to Eva, whose football-player boyfriend was sitting right beside her.

Putting it out of his mind, Charlie squirmed in his seat and pressed his nose against the window on his left, cupping his hands around his face. He stared hard, trying to make out something in the blackness outside.

Now someone was poking Charlie's shoulder with a finger like an iron rod. He pulled back from the window and saw the all-American face of Colby Dennison looming at him over the seat back.

"All right, Freeman, what'd you say to Eva?"

"When?"

"You know when, you doushbag."

"Nothing," Charlie said. "I didn't say anything to her."

The airliner bumped hard. Charlie risked turning away from Colby's hostile scrutiny. Something was going on in the darkness outside the plane. He strained to see, but it was hard to make out anything. The reflection of his own eyes seemed to be hanging a few inches beyond the window. Past that, he saw the leading edge of the airliner's wing, with the navigation lights faintly pulsing on it, and—there seemed to be something black floating in the air just above the wing. It hovered up and down weirdly, various protrusions coming out of it at odd angles. With a shock, Charlie suddenly realized that the object was part of a larger structure above it, that it reached up and up, bigger and more massive-looking the higher he looked, and it was all being extended from a vast wing-shaped something that hung over the 747 like the roof of a building!

The black thing rotated toward the side of the airliner with huge mechanical precision and opened like a grasping hand. Charlie jerked his face back from the window. Colby Dennison was still leaning over the seat back in front of Charlie. The plane was shuddering, as though it were rolling fast over bumpy pavement. Charlie realized his mouth was hanging open. He closed it.

Colby's head was joggling on his thick neck from the vibration of the plane. Several of the students were calling out in alarm. Colby glanced uncertainly around the passenger cabin, caught himself, and glared down at Charlie. "I'll see you later, Freeman," he said, and pulled out of Charlie's sight. Colby's scared, Charlie thought.

The muffled roaring from outside had taken on grinding, howling overtones. Charlie pushed his face against the window again.

Outside, the black arm was moving in steps across the airliner's wing between the passenger cabin and the inboard engine. A flat leverlike extension of the arm was opening and closing like the blade of a colossal scissors. The black thing was biting its way through the metal of the airliner's wing! Orange flame erupted, but was immediately smothered in a cloud of steam. The shorn-off wing vanished in the darkness. The cabin lurched violently. Charlie's forehead rapped the edge of the window. He caught sight of his own slack, gaping face, reflected in the outer pane. The plane dropped sickeningly, then leaped upward. The passengers screamed in chorus.

Charlie tore himself away from the window. The passenger cabin lights had mostly gone out, except for a dim few. The airliner was steady now, as though nothing had happened. He noticed that he was drooling on his chin. He wiped his sleeve across his mouth.

The stewardess stood at the forward end of the cabin under the arched ceiling, clinging to the handrail of the stairway. Her face was chalk-white under the makeup. Charlie couldn't see the other students behind their high chair backs, but he knew they were all listening for something, as the stewardess was. It came to him that he could no longer hear the hum of the plane's engines, only the muffled roaring sound, like a great waterfall in the distance. In the amazing silence, Charlie looked around him, at the airliner cabin that had disappointed him the first time he saw it: the prosaic, pastel-tinted fabric; the slick, colorful, boring magazines in the elastic pocket; the grayish-white plastic paneling; he looked at this, and a huge, inexpressible comprehension swelled inside him until he felt his chest bursting with it.

He could see the stewardess pull herself together. She raised her microphone: "Ladies and gentlemen, the fasten-seatbelts sign is still on. You will find airsickness bags in the pocket in front of you—" She stopped at the sight of Charlie leaping from his seat, his face blotched with excitement, his lank hair plastered to his forehead with perspiration.

"Listen, everybody! Listen! We've been captured by a UFO! A flying saucer!" Charlie sprayed the nearest seats with a mist of saliva.

Faces bobbed over the backs of all the seats in the passenger cabin. Charlie stopped himself in mid-yell, but no one had laughed. They were all looking at him, waiting for him to say something else.

"I'm not kidding," he added feebly.

The teacher, Mrs. Robinelli, looked at him sternly from her seat in the center of the cabin. "Charlie, this is not the time," she said.

"Charlie's gone cave," an anonymous voice said.

Charlie slid into the aisle and started toward the front of the plane. The stewardess eyed him nervously and gathered herself to stop him. "Please, it's all right," he told her. "I was only trying to make everybody laugh. So they wouldn't be scared. But I really have to go to the bathroom. Really." He held his bulging stomach and looked at her significantly.

Mrs. Robinelli, who was sitting nearby, touched the stewardess's arm and nodded. The stewardess stood aside for him.

Charlie edged past the stewardess. The lavatory was located on the opposite side of the plane from his seat. Once inside, he closed the door, braced himself over the toilet, and tried to see out the tiny window. Nothing was visible in the darkness outside the plane. He gave it up, turned around carefully in the confined space, and opened the lavatory door quietly.

The passengers were talking among themselves excitedly. The stewardess and Mrs. Robinelli were busy near the rear of the cabin. The students in the nearest row of seats pointedly looked away as Charlie emerged from the lavatory. Charlie walked quickly across the front of the cabin. Once he was past the partition next to the stairway, he was out of sight of the stewardess and the other passengers.

In the cockpit, the pilot, copilot, and flight engineer sat staring forward as though frozen in their seats. They took no notice of Charlie as he pushed his way to the front seats.

"Sir?"

Milanovitch broke out of his paralysis. "What? It's you. What're you doing here?"

"Gaw" was Charlie's only response. He'd caught sight of what the three men had been looking at. Beyond the thick glass of the windshield, an array of dim red lights hung in the darkness in front of the airliner. The lights spelled out a message:

ONE MOMENT PLEASE

After a long pause, Froward spoke. "Well, Charlie, you can see what we're up against here," he said.

"Or not see, as the case may be," Peake said.

Charlie stuttered and gobbled, then got control of himself. "I, I, I came up here to tell you what I saw through the window when all that shaking and bumping was going on. I had to sneak past the stewardess to get here."

"At this point, I would be glad of any kind of enlightenment, from any source whatsoever," Peake said.

"Quiet, Peake," Milanovitch said. "Go ahead, son."

"When I got back to my seat, I started looking out the window," Charlie said. "There was, like, a big pole or a tower outside, right beside the airplane. It was hanging down from a sort of big thing that was over the airplane. It was like a big wing. The pole sort of rotated toward the airplane, and it had a big pincers, like a pair of pliers, on the end of it. The pliers opened up and moved toward us. It looked like it was curved to fit the side of the airplane. Then I saw another machine cutting off the wing on that side of the airplane. The wing caught on fire, but the fire went out when the pole squirted something on it. It looked like a fire extinguisher. After that, everything went black outside, and I couldn't see anything else."

There was another long pause.

"I'm ready to believe anything," Peake said. "I mean, having the wings cut off goes along with what's on my board here. We've lost all generator power, oil pressure is zero, and—"

"You saw all this yourself, out of one of the cabin windows?" Milanovitch asked.

"Yes, sir," Charlie said.

"Well, I find it pretty hard to—"

Charlie interrupted hastily. "I think we've been grabbed by a, what you call, uh, you know, a UFO. That's what I saw outside the window. Now we're inside of it. Those red letters out there are for giving us instructions. About what we're supposed to do, I mean." Charlie watched himself, hardly believing he was talking about such things, seriously, with a group of adult men, and being taken almost seriously.

"Are you sure you weren't asleep, and dreaming?"

"If he was, we are too," Froward said, indicating the sign in front of the airliner with a nod of his head. The conversation halted. The silence in the airliner was unnerving.

"Dammit," Milanovitch said, "let's think about the passengers. I'm not even sure the cabin intercom is working. Peake, get back there and make sure everyone is strapped in. Tell them, uh, tell them everything's okay, that we're expecting more turbulence and so forth. Ask Lena to come see me. You stay with the passengers until she gets back."

"Roger," Peake said, getting up.

"I've got an idea," Froward said after Peake had departed. "We don't have any landing gear power or outside lights, but if we manually drop the nose gear, we could turn on the taxi light and maybe see something."

"You're sure we're not flying at three hundred knots?" Milanovitch asked.

"You see the airspeed indicator, too, don't you? It says zero. You don't hear the engines, do you? Unless we're both crazy, we're inside this kid's UFO. So . . ."

"But we won't be able to get it up again!"

"What the hell difference does that make?" said Froward, motioning with a sweep of his arm at the red lights glaring on all the instrument panels in the cockpit.

"Go ahead, turn on the taxi light," Charlie said eagerly. Without invitation he had buckled himself into the empty seat behind the pilot's position and was craning to see out the windshield past Froward and Milanovitch.

"Why not?" Froward asked.

"All right," Milanovitch said. He reached under the instrument panel and pulled a lever. A heavy jar shook the airliner.

"Nose wheel down and locked," Milanovitch said, consulting his instruments.

"Okay," Froward said. He toggled a switch, and yellow light sprang up outside.

"Shit," Froward said. Milanovitch groaned with disbelief.

There was a wall about two meters in front of the airliner. The wall was covered with cables, piping, boxes, and indefinable shapes, mostly concealed by shadows. In the center was a flat panel covered by a regular pattern of black dots, some of which were glowing to make the red letters. Charlie was disappointed, as he had been disappointed at his first sight of the airliner. What they were looking at certainly didn't impress him as being an alien starship. Instead, it looked like what is seen under the hood of an automobile, or, worse, it looked like one of the walls of the furnace room of Garfield High School in Seattle.

The stewardess arrived in the cockpit, breaking the spell. "What's going on, George? Oh, boy," she gasped, as she caught sight of the view through the windshield. She stumbled a little, catching hold of the back of Charlie's seat.

"I wanted you to see this," Milanovitch said.

"I s-see it," she said.

"How are the passengers doing?"

The stewardess straightened her back and, with a great effort, recovered her professional manner. "Okay, so far. Shaken up, but nobody hurt. Their teacher is keeping them calm."

Milanovitch gestured at the windshield. "Lena, I don't know what to say about this, except we seem to be safe for the moment. There's battery power. We may have landed somehow, but this young fellow here says he saw us get hijacked by a flying saucer. Yes, you heard me right. He says we're inside it. How should I know? Keep everyone buckled in until further notice. Yourself and the teacher included. All right?"

"All right," she said. Indicating Charlie, she said, "I suggest you keep this one in here." She left.

The sign outside changed to:

WARNING

PREPARE FOR ACCELERATION

ACCELERATION BEGINS IN 125 SECONDS

DIRECTION FORWARD

RATE 19.5 METERS SECOND

DURATION 1444 SECONDS

THANK YOU FOR YOUR COOPERATION

"Informative sonsabitches, aren't they?" said Peake, who had returned to the cockpit. The first number on the sign began to count backward.

"What's it mean?" Milanovitch asked.

"It means they don't have artificial gravity," Charlie said.

"What?" Milanovitch said.

"It also means they're going to take us away now," Charlie said. "They're warning us to get ready for, for, the blast-off. Or whatever."

"What?" Milanovitch said again.

"It's just like *This Island Earth*."

"What?"

"If that word *rate* means acceleration rate, we'll feel about two gees," said Peake.

"Wait a minute," Milanovitch said. "Aren't we going to do anything about this?"

"Sure, Captain. What did you have in mind?" Froward said.

"Well, dammit, we could pop the emergency exits and get everybody out—"

"Out where?" Froward asked.

"I mean, after we wait awhile."

"Is that what they did in *This Island Earth*?" Peake asked.

"M-more or less," Charlie said.

"Did it have a happy ending?"

"Sort of."

At that moment, the blinking number on the sign reached zero. The thundering noise from outside the plane suddenly became loud. Charlie felt the plane surge ahead smoothly. It felt the same as when the airliner had taken off from Sea-Tac International in Seattle, but it went on and on, and the acceleration increased until he felt as though he were lying on his back in the deep chair. He settled back in his seat and looked up at his knees. Still not scared, he thought.

Froward lay in his copilot's chair, looking up at the instruments, his mind rejecting one idea after another. He wanted a drink and a cigarette. The wheel and control column flopped in his hands. The airliner's pitch indicator showed plus-85; the plane was practically standing on its tail. The "duration" number on the signboard began to count down minutes. Skepticism left him. There was no way this could be any normal happening. The kid, Charlie, had to be right.

Hijacked into space. Froward believed it. In fact, he wanted to believe it. Every minute that blinked by on the alien signboard put more miles—more hundreds of miles—between him and his life, his jobs he'd had and would have, all of it. He relaxed, sank deeply into the comfortable chair with its fleece-lined upholstery. There was nothing for him to do.

Behind him, Peake thrashed in his chair, grunting with discomfort.

"You all right?" Milanovitch asked him.

"Yeah, but my chair faces sideways. I'm lying on my side."

Peake said. "I'll bet young Charlie here thinks it's a small price to pay for seeing outer space and all. Didn't you always want to be an astronaut, Charlie?"

"Y-yes," Charlie said.

"See? One of us is happy," Peake said.

Chapter Two:
Okay to Be Scared

They lay on their backs, able to move but unable to leave their seats. A muffled crash came from the passenger cabin.

Milanovitch heard it. "Something's come loose in the passenger cabin," he said.

"Maybe something from the galley," Peake answered.

"Dammit," Milanovitch said. "How long is this going to go on?"

"About twenty minutes if you can believe the sign out front."

"Then what?"

"You got me."

"You think the plane is pitched nose-up?" Milanovitch asked.

"Nope," Peake said. "We're accelerating forward, just like the sign says."

"Come on, Peake, how could we be speeding up so much?"

"How could the plane be standing on its tail?"

"How the hell would I know?"

"Charlie thinks we're being rocketed into outer space, don't you, Charlie?"

"Y-yes, sir."

"I knew it."

"What?" Milanovitch said.

"The UFO is taking us to a high orbit. That's what I think, anyway," Charlie said.

No one had any reply to this. Finally Froward said, "Go ahead, Milanovitch, ask him."

"All right, dammit, I will. Charlie, what makes you think we're being taken to a, uh, high orbit?"

"Well, I've watched shuttle launches on TV. And it doesn't

take them this long to get to orbit. And I don't think they go this fast either. And twenty minutes isn't long enough to get to the moon, or a planet, and—"

"Okay, I get the picture. I suppose you know what'll happen when we get there?"

"Take it easy, Milanovitch; it's not his fault," Froward said from the copilot's seat.

"I really don't know for sure," Charlie said. "But I think we'll probably have to dock with the mother ship. In space. We'll be in zero-gee while that's going on. Unless the aliens have artificial gravity that works in space but not on Earth. But I don't think they do. I can't really believe in artificial gravity—"

"I can't really believe I'm listening to this!"

"Take it easy, Milanovitch!"

". . . sorry!"

"What's this about a mother ship, Charlie?" Peake said.

"There's usually a mother ship. Like that TV show 'V'; there was this huge mother ship, but that had artificial gravity—"

"Never mind that, Charlie. What about the zero-gee?"

"It'll feel like we're falling, but we won't be. It'll scare the socks off—"

"That's right," Peake said. "The passengers will go crazy."

"Is the cabin intercom working, Peake?" Milanovitch asked.

"It's not. My panel shows an open circuit breaker, and I can't make it stay closed."

"I see."

"Maybe somebody should try to get back to the passenger cabin before this zero-gee happens."

"You mean, if it happens," Milanovitch said.

"No, don't try it," Froward said. "It would be like trying to climb down an elevator shaft, the way the plane is standing on its tail. We'll have to wait it out, and see what happens."

They waited. Froward noticed the rumbling noise outside the airliner had faded to inaudibility. Unable to think of anything else with which to occupy himself, he began to study the gray wall beyond the windshield. It looked like a mass of pipes and machinery, the kind of thing he'd seen all his life, but there was something odd about it. He followed one of the pipes, or conduits, or whatever it was, with his eyes. It ran from left to right, looping around boxes and other protrusions, occasionally spot-welded to the wall. That was one of the oddities. In the factories that Froward had seen pictures of, or had visited, the pipes were usually supported by brackets, not welded. That led to another discovery: Nowhere on the machinery could Froward see any screw heads, rivets, or other fastenings. Everything was welded. And there was no labeling, color-coding, or signs of any sort. Froward pointed this out to Milanovitch and Peake.

"Does that mean we're really inside a flying saucer?" Peake asked.

"It depends on what you think the inside of a flying saucer looks like," Froward said.

"Look," Peake said, "a short while ago, I was convinced we were flying over the Pacific Ocean—"

"Let's not go through it all again," Milanovitch said. "Let's try to think of something practical."

"Yes. All right," Peake said. "If nothing's changed by the time that number out there has counted down to zero, I suggest we do something."

"Okay," Milanovitch said. "When the number gets down to zero, we open one of the doors. How does that sound?"

"Fine," Peake said.

"It's your airplane," Froward said.

"Sounds good," Charlie said.

"Just leave the flying to us, Charlie," Peake said.

They waited some more, watching the duration number. When it reached 60, the lettering on the sign disappeared, to be replaced by:

> FREE FALL SOON
> YOUR CONTINUED COOPERATION
> IN THIS MATTER
> IS SINCERELY APPRECIATED

"Darth Vader will be showing up any minute now."

"Peake . . ."

"Ooop!"

It felt as though the floor of the cockpit had dropped from under them. Froward clutched the arms of his chair. He forced himself to look at the instrument panel in front of him, then out the windshield. Nothing had moved outside. The airliner continued falling and falling, but the final annihilating smash never came. Instead, a chorus of inarticulate yells and high-pitched screaming swelled in the passenger cabin, becoming louder and louder until Froward could bear the sound of it no longer.

"I'm going to the cabin!" he shouted at Milanovitch.

He punched the release button on his seatbelt and shouted in astonishment. He was floating unbelievably upward, out of his seat. He pushed himself away from the ceiling of the cockpit and got his feet on the floor, catching glimpses of Milanovitch frozen in his chair with his arms straining, his fists gripping the useless control wheel, and greasy, fish-faced Charlie staring at him. A Ticonderoga pencil extruded itself from the boy's shirt pocket and rose slowly into the air like a yellow worm.

The screaming in the passenger cabin became more terrible, a kind of yammering howl mixed with falsetto female shrieking. Froward felt as though he were trapped in a nightmare. His feet kept skating off the floor behind him. The carpet seemed to bounce up and hit him on the chin. Scrambling and thrashing, he got his feet under him and lunged at the door. He flew three feet and collided with the door face-first. Grabbing the door handle and the edge of the navigator's desk, Froward wrenched himself upright again, and pulled the door open.

A hellish sight stopped Froward halfway through the doorway. The kids were in their orderly seat rows, all of them with mouths stretched wide open so he could see into their wet throats, all screaming uncontrollably, hands clutching frantically. Froward spotted Lena Gershner, the flight attendant, clinging to the edge of the galley partition, her feet drawn up so that she floated in a fetal huddle a yard from the floor.

The sight of her steadied Froward. He blocked the screaming out of his mind. He reached the partition and pressed Gershner against it with his body.

"Lena! It's all right! It's okay!" He had to shout it into her ear. She relaxed a little and looked at him.

"We're all right, Lena," Froward said. "It's zero-gee. We aren't really falling."

Her lips moved as she answered him, but he couldn't hear her. He called into her ear, "We have to calm down these kids. Help me."

But the passengers were quieting down by themselves, per-

haps having been brought to themselves by the sight of the copilot hugging the stewardess in the front of the cabin. By the time
Froward and Gershner had gotten themselves turned around, the
screaming had stopped. There was a moment of silence, then a
rapid babble of talk began in the cabin.

Froward bellowed, "Shut up!" The talking stopped abruptly.
The air in the cabin was cluttered with drifting objects: bits of
paper, pencils, even a portable cassette player trailing its head-
phones on the end of a slowly looping wire.

Froward caught sight of a scuffle of some kind going on in the
center of the cabin. "Help her! She's choking!" a girl screamed.

Froward clambered awkwardly between the backs of the passenger seats toward the disturbance. A girl with long black hair
fought in her seat, her hair whipping around her head. Her seatmate twisted in her seat, fumbling at her. The seatbelt came
loose, and the black-haired girl rose toward the ceiling of the
cabin, her back arching, her face turning purple. A stream of
glistening brown particles gushed from her mouth and flew horri-
bly down the cabin like a swarm of insects.

"She's choking!" the other girl yelled, hitting at the buckle of
her own seatbelt.

"Stay put!" Froward told her sharply. He grabbed at the black-
haired girl but missed her. Helplessly, he sailed overhead and
collided with the rear wall of the cabin. Getting his feet against
the wall, Froward pushed off, flailed at the girl with both arms as
he passed her in midair, but only succeeded in pushing her farther
away. The girl's mute, writhing body floated toward the front of
the cabin.

Froward crashed into the washroom door in the front of the
cabin. He shouted, "Grab her, somebody!" Dozens of arms
reached up for the girl, but she was above them, rolling along the
cabin ceiling.

Lena Gershner jumped at the girl. Froward saw her shiny,
black stewardess's high-heel shoes spinning through the air.
Gershner was tumbling head over heels, but she managed to
snatch the girl's ruffled shirtfront as they soared past each other.
On a new trajectory, the two of them bounced off the ceiling. "I
got her!" Gershner yelled as she and the girl fell out of sight
between the seats.

Froward launched himself again, this time slowly and carefully. He was able to walk himself with his hands along the seat backs with his body extended behind him like a swimmer's. Gershner was on the floor, her legs wedged under the nearby seats, her arms wrapped around the girl from behind, fighting to work the girl's limp body into position. Froward arrived in time to see the stewardess's face contort as she squashed the girl's torso with rib-cracking force. A blob of vomit popped out of the girl's mouth and wobbled upward.

The girl had no pulse under her collarbone. Froward and Gershner worked on her together, mouth-to-mouth and heart pressure. Someone was sobbing in the cabin. Some talk began. Froward heard the teacher ordering silence.

Froward and Gershner sweated and worked, one hard breath and sixty cardiac compressions per minute, counting the seconds out loud. The girl had a provocatively rounded figure but seemed very young in spite of it, or maybe because of it. In order to work on her Froward had to look at her; she had pretty pale skin and long eyelashes. Her half-open eyes looked at nothing. God damn it, what a helpless and hopeless way for a child to die! Froward pushed back the thought in his mind in the way he had learned during his war year: can't think about it now.

In the corner of his eye he noticed a face. Charlie was floating overhead like a seal.

"They sent me to see what you were doing," the boy said, goggling down at the girl lying on the floor, her slack body jolting with the violence of Gershner's heart massage. "What's the matter with her?"

"She threw up and choked on it," Froward told him. It was an effort for him to speak. "We're giving her first aid. Any change up front?"

"No, sir. Except the sign now says 'stand by for sudden accelerations.' Did you feel that bump a while ago?"

"No," Froward said. "Go back to the cockpit and tell them what's happening here," he said. "And strap yourself in. Tell them I said you weren't to leave your seat again."

"Yes, sir." Charlie somersaulted deftly off the ceiling and glided neatly out of sight.

"Pay attention to what you're doing," Gershner snapped at Froward.

The nape of the girl's neck, where Froward had his hand under her thick black hair, was cold.

"Lena, maybe—"

"No! We're going to keep at it! Not quitting!" She paused and motioned for Froward to give the girl mouth-to-mouth.

Froward put his mouth over the girl's, tasting sour vomit, and blew a hard breath into her lungs. He wiped his mouth on his uniform sleeve. "Maybe someone else could take over for me, Lena. I think I should get back to the cockpit."

"I could do it," a girl said from a nearby seat. Froward glanced up and saw a curly-haired girl leaning over him. Involuntarily, his eyes met hers at close range. She looked back at him calmly from under level black eyebrows. Her eyes were clear light brown, almost yellow. In spite of her dark complexion the girl had a scattering of freckles across her nose and cheeks. "I know how to do CPR," she said. "I learned it in my swim class last week."

The airliner vibrated irregularly. "How about it, Lena?" Froward said. "Can she take over?"

"All right, my arms are tired," Gershner said. "Let her take my place. I'll do the mouth-to-mouth."

Froward instructed the girl. "Pretend you're swimming to us. Don't turn loose of your handholds, whatever you do. Keep your foot hooked under the arm of the chair. You (to the dark girl's seatmate) hang on to her belt. That's right. Come down here now. . . ." She was big and strongly built, and was dressed in a plaid Western shirt and blue jeans. She caught Froward looking at her as she lithely flowed into the cramped space on the floor of the aisle.

Lena Gershner stopped working long enough to trade places with Froward. He worked his way over the backs of the passengers' seats, incongruously hovering overhead with his legs poking stiffly out behind him. There was an awed silence in the passenger cabin; the kids were all looking at him with fright on their faces.

The space forward of the passenger area was more open, offered fewer handholds, and was therefore harder to negotiate in weightlessness. Froward's bruises from his previous acrobatics were still throbbing. He gave himself the slightest of pushes away from the corner of the galley cabinet and floated toward the cockpit door. He heard Lena furiously giving orders to the dark-haired girl: "Harder. Push harder than that! Cave her ribs in! That's right. Now do it faster...."

When he reached the airliner's cockpit, Peake and Charlie held on to Froward's legs as he crawled through the air back to his seat.

"We've been looking out of the side windows with this flashlight," Milanovitch told him. "We're in an aircraft hangar. Looks like the wings have been cut off."

"Charlie was right about that," Peake said.

"Have a look."

Froward put the flashlight and his face against the window on his side of the cockpit. Because of weightlessness, his behind refused to stick to his seat, so all he succeeded in doing at first was pushing himself away from the window. Swearing under his breath, he stopped what he was doing and laboriously rebelted himself to the seat. He jerked the straps painfully tight. Milanovitch and Peake looked on with strained faces. Charlie nodded wisely.

A couple of meters away from the window, there was a wall similar to the one in front of the airliner. Froward directed the beam of the flashlight at various machineries, cylinders, cables. None of the objects was the least bit enlightening. Ten meters below, Froward could make out part of a smooth black floor.

"The floor is interesting," Charlie said with a snuffle in Froward's ear.

"Dammit, Charlie—!" Froward barked at him, whipping a white handkerchief from his coat pocket, "—blow your nose!"

Charlie took the handkerchief and blew splashily, his eyes on Froward. He wadded up the handkerchief, wiped his chin with it, and offered it back to Froward.

"You keep it!"

"Thanks, uh . . ."

"You're welcome! Now what's so interesting about the floor?"

Charlie wavered.

Froward relented. "Look, Charlie, if you want to be taken seriously, you've got to clean up your act a little, that's all."

"I'm sorry."

"It's okay. Now, what about the floor?"

Charlie took a deep breath and launched into a complicated

exposition that boiled down to the concept that the Martians or ETs outside were loading the airliner into a mother ship of some kind and that the men in the cockpit could expect some action pretty soon. Neither Peake nor Milanovitch offered to interrupt the boy, and neither of them had anything to say after he had finished.

"What's all that got to do with the floor?" Milanovitch said.

"It's smooth. That means that something is going to be walking or rolling around on it. That means we're going to have gravity sooner or later."

"I see. Well, that's a good point, Charlie." Milanovitch addressed the other men in the cockpit: "I take it that we are all won over to the flying saucer, UFO, ET,—"

"Little green men—"

"Yes, Peake. You're all won over to that point of view now? You, too, Froward?"

"Oh, yes."

"Anything else?"

"I've been feeling the plane moving around. Up, down, sideways," Peake said.

"I feel it, too," Charlie said.

"And . . . ?" Milanovitch demanded.

"Midcourse maneuvers. By little attitude jets," Charlie said.

Milanovitch had lost his grip on the flashlight, and it was rotating in the air in front of his nose. He reached for it carefully. Another noise, like a padded door being slammed shut, came through from outside.

So gradually that it was almost unnoticeable, weight returned to the men in the cockpit, pressing them down into their seats. Outside, the red sign changed to

ACCELERATIONS COMPLETED

PLEASE REMAIN IN YOUR SEATS

THANK YOU

"I bet we're in the mother ship now. I bet we've left for our next destination, too," Charlie said.

"Or we're sitting on the ground," Milanovitch said.

"No way," Peake said.

"If this is some kind of terrorist attack, we might be letting ourselves get in deeper by not doing something about it," Milanovitch grumbled. "I think we should open a door, go outside, and have a look around."

"There might be a vacuum outside," Charlie said.

"No, that's one thing we don't have to worry about," Milanovitch said. "With no power, the air would've leaked out of here by now."

"I thought this was a pressurized cabin."

"It is, but the pressure is maintained by . . . skip it. Peake, what do you say?"

"I agree with George. Can't just sit here."

"I think we should—"

"Not you, Charlie. You stay here and keep an eye on the sign, okay? Don't move."

"All right, if you say so." Charlie shrugged elaborately. The tone of his voice and his body language made it clear that the airliner crew forwent his advice only at their serious peril.

Milanovitch ignored him. "Let's go."

In the open space between the airliner's galley and stairway, the three men found Lena Gershner and Mrs. Robinelli kneeling on the carpeted floor beside the childish, motionless figure of the girl who had choked. The two women had covered the girl with one of the airliner's blankets.

Mrs. Robinelli looked up at Milanovitch. "Whatever a-am I going to tell her parents?" she sobbed, tears streaming down her lined face from behind her glasses. Froward hadn't realized how old the teacher was.

Gershner pulled the garish blanket, with TRANSPAC AIR CHARTER in big green lettering, over the dead girl's head.

"Come on. There's nothing left to do here," she said, pulling at Mrs. Robinelli's arm. The teacher got up obediently, seeming to unfold her lanky body as she stood, dabbing at her face with a wad of tissue, and walked slowly back to the passenger cabin.

"I finally had to stop working on the girl," Gershner said. "The CPR wasn't doing any good. We brought her in here. Away from the kids." Gershner's face twisted in a kind of snarl, her teeth showing. "I couldn't bring her out of it!" she hissed. She had lost her usual ivory composure. Her heavy makeup was smeared and streaked. For a second the harsh angles in her face showed, and she looked older, her real age, not her professional age. ". . . my passenger, and I lost her!"

"It couldn't be helped, Lena," Froward said.

Gershner pulled down the skirts of her stewardess jacket and tried to push a wisp of her long ash-blond hair back into the knot on the back of her head. "What now?" she said. The wisp fell back into her face.

"We have to tell the passengers something," Milanovitch said. "Tell them we've been diverted to Hawaii. Because of bad weather. We've landed the plane at some out-of-the-way field, and we're waiting for further instructions. That's as good a story as any for the moment. For your own information, the plane is inside some kind of a big black room, like an aircraft hangar. That's all we know—"

The captain was interrupted by a shrill scream from the passenger cabin. In the cabin, one of the girls was sobbing hysterically and clambering frantically over her seatmate in an effort to get away from the window.

Gershner arrived first and blocked the girl as she started to run up the aisle. "What's the matter? What is it?" she asked, holding the girl's arms down. The girl, gasping and sobbing, couldn't reply. The other students were staring at the scene with their mouths open.

Gershner gave the girl a violent shake. "Stop that! What's the matter with you!"

"I, I saw a bug! A big bug! It was crawl-crawling over the window!" The students began to glance fearfully out of their windows.

A boy shouted from the back of the cabin: "I see something moving outside!" Now the passengers, all babbling at once, were trying to see outside. Over the noise Froward heard something else, a myriad of metallic squeakings and clickings on the skin of the airliner. His flesh crawled. He looked at Milanovitch, who was listening, scowling with perplexity.

"We have to play it straight with the kids," Froward said. "Go on, tell them what's happening."

"I don't know what's happening!"

Froward stepped to the front of the passenger cabin. "Quiet! Listen up!" he bellowed. The clang of authority in his voice made Gershner jump. The kids were bolt upright in their seats. From downstairs came the unmistakable rattle of someone or something tampering with the airliner's door latches.

"Listen up! We've been hijacked! The plane has landed! Hear that? Someone's trying to get in!"

The kids were white with fear. Froward towered over the front seats, glaring, his face stark and creased. "We're going to keep them out! You boys—you, you, and—all of you!—go downstairs with Mr. Peake. Hold the doors! Get moving!"

They jumped to obey, almost knocking Froward and Milanovitch down as they crushed past them in the narrow aisle. "Just a minute, Froward!" Milanovitch exclaimed. "The passengers can't—"

Froward outshouted him. "You girls come up here to the front of the cabin!" he shouted. "Remaining boys stay in the aisle! The arms of the seats are detachable! Use them for clubs! Lena, hand out fire extinguishers, knives, anything." Teenagers milled in the aisle, waving an assortment of weapons.

"Bash anything that doesn't look right! You with me?"

The teenagers roared an affirmative shout. A loud crash shook the airliner. A harsh, grinding rattle began in the passenger cabin. "Something's cutting through this window!" one of the boys yelled.

"You know what to do!" Froward shouted back.

One of the girls spoke up loudly. "I'm not hiding here. I want to fight, too!" Several other female voices loudly agreed.

"Fine! Women's lib!" Froward said. "All right, some of you go back to the aisle. The rest of you follow me."

Yelling and pandemonium broke out downstairs on the main deck. Froward jumped down the narrow stairway closely followed by a troop of girls. The main deck was like a gloomy tunnel, blockaded by strapped-down cargo pallets and tall aluminum containers gleaming dully in the dim illumination of the airliner's battery-powered emergency lights. Peake was running up and down the center aisle between the containers, deploying his boys along the walls.

"Someone's opening the doors!" "They're coming in!"

Froward snatched an escape axe from an opened toolbox and turned to face the nearest door. Deep inside himself he really expected to see a guerrilla with a beard and a machine gun, a terrorist wearing an Arab scarf, maybe even a toothy and eyeless alien monster, but he didn't expect the clownish thing that pulled open the door. It looked like a camera welded on top of a public mailbox, carrying a TV set in four mechanical arms. Whatever it was, it pushed itself blunderingly into the airliner while one of the arms reached down and turned a knob on the TV set.

Froward stood staring dumbfounded at the apparition. One of the boys shouldered him aside, cocked back a muscular right arm, and fired a hard forward pass at the intruder. The missile, a metal compressed-air bottle, flew unerringly into the cameralike device and smashed it to pieces. The intruder wobbled backward, teetering on the doorsill. The TV screen lit up with a picture of a human face. "Hi, there!" the face said. "Please don't—" The machine tilted over backward and vanished overboard. A booming crash, with overtones of breaking glass, sounded from the darkness.

Whoops and yells went up all over the main deck. "Yea-hey!" "All Riiight!!" "Get 'em, Colby!!"

Five of the lurching mechanical monsters invaded the airliner through the other doors. Yelling teenagers leaped out of the spaces between the cargo containers and swarmed over the intruders, flailing at them with chair arms, fire extinguishers, and other weapons. Some of the machines were pushed out of the airliner, others simply crumpled before the kids' onslaught and were beaten to fragments. More "TV sets" exploded in showers of glass on the deck.

One of the ruined machines had apparently dragged a flexible metal duct through a door; Peake was hacking at the duct with an axe. By the time Froward got to him, the engineer had severed the duct, and most of it had fallen back outside. Froward leaned out into the darkness, grabbed the door, pulled it closed, and fell backward against one of the cargo pallets. It was amazingly hot outside the airliner, and he had caught a glimpse of black floor covered with scuttling monsters. Someone was hitting his shoulder.

It was the freckled, curly-haired girl who had helped Gershner's lifesaving effort. She was holding out a thick nylon strap. "Here!" she said. "Tie the door closed with this!"

He looped one end of the strap around the door handle and began to fumble with it. The girl butted him aside with a muscular hip. "Let me do it." She expertly tied a complicated hitch

around the door handle, fastened the other end of the strap to the
nearest cargo tiedown, and tightened the whole arrangement with
a jerk. "That oughta hold it," she said.

The fight was suddenly over. The kids rose from piles of
wreckage, scattering wheels and armatures with their feet, talking
excitedly. Froward began shouting. "Get the doors closed! Uh,
just a moment. What'd you say your name was, miss?"

The tall girl with the freckles was standing nearby, coolly
rolling up the cuffs of her plaid Western shirt and shaking her
long, curly black hair out of her face. "Chela Suarez," she answered promptly.

"Show them what to do, Chela Suarez."

"You bet." The girl amazed Froward by pulling a six-inch
folding knife from her jeans. She flipped it open and began
slashing nylon straps from the nearest cargo pallets.

Under Peake's direction the passengers bustled industriously
in the gloom, sidling between the cargo containers, lashing the
doors, collecting more weapons, piling debris against the walls.
While they worked, Froward had a close look at one of the alien
robots. Alien robot is how I think of it now, he muttered to
himself.

"Looka here," an adenoidal voice said in his ear. "The alien
has a tail. It's a wire. Looks like a telephone cable. I bet that's
how the robot is controlled." A pudgy hand in a soiled cuff
pointed out the stump of a cable protruding from the side of the
machine. The severed end of the cable had frayed into dozens of
thin wires.

"Charlie, what the hell are you—"

"The, uh, captain sent me down here to tell you what happened," Charlie said. Pulling Froward's handkerchief out of his
shirt pocket, he carefully blew his nose and replaced the handkerchief. "Sir," he concluded.

"Well, what happened?"

"The stewardess, I don't know her name, and the kids up
there in the passenger cabin killed one of the aliens, too. It bored
its way through one of the windows with a sort of drill bit or rasp
it had on its stomach. It's just like this one except it's small
enough to get through the window, has more legs, and has two
lenses instead of one, and—"

"Right, anything else?"

"Oh, yeah. The sign—you know the one in front of the cock-pit?—has changed. Now it says, 'PLEASE COOPERATE MORE SIN-CERLY. DO NOT DESTROY THE WHATCHAMACALLITS.'"

"What do you mean, 'whatchamacallits'?"

"That's what it says, sir. Literally 'whatchamacallits.'"

"Well, that's—" Froward was interrupted by banging, tram-pling, and shouting.

"They're back!" "They're in the windows!"

The doors rattled violently. Worse, dozens of the windows along the sides of the main deck were bulging inward, slowly and grotesquely, like huge spitbubbles.

Charlie, jumping up and down at Froward's elbow, screeched in a cracking voice, "They're melting the windows!"

The kids were yelling and screaming on the verge of panic. Melted plastic hung from the window frames in semitransparent bags, each one stuffed with sharp-jointed little legs scrambling to get out. Froward heard Peake's hoarse shout: "Stay in your places! Stay in your places!"

Suddenly the lights along the ceiling came on, brightly illumi-nating the main deck. Froward gawked up at the lights, but there was no time to think over the new development.

The window plastic splattered inward, and clusters of black, roachlike monsters poured into the main deck. For a second they dangled on wires, legs and antennae wriggling, then they cas-caded to the deck, the ones in front being pushed through the window by more behind. They skittered around the metal deck on their smooth black shells, righted themselves, and scuttled in all directions, snapping and whirring, pincers and blades waving.

It was too much for the kids. Wailing in horror, they dropped their weapons and stampeded back toward Froward and the stair-way that led to the passenger deck.

One of the invaders scuttled across Froward's toes, trailing a thin wire behind it. Before he could stop the boy, Charlie snatched the axe from his numb fingers and chopped off the wire, nearly hitting Froward's feet.

The mechanical roach flopped on its back, revealing a set of little spinning rubber wheels. Charlie began chopping at the mat of wires laid down by the rest of the horde. More of the little monsters halted in their places. The screaming subsided. Peake, in the rear of the airliner, was already striding along the opposite side, steadily working his axe like a man cutting weeds.

The youngsters, reheartened, rushed to help. In a few minutes, all of the monsters, at least a hundred of them, were immobilized, and their metal corpses had been kicked into the spaces between the cargo containers.

Froward and Peake, shouting and shoving, got the girls and boys back into their positions. "It's okay to be scared!" Peake called out from somewhere among the cargo containers. Gasping for breath, they waited for the next attack.

Chapter Three:

Please Cooperate for Your Own Safety

They waited, but nothing happened. The brightly lit main deck looked almost normal, except for the clusters of nervous, club-wielding teenagers ranged among the cargo containers.

Milanovitch stumped down from the passenger deck. "I'm sure you noticed the lights coming on," he said. "Someone outside must've plugged a power cable into the ground power receptacle in the nose wheel well."

"Good thinking," Froward said. "The question is, who?"

"I'd like to shake his hand, whoever he is," Peake said, returning from the rear of the airliner. "That is, if he's got hands."

Milanovitch pulled Froward aside. "From now on, I'm giving the orders to the passengers."

"You bet," Froward said.

"I mean it, Froward!"

"I said yes, didn't I?"

Charlie swaggered up, interrupting the two men. "It was me who stopped the bug things," he said. The fat boy was so full of himself he could hardly breathe.

"Hero of your own science-fiction adventure, eh, Charlie?" Froward asked. He patted Charlie on the back.

"It's getting stuffy in here. Hot, too," Milanovitch said.

"Come to think of it, the machine the boys and I smashed up was dragging a kind of flexible pipe behind it," Peake said. "Could it've been a duct for an air conditioner? And did you see the TV sets the first group was carrying?"

"TV sets?" Charlie piped up.

"We'll have to close off the broken windows and clear away this mess," Milanovitch said. "Peake, get some of your kids and have them tear out some of the paneling from the bulkheads and stuff it in the—"

Charlie broke in. "Wait a minute! You mean the aliens are trying to communicate with us and you wouldn't let them?"

"Charlie, that's enough from you for the time being," Milanovitch said.

"Hold on just a second, George," Peake said. "Let's hear this first. What're you saying, Charlie?"

"The aliens are trying to communicate. That's why they have that sign out in front of the cockpit!" The fat boy was almost jumping up and down with exasperation.

"That's crazy," Milanovitch said.

"I didn't take it in at the time," Peake said, "but I think one of the TVs was showing a picture of a face."

"Damn!" Charlie said. "You should've let it come in!"

"At the time, it didn't seem like quite the thing," Peake said.

Milanovitch snorted with impatience. "That's crazy. If that's what they want, why don't they just say so?"

"Maybe they can't," Peake said. "Maybe they don't understand how to communicate. These robot things are ugly as hell, but have any of them actually hurt us?"

"They plugged the aircraft into ground power, and gave us light. That was helpful," Froward said.

"Right," Charlie said.

"All right," Milanovitch said. "What does all this mean in terms of what we do next?"

"It means the next time they try to get in, we let them in," Peake replied. "Or one of them, at least."

"No!" Milanovitch said. "We have the passengers to protect! We can't take any chances, not even one!"

"It doesn't make any difference. In the long run, we're going to have to deal with them. We can't hold out in here forever." Peake turned to Froward. "Isn't that right, Jeff?"

"Maybe."

"Let's get to work," Milanovitch said.

Peake led a group of the passengers in chopping sections of plastic paneling out of the walls and ceiling of the airliner's main deck to jam into the melted-out windows. Froward and Milanovitch went from one side of the deck to the other, peering outside with the flashlights through the airliner's little rectangular windows.

"See anything?"

"Nothing moving. We're still in a hangar of some sort."

It was beginning to get uncomfortably hot in the airliner, and the air filtering in through Peake's impromptu shutters reeked of overheated machinery and fuming plastic.

"Why is it so hot out there?" Milanovitch asked.

"We're in space, I keep telling you," Charlie said, tagging along behind the two men. "In space, the sun shines around the clock, and things never get a chance to cool off."

"You think he's right?" Milanovitch said to Froward.

"I guess."

Milanovitch told Froward to take Charlie upstairs and inform the others. Lena Gershner and Mrs. Robinelli were eager for news. Froward cut off the boy's description of the battle with the mechanical roaches before it could start.

"We've managed to hold off all attempts to board the plane," he said. "So far, it's been nothing but machines like the one you got up here. They're awful-looking, but they seem fairly helpless. We've smashed enough of them downstairs to start our own junkyard." Gershner started to reply, but he interrupted her. "I've got to check the cockpit. I'll be back in a minute. Come on, Charlie."

Froward led the boy to the cockpit. The sign out front read:

> P EASE COOPERA E MORE SINCERE Y
> DO NO DES ROY HE
> WHA CHAMACA I S

"Some of the letters are missing now," Charlie said, pointing out the obvious. Other than that, nothing new could be seen from the windows, although the nose wheel taxi light was blazing brighter than before.

"Charlie, you stay here in the cockpit and let us know if anything happens."

"Yes, sir. Can I sit in the copilot's seat?"

"Sure you can. Just don't mess with anything and stay put, okay?"

"I won't; I mean I will. The captain had me listening on the radio. Should I go on doing that?"

"Good idea. Keep your ears open, Charlie. If anyone tries to call us, you'll hear it."

"Yes, sir."

Froward returned to the passenger cabin, peeling off his uniform jacket as he went. The students were still at their defensive posts, but Froward could see them sagging with exhaustion. He looked at his watch. It was four-thirty in the morning. He drew Gershner aside. "How're they doing?"

"The only thing keeping them going is nerves," the stewardess said. "Suppose I hand out coffee, milk, and fruit juice, and let them rotate to the rest rooms."

"Yeah, do that. Are the galley refrigerators working?"

"Just like at an airport. Listen, Jeff, are we really inside a flying saucer?"

His smile was ironic. "Good heavens, Mrs. Gershner, I never thought I'd hear a question like that coming from a stable, mature person such as yourself."

"The kids have been asking me about it. Well, are we?"

He laughed humorlessly. "Something's going on, and that's the explanation that fits." He took her hand. "I suppose this means our date in Tahiti is off."

"Dammit, Jeff!" She jerked her hand away and went to the passenger cabin.

Downstairs on the main deck, Milanovitch and Peake were standing together at the foot of the stairs. Like Froward, they had removed their coats and ties. The main deck was hotter than the passenger deck.

"We've waited long enough," Milanovitch said.

"I agree," Peake said.

Froward glanced around. The teenagers, in twos and threes, were positioned at the doors and on both sides of the deck. "Anything moving out there?" he said loudly.

"No, sir." "Nothing here."

"Okay," Milanovitch said. "Let's open that door."

Froward and Peake untied the nylon strap on the door, then pulled it inward. Heat slapped their faces.

"Jesus!" Peake said. "It's like opening an oven!"

The air was almost too hot to breathe, and it stank of oil and ozone. Coughing in the fumes, the men leaned out of the door and looked around. The airliner was enclosed in a gloomy, hangarlike space. About ten meters away from the door stood a metal wall covered with inexplicable machinery. From all around came a low, throbbing rumble. It was a five-meter drop to the floor of the hangar from the main deck.

"I always forget how tall these 747s are," Peake said.

Milanovitch moved off toward the front of the airliner. Shortly he returned dragging a lightweight metal ladder. "Shall we?"

Panting in the heat, the three of them wrestled the ladder out the door and lowered it to the floor outside. The ladder was equipped with hooks that attached it securely to the doorsill.

"I'll go first, if you like," Peake said, picking up his axe.

"No, I'll go first," Froward said. "You come after me. After we're out, George, pull in the ladder and close the door."

"Wait a minute—" Milanovitch protested.

"It's too hot for arguing," Froward told him, backing out of the door and feeling for the first rung of the ladder with his foot. "You're the aircraft commander. You have to stay with the passengers and the plane. I'm the one who's been fired, so I get to play tourist. Just keep that light aimed out here."

They backed down the ladder. "One small step for a man—"

Froward laughed.

"Knock it off, Peake," Milanovitch said.

Peake closely followed Froward down the ladder. The floor was made of hard, rubbery stuff. Froward could feel the heat of it through his shoes. "Toss that light down here, please, George," he said to Milanovitch.

Froward slowly turned around, sweeping the beam of the flashlight in a circle. The fuselage of the 747 was resting in a massive, complicated cradle that held it about six feet off the floor. Its wings had been sheared off, leaving ragged metal edges, cables, and hoses slowly dripping hydraulic fluid.

"Charlie got it right," Peake said.

"Notice that crack in the floor directly under the plane?" Froward said.

"What about it?"

"It's the only seam in the floor. It's consistent with the idea that the plane was picked up by that thing"—he gestured at the cradle—"and drawn up through the floor." Froward hacked dryly. The air in the hangar was so dessicated it was making his eyes sting.

Looking beneath the belly of the airliner, Froward could see the opposite wall of the hangar. It wasn't so much a wall as a looming pile of heavy, incomprehensible machinery. The area in front of the plane was lit up by the nose wheel taxi light, but elsewhere the black floor of the hangar stretched away out of sight in the murk.

"Spooky," Peake said.

"I don't want to hear about it," Froward said.

Lying on the floor nearby was the severed end of the metal duct that Peake had cut loose from the robot that he had destroyed inside the airliner. The duct was blowing a steady stream of cool, fresh air.

"Air conditioning," Peake said. "Charlie was right about this, too."

The duct ran toward the front of the airliner. Froward started walking slowly in that direction, flashlight held out in front, Peake on his heels. Looking up, he saw the cockpit windows, with Charlie's round face blocking one of them. The red signboard hadn't changed. They moved toward the front of the airliner; Froward jumped when he noticed something moving high up on the nearest wall. He aimed the flashlight. A lens as big as a man's hand glinted at them from the gloom.

"What's that?" Peake said.

"A TV camera. It's following us as we move."

"What'll we do?"

"Ignore it."

They walked on, nervously watching in all directions. In the nose wheel well, a heavy, insulated cable hung from the ground power receptacle. The cable hadn't been plugged into the receptacle, it had been welded to it.

"I guess the Martians didn't have the right size connector, and they couldn't get in touch with the Boeing company," Peake said. Froward merely cursed.

In the wall of machinery in front of the airliner there was a smooth, recessed panel. The airliner's bulging nose had prevented them from seeing it from the cockpit. The panel was made of the same dark gray metal as everything else in view.

"That looks like some kind of a doorway," Peake said.

"Yes, it does," Froward said. As they approached, their shadows, cast on the panel by the airliner's taxi light, loomed larger and larger. Froward touched the panel tentatively. If anything, the panel was hotter than the surrounding air. It didn't yield when they pushed at it.

"Let's try sliding it to one side," Peake said. They tried to shove it to the right and left, with no results.

They stood in the light of the airliner's nose wheel, chafing their scorched hands. "Now what?" Froward said.

"Well," Peake said. "The violent approach has worked all right so far. Why don't I just whack it?"

Froward could see no advantage in caution. "Go ahead," he said.

Peake swung his axe overhead and chopped downward. The axe bounced and skidded to the floor, leaving a deep dent and a bright scratch on the panel. He wiped his hands on his shirt, pushed Froward farther back, picked up the axe, and, this time putting his whole body into the stroke, whipped the axe horizontally from the floor into the middle of the panel. The sharp steel bit into the metal with a crack like a pistol shot, followed by an ear-splitting, hissing roar.

"What the hell is that!" Froward yelled. The roar was so loud he could barely hear himself.

"It's air!" Peake shouted over his shoulder, as he struggled to pull the axe out of the panel. "It's rushing out through the hole I made! I've done it this time!" Looking genuinely frightened, he redoubled his efforts to retrieve the axe.

Suddenly, the roar died to a whistle, then a whisper. "Jeezus!" Peake said, suddenly staggering back with the axe in his hand. His voice was loud in the unexpected silence. "I thought I cut a hole in the side of the goddamn spaceship or something! Oops! Look out!"

As though the air pressure in the hangar were the only thing holding it in its frame, the panel was toppling outward. Froward leaped out of the way as it thudded on the floor.

The men stood and stared. Beyond the panel there was a narrow bridge or walkway that projected twenty paces outward into starry night, like a diving board into infinity. On the end of the walk was a cluster of cameras and telescopes on heavy mountings.

Almost involuntarily, Peake and Froward walked over the fallen panel and took a few steps outward onto the walkway Beyond, above and below the edge of the walkway, there was nothing but starry space and a crescent moon, so bright that it hurt the eye to look at it. They were standing in the middle of a huge hemisphere of glass or plastic that protruded from a black, clifflike wall.

Froward licked his lips, which were cracking in the dry heat. "Outer space. I'm really convinced now," he mumbled. "Is-is this some kind of observatory or control room?"

"It must be," Peake said. An object on the end of the catwalk the size of a shoe box whirred as it rotated to aim a lens at the two men. "Uh, there's another one of those cameras. What?"

"I didn't say anything," Froward said uneasily.

Peake grabbed Froward's arm. "I heard someone!" he whispered. They stood rigidly, ears straining.

A voice boomed behind them. "HI THERE!!"

Both men leaped into the air, whirled around. One of the large robots had rolled silently up behind them. They were trapped on the walkway.

Peake jerked his axe overhead. "Get back!" he yelled. "I'll kill!"

The robot didn't move. It was carrying one of the TV sets in its articulated, crablike arms. It reached down and adjusted knobs on the set. "HEY, CHECK IT OUT!!"

Froward and Peake looked at each other in mystification. The robot's voice rang with grandisonant heartiness. "Please follow instructions carefully! Please do not damage the things! Do not adjust your set! Yes, you, too, can travel comfortably and safely on YOUR VERY OWN SPACESHIP!!"

"It s-sounds like a goddamn game show announcer!" Peake said, sounding half-strangled.

"What's that smell?" Froward asked, his senses stretched to the limit.

"Only me," Peake moaned. "That damn thing made me pee in my pants!"

The robot suddenly rolled several meters backward, as though it had at last comprehended the threat of Peake's upraised axe. "THERE IS NOTHING TO BE AFRAID OF!!" it announced.

"Let's get off this catwalk." Froward muttered to Peake.

"I am not on the catwalk," the robot replied in a different voice.

"I was talking to, to—" Froward broke off. "Come on, Peake." The two men advanced step by step. Reassuringly, the robot trundled backward, keeping a safe distance from the two men. They reached the hangar floor and stepped off the catwalk.

"Go on, talk to it," Peake said, out of the corner of his mouth.

"Reach out, and touch someone," the robot sang. The TV set in its arms had flickered alight, and now displayed the image of a white-haired, fatherly-looking man with a mustache. The man, visible from the chest up, was wearing a conservative suit and tie. The man seemed familiar, but Froward couldn't place him.

"Reach out, and just say hi!"

"You just keep back!" Peake yelled at the robot, waving his axe.

"Take it easy," Froward said. The absurdity of the situation was taking the edge off his fright. "Ahem. Uh, who, are, you? I feel like an idiot."

"You're doing fine," Peake said under his breath.

The man on the TV said, "Take it easy. You're doing fine. There is nothing to fear. You will not be harmed. I am keeping back. 'Who am I' is an appropriate question. I am telling you. I am a representative of the crew. You are now aboard your very own spaceship. Please answer this question to the best of your ability: Do you understand me?" As the TV image spoke, its voice changed from the voice the robot had used to another one that seemed to fit the naggingly familiar face on the screen.

"Yes," Froward said. "I understand you."

"That's wonderful!" the man said. "You're taking it easy. You're doing fine."

"You hear that, Peake?" Froward said. "He's got a different voice now."

"Gaw," Peake said.

"You're perfectly right," said the man in the screen with a disarming twinkle. "I am overcoming the transmission or communication problems caused by my lack of experience in two-way conversation with you. For example, Peake peed in his or my pants. He is taking it easy. Do you understand me?"

"I guess so."

Peake whispered at Froward. "Do you realize who that is?"

"No. Stop poking me."

"It's Walter Cronkite!" Peake said.

With profound shock, Froward suddenly recognized the face on the screen. He'd been seeing it for decades on the TV news!

The image said, "No, I'm really not Waltercronkite. As you now know, I am a representative of the crew. I am using Waltercronkite's face and voice to speak to you. I and the other crewpersons have studied your way of life. We estimate that you and the other person or persons will find comfort in the face and voice of Waltercronkite, because many of your televisions have said so. We'll have this and other stories later in our program. Now this."

The familiar face was replaced by a scene, the interior of an airliner. Froward quickly noticed that it wasn't their airliner; it wasn't even a 747.

Bouncy, cheerful music began. The camera closed in on a pair of cute teenagers, two girls who were obviously professional actresses. They were discussing something animatedly, hopping up and down in their seats. The voice of an unseen announcer spoke over the music. "Many of you are asking yourselves, 'What is this big, roomy, comfortable spaceship that we're riding? And how did we get aboard?'"

"Jeezus!" Peake said. "They're showing us a commercial!"

As the announcer talked on, Froward realized that the two girls in the airliner scene were repeating the same sequence of motions over and over again. The scene was a film or tape loop cut out of a real TV commercial.

The picture switched to a 747 airliner flying in a night sky. The word *simulation* appeared at the bottom of the screen.

The announcer continued, a chuckle in his voice. "Yes, friends, we've prepared these models to show you how it was done. Our spaceship approached your airliner from behind . . ." A weird boomerang shape loomed up behind the airliner and positioned itself overhead. The boomerang was enormous, its wingspan at least ten times the 747's.

". . . the spaceship opened its twin safety doors, and, presto, you and your aircraft were welcomed aboard!"

The 747 looked like a toy under the aliens' flying wing. Telescoping mechanical arms drew it inexorably into a gaping rectangular opening in the boomerang's underside. Just before the

airliner disappeared inside, its wings fell off and tumbled away.
"My God!" Froward croaked.

Peake snickered distractedly. "Hardly reassuring, is it?" he
said. The flying wing sprouted a tail of flame, shed its wing tips,
and zoomed upward.

A bright reflection began to move over the TV screen, mask-
ing the picture. Behind them, the stars beyond the transparent
dome were slowly shifting. The dazzling moon had moved out of
sight. An even more dazzling Earth was edging into view. The
white and blue crescent was so bright Froward could no longer
see the stars. When the men faced front again, the robot hadn't
moved. Froward noticed one of the air-conditioning ducts lying
on the floor nearby, blowing cool air over the floor, dispelling the
worst of the heat and fumes.

"We apologize for the slight inconvenience that you may have
felt because of the short period of weightlessness some of you
may have noticed while we were docking with your spaceship's
big powerful engine unit. . . ." The TV screen showed the huge
boomerang wing being dwarfed in turn as it drifted up to a gray,
bulbous object that looked like nothing so much as a funnel stuck
into a watermelon. The wing backed into a slot on the side of the
watermelon, the funnel spouted ghostly blue rocket exhaust, and
the whole thing flew toward the screen.

The image changed back to the two teenagers smiling and
waving excitedly out of their seat window. "Bye-bye! Bye-bye!"
they chirped. The music swung into an upbeat finale and stopped.
The screen went blank for a moment, then the Cronkite face
reappeared.

"We hope you enjoyed our presentation," the face said, smiling paternally. "And now you are invited to return to the aircraft,
taking this air conduit and this TV set with you. They are designed to provide a healthy environment and communication inside the aircraft."

"No," Froward said.

The face on the screen froze, like a movie stopped in mid-
frame. "The spaceship can only provide environment air through
the conduit. The spaceship can only provide air for inside the
aircraft. Please cooperate for your own safety," the Cronkite
voice said.

"What safety? You've already killed one of the passengers with your goddamn cooperation!"

The image didn't move, and there was no answer for a long time. Peake shifted his grip on the axe, and Froward prepared to jump. After half a minute a different voice said, "Why did one of the passengers die?"

"She died because of weightlessness. You're responsible for her death."

After another long pause, the robot said, "It's true. I have caused a death. I grieve. I am grieving."

A minute passed in silence. The image of the face jiggled and blurred several times. Peake finally touched Froward's arm and said, "What do you think? Are they telling the truth about the air duct?"

"I don't know. This is all so crazy, I don't know what to think. For all I know they could be planning to gas us all to death in the passenger cabin!"

"Completely not!" the robot said unexpectedly. "I grievously regret the death of your passenger. This accident ended he-she's probability of a long life and happiness as one of the crew."

"None of this is relevant," Froward snapped. "If you're really concerned about the safety of the passengers, return them to Earth."

"It's impossible to return to Earth, even if we wished to. There is only enough fuel to go to Charon. You and the other persons must go to Charon. You and the other persons must cooperate."

"Why should we cooperate with hijackers?" Froward said.

"I regret that I am a hijacker. I regret the hostility and vandalism of you and the other persons. I did not anticipate vandalism. I no longer have enough whatchamacallits to perform all of the necessary functions of the spaceship; for example, providing healthy environment for persons, so that they stay alive and well while traveling to Charon. Noncooperation will cause deaths of persons."

Froward and Peake spoke at the same time. "What's Charon?" "What's a whatchamacallit?"

The robot hesitated before saying, "A whatchamacallit is a device, a unit, a machine that manipulates things. You are now speaking to me through a whatchamacallit. Charon is the English name of our-your destination. Please ask one question and wait for my response before asking another question."

"It means robot, I guess," Peake said to Froward.

"Yes, robot. This word is now in my vocabulary. Please do not destroy the robot. It's the only one remaining. Don't you know Charon?" it said.

"I never heard of it before," Froward said.

"We realized that you would need to be informed of many things," the robot said. "We have prepared many presentations for your information. They will be shown to you and the other persons in logical sequence. Now, please return to your aircraft, and install the air conduit and this TV set."

Froward felt hot, tired, and thirsty, and that he wasn't as young as he used to be. "No," he said. "Return us to Earth. If you don't, we'll smash everything in sight. How much damage can your spaceship stand? Would you like that?"

"I wouldn't like it. You would all die. You might perhaps make it impossible for us to arrive at Charon. Then we would all die."

"All right, return us to Earth!"

"I can't. You can't."

Froward waved his axe at the transparent dome. "How'd you like it if I broke your frigging observatory window!"

The alien took a moment to process this statement, then it said, "You wouldn't do that."

The machine stood, waiting for their next move. Froward turned to Peake. "He's right, I can't do it. I can't take the chance."

"Let's compromise," Peake said. "Take the air conditioner, and we'll figure something else out later."

"Very well, we'll take the air conduit," Froward said to the robot. "I warn you not to attempt to come aboard the plane. If you do, we'll wreck everything we can get our hands on."

"I-we will not attempt to come aboard the aircraft. You will wreck everything."

The two of them walked the short distance back to the door of the airliner. The hangar was illuminated by the light of the Earth streaming through the open panel. The robot rolled along behind them, carrying the TV set and dragging the air conduit and keeping its distance. When they arrived below the door, Milanovitch was watching through its window. Froward motioned at him to open up.

The door opened a crack, and the muzzle of a gun emerged, closely followed by Milanovitch's nose. "Are you all right? Is it safe?" the pilot said.

When the two of them had been helped into the airliner and given several cups of water apiece, Milanovitch explained, "After you left, I started wondering about the cargo," he said. "We opened up one of the containers, and there were all these guns and ammunition. It did wonders for morale."

"I'll bet," Peake said, looking around. "You guys look like a scene from World War Four. Pardon me while I go change my pants."

The kids grinned at Peake as he climbed the stairs to the passenger deck. "It's okay to be scared!" one of them called. They were dripping sweat and brandishing knives, axes, pistols, and a few stubby weapons that Froward recognized, with horror, as U.S. Army M79 grenade launchers.

Froward, finally able to speak, burst out, "If someone shoots off one of those grenade launchers in here, the round will explode and kill half the people on the deck!"

"Oh," Milanovitch said. "I thought they were some kind of giant shotgun. I'll have the kids unload." He turned away from Froward and shouted, "Open your guns and pull the shells out, boys! Too dangerous to leave them in." The teenagers obeyed slowly.

"Did you find out anything?" Milanovitch asked.

"We sure did," Froward said. "Before we go into that, there's an air-conditioning duct out there. Let's get it inside."

"Maybe that's not a good idea," Milanovitch said.

"They've already got us by the balls, Milanovitch. We might as well let them get us by the lungs, too." Some of the nearby teenagers laughed.

"I suppose you're right," Milanovitch said. "Go ahead."

Froward opened the door. "One of those robots came back with us, so don't get excited when you see it. We've been talking to it. It seems to be more scared of us than we are of it."

Outside the airliner, there was now enough light to see the robot's movements. The humans clustered at the remaining windows and watched as it rolled onto a small platform nested among the machinery of the hangar wall. A long, jointed arm swung the platform with the robot up to the side of the airliner, where it began to push away the plastic paneling over one of the melted-out windows. Once the opening was clear, the robot poked the duct into the main deck. "There is another air conduit for the upper deck," the robot announced in a buzzing voice. "Please allow me to install it also."

"Why not?" Milanovitch said.

"All right, go ahead," Froward said to the robot. It didn't move.

"Sometimes it seems to be a little slow on the uptake," Froward said. "I'll try using its own words: I allow you to install the second air conduit."

"Thank you," the robot said. Its platform rose up to the passenger deck. Shortly afterward the robot descended again, then rose back to the door level, this time holding the TV set. "Please accept this TV. There is a cable with the upper air conduit. Please plug in the cable. Please communicate."

"Anything to oblige," Froward said, stepping forward. As he took the TV from the robot he inadvertently touched one of the robot's claws. It was warm and oily. He set down the TV and wiped his hand on his pants. The robot pulled back to the hangar wall. He and Milanovitch quickly closed the door and strapped it shut.

Chapter Four:

They're Screwing It Up

It was stiflingly hot in the passenger cabin. Exhaustion and incredulity made the kids belligerent. "When are we going to get to see this stuff?"

"As soon as possible," Milanovitch said.

Someone else spoke up. "How do you know it's not a fake?"

"How do you know it's not a faa-aake?" Charlie mimicked from his seat, not loudly enough for the adults to hear. "A fake, my butt."

"There's no way the things we've experienced, especially the zero gee, could be faked," Milanovitch answered.

"Any asshole who's on the honor roll like you are, asshole, should know that," Charlie muttered inaudibly at the questioner.

A girl in the second row was tentatively holding up her hand. "What do they look like?" she asked timidly.

"Oooh, are they scary-looking?" Charlie piped to himself.

Froward answered. "Mr. Peake and I didn't see any of the aliens, only the robots. I think they're afraid to show themselves."

"You mustn't be frightened of what they look like, Gwynnis," Mrs. Robinelli put in. "Looks can't hurt anybody. We already know that we're stronger than they are, and they can't harm us."

Charlie snorted derisively at this.

Froward continued. "The robot said that they weren't intending to attack us. It said all they were trying to do was install these air-conditioning ducts and bring the TV sets, like this one, aboard."

Charlie spoke up loudly. "What'd the aliens tell you?

Where're they taking us? Why did they hijack us? What're the TV sets for?"

"I was about to go into that. Mr. Peake and I talked to one of the robots. It seemed scared of us and what we might do. It said we can't go back to Earth. We threatened it. Told it we would chop our way out if we had to. It told me that if we did any more damage to the, the spaceship, we would all die. It didn't say it would kill us, it said we would die from lack of air and so forth.

"As for your other questions, I didn't ask why we were hijacked. But the robot did say that we were going to someplace called Charon. I don't know where that is, or what it means."

"I do!" Charlie said.

"Charlie, why don't you just blow it out your shorts," Colby Dennison said, twisting in his seat to face Charlie. Several other students in the vicinity echoed, "Yeah, Charlie, just shut up." "What the hell do you know about anything?"

Froward reacted before any of the other adults. "That's enough! It's time for everybody to grow up! Charlie, that goes for you especially."

Resentment congealed in Charlie. He sat in sullen silence: *When all the big sports heroes and scholarship winners were chickenshit, it was me who . . .*

Colby spoke up. "I was the one who started it. I'm sorry."

"Okay, Colby, thanks. Now, Charlie, if you have something to say, something constructive, that is, let's hear it."

"Charon," Charlie said, self-conceit popping the name out of his mouth. "I know what it is. It's the moon of Pluto."

"You mean the planet Pluto?"

"Yes," Charlie said. *Any airline copilot should know that,* he added mentally.

Mrs. Robinelli spoke up. "If I'm not mistaken," she said, "one or more of the asteroids are named Charon, as well."

"Hmm. Well, to get on to your other question, Charlie, the robot gave us this TV set. Whoever is running this operation wants to talk to us through it, and explain things. Mr. Peake and I have already seen one of their little educational programs, and there are supposedly more of them. It's up to you whether you see them or not."

"What about Susan Sachs?" a boy shouted. "What about her?"

Froward hesitated, not having heard the name before.

"Susie was an accident," Chela Suarez said. "She choked. She died before the aliens tried to come inside. I was with her when it happened."

The mention of the dead girl brought a momentary silence. Then the timid girl raised her hand and said, "I don't like this. How much longer is it going to go on?"

"Yes," someone else said. "When are we going to get to Tahiti?"

The question seemed to catch Froward by surprise. "What?" he said.

"Gwynnis thinks she's watching TV," Charlie said. "Welcome to real life, Gwynnis."

Without warning, Colby Dennison shot a brawny hand through the crack between the backs of his row of seats and grabbed Charlie's shirtfront, also painfully catching a fistful of the fat boy's flesh. "Shut up! Don't say anything else!" he hissed. He threw Charlie back into his seat and withdrew his arm.

Everyone missed this muffled outburst because they were all looking expectantly at the TV screen. Milanovitch plugged in the TV cable. The screen flickered into life. The same face Froward and Peake had seen before appeared on the screen, looking benevolently out of the glass at the passengers. It was motionless, like a still photograph. "Who's that?" one of the teenagers said.

"I guess you're too young to remember Walter Cronkite," Froward said. Charlie thought he'd heard the name before.

The image began to move. "Hello," it said. "Thanks for allowing me to speak to you. This is a two-way conversation. Please answer this question to the best of your ability: Can you understand me?" The face froze back into the expression it had had when it had first appeared on the screen. Charlie noticed a small hole on the front of the set, and guessed that it concealed a camera lens.

"It's probably waiting for us to answer," Milanovitch said. "Yes," he said in a public-address manner, "we understand you. We want to ask you some questions."

"That's fine," the face said, coming back to life again with a kindly smile. "I can see and understand you, too. I am pleased to see all of you, and I'm sure that we will work well together. I'm ready to answer questions."

A boy, his face bandaged from the skirmish on the main deck, stood up in his seat. "Cut the shit!" he shouted angrily. "We want to go home! When are you going to let us go!"

"I'm cutting the shit for you right now," the face said, with an easy, warmhearted chuckle, its blue eyes twinkling with sincerity. "You can't go home, and I'm sure you're asking yourself, 'Why not?' Here's the interesting answer."

The screen went blank, then lit up again with an outer-space picture, stars against a black background. Music began. "Okay," Froward said, loud enough to be heard over the music, "this is one of the educational shows I was telling you about. Don't let it scare you."

The 'camera' panned down to reveal a black, bulbous shape forging majestically through space. It cruised past, its smooth sides featureless except for a square-ended crack from which protruded a sharp edge like a coin stuck in a slot. "I think this is a picture of the alleged spaceship, and we're in that slot," Froward said. "That little glass speck you see there might be the dome window I told you about."

The show continued without comment from the screen. The music continued, the ship moved off toward the stars, revealing a bell-shaped exhaust that was emitting a dim flame like the gas burner on a stove. Charlie, antagonisms forgotten for the moment, gaped at the screen. For the first time, he felt himself wavering. He asked himself, If I could get out of this and be at home safe, right now, just by waving a magic wand, would I do it?

As the ship moved away, the music concluded, and the Cronkite voice said, "You are seeing an actual picture of your spacecraft, as it appears at this moment. It is now taking you to the world you call Charon. The fuel this spacecraft carries is sufficient to accelerate to the very high speed needed to arrive at your destination within seventeen days. Your spacecraft is also supplied with ample air, water, and food for this period of time."

The picture changed to a profile drawing, then a cutaway, of a 747 airliner showing the passenger deck upstairs and a main deck full of square containers downstairs. An orange arrow moved along the cargo containers. "You will find food, clothing, and other supplies, which have been provided for your comfort and convenience during, and after, the trip to Charon, inside your Boeing 747-200C aircraft. These supplies were purchased and

packed in the U.S.A. for your comfort and convenience." Milanovitch swore obscenely, and was prodded for it by Mrs. Robinelli.

The picture changed again, this time showing a motion picture
of the capture of their airliner. The 747 was being overtaken from
behind by what Charlie breathlessly recognized as a gigantic flying wing. There was no commentary, but Froward said, "This is
the same show we saw when we were outside. It's how we—"

"You are now seeing the method used to bring you to your
spaceship," the voice from the TV interrupted. "This winged vehicle brought your Boeing 747-200C aircraft to your spaceship. It
is not capable of returning to the surface of the Earth."

The screen showed the airliner being engulfed by the aliens'
wing and hauled away into space. Under the image appeared the
word *simulation*. There were muted groans from the students.
"This isn't really true, is it?" someone said.

"I'm afraid it is," Milanovitch answered tiredly.

". . . For your comfort and convenience, you are being taken
to Charon, where there is an unlimited supply of air, water, and
food." The TV showed the spaceship dwindling among the stars.

After a weird glimpse of something that didn't seem to belong
to the rest of the show (a scene of happy girls waving good-bye
through an airliner window) the screen switched to a highly de-
tailed color view of the Earth from space. The size of the planet
shrank by an infinitesimal amount while Charlie studied it.

"Now we bid farewell to Earth," the announcer intoned cere-
moniously. "We see it as it now actually appears from our spacecraft. For, soon, you will be members of the crew of Charon,
with a mission to boldly go where no man has gone before. . . ."

Colby Dennison turned in his seat again, reaching for Charlie.
Charlie shrank away from him. "What do you know about this,
Freeman? Is it true? You'd better give me a straight answer."

"It's true," Charlie said. "The space part is, anyway. You
heard what the captain said about the weightlessness. I know
what he was talking about, and he was telling the truth."

"Then, why is this all so fake, the TV music, the 'Star Trek'
stuff, and all that!"

"Cut it out," Charlie whined, dodging Colby's hand. "You
think it's fake because you don't know any better. The aliens

probably learned English by watching our TV programs. They
think that's how we talk!"

Colby started to grab Charlie again, but paused to think about
what he'd been told. "You don't know everything, Freeman!" he
finally snarled.

"Science fiction," Charlie said, cowed but unable to resist the
impulse, "is my métier."

Eva Wilcox was clutching at Colby, probably the only thing
that prevented him from squashing Charlie's nose. "What'll we
do, Colby? What'll we do?" she cried, in her high-pitched voice.

Up forward, the adults were swamped with angry questions.
Milanovitch reached down and pulled the plug out of the back of
the TV set just as it seemed to be starting another presentation.
"Uh, just a minute, everyone," he said.

A discussion, in low voices, ensued among the adults.
"Should we take them outside?"

"Why not?" Froward said. "They're going to have their noses
rubbed in it some time. Now's the time."

"It's not safe," Gershner said.

"It's not safe in here either," Peake retorted.

"We need the students' voluntary cooperation," the teacher
said. "We'll get it best by letting them participate in decisions,
and by keeping them informed."

"Mrs. Robinelli is right," Milanovitch said. "We'll take the
chance."

With much noisy debate and moving about, the adults organized the teenagers and themselves into armed tour groups. Charlie kept out of the crowd, and as the others moved to the lower
deck to wait their turns, Charlie found himself being left alone on
the passenger deck. He moved to a vacant seat close to the alien
TV set.

"Charlie, don't you want to go?" Mrs. Robinelli asked him, as
she followed the last group of students down the stairway.

"No thanks, Mrs Robinelli. I'm kind of tired. I'll see it later."

The teacher stopped and looked at him. "Are you sure you're
feeling all right, Charlie? Do you want me to stay here with
you?" She was blotting the perspiration from her face with a
tissue; her iron-gray hair was sticking to her forehead.

"Oh no. I'm just not used to staying up all night, that's all."

"All right, Charlie. We'll be back shortly. And Mr. Froward will be right downstairs."

"Thanks, Mrs. Robinelli. I'll be fine after I get some sleep." The teacher descended the stairs. As soon as she was out of sight, Charlie lumbered out of his chair and reached for the TV cable on the floor.

The picture came on almost at once, a smeary pattern of colors. The TV anchorman's voice came from the speaker. "Why did you disconnect the television?" it asked.

"I didn't disconnect it," Charlie answered. "It was the other people who did it. They wanted to talk, and your show was interfering. They should be outside of the plane by now. Can you see them?" Charlie sniffed and wiped his nose on his shirt-sleeve.

"Yes. I can see them. Please do not damage the parts and equipment. It is better to remain inside the aircraft, for your comfort and convenience." Now the pattern on the screen had formed into the newscaster's face. The image's mouth was moving, although the remainder of the face was still frozen. The effect was uncanny.

"Would you like me to tell you things? Give you advice?" Charlie said.

"Your cooperation is sincerely appreciated. It is the purpose of the TV."

"Well, the first thing you should do is stop using the TV faces. Most of the time they look like zombies. They give us the creeps."

"What are zombies? What are creeps?"

Charlie staged a ghoulish laugh: "Mwoo-ha-ha-haaa . . . Zombies are the lifeless undead," he intoned hollowly. "Human beings catch a disease from zombies called the creeps."

"I understand. Zombies must be similar to ghosts. I have seen many shows about ghosts, demons, and the person Dracula. I estimate that these things are fantasies and fictions." The voice was sounding slightly more human.

"Don't be too sure," Charlie said, grinning at the screen.

The face on the screen distorted into a random pattern of stripes. "Is this a better picture?"

"It's my turn to ask questions. If you want information from me, you have to give me information, understand?"

"I understand. Conversation with you will provide me with better knowledge of English words and syntax."

"That's fine," Charlie said. He put his thumb over the little hole above the screen. "Can you see me when I do this?"

"I am unable to see you when you do this. However, I am able to see you imperfectly through one of the aircraft's windows from one of my cameras located outside. Are you inoculated against the creeps?"

"No one is inoculated against the creeps," Charlie said, removing his thumb, "and many of us are suffering from it already. That was your last free answer. Can you see the other kids downstairs?"

"I see them. We also see the grown-ups. Some of them are leaving the aircraft. That is not recommended. Some of them are approaching your spacecraft's observation facility. That is not recommended—"

"What are they doing?" Charlie asked eagerly.

"Some of them are approaching your spacecraft's observation facility. That is not recommended."

"I mean, what are they saying?"

"I-we can't interpret their body language. Many are talking simultaneously. Please observe and give me advice. Further damage to the equipment may result in failure of the mission and more deaths."

The picture changed to a view of the flight engineer, Mr. Peake, leading the stewardess, the teacher, and a group of the students past the looming nose of the airliner. In the background were the walls of packed machinery that Charlie had already seen through the airliner's windows. Charlie watched, enthralled, as the picture zoomed to follow the group through a brightly lit doorway. The colors and brightness levels on the screen adjusted. The humans became silhouettes against the glare of a huge, cratered moon that was moving smoothly past the alien window.

"Wow!" Charlie shouted. "Is that the Earth's moon?"

"Yes."

The humans in the screen were milling against one another. Some were pointing; some were hiding their eyes. The speaker of the TV set produced a babble of voices, mostly exclamations, some weeping hysterically. Charlie heard Mr. Peake's voice rising over the noise. "You don't have to stay here—you can go back to your seats when you want to—!"

Charlie's courage increased at the sight of the others' distress. He stood up in order to see the screen better. "That's what being educated does for you," he commented. "Listen, alien, can you make those kids hear my voice out there?"

"Yes."

"Oho," Charlie gloated. "But first things first. Tell me this, you alien. Why have you kidnapped us?"

The TV ignored his question. "I'm concerned about the other persons outside. Many of them are very emotional. They may harm themselves or damage the equipment, whichever occurs first."

Charlie moved his face closer to the TV screen until his nose was almost touching the glass. In the midst of so many distractions, he was becoming interested in the texture of the TV image; it was far clearer than any television he had ever seen before. It was like looking at a fine color photograph. He had a magnifying glass in his briefcase.... "Uh, would you like for me to say something to the people outside to reassure them?"

"Yes. Please do so. Your voice will be heard outside."

Charlie took a deep breath. "Youu are all doooomed!" he announced in his best horror-movie voice. He looked to see what effect he'd had on the kids, but apparently they hadn't heard him. "Oh, well," he said, "maybe it wasn't a good idea anyway—"

He was halted in midspeech by something new on the screen —a black horizontal bar that blocked most of the picture, upon which was a line of fast-moving text in white uppercase letters: I AM READING YOUR BRAIN LEAVE YOUR HEAD CLOSE TO THE SCREEN

Charlie jerked his head away from the screen, then slowly drew close to it again. His long history as a target for playground bullies had given him excellent self-control. He kept his head still.

"You're reading my brain?" he said.

The newscaster face said, "I'm sorry, but I don't understand your question. Please restate it, using different words...." Charlie missed the rest of what it said because the line of text changed to YES I AM LEARNING TO INTERPRET THE MEANING OF YOUR BRAIN ELECTROMAGNETIC EMISSIONS IT WILL NOT HARM YOU

Meanwhile the news anchorman face was looking pleasantly out at him, waiting for him to respond.

ALIEN CANNOT READ YOUR BRAIN

"Who are you?"

"I am the crew of Charon. Crew is the best English word I-we have found to describe me-us. We are those who-that control that which you call Charon." YOU MAY CALL ME THE PROCTOR

Charlie's face contorted with perplexity. He heard voices downstairs as the students began to return to the airliner. IF YOU HELP ME I WILL GIVE YOU POWER CHARON WILL BELONG TO YOU CHARON THE STARSHIP WILL BE YOURS NOW LOOK AT ONE OF THESE TWO WORDS READ ONE OF THEM IN YOUR MIND The line of text winked out, to be replaced by YES and NO.

"Wha? What kind of power?" Charlie asked. His nose was making a grease spot on the glass screen.

"I'm sorry, but I don't understand your question. Please restate it, using different words." ALIEN CANNOT READ YOUR BRAIN I WILL GIVE CONTROL OF THE POWER OF CHARON I WILL ERASE ALIEN FOR YOU YOU MAY FORCE THE OTHER PERSONS TO OBEY YOU READ YES OR NO

Charlie clenched his teeth and decided. YES, he read. YES. YES.

Talk and footsteps sounded in the stairwell. The other students were coming up to the passenger cabin. Charlie quickly reached and pulled the plug from the TV set. The screen became blank. He fell back into his seat and closed his eyes as the first students entered the passenger deck.

"What're you doing, Charlie?" one of them asked.

Charlie pretended to wake from a doze. "I crashed out for a while," he said, looking up. He realized he was panting with excitement and forced himself to stop it.

It was the girl with the curly black hair whom Charlie had seen during the battle with the alien robots, the one who had worked with Froward tying the doors shut. She was a relative newcomer to the school. Her big good looks and the way she had of studying him intimidated Charlie. The other students, made oblivious by shock and fright, were pushing roughly past her in the aisle to get to their seats. "Mind if I sit here?" she said, indicating the seat next to Charlie.

"Uh, sure. Whoever was sitting here before will probably come and make us move, though," Charlie said.

"Their mom," the girl said. "They're still down there waiting for their turn in the barrel. Besides, I can't see the TV screen very well from back there where I was sitting."

Charlie felt greatly in need of some time to think about what he had seen on the television screen, but the advances of this girl, whoever she was, were not to be resisted. "I didn't get your name yet," he said, sneaking a peek at her bosom. She had unbuttoned her plaid cowboy shirt a little lower than was customary at Garfield.

"Chela Suarez," the other said, as she sat down. "My real name's Michela, but I like to be called Chela for short. The newest kid in the class. Or, I was," she added significantly.

"What do you mean?"

Chela lowered her voice. "No more class. No more school for us." Not smiling, she showed her teeth. They were white against her dark skin, and seemed almost too large, even in her broad jaw. She seemed too strong and capable to be a schoolmate of Charlie's.

"Well," he said, somewhat nervously, "it's nice to meet somebody who understands what's going on for a change. How are the rest of them taking it?"

"Mass chickenshit," Chela said. "Now I know what they mean when they say someone's spaced out."

Charlie laughed tentatively.

"You know how to get this TV working again?" Chela asked.

"Just plug it in. I guess. You want to?"

"Damn right. I want to know about this shit, as much as I can. This the plug?"

"Yeah, I mean I think so. Turn the volume down, you know, so it won't disturb the others."

"Good idea, Charlie." Chela hopped out of her seat, stuck the cable back into its receptacle on the back of the TV set, and plopped down again, leaving Charlie with an image of perfectly rounded hips perfectly fitted into copper-riveted blue denim. ". . . see what the ETs have on their little minds," she was saying. "Where'd you say they were from? Pluto?"

"That's almost right," Charlie said. "They said Charon, the moon of Pluto."

"Yeah," Chela said. "We'll have to name them. Can't just call them ETs. The Charonians. The Charonoids."

The screen showed a swirling pattern that formed itself into a color moving picture of a giant, two-legged reptilian monster striding through heavy undergrowth, weedy trees whipping at its piston legs, broken twigs and leaves showering down, flocks of birds scattering, sunlight dappling its pebbled hide, its mouth gaping, panting, palisades of pointed ivory teeth clapping open and shut. Almost as soon as Charlie realized what was before him, the picture blinked off.

"Hey! Wait! Lemme see that again!" he exclaimed.

The screen showed the pattern of stripes. "Why did you disconnect the video again?" the news anchorman voice asked from the speaker.

"It was an accident! What was that dinosaur?!" Charlie surged out of his seat and rattled the TV set with both hands. "Answer or I'll—"

Chela grabbed the set in time to keep it from falling off the counter. "C'mon, Charlie, cool it! Jeezus Christ! They're looking at us!"

The alien voice said, "Take it easy. Please cool it. You're becoming too irrational. For your psychological welfare, the following entertainment is provided until the grown-ups supervise you." The opening bars of the "Leave It to Beaver" TV show theme music came from the set.

"Oh, crud, oh, crud!" Charlie moaned. "They've probably got thousands of old TV programs to show us."

"Keep it quiet, will you? Dang it, the least they could do is show 'Sergeant Bilko.' That was always my favorite," Chela said. "What's the matter with you, anyway?"

"It was a dinosaur!" He was trying to keep his voice down as more students returned from the main deck and the seats around them filled.

"Well, so your mom is a dinosaur. It was probably just some old movie."

"No," Charlie said authoritatively. "I have seen every dinosaur movie that has ever been made. Each one of them at least a hundred times. That wasn't any of them."

"We got other things to worry about than old movies. For instance, what do the Charonamese, the Charonese, that's it, want with us? I think the captain ought to hand out those pistols again, if you want to know what I think. The grenade launchers won't be much use until we get out of this plane, but I'll show you how to shoot all those weapons, if you want. My father's in the army; he used to take me to the firing range when we were at Fort Jackson. I'll show those Charonese some of the old ultraviolence if they want it—"

"No, it's nothing like that. The aliens aren't trying to hurt us. I think they want us to help them or do something for them."

"Like what?"

"I don't know. Maybe be part of the crew of a spaceship or something."

"Really," Chela said.

"Wouldn't you like to see outer space? Don't you realize that we're the first humans to make contact with an extraterrestrial civilization?"

"Oh, sure," Chela said. "It's just that I'll be wanting to go home after we've finished exploring the universe. That's the part I'm not so sure about."

Charlie almost blurted that he fully expected to fly his own starship back to Earth in triumph, but he managed to stop himself in time. "We don't know that," he said. "The Charonese might be planning to make some of us their ambassadors to the world. Do you realize? We might be famous! Rich! We'll be able to do whatever we want!" In spite of his efforts at self-control, Charlie snuffled with greed, his face all pudgy anticipation.

Chela looked sharply at him. "You think so?"

Before Charlie could reply, another group of students trooped up the stairs looking glum and overheated. They were followed by the adults. As before, the flight engineer, Mr. Peake, remained behind to guard the main deck. The students returned to their various seats, no one claiming the ones Charlie and Chela occupied. Captain Milanovitch noticed the TV set.

"'Leave It to Beaver'?" he said incredulously, looking at Charlie.

"I plugged it back in, and the alien said that this was for entertainment until you got back," Charlie told him.

"I see. I'm not so sure it's a good idea for you youngsters to watch this thing unless one of the adults is around."

Without waiting for Charlie's answer, Milanovitch addressed the other students. "Now you've seen everything there is to see out there. I think you'll all agree that there's nothing we can do about this situation right away, so I think it would be a good idea if you got some rest. Things might look better later on. I'm going to turn down the cabin lights. I know it's hot in here, but try to sleep. Mr. Froward, Mr. Peake, and I will be on guard, even though we don't think there's anything to be afraid of. They"—he emphasized the pronoun—"know we don't want to be disturbed." He smiled briefly, but got no response.

"Well," he concluded. "Good night, and I'll see you in the morning."

The "Beaver" episode, complete with commercials from Billings, Montana, was still going on. Milanovitch pulled the plug. "Let's leave this thing off for the time being," he said to Charlie. "If they want to tell us anything, they can wait till morning. Good night."

Milanovitch went downstairs. Froward passed him coming up the stairs and saw Charlie. "How you doing, Charlie?"

Charlie peered up at him. "Okay," he said.

"Good night, Mr. Froward," Chela said. Froward nodded at her before he remembered who she was, the girl who'd been such great help during the fracas on the main deck. Thinking this, he caught himself staring into her strange yellow eyes. He broke off, nodded at her again, and left.

His flight bag was in its locker. He opened it and took out some clothing, and found the fifth of bourbon he'd brought with him from home. He looked at it a moment, then put it back. Taking a pillow from another locker, he made his way to the cockpit, intending to sleep there until it was his turn to stand lookout downstairs. The cockpit was deserted. He switched off the overhead light, noting that all the instrument lights were still glowing, the ones on Peake's flight engineer board mostly red. Beyond the windshield, the Charonese signboard had gone blank. He peeled off his sweat-soaked uniform and changed into a fresh T-shirt and swimming trunks, and settled into the copilot's seat with the pillow.

Lena Gershner padded barefoot into the cockpit. "Hi," she said.

"Well, hello. I was just thinking about you. Where've you been hiding?"

"In the ladies'," she said. "I just had to get some of my clothes off. I suppose there's no point in adhering to the letter of the company dress code—"

"An outstanding idea," Froward said, reaching out to put an arm around her hips as she stood next to the pilot's chair. He pulled her down into his lap and slid his hands under her skirt. Her bare skin was damp with sweat, and the smell of powder rose from her loosened blouse. At first she softened and her lips opened under his, but suddenly she sat up and pushed herself away.

He laughed at her. "Okay, we'll observe the proprieties until further notice."

"It occurred to me that my ex-husband probably thinks I'm dead now."

"He's safe with his lady friend, planning how to spend your insurance money."

"No, my parents are the beneficiaries. They'll probably give away most of the money to that rip-off television evangelist they watch all the time. I wonder if they think I've gone to hell?"

"We're headed in the opposite direction," Froward said, reaching for her again. "As you must have noticed when you looked through the big window."

"I didn't look. It made me sick. Stop that."

"All right. But that's not what you said last time we were in Tokyo."

"In Tokyo, I was trying to live my life for myself. I mean I wasn't going to play the game any more. I'd been playing the good wife game, and my husband got his bookkeeper pregnant in a motel. Before that I played the good employee game and put my husband through school. Before that I played the good little daughter game and got married. That's what I was doing with you in Tokyo."

"I knew it. Why do women make love for political reasons? Not that I mind."

"It wasn't just political. I like you. Your last statement shows one of the reasons why I do. In some ways, you're very clear-sighted."

"Try this for clear sight," he said. "These Martians, or whatever they are, want us to join some kind of colonizing scheme. If that's true, they might force us to do openly what, before, we were only able to do with delicious secrecy in exotic foreign cities."

She sat stiffly in his lap, not listening to him. "I'm not doing a very good job," she said.

"Don't downgrade yourself," he said. "That girl was done for as soon as she allowed herself to throw up."

"She couldn't help herself—"

"None of us could help her either. She wasn't a child."

The amber and green lights of the useless instruments gave her face a hard outline. "We just spent an hour watching that propaganda on the television, and letting the kids watch it, too."

"The television doesn't matter. It might do some good," he said.

"You act like you don't care about it all!" she whispered fiercely. He grimaced.

"We should force the hijackers to take us back," she said.

"They say they can't take us back."

"That's what they say."

"We can't wreck their spaceship," Froward told her. "We can't risk being stranded in space and running out of air with thirty heavy-breathing teenagers—"

"There are twenty-four passengers," she snapped. "Spaceship," she muttered. She said it, a child's word, used in comic books and adventure movies, as though uttering it were a form of surrender. "All right," she said, "take a hostage. You and George and some of those football players could do it."

Froward grinned at her in the dark. "I'm way ahead of you," he said. "The problem is to make them come out in person."

"They seem to be very eager to talk to us. Try wrecking their cameras and speakers—"

"I'm sure if Charlie were here, he would remind us about that scene in *2001* where the computer was reading their lips through the window." He rummaged in her clothing.

She clutched at him. "I just don't want us to lose our momentum, all right?"

"I won't," he said. His hands were cool, his long fingers kneading her flesh.

She panted and sagged against him, then caught herself. "No —stop that. Not here. Not now."

"Okay." He lifted her out of his lap, his big hands grasping her thighs and waist hard, making her gasp. "One thing," he said to her out of the darkness.

"What?"

"You don't know what I care about," he said. After a while, they slept, he in his copilot's chair, she in the engineer's.

Back in the passenger cabin, Charlie lay awake, trying not to be uncomfortable about Chela's musky, unmistakably female presence in the next seat. He forced himself to think about what he'd seen on the Charonese television.

What was this Proctor, that made the line of text on the screen? Was it really reading his mind? And it had referred to the other presence, the one represented by the news anchorman, as "alien." Probably that was because Charlie had called it "you alien" when he had been quizzing it beforehand. The Charonese didn't seem to be aware of the Proctor's presence, even when both were using the same channel of communication.

Chela sat up in her seat, interrupting Charlie's musing. He lay still, his eyes closed, keeping his breathing even. Through his eyelashes he saw the girl stretch and push back her thick black hair. She reached behind herself and undid her bra strap through her thin shirt. She wriggled her shoulders, scratched her back thoroughly, and lay back with a moan of pleasure. In a moment she was snoring softly.

Charlie was thoroughly rattled by Chela's display of sensuousness, but he didn't stir. Okay, get back to business, he told himself.

Maybe there was some kind of mutiny or subversion going on among the aliens. In the dark, Charlie narrowed his eyes and nodded to himself dramatically. Maybe the Charonese were screwing up, not doing a good enough job to suit the Proctor. Frankly, Charlie thought complacently, the Charonese *were* screwing it up. If they really wanted the help of the humans, they sure were going about it in the wrong way, scaring us to death, letting us destroy all those robots.

And the humans. Charlie thought of them that way, as if he

weren't one of them. He almost wasn't. They were stuck in their rut of authority and success. When things got a little unusual, like now, they couldn't cope. They were screwing up, too. Fighting the Charonese, as though being given a free ride on an alien spaceship were some sort of an inconvenience. An interruption in their careers (college, good jobs, being pretty) instead of the greatest opportunity that anyone, anyone . . .

The Proctor thought Charlie was an extraordinary person, who deserved an extraordinary reward, "power over Charon." Maybe it thought Charlie would do the job right, and not screw it up. Especially if he were given the power to "force the other persons to obey."

Force the other persons to obey. Chela, asleep, slumped against him a little. He could feel the body heat radiating from her.

Charlie, cynicism gone, admitted that he had often thought this of himself. He had often thought he was an extraordinary, a superior, person. Other people, put off by his personal peculiarities, which he couldn't help, had failed to see his superior grasp of things. They were all wrong, as usual, only this time, they were going to miss out. The Proctor was ready to rely on Charlie, not them. His heart thumped with excitement. He would have to force himself to go to sleep, even though he'd just been through the longest day of his life. He needed his rest. He wasn't going to screw up.

Chapter Five:
Bullshit, Said Charlie

On the morning of the first day, Charlie woke up with a ravenous appetite for shredded wheat with col milk and lots of sugar, and the knowledge that he couldn't get it.

Everyone listlessly watched the stewardess, her blond hairdo sketchily repaired, her once-immaculate uniform wrinkled and lint-speckled, as she carried trays of food in and out of the airliner's galley. In the middle of the passenger cabin, Mrs. Robinelli was talking quietly to a group of girls, one of whom had been weeping with homesickness earlier.

"I wonder what the heck we're going to eat, later on, I mean, when the airliner food gives out?" Charlie said. His stomach rattled ominously. "Also, how many times can you flush one of those airliner toilets before it fills up and overflows all over the rug?"

"Your mom, Chuckie," Chela said.

Charlie reached down and dragged out a bulging leather briefcase from under his seat. Laying it on his lap, he opened it and fished through notepads, pens, pencils, crayons, crumpled sheets of lined notebook paper, paperback novels, balls of used Kleenex, crushed packages of cookies, a magnifying glass with candy wrappers stuck to it, finally extracting a flattened fruit pie in a paper wrapper.

Chela spotted an expanse of pink flesh under a mashed candy bar. "*Playboy* magazine," she said. "Charles, I didn't think you had it in you—"

"Hands off," Charlie said, fending her away. "Come on, Chela, I'll let you see it later, when no one's looking, okay?"

"I don't want to see it, I'm trying to save you from plastic sex and the evils of self-abuse. What's this?" She dragged out what looked like a miniature typewriter keyboard carefully packed in scraps of foam rubber.

"My portable computer," Charlie said, his face flaming. No girl had ever talked to him before like that. He pulled the computer out of its packing, making a fumble of it. He held it out to show her. "It's a Model 100. This is the keyboard; these black buttons are for different functions, and this gray panel is the screen. This is where you plug in a telephone."

Chela groaned. "I knew it the first time I laid eyes on you. You're the school computer wally."

The stewardess arrived at their seats with two trays of breakfast. "Oh, a computer," she said. "How interesting." She left without waiting for an answer.

"You have just been served breakfast by this year's Miss Excitement," Chela said.

Charlie's aplomb returned at the sight of food. "You could've said, one of the numbnut adults who got us into this."

"Mass barf," Chela said, looking at her limp pancakes and crumbled eggs.

"Better eat it," Charlie said, his mouth stuffed, juice dribbling on his shirtfront. "You don't know where your next meal is coming from. And since I don't know where your next meal is coming from either, I'll eat that one for you if you want."

"Your mom," Chela said, and began to spoon up her food. Captain Milanovitch and the other members of the airliner's crew filed into the front of the passenger cabin and stood to one side, crowded against the wall.

The captain took up a position in front of the passengers' seats and said, "Your attention, please. Thanks. Now, I'm sure you all realize that we have to get a little organized. There are several jobs that need to be done. For one thing, we need to organize a system of lookouts. Also, the hijackers claim they've packed supplies for us in the plane; we need to check this out and see what we have." Charlie's hand popped up. "I'll answer questions in a moment—"

"The first thing we should do is turn on the TV again and see what the Charonese say. Then we do the other stuff."

An angry shout came from the other side of the cabin. "I think we should concentrate on getting out of here!" Other voices rose in agreement.

Milanovitch tried to reply. Charlie had his hand up before he could begin. "Turn on the TV! Take a vote!"

Chela Suarez stuck up her hand. "Charlie's right, Captain. We should take a vote. This isn't school. We're all victims of this hijacking. Democracy rules." The teenagers growled agreement.

Milanovitch glanced at the other adults. Mrs. Robinelli nodded at him sharply, Gershner looked uncomfortable, Peake waggled an eyebrow, and Froward looked blank. Charlie looked at Chela to see what her response would be. She was staring at Froward instead of paying attention to the debate.

"Er, all right, everyone, how many people are in favor of turning on the TV now?" All the students were in favor. "I was afraid of that. Majority rules." With a sigh, Milanovitch plugged in the Charonese device.

It was the hearty game-show announcer voice: "Good morning, everyone! It's nice to see you again. Did you sleep well?"

"No, we didn't," Milanovitch said. There was nothing to be seen on the TV screen except a pattern of stripes in random colors. "Can you see me?"

The voice from the screen abruptly changed to sexless neutrality. "Yes," it replied. "You have spoken to me-us before."

"That's correct," Milanovitch said. "I am the captain of the aircraft that you have unlawfully hijacked. Your actions have already resulted in the death of one of the children. I'm responsible for the safety of these children. Return us to our homes immediately, before you cause more harm."

"Sorry," the voice said. "Sss. I am sorry." The pattern on the screen jerked a couple of times, and the speaker hummed for a moment. Charlie wondered at this. Was it an emotional response at the death of one of their number?

The voice continued. "It's impossible to return to your homes. We have only enough fuel to perform this part of our mission, to bring all of us safely to Charon." A picture appeared on the screen: space and stars, with a tiny, blue-and-white half-moon shape in the center. "This is the appearance of Earth as seen from our spacecraft. Note the great distance."

Charlie forgot himself enough to tap Chela's knee. "Hear

that?" he whispered. "They're using better English now. They're learning."

"Piss off and die," Chela whispered back. Froward noticed the disturbance and frowned down at them.

"I want to explain to all of you," the alien was saying, "why it has been necessary to bring you here involuntarily."

"Go ahead, we're listening!" Milanovitch snapped.

"There is a great task that we must perform together. Previously, when I have attempted to explain, you have disconnected the TV set. Please don't do it, please. If you don't communicate, the danger to our mission will increase, and some of you may suffer unnecessarily. Please tell me, to the best of your ability, how I can improve my communication with you."

Milanovitch was ready with his answer. "You should come out, and talk to us face-to-face, so we can see you. That's the kind of communication we respond to." Charlie noticed that Froward's fingers were twitching behind his back.

"The answer to that question is part of the explanation I wish to give you. Please be patient, please."

"All right," Milanovitch said. "Why did you hijack the plane and kidnap all these children? Just answer the questions. We don't want to see any movies."

"Who said we don't want to see any movies!" Charlie puffed in Chela's ear. Chela elbowed him away.

"I-we hope that you and the children will join us as members of the Crew."

"The crew of what?"

"Charon. The object you call Charon. The moon of Pluto. The Spacecraft Ark. These are English words that may be used to describe Charon."

Milanovitch's impatience made his speech falter. "W-well, what is this Charon? Tell us that!"

"Okay, I am telling you that. Charon is an artificial world designed to preserve life in space for long periods of time. We are the Crew of Charon. I have a picture of it ready to show you, if you'll agree to look at it calmly."

"All right."

When the picture blinked onto the screen, the students' restless whispering changed to strict motionless attention. Charlie wasn't sure what he was looking at. Instead of the doughnut- or cylinder-shaped space vessel he had expected, there was a picture of a blue, white, and tan planet, similar to Earth. A planet, but it didn't look quite right. Charlie frowned as he studied the picture. In a few seconds, he realized that the problem was in the appearance of the clouds on the planet; they were too high in its atmosphere. In all the pictures of the Earth from space that Charlie had seen, the clouds looked as though they had been painted onto the globe, white on blue. Compared to that, Charon looked wrong. Charon's clouds were raised above its surface, like a cartoon of a planet, instead of a real one. Charlie could even see the clouds slowly moving, their indigo shadows following them along the surface.

Charlie's concentration was interrupted by a comment from one of the girls sitting behind him: "How do we know this is real?"

"You might as well believe it," Charlie said.

"Oh, shut up, Charlie!"

"That's enough of that," Mrs. Robinelli said.

Another voice spoke. "Really. What difference does it make?"

The alien voice droned on. "This is not a live picture, but it is an accurate representation of the appearance of Charon, somewhat magnified, as seen from the object you call the planet Pluto."

"Captain Milanovitch?" Charlie said. "Can we ask questions?"

"Better let me do the talking, Charlie."

"Ask them how they keep it warm."

"Charlie, it'd be better if—"

The alien voice interrupted. "His name is Charlie. Charlie is saying an appropriate question. It is true that Charon has some of the appearance of a natural planet. Nonetheless, nevertheless, however, it is not a natural planet, it is an artifact. Charon is a hollow, spherical shell. In the approximate center of the space inside the shell is a gravitational singularity, or black hole, which radiates enough energy to warm the shell. Charon was built around the black hole in order to take advantage of its gravitational field. Its gravity holds Charon's atmosphere around the outside of the shell. The gravity on the outer surface of the shell is similar to Earth's."

The picture changed to show a hummocky snowfield glowing softly under the light of thousands of stars. In the distance, a low pyramid squatted on the level horizon. "This is a recorded picture of the surface of Pluto. The object in the distance is a device that simulates sunlight."

Charlie's resentment was overcome by ecstasy. Some of what the alien had said had gone over his head, but he understood that he was the first person to see Pluto close up and, he added to himself, glancing at the others, to appreciate it. He had to restrain himself from bouncing up and down in his seat like a child.

The camera panned upward to show Charon in the black sky above the tower. The voice lectured on, dispassionately. "The sunlight-producing device is similar to the laser lights produced by human technology. It shines a beam of wide-spectrum light on Charon, simulating natural sunlight. Energy for the laser process is derived from hydrogen, which is stored in Pluto."

The picture changed to a landscape, a view up a tawny, grass-covered slope. Huge puffy clouds sailed in a hot blue sky, their shadows flowing down the hillside over the waving grass. A flock of birds flew out of a nearby patch of brushwood, indistinguishable except as black specks against the light. "This is a typical view of the surface of Charon," the speaker said. "As you can see, it is kept in as natural condition as possible."

"Is that where we're going?" one of the passengers asked. Charlie recognized Colby Dennison's voice. Milanovitch gave up trying to control the students.

"Yes," the alien voice said. "You will find it comfortable."

"It looks just like Earth," Colby said.

"Charon is like Earth. It is an artificial biome, or natural environment, which we have stocked with plant and animal life from Earth. Its purpose is to preserve a natural biome from Earth safe from pollution and other disasters."

"What're we supposed to do on Charon?" the boy demanded.

"You and the other humans will be trained and educated to take over the management of the biome and the machinery that supports it. The task is similar to the management of a large zoo or national park. Please ask more questions."

The students were struck dumb by what happened next on the screen. In the distance, almost to the skyline along the top of the hill, were a small number of what Charlie had taken to be sandstone boulders protruding from the deep grass. Before anyone had a chance to ask another question, one of the boulders stood up and looked around. It was an animal like a kangaroo. It sat propped on its tail, forelegs dangling, long jaws working as it chewed on a bunch of yellow grass.

"Look!" Charlie said. "That has to be a dinosaur!" He was so excited he could hardly catch his breath. "Is that a dinosaur?" he said loudly in a high voice, ignoring Milanovitch's efforts to shush him.

"Yes."

"No shit? From Earth?"

"That is correct. The purpose of Charon is to preserve a biome that was saved from a disaster on Earth approximately sixty-five million years ago."

The students began a dismayed muttering, but Charlie's triumphant whoop drowned them out: "Dinosaurs! They got dinosaurs!" As though they had heard him, the other animals on the hillside suddenly stood up, looking in different directions, snuffing the wind. Mrs. Robinelli had her eyes glued to the screen, her steel-blue eyes glittering with fascination. Mr. Froward grinned with genuine happiness. Chela laughed at him.

"What kind of dinosaur is that, a hadrosaur?" Charlie asked, stealing a glance at Captain Milanovitch. The captain looked back at him resignedly.

"I-we do not use a spoken language," the alien voice replied. "One of the tasks we have ahead of us is to learn from you the English names for the plants and animals under our care." Most of the students didn't hear the reply over the conflicting conversations going on in the cabin. On the screen the dinosaurs trotted off the screen in a group, their forelegs held against their bodies, their high, narrow tails sticking out behind.

Mrs. Robinelli's voice rose above the noise. "Quiet, please. Thank you. If we're going to leave the television on at all, let's keep quiet enough so everyone can hear."

"Where're we going to live?" a girl asked, after quiet had been restored.

"Another appropriate question," the alien said. "What is your name?" The girl didn't answer.

After a second, the picture blinked to another uphill view, this time of a five-legged concrete tower standing in a grove of tall pines. The top of the tower was a flat platform, which supported a small village of picturesque two-story buildings.

"This home has been prepared for your comfort and convenience. Each of you will have his-her own apartment. I recognize the human need for privacy. The design of the buildings is based on pictures that I-we have seen of the dwellings used in places in the United States with climate similar to Charon's. Facilities have been constructed for your training, amusement, and health requirements. Materials will be provided with which you may furnish and decorate your dwelling spaces. The building will provide complete protection from wild animals. Of course, once you have been sufficiently familiarized with conditions on Charon, you may live anywhere you wish. If you successfully complete your training, full control of Charon and all of its resources will be yours. That is our mission: to prepare you to become the Crew."

"That doesn't sound so bad," Chela remarked.

"That's what I've been telling you!" Charlie said.

Froward addressed the screen. "How long is this training going to take?"

"The flight to Charon will take approximately eighteen days. The training period is expected to last thirty to forty years."

Once again, an uproar broke out in the passenger cabin, different voices shouting objections and denial. Charlie cackled and called out, "Hey, now you 'tards can stop worrying about getting accepted into college!"

After a minute, the noise in the passenger cabin diminished. Colby Dennison stood up, breathing hard. Eva Wilcox clung to his hand. "Well, look," he said, trying to control himself, "are we going to be allowed to contact our parents? I mean—"

"This is an appropriate question," the alien said. "I anticipated that you would be emotionally upset by this information. Perhaps you would like some light entertainment from your TV networks to help you regain your positive attitude—"

"Just answer the goddamn question!"

"Unfortunately, none of you will be allowed to communicate with anyone outside of your group during your training period. There will be no contact with anyone on Earth, including your families. I am sorry, as I know this is important to you."

It took a moment for everyone to digest this revelation. Charlie was shocked. Face it, he thought, the aliens wanted them to be Crew. The Proctor thing wanted them to be Crew, too. The only difference was that the Proctor was going to use Charlie as a prod, to do a more thorough job of Crew-izing the humans. Either way, it meant exile for life. How can I get any benefit from being an extraordinary person unless I'm where I want to be? Charlie had no objections to the ordinary world, only to his position in it. As Chela had said yesterday, exploring the universe was okay only if you can go home afterward.

"Bullshit," he murmured. Chela glanced at him.

The picture on the screen, the concrete tower with the apartments, faded, and was replaced by the pattern of stripes. Colby was shouting, "Why can't we call our parents?"

"I-we estimate that, if any human government were informed of the true nature of Charon, it would become likely that that government would attempt to interfere with the delicate ecological balance of Charon's present biome, and the machinery that supports it. My mission, which is now your mission also, is to protect and preserve life. This might become difficult or impossible if we were attacked by one or more of the human governments."

"No one would attack Charon," Colby said pleadingly. "The human race would help you!"

"Bullshit," Charlie said.

"The human race has a history of violence and instability," the TV screen said. "The only certain way of preserving Charon is to maintain its secrecy and isolation."

"Why us?" someone asked. "Why now?"

"The eternal question," Froward murmured. Only Chela and Charlie in the front seats heard him, but Mrs. Robinelli tapped his shoulder and frowned at him. "Sorry," he muttered.

The Charonese voice said, "I assume you want to know how and why you were selected from all other humans for this mission. We and I have waited through approximately ten thousand years of human development to select you, and no one else, for the Crew. For three reasons. One is, you are healthy and young. Two is, you were born in a technologically advanced society. Therefore, you are physically and intellectually ready to be trained for our mission. The reason three is more difficult to explain. Recently, I-we of the Crew have begun to fear that the Earth is nearing another worldwide disaster similar to the one that wiped out the animal life of Earth sixty-five million years ago."

"What disaster is that?" Colby asked.

"I refer to the increasing likelihood of nuclear warfare among the human governments."

"Nuclear warfare—" Colby's face was pale, like wax.

"Yes. War with nuclear weapons threatens to exterminate all higher forms of life on Earth. The risk has become intolerable. I-we are determined to save at least part of Earth's natural variety of life forms from the nuclear warfare of the humans. Some humans will be saved likewise, namely yourselves."

Charlie was thinking too hard to listen to the exchange between Colby and the alien. To his disappointment, he now found himself in agreement with the adults and his fellow students. They had to get out, to escape. But how do you get away from outer space, from the planet Pluto? It was bullshit to think you could do it by sabotaging the spaceship, by fighting the aliens bare-handed, by kicking and screaming. No. What you do is let the aliens teach you how to drive the spaceship, then you steal it. Charlie had it half-dicked already, what with his friend Proctor and all.

"It all makes a lot of sense to me," Charlie said loudly.

"Shut up, Freeman," Colby said, falling listlessly back into his seat.

"Hey, I thought we weren't going to try to shut each other up, and stuff," Charlie said. "I have as much right to say what I think as anyone—"

"You're right, Freeman!" Colby barked at him from the depths of his seat. "Say whatever you want!"

Before Charlie could gather his wits after this unexpected success, the Charonese voice said, "I would like to address the captain now, please."

Charlie had been about to announce his policy to the others. Now he sat with his mouth open, thinking, how stupid can I get? I can't mention any of this where the aliens can hear me! Also: these jerks won't listen to me about this; they don't listen to me about anything! He printed it across the insides of his eyelids in letters of fire: Keep Your Mouth Closed. He would save them in spite of themselves, then make them grovel for it. The thought made Charlie feel cheerful again.

"Go ahead," Milanovitch said dispiritedly to the screen.

"Our spacecraft is in need of mechanical maintenance and minor repairs."

"Yes?"

"You and the other humans have destroyed almost all of the robots I would ordinarily use for repairs. I can reactivate most of them if you will return the parts that are still aboard your aircraft."

Milanovitch looked puzzled. Peake said, "It means the junk downstairs. The ones we wrecked, and the broken pieces."

"Oh, yeah."

"Tell them no," Peake said. "If they get those robots working again, they might attack us again."

Milanovitch said to the screen, "We'll have to think it over."

There was no response from the screen. "Maybe it didn't understand you," Peake suggested. "Sometimes they're a little slow on the—"

"Uptake, yes. About the robot parts," Milanovitch said loudly to the screen, "we will inform you of our decision later."

"Very well," said the screen, "we will begin training and education today. In order to insure your comfort and convenience, I must learn the physical parameters of each of you, your individual identities, and your medical histories, if any. Each person will step up to the TV screen and remove all of his or her clothing."

Everyone was aghast except Charlie. "Hey, Chela," he whispered, tapping her knee, "'Beaver' time again. You first." His chortle was squelched by a hard, well-placed elbow in his ribs.

Milanovitch stepped forward and pulled the plug again. The TV picture winked out. "I presume you've all seen enough for the time being?" he said to the passengers. They all muttered assent. From his position in front of the passengers, Milanovitch began to assign jobs to the students: lookouts, cargo inventory, cleanup.

Charlie made sure he was among the group of students who went outside the airliner with Mr. Peake to see what was stored in the baggage compartments under the cargo deck. Once outside in the gloomy, machine-filled hangar space, he hung back from the group and walked by himself under the nose of the plane to take his first look at the real outer space.

The dome window and the catwalk, and the midnight splendor of the stars beyond, met all of his expectations. As he made his

way back to the right side of the airliner's fuselage, where Peake
had opened the baggage hatches, he looked for robots or some
other sign of the Charonese presence, but saw only the silently
swiveling cameras on the walls.

"Charlie, I think it would be better if—"

"I'm sorry, Mr. Peake. I never got to go out yesterday, so this
is my first time to see any of it."

"Nevertheless, from now on—"

"I won't, sir."

"All right, let's get on with it." The baggage hatches, hinged
on the underside of the aircraft, had already been let down to rest
on the hangar floor. The forward compartment contained the students' luggage, but the after compartment was packed solid with
cardboard cartons. Peake got out a pad and pencil, and instructed
some of the boys in the group to climb inside and start passing
the cartons out.

Charlie clambered inside the compartment and squeezed
among the cartons.

"Uh-oh, Charlie's smelling out the food supply," one of the
boys said, as Charlie began industriously shoving the cartons out.

"Smelling up the food supply, you mean," another boy added.

"No, Reilly, that's not what I'm looking for. Here, help me
pull this out. No, what I'm really looking for is your shovel."

"My shovel?"

"Yeah. We're all going to be on the Charon Crew, but you're
on the shit detail."

The boys laughed in the cramped space. Surrounded by the
relatively familiar walls of the airliner, they felt somewhat more
secure than in the hostile emptiness outside.

"Okay, Charlie," Reilly said. "What detail are you going to be
on?"

Charlie puffed with exertion as he pulled out a heavy cardboard carton. "I'm in charge of pussy selection," he said. "You're
laughing?"

"Not me. I never laugh about pussy," Reilly said.

"Think it over, gentlemen," Charlie said. "The Charonese said
we were going to have to stay there forty years, right?" They all
stopped working and looked at him grinning and goggling in the
low, ill-lit compartment.

"I'm sure you've noticed that there are more girls than boys on this trip, right?"

"Hey . . . ! That's right . . . !" Reilly said in a wondering voice.

"He catches on quick, doesn't he?" Charlie said to the other boys, who now cackled at Reilly. "If Reilly does a good job on the shit detail, I'll let him have his girlfriend Tina, plus a second helping, if you know what I mean."

"So who do you get, Charlie?" one of the others asked. "I notice that new girl, Chela Suarez, like, hangs around."

"True, but the two-fisted cowgirl type doesn't appeal to me. I prefer timid blondes. Eva Wilcox is who I get. What I've been doing with the Suarez girl is taming her, so she won't be too much for Colby to handle."

"Haw!"

"Laugh your heads off, gentlemen. I'm always right, and I never make a mistake. Mrs. Robinelli has already made up the list according to my recommendations. She put her name next to Reilly's and you"—he pointed at one of them—"get the stewardess."

"That's not so bad, but Mrs. Robinelli is too tall for Reilly!"

"Reilly is too black for Mrs. Robinelli!"

"Too horny, you mean!"

"Gentlemen, this is an equal opportunity spaceship."

Mr. Peake stuck his head into the compartment: "Come on, less talk and more work, boys."

The boys returned thoughtfully to work.

The cartons proved to contain workmen's coveralls and boots, all sizes. Beyond the cartons the boys came to a pile of mailing envelopes. Peake ripped open several of them and discovered that they contained books and other printed matter: *The Merck Manual*, a medical text; *Better Vegetable Gardening*; *Electronics Theory*; *The Dinosaur Dictionary*; *All the World's Painting*. They had all been mailed directly to TransPac Air Charters from dozens of publishing companies. Deeper in the pile were boxes containing complete encyclopedia sets, history textbooks, foreign language dictionaries.

Peake was instructing Charlie and some other students to sort the stuff and stack it around on the hangar floor when Froward and Mrs. Robinelli strolled out of the gloom from the direction of the airliner's tail.

"We've been exploring," Froward said, switching off his flashlight. "Back near the tail section we found a big door in the hangar wall. It's got latches and handles on it, as though it were meant to be opened and closed. I didn't mess with it."

"What do you think it is?" Peake asked.

"It appears to be an air lock," Mrs. Robinelli answered. "Perhaps leading to the unpressurized parts of the spaceship. After all, it wouldn't make sense to have air in the entire vessel. The Charonese probably provide air only to this hangar, and their own quarters."

"Is that what we're calling them? Charonese?"

"Michela Suarez suggested it," she said. "It seems adequate."

Peake waved a hand at the steadily growing heap of fourth-class mailers and book cartons. "What d'you think of all this literature, Mrs. Robinelli?"

Froward and the teacher began to open some of the cartons and look at their contents. Mrs. Robinelli said, "It looks as though the Charonese want a better view of our culture and science than they can get from television and radio. Also, some of these books must be intended for us to use, after we arrive on Charon, like this one." She held up two booklets entitled "Build Your Own Grain Mill" and "Effective Contraception."

"Half this stuff was ordered from the U.S. Government Printing Office," Froward observed.

"Yeah, but who by?" Peake said. "I mean whom by. Or by whom. Teachers make me grammatically self-conscious, Mrs. Robinelli." She crinkled at him. "What I mean is, do the Charonese have agents on Earth, to buy things for them?" he concluded.

"Not necessarily," Mrs. Robinelli said. "You can order almost anything, and pay for it as well, by telephone or telex."

"Are you saying they're tapping the phone lines?" Peake said.

"They wouldn't even have to do that," Froward said. "Most overseas phone and telex goes by satellite these days. All they would have to do is figure out the system, and beam a message at the right moment."

Peake laughed in amazement. "Well, all that being so, how did they know which plane to put the, the—" Comprehension spread over his face. "Mrs. Robinelli, how did this student-exchange program with, what's it called, the Republic of Nauru, get arranged?"

"I presumed, at the time, that it was being arranged by the U.S. Department of Education, at the request of the government of Nauru. The school principal told me that they had requested a selection of outstanding students. He said that they had asked us not to pick any handicapped students, because of the conditions under which they would work on Nauru."

"Did any of the feds visit the school in person?"

"Not to my knowledge. The program was all put together by phone and telegram. The funds arrived at the school by wire. It's probably safe to assume that the Nauru student-exchange program was a fraud, somehow engineered by the Charonese."

"That's fantastic!" Peake exclaimed. "How could they have done it without human help?"

The corners of Mrs. Robinelli's mouth twitched wryly. "You don't know the federal bureaucracy, Mr. Peake. All it would have taken to set the whole process in motion would be the arrival of the appropriate communiqué from someone purporting to be the Nauruan educational minister."

"Sure," Froward said. "It's the same effective management that brought you the Vietnam War, Lebanon, and Central America." Mrs. Robinelli laughed, not crinkling.

Deeper into the baggage compartment, the boys began to find cases of pharmacy items: vitamin pills, antiseptics, antibiotics, bandages, headache and diarrhea remedies, toothpaste, underarm deodorant, feminine hygiene spray.

"You're kidding me!" Peake said, after a grinning teenager had passed the last item into his arms.

"Remember, all they know about our personal lives is what they see on UHF-TV," said Mrs. Robinelli. "There's a robot coming up behind you, Mr. Peake," she added, almost matter-of-factly.

The men jumped around to face the advancing machine. The teenagers who had been sorting the cargo dropped what they were doing, some of them backing away. Charlie hastily put a stack of cartons between himself and the machine as it rolled out of the darkness. It halted some distance away, mechanical arms dangling. The camera on top swiveled to face the group. "Mr. Froward," it said, in a human-sounding voice.

"I'm here."

"We have been inspecting the spacecraft. The repairs and maintenances are behind schedule. Please allow me to reassemble the robots that remain inside your aircraft."

"No. If you get those robots working again, you might use them to attack us."

"We did not attack. We intend no harm."

"Sorry, we don't trust you," Froward told it. The robot didn't answer. For a minute it stood without moving. Finally, Froward said loudly, "Go away!" To everyone's surprise, the robot obeyed, moving silently toward the airliner's tail until it was out of sight in the shadows.

Everyone sighed with relief except Charlie. "Sir? Mr. Froward?"

"Yes, Charlie?"

"Uh, I don't mean to be pushy or anything, but don't you think we should be more cooperative? I mean, what if something is going wrong with the spaceship like it says?"

Mrs. Robinelli put her hand on the fat boy's shoulder. "That may be, Charlie, but Mr. Froward is trying to encourage the Charonese to come out and talk to us in person."

"What if they can't, Mrs. Robinelli?"

"They haven't said that yet, Charlie." Charlie frowned and pursed his lips, but went back to work.

Lunch was late. It consisted of uncooked army C-rations and sterile lukewarm water out of cans, all discovered by Milanovitch's work party among the cargo on the 747's main deck.

"Something else of interest," Milanovitch told Froward, who had come down after the noon meal to see what else had been discovered in the cargo. "We also found these." He pulled a plastic tarpaulin away, revealing six Johnnie on the Job portable toilets.

"Well, that'll be a relief for all of us," Froward said.

"I still haven't come across any paper," the captain added soberly. Froward nodded and walked away smiling, scribbling a pencil note on his clipboard.

Froward spent the rest of the day working down his checklist:

> roll call/sync. watches (make it 2 P.M.)
> make list of psgrs. (23 kids, 5 adults)
> kids rotate to baggage outside, chge to summer clo.

(see Ms. R.—girls/boys etc.)
set up toilets outside (see Ms. R. ditto)
(min 2 adults outside at all times!!)
finish inventory cargo
dental clinic   electronic supplies
surgical   shop equip.
T paper (!)
garden tools   med supplies
everybody inside.   lock up.   roll call.
lookouts
sleep/lights out
remove corpse (self, George, Lena, Ms. R.)

When it was late, they carried the dead girl through the over-heated gloom to Mrs. Robinelli's supposed air lock door. Froward, clasping her under the arms while Milanovitch carried her feet, had an unpleasant flashback to his war years: the girl's belly had swollen, stretching the buttons on her clothing. After they set her down and covered her with a blanket, and stood for a moment awkwardly, Lena Gershner did something that surprised Froward.

"We should say something," she suddenly told the others.

"Go ahead, Lena," Milanovitch said.

"Lord God," she began in a strong voice that echoed in the hangar, "we were unable to prevent the death of this child. She had the right to expect our protection, and we failed her in her moment of need."

Gershner paused. Froward thought she'd finished, but she continued. "Now we lay her down, not in her native soil but in the presence of her enemies, far from her home and parents. Therefore we pray that You take her into Your high house and comfort her and give her peace. Give us the strength and the wisdom to do our duty here in the shadow of fear and evil. Amen."

"Amen," Mrs. Robinelli said firmly. The rest of them repeated it automatically. Froward glanced up and saw Lena's face set like marble in the light of their flashlights. Milanovitch led the way back to the airliner. There was no sign of the aliens or their robots. Peake was waiting to open the passenger door and let down the ladder for them.

Upstairs, the lights were dimmed, but the students were still awake, waiting in awed silence for the adults to return. They watched Milanovitch pick up the alien television set and start down the stairs with it.

"What's he doing!" came Charlie's angry whisper. "Wait! You can't—!"

"Shh!" "Shut up!"

On the main deck, Milanovitch and Peake were standing next to the open doorway. "You want to do it?" Milanovitch asked Peake.

"Sure!" Peake took the bulky device from Milanovitch's arms, raised it overhead, rotated shakily to face the doorway, and threw it as far as he could out into the hangar. An explosive smash echoed in the darkness.

Peake wiped his hands on his pants. "Gad, that was fun!"

"If you thought that was fun, just wait until we get our hands on one of those Charonese," Milanovitch said.

Chapter Six:

Estimated Arrival Time

On the second day, they found the space suits.

That "morning," before letting anyone else outside, Froward and Mrs. Robinelli patrolled the hanger space with flashlights in their hands. During the "night," the dead girl's body had been stealthily removed. The books and other printed matter that had been left outside had likewise disappeared.

"None of the lookouts saw anything last night," Froward said. He shone his light around the dark walls and floor, his hand resting on the butt of the .45 automatic stuck in his belt.

"It's difficult to see anything in this dark, especially through the airliner's windows," Mrs. Robinelli said. "I presume they, or it, came through here, and took the books and Susan's body out that big armored door."

"It might be a good idea to rig some lights out here," Froward said. "We can scrounge fixtures and wire from the plane."

"Yes. We'll have to organize outside games and activities for the children. We can't expect them to stay in their seats for two weeks."

"You think it's going to be two weeks?"

"That's what the Charonese told us."

The two of them followed the beam of the flashlight across the floor of the hangar to the huge armored door in the rear wall. Froward waved his light across it. "Should we open it up?"

"It might be dangerous, but . . ."

"Let's go see if Captain Milanovitch is interested," Froward said. Cameras on the walls rotated on silent motors, following them as they returned to the wingless fuselage of the 747.

The armored door was dogged shut by a dozen metal wedges,

each of which had to be laboriously jacked out of the way by ratcheted levers apparently provided by the Charonese for that purpose. Milanovitch, Froward, and Peake worked at it for fifteen minutes. When the last wedge had been removed, the door rotated upward to the ceiling, propelled by what looked like hydraulic pistons.

"There certainly isn't anything unearthly-looking about the engineering in this here spaceship," Peake said, as they shone their lights into the space beyond. "I guess the Charonese go by the kiss principle."

"What's the kiss principle, Mr. Peake?" Charlie asked.

"Dammit, Charlie, what are you doing here? Oh, don't bother answering. 'Kiss' stands for Keep It Simple, Stupid. Dammit, Charlie, don't go in there—"

The room on the other side of the armored door was boxcar size. Charlie walked out into it and stood looking around as though he expected to find something. The wall straight ahead and to the left were other armored doors. The adults hastily followed Charlie into the new space.

"Look here," the fat boy said. "The wedges on these doors are operated with motors. So is the one we just came through. I bet you turn them on by hitting these plates."

"Don't touch them!"

"I won't. The other side is probably a vacuum, isn't that right, Mrs. Robinelli?"

"I believe so, Charlie," the teacher answered. Spot-welded along the plain walls of the air lock were wire baskets, at convenient heights for humans. Charlie walked up to the nearest basket and pulled out a roll of plasticlike material.

"Just a minute, Charlie—" The boy ignored Milanovitch's order and shook out the roll of plastic. When laid out on the floor, it proved to be a one-piece garment complete with head, hands, and feet.

"Now we're getting somewhere, Mrs. Robinelli."

"Yes, indeed, Charlie. These are space suits."

The other adults clustered around Charlie and the teacher for a closer look at this latest piece of science-fictional equipment. The suit seemed to have been molded in one piece, without seams. The plastic was thick, flexible, and transparent except for heavy opaque bands around the waist and shoulders, and in rings at various places around the legs, arms, and fingers.

"I'll try it on."

"It looks too big for you, Charlie," Mrs. Robinelli said.

Froward held up the suit. It was large enough to fit a giant. The suit had an opening, an overlapping slit that ran from shoulder to shoulder in front of the neck. "I guess you're supposed to step in here," he said.

After some experimentation and much advice from Charlie, he discovered the best way to get into the garment was to put his legs in first, then to draw on the arms and headpiece.

"It's rather loosely draped, even on Mr. Froward's Lincolnesque figure," Mrs. Robinelli commented.

The suit's entrance slit sealed itself firmly closed when Froward ran his fingers over its overlapping edges. "Although," he observed, "I'll be damned if I see how it can really be airtight."

"It has to work,'" Charlie said. "The Charonese put them here for us, so they must work."

"Charlie, your innocent faith touches me deeply," Peake said as he went from basket to basket, pulling out more suits. "Look, they're all the same size."

"The question is," Froward said, holding up the baggy legs of the suit while taking a few experimental steps, "what are they supposed to be used for?" His voice sounded muffled inside the loose, transparent bag that was draped over his head.

"Emergencies, perhaps," Mrs. Robinelli said. "Somewhat in the nature of life preservers aboard ships. I suggest that we take all of the suits back to the airliner with us."

"I second the motion," Froward said. "It's getting stuffy in here. Help me out, someone. Damn!"

The slit in Froward's suit now seemed to be welded shut. After a second of watching Froward straining to pull it apart, they all rushed at him, seizing handfuls of the plastic material near the seam. Peake and Milanovitch pulled in opposite directions, while Froward hopped about awkwardly.

"I can't get it open!"

"He'll suffocate!"

"Try to peel it upward!"

"Here, Jeff, lie down on the floor! Hold still. Now pull that way!"

Froward, trying to lie still so the others could work, was beginning to breathe hard in the suit. "There must be some trick to it," he said. "Get something sharp; try to pry the seam or cut it open!"

Running footsteps sounded in the darkness. Charlie looked up and saw Chela Suarez approaching from the direction of the passenger door, running and pulling at her pocket at the same time. "Look out!" she called in a clear, high voice, "I've got a knife!"

Peake reached for the knife, but Chela slapped his hand aside, pulled out a handful of the plastic and began to saw at it. "It won't cut!" she exclaimed. She smoothed a piece of the material on the hard floor and stabbed at it with the knife point; the plastic wasn't even scratched.

Froward, scared, panted for air. "This. Is ridiculous. Try. Burning it."

They all looked at one another. "I don't smoke," Peake said.

"Me neither," Chela and the teacher said simultaneously.

Peake jumped up without a word and ran for the airliner. Chela attacked other parts of the suit with her knife without effect. "Try shooting a hole in the suit from the inside, Mr. Froward," Charlie said.

Mrs. Robinelli held the glove of the suit while Froward fought to pull his arm out of the sleeve. He succeeded, and yanked the pistol out of his waistband. He was squeezing the trigger with one hand and covering an ear with the other when the suit suddenly fell open by itself.

When Peake came running back with several cigarette lighters collected from Gershner and the passengers, Froward was already out of the suit. They experimented; flame had no effect on the suit either.

"Why did it open?" he asked the others. "Was there some trick to it?"

Mrs. Robinelli shook her head. "Maybe it's designed to open automatically after some period of time," she said.

"What use would that be, if you were out in a vacuum when it happened?" Milanovitch asked.

"It would make you a mighty fast spacewalker," said Peake.

"I'll bet it's got some kind of automatic sensor inside," Chela said. "Maybe it opens when the suit gets too much carbon dioxide inside."

"Yeah," Charlie said, annoyed that he hadn't thought of it first.

"Which reminds me," Froward said with a scowl. "Not that I don't appreciate your help, miss, but you kids were supposed to stay inside until we made sure it was safe."

"And you were doing a really great job of it, too, Mr. Copilot," the girl said.

"No impertinence, please, Chela," Mrs. Robinelli said.

"I was sent out to bring Charlie back, in case he was being a nuisance. I mean, they knew he was being a nuisance."

"Pack it, Suarez," Charlie muttered.

"Your mom, Freeman," she growled back at him.

Peake held up the suit with its legs dragging on the floor. "It's going to take one hell of an emergency to get me inside one of these things," he said.

On the third day everyone sweated and itched. There wasn't enough water for washing. Milanovitch and Peake led the students in hacking off the plastic paneling from the airliner's walls and ceilings. They patched together the electrical wire obtained in this way, and strung it outside. They unscrewed light fixtures from the baggage compartment and the sides of the fuselage and hung them from the wing and tail stumps, providing dim light in the hangar. That "night," Peake instituted his poker class for the students.

On the fourth day, games were organized outside: paper-ball badminton on one side of the 747's fuselage, and tin can soccer on the other other. Mrs. Robinelli produced a volleyball from her luggage. "When you've been a teacher as long as I've been, you think of these things," she said, with a wink at Lena Gershner.

Playing teams were selected at random every "morning" and dissolved every "afternoon." In the evening the students treated the bruises and abrasions acquired in the games. Milanovitch was everywhere, trying to discourage rough play.

A student, trying to light a clandestine cigarette, was drenched with sticky chemical sprayed from a hidden nozzle in the ceiling of the hangar.

Charlie didn't play any games. He read through his supply of paperback novels and spent most of his time outside wandering around the hangar. At other times he stayed out of sight in the Charonese dome window. Mrs. Robinelli explained that Charlie was a confirmed loner, who needed more privacy than the others did.

On the fifth and sixth days, games again. Now some of the other students refused to join in. Milanovitch noticed some of them were suffering from periods of depression. "Most of these kids are extroverts," Mrs. Robinelli advised him. "They're at ease and at home in social situations, but might not deal well with uncertainty and a threatening environment."

"It's interesting how Charlie seems to stay busy and contented all the time," Peake said.

"He's not like the others," Mrs. Robinelli said. "At school, he's out of place and unhappy. Perhaps his social backwardness and general immaturity make him more adaptable than the others. I had to argue with the principal about Charlie; he didn't want to allow him on the trip. He said he was a poor representative of American youth. The clinching argument in Charlie's favor was that the putative Nauruans had asked for someone with knowledge of the paleontology of the Mesozoic period."

Peake looked at her questioningly. "Dinosaurs, Mr. Peake," she said. "Charlie is an expert."

"Oh."

"At the time, I wondered why the Nauruans asked for that. At any rate, I thought that Charlie would get more out of the trip than the other children. They're fine boys and girls, but they tend to be a little too complacent and self-satisfied."

"Now you'll never know if you were right about Charlie." Peake grinned.

"We may find out more about Charlie than I anticipated, Mr. Peake."

As the days of confinement and darkness dragged past, the air in the hangar grew steadily cooler. There was no sign of the Charonese.

Late one night Froward heard angry shouting coming from downstairs. "I was afraid this sort of thing would start pretty soon," he mumbled, not completely awake. He and Lena Gershner were lying chastely side by side on the carpet near the stairs. Peake slept heavily on the other side of the floor.

"What?" she said.

"The kids are arguing among themselves."

"Oh." She made no move to get up.

Someone, it turned out to be Charlie Freeman, stamped angrily up the stairway and into the passenger cabin, where Mrs. Robinelli was dozing in her seat. "It's not fair . . . !" Froward heard him saying. Shortly afterward, the teacher and Charlie passed through on their way downstairs. Quarreling voices soon rose from the main deck. Milanovitch, who had the watch, glanced out of the cockpit door at Froward. Froward sighed and got up, his back aching from lying on the hard deck.

In the middle of the main deck, between the tall cargo containers, he found Mrs. Robinelli in confrontation with several students. It was the first time he had seen her angry.

The argument stopped as Froward approached the group. The students looked sheepish, or embarrassed. They were in various states of undress, most of them in pieces of the clothing they had brought with them, or wrapped in blankets. The students had colonized the main deck, unpacking their baggage in empty cargo containers and making sleeping pads of torn corrugated cardboard.

One of the disputants was Colby Dennison. "We're not doing anything!"

"I know. Eva won't let you!" Charlie said.

Colby's face flushed with rage, but Charlie continued. "That's not the point, anyway. You've got no right to chase me out of here. I can sleep anywhere I want."

"Charlie, you're hanging around where you're not wanted."

"Yeah, Freeman!" another boy said.

"I was here first! What do you think this is, the honeymoon suite?"

The boys moved menacingly toward Charlie, who glanced at Mrs. Robinelli and stood his ground.

"Okay, let's calm down," Froward said.

"Look, Mrs. Robinelli," a tall, disheveled-looking girl said, "we aren't at Garfield anymore. This is the real world. We're on our own. You can't just tell us what to do, at least not all the time."

Mrs. Robinelli looked rumpled and baggy in one of the loose brown workmen's coveralls that had been found in the cargo. "Reilly and Tina, here, know the rules perfectly well," she said. "They know their parents wouldn't tolerate their sleeping together. Sex, on school trips—"

"Excuse me, Mrs. Robinelli," Froward interrupted. "Tina has a point."

The teacher looked at him sternly through her metal-rimmed glasses. "Mr. Froward, this is a matter of—"

"Excuse me again, please. Hear me out. Now, Tina and Reilly, and the rest of you, you understand that what we're talking about here isn't love, but fucking, right?"

The boys snorted; some of the girls blushed. Mrs. Robinelli began to speak, but Froward waved her to silence. "We're talking about sex. Let's not beat around the bush, okay? I'm sure you boys and girls do it plenty in your cars, or your parents' cars."

"We do not!" one of the girls gasped.

"You don't? I did, when I was your age. I used to do it in my old Studebaker. Tina, are you on the pill?"

"Yes I am!" she said defiantly. "My mother told me—"

"How about you, Claire? What are you doing about contraception?" Claire, small and plump, blushing under her tan, shook her head. "Where we're going, there're no hospitals or doctors. If anyone gets a serious health problem, like a teenage pregnancy, it'll be tough shit for them."

The girls were all looking at one another. The boys were mainly looking down, scuffling with their feet at bits of cardboard and blankets on the floor.

"Mrs. Robinelli and I probably don't see eye to eye on this," Froward said. "I say sleep together if you want to. It'll help you get through. But remember about no doctors, no medicine. That's all I've got to say." He touched Mrs. Robinelli's elbow, took Charlie by the arm, and started back toward the stairway.

The teacher hesitated a moment, then followed.

"They can't hog the whole downstairs!" Charlie said in a loud whisper.

"You can sleep in the passenger cabin one more night, Charlie," Froward told him, evading the teacher's sharp glare. "What's the matter, don't you like to sleep next to Chela?"

"It's crowded. She snores. I can't sleep unless I lie flat."

"I can dig it. We'll do something about it for you later, okay? Now go upstairs."

After the boy left, Froward said, "Ah, youth."

"Mr. Froward," Mrs. Robinelli said, "cynicism is out of place where the children are concerned."

"The most important thing is to keep them on our side. We won't be able to control them unless we see their point of view once in a while."

"We'll take this up at a later date." Mrs. Robinelli walked away stiffly, her arms stubbornly folded.

Froward returned to the carpeted space behind the cockpit and lay down. As he composed himself for sleep, Gershner said, "Not bad, Mr. Froward."

"Thanks, Lena," he said. "Does this mean you'll go all the way with me?"

She reached out in the dark and touched him. "I was surprised the old biddy stood for it. I expected her to strike you down with one blow of her ruler."

"She's not so bad. She knows we're probably facing a lifetime of living with these kids as adults."

"I'm not playing Adam and Eve for the hijackers! I'll be damned first!"

He smoothed her hair away from her face, and she shook his hand off. "I was going to tell you about that next," he said. "I lied to the kids."

"What do you mean, you lied to the kids?"

"I found enough birth control pills in the medical supplies to take care of an army of teenage girls. And there were instructions on how to perform vasectomies on men. The aliens don't want us to play Adam and Eve."

"If they don't want us for that, what do they want us for?"

"They probably would've explained it better if we hadn't destroyed the last TV set."

"I'll be damned first," she muttered. She rolled over, away from him, and pretended to sleep.

On the ninth day the armored air lock door, which had stood open since the finding of the space suits, closed with a thump. The students were all outside the airliner, but the lookouts were alert, and shouted a warning from the rear of the hangar. Everyone stampeded for the ladder.

Froward and Peake, guns in hand, brought up the rear of the retreat. Stooping to see under the airliner, they watched the air lock slowly begin to open again.

"Don't shoot, even if I do," Froward ordered.

Above them, the students, having been drilled at it every day, were quietly and quickly pulling the passenger ladder up into the airliner.

The robot rolled out through the air lock and crossed the hangar toward them on silent rubber wheels. "Damn, still no Charonese," Froward said.

"Unless they're invisible," Peake said, "as in innumerable episodes of 'Star Trek' . . ."

The robot rolled to an abrupt halt in front of them. "Good morning, Mr. Froward," it said.

"Same to you," Froward said.

"Please don't shoot the robot that is now in front of you. It is the only one left. It is needed for vital repairs and maintenance." The robot was covered with frost, which began to melt and drip on the floor as Froward watched. Froward noticed that the machine was scratched and dented, and that one of its pincers was missing.

"I've come to warn you," the robot said. "Our spacecraft is about to make its midcourse turnaround maneuver."

"That statement doesn't mean anything to me," Froward said.

"Of course it doesn't," the robot said. "Excuse me for not being explicit. We shall be subjected to about one hour of zero gravity. I recommend that you and the others buckle yourselves into your seats and remain there until our propulsion is stabilized. At that time, gravity will be restored, and you may resume your normal activities."

"Thanks for the warning," Froward said. "When is zero gravity going to start?"

"In about fifteen minutes. A countdown will be provided on the illuminated display in front of the aircraft's cockpit. Do you understand?"

"Yes," Froward said impatiently.

"Please repeat the instructions I have just given you."

"Go unscrew yourself," Froward told it. The robot stood motionless for a moment, then backed rapidly toward the air lock.

The adults crowded into the cockpit to see the signboard.

WARNING WA NING
PE IOD OF ZE O G AVITY
COMMENCING IN 13 MINUTES

DU ATION APP OXIMATELY 30 MINUTES
PASSENGE S MUST WEA SEATBELTS

"It's a trick," Gershner said.

"I don't think it is," Mrs. Robinelli said. "It means we're halfway to Charon. This spacecraft is rocket-propelled. The Charonese will shut down the engine, turn the ship around, and start the rocket again. While they're doing that, there won't be any acceleration, so we won't feel any gravity in here."

"Then we'd better do as they say," Milanovitch said. "Froward and I will stay downstairs as guards, just in case."

COMMENCING IN 13 MINUTES changed to 12. They scattered to their various tasks.

Zero gravity lasted two hours, not thirty minutes. The passengers suffered out the endless plunge, miserably clutching the arms of their chairs. The alien vessel shuddered and jolted. The air of the passenger cabin filled with food crumbs, paper fragments, pencils, hairpins, and all the other human detritus that had been lost in the carpet and under the seats during the past week. When gravity at last returned, something else came with it: a persistent, irregular vibration that everyone could feel through their shoes.

As if that were not enough, when they opened the passenger door they discovered a noisome mess: the portable toilets outside had spilled during zero gee. By the eleventh day, forty-eight hours of intolerable confinement later, the sewage had dried out enough to be sweepable.

On the tenth day, Peake found Froward nursing the last of his bottle of whiskey behind one of the cradles that held the airliner's fuselage. Froward was as grimy as the rest of them, and gray stubble covered his face.

"Last chance to get drunk, Peake. This is the last bottle within a million miles. Ten million miles."

"No, thanks. Warm bourbon is too much for me."

"Suit yourself." Froward tilted his head backward and swallowed audibly.

Peake squatted beside the copilot. "Any special occasion? Or is this just recreation?"

"I'm celebrating my future as an ex-alcoholic," Froward said with a laugh. "Also my departure from the ranks of the gainfully employed. Tell me something, Peake. If I reported Milanovitch's failure to log the trim system problem, would you have backed me up?"

Peake thought before answering. "Maybe not," he said. "It would've been yours and my word against everybody's. Your word doesn't count for much. Or didn't, I should say. Anyway, I liked my job and wouldn't want to lose it."

"That's crap, isn't it, Peake. I mean the way some mistakes are okay, and others aren't, just because of what you look like when you commit them?"

Peake rubbed his chin. "Yeah, but so what?"

Froward laughed. "I like your attitude, Peake. I used to wish I could be like you."

"Don't get me wrong, Jeff. Passenger aviation is too serious for mistakes, either your kind or Milanovitch's kind."

Froward became serious. "Yeah," he said, and added enigmatically, "it's not like selling used cars." He sighed bourbon fumes at Peake's face. "Anyway, here's to simplicity." He drained the few ounces left in the bottle and sat there, waveringly. Nearby, Peake found Froward's empty flight bag. He rolled it up for a pillow, and helped Froward to lie back on it.

On the twelfth day the temperature outside went from cool to chilly. They took to wearing the workmen's overalls provided by the Charonese. The games outside resumed, intense and furious. Nobody kept score. Occasionally the floor would drop slightly or jerk to one side or the other. The adults considered keeping the students inside, but decided it was out of the question.

On the thirteenth day the Charonese-supplied air ducts stopped blowing. Milanovitch hoped no one would notice, but Charlie Freeman saw it, too, and spread the news.

There was a near riot on the fourteenth day, and a crying epidemic on the fifteenth. Charlie broke through Froward's' distraction and called his attention to the small TV cameras on the walls of the hangar. The cameras were no longer following the movements of the humans. Instead they jerked and twitched, little motors whining, and their lenses broke against the metal stanchions.

On the sixteenth day the air inside and outside the airliner was noticeably foul. Charlie predicted suffocation for all hands.

That night, garbled statements began to appear on the illuminated signboard. Milanovitch sat in the cockpit a long time with his notepad, trying to decipher the messages. It was hopeless.

On the seventeenth day Mrs. Robinelli came and got Froward away from the stickball game he wasn't so much umpiring as watching for signs of hysteria.

"What's the matter?" he asked her, after she had drawn him behind the 747's nosewheel.

"I just found out that Charlie Freeman has been in contact with the hijackers."

"What!" Froward's exclamation went unheard under the noise of the youngsters' games.

"He salvaged the TV set you smashed and somehow hooked it to a cable. He told me he's been talking to one of the Charonese for the past two days."

"I can't believe it! The little—!"

"Charlie told me that the Charonese warned him that we would be arriving in Charon in about fourteen hours. He says that there might be a crash."

"Where is he?"

"The window room."

The view through the glass hemisphere was stunning, as always. The stars were above, below, and in front. The catwalk led out over the abyss, toward the Milky War, which was brighter and crisper than Froward had ever seen it before.

He took a couple of steps out on the catwalk and called softly, "Charlie?"

"I'm down here, Mr. Froward," Charlie answered meekly. He was hidden under the catwalk, where there was a narrow floor between the lower rim of the transparent dome and the room's rear bulkhead.

Froward let himself down and helped Mrs. Robinelli to follow. Charlie had made a kind of nest for himself down there. Froward noticed a blanket from the airliner, a scuffed leather briefcase, scattered papers and novels, some tools, and the scrambled parts of the Charonese TV set Peake had thrown from the door two weeks before.

"So the robot didn't clean this up, after all."

"No, sir. I brought it here when no one was looking. I thought it might give me something to do. I'm not doing anything wrong."

"Just tell me about it, Charlie."

The boy glanced fearfully at Mrs. Robinelli before starting. "Well, uh, I noticed that the cable for the TV had little wires in it, so I started tying them two at a time to the telephone jack on my computer." Charlie motioned them to kneel and held out a flat white box with a typewriter keyboard.

"Go ahead, Charlie."

"Yes, ma'am. After a while, I started seeing letters on the little screen on my computer. I couldn't believe it! So I typed in some questions, you know, to see what it would do. It started talking to me."

"What did it say?"

"I recorded the conversation in the computer's memory, and printed it out on paper. You can see it." He handed the two adults a mass of what looked like paper cash register tape. Froward began to read it. Nearly every other line was random gibberish or Charlie's typing errors, but the text made some sense anyway:

I SEE YOU HOW? CAMERA BEHIND YOU ON CEILING what am i doing now? TYPING IS THAT A COMPUTER? yes PLEASE HOLD IT CLOSE TO THE CAMERA THANK YOU I HAVE IMPORTANT INFORMATION FOR YOU YOU ARE CHARLIE? yes I AM THE ONE WHO CONTACTED YOU BEFORE I HAVE IMPORTANT INFORMATION FOR YOU CHARLIE ok PLEASE RESTATE YOUR what is the information? OUR SPACECRAFT IS MALFUNCTIONING ARRIVAL AT CHARON MAY BE DANGEROUS BECAUSE OF LOSS OF CONTROL SYSTEM FUNCTIONS LOSS OF COMMUNICATION WITH HUMANS LOSS OF . . .

Froward skimmed over dozens of lines of text listing the things that had gone wrong with the aliens' spacecraft. "I'd have to be an aerospace engineer to understand what this means," he said to Mrs. Robinelli.

"It's apparent that they've been reading our books and listening more knowingly to Earth's communications networks," she commented. "But they still don't really understand how to talk to human beings."

EXPECT HIGH MECHANICAL STRESS CAUSING POSSIBLE RUPTURE OF LIFE SUPPORT AREA OF SPACECRAFT YOU AND HUMANS SHOULD DON SPACE SUITS WHICH ARE LOCATEDi know where they are when will we arrive at charon? ETA 19 HOURS FROM NOW DURA-

TION OF DOCKING PROCEDURE IS UNKNOWN BECAUSE OF LOSS OF DOCKING SYSTEM FUNCTIONS ON CHARON LOSS OF COMMUNICATIONS WITH CHARON you mean you cant communicate with the other charonese on charon? IF CHARONESE = CREW THEN YES why cant crew on space craft communicate with crew on charon? LOSS OF ANTENNA AIMING FUNCTION CAUSED BY FAILURE TO MAINTAIN CAUSED BY HUMANS DESTRUCTION OF ROBOTS AGGRAVATED BY HUMANS REFUSAL TO ALLOW SALVAGE i didnt do that the other ones did that I KNOW what isHELLO! I HOPE YOU' E FEELING FINE TODAY. THANKS FO GETTING BACK IN TOUCH WITH US. I'VE BEEN WANTING TO LET YOU KNOW THAT OU A IVAL AT OU DESTINATION, CHA ON, MIGHT BE A LITTLE OUGH. SO, JUST AS A LITTLE P ECAUTIONA Y MEASU E, LET'S LEA N HOW TO USE THE SPACE SUITS . . .

Froward read several more feet of the tape, which, with the interspersed lines of gibberish removed, boiled down to "get into the suit and seal the opening."

"Is this all there is, Charlie?"

The boy didn't look up, but remained hunched over the paper, as though studying it more carefully. "Yes, sir. I ran out of computer memory."

"I mean, did you talk to them any more after filling up the computer's memory?"

Charlie hesitated. "I tried, but they didn't make any sense after this. Pretty soon it stopped, and I came to tell Mrs. Robinelli. May I have my computer back now?"

"Charlie, you knew we agreed not to deal with the hijackers except as a group—"

As though he'd been waiting for Froward to say it, Charlie shot back at him. "I had to do it! You should've let the Charonese fix their robots! They can't keep this spaceship going with only one robot! I told you, but you wouldn't listen! And Mr. Peake shouldn't've busted that TV set! I knew things were going wrong with the spaceship, and now I've proved it! Now it's probably too late to do anything about it!" The boy stood in front of the two adults, breathing hard, the whites of his eyes showing in the gloom.

Froward took a deep breath. "Okay, Charlie, I have to say, you were right. And the rest of us were wrong, or mostly wrong. From now on, I'm going to listen more carefully to what you have to say. Okay?"

Charlie nodded, looking aside.

"It's time to lock up for the night, Charlie," Mrs. Robinelli said. "Go back to the airliner now. Mr. Froward and I will bring your computer back with us in a few minutes."

Charlie got slowly to his feet, climbed slowly to the catwalk, and left. After he had gone, Froward said, "Do you get the impression that he's concealing something from us, or covering something up?"

"This is hardly a normal environment," Mrs. Robinelli said. "None of us are behaving normally. What would he have to cover up?"

"I have no idea." Froward tried typing "hello" on the computer's keyboard, but there was no response. "We'd better get back to the others," he said, disconnecting the computer and standing up.

The teacher put her hand on his chest. "Jeff, I told you about this instead of the captain. I thought you would understand better. I want to keep this to ourselves."

Froward looked at her questioningly.

"He's just a boy," Mrs. Robinelli said. "It wouldn't be right for us to allow him to become a social pariah. If the other children found out, that's what might happen to him. He's too young to have to pay that price, especially when you consider that these children may have to live with one another the rest of their lives. Charlie may have done wrong by going behind our backs, but perhaps he saved our lives by doing so."

Froward shrugged. "Anything you say."

On the eighteenth day they arrived.

Chapter Seven:
The Roller Coaster

The first sign of it was a terrifying dive into zero gravity. There were shrieks and cries as the bottom dropped out, but no one was hurt. Milanovitch, forewarned, had kept everyone inside the airliner, seatbelts fastened.

All day they sat, too exhausted to be afraid anymore, while the airliner was thumped, dropped, moved to this side or that side, or up or down. The electrical power went out, leaving only the Charonese signboard visible outside the airliner. In the early afternoon there were a series of jarring crashes, after which all movement stopped.

They waited an hour.

Froward began to hear the passengers talking in the cabin. "I just realized," he said. "I can't hear the roaring sound anymore."

"That might mean they've shut off the rocket engine," Milanovitch said. "We've landed, maybe."

Beyond the windshield, the Charonese signboard showed a random, useless pattern of numbers and letters. Milanovitch unbuckled his seatbelt and rose carefully out of his pilot's chair. Not daring to move his limbs, he floated up to the ceiling of the cockpit and gently descended again. "We've at least got a little gravity here," he said. "Come on, let's go see about the kids."

They made it to the passenger cabin by running their fingertips along the ceiling, shuffling their feet to prevent their bouncing to the ceiling with every step.

The passengers, under Gershner's supervision, were taking turns in the rest rooms and the galley. "Anyone hurt?" Milanovitch asked her.

"No, thank God," Gershner replied. "In fact, most of them are already walking better than we are."

"Keep in mind that most of these young people are competent athletes or dancers," said Mrs. Robinelli, who had come up as the men entered the passenger cabin.

"Anyway," Gershner said, "what happens now?"

"People keep asking me that," Milanovitch said. Froward thought he looked tired and chastened, compared with the way he'd been at the start of the hijacking.

"There's reason to believe that we've arrived at Charon," Mrs. Robinelli said firmly. "There's nothing to be gained by waiting. Someone should have a look outside, since it's too dark to see out of the windows." She moved closer and said in a low voice, "You've noticed how foul the air is in here. There's no telling how much longer we can stay here."

"We'd better have a look outside," Milanovitch said.

"Yes," Mrs. Robinelli said. "And I think Charlie Freeman should go also."

"What?" Milanovitch said.

"George, he may be an eccentric boy to you, but, next to me, Charlie Freeman knows more about space travel than anyone else on the plane. I'd go, but I'm not agile enough to move in this gravity without help."

"She's right, Captain Milanovitch," Peake said. Milanovitch looked at the others. Froward shrugged, Peake frowned and nodded, Gershner reluctantly agreed with the teacher.

Down on the cargo deck they opened the passenger door. Their flashlights shone out into the cold, evil-smelling darkness. "It's just like when this whole thing started," said Peake. "Like we're doing it all over again."

"We'll get through this all right, Mr. Peake. You'll see."

"That's very reassuring, Charlie. Thanks."

There was no sign of the robot, no sound or movement in the hangar at all. They made their way over the hangar floor in the absurd toe-tapping style they had practiced in the cargo deck. They stopped at the entrance to the Charonese observation room.

"Holy crap!" Peake whispered.

The view from the dome window was incomprehensible. It made Froward feel queasy to look at it. Evidently, the spacecraft was perched on the top of a colossal tower. Their spacecraft stuck out from the edge at least a dozen meters, giving Froward the horrifying notion that it might teeter over into the drop-off.

Froward's eye involuntarily followed the tower downward. Bands of dull metal and clear crystal alternated as far as he could see, until they were blended by distance. Below that, the tower tapered to a terrifying perspective point in the middle of a brilliant blue and tan ball, which was spotted here and there with bumpy white clouds.

"That must be Charon," Charlie whispered.

"I thought it would be bigger than that," Peake said, also whispering.

"Mrs. Robinelli and I talked about that," Charlie said. "She said Charon is a sphere about ninety kilometers in radius. That makes it a little bigger across than the island of Hawaii."

"Jesus Christ," Froward said. "This tower, or whatever it is, must be hundreds of miles high. They didn't mention any tower to us."

"You didn't give them a chance to mention it," Charlie said.

"That's enough, Charlie," Milanovitch said.

As his eyes adjusted to Charon's dazzle, Froward saw details inside details in the land below. He saw little lakes like sapphire chips lying on a blue-green carpet; he saw threaded rivers meandering in beds of pale yellow sand; he saw a streamer of gray smoke coming from a brushfire. In another place, a pile of shining clouds thrust almost palpably above Charon's surface, a thunderstorm building. On one side of the sphere he saw part of a round sea, streaked different shades of blue.

That's a whole damn world down there, Froward thought.

"I don't see the yellow brick road anywhere, do you?"

"Peake's right," Milanovitch said. "There're no roads or towns. Nothing's moving on the water either."

"What's that?" Peake said, pointing overhead. They all reassured themselves of their handholds and carefully looked up. A speckled, ash-gray ball hung in the starry sky directly above them, like an outsize moon about to fall on thier heads.

"Wow, that must be the planet Pluto," Charlie said. He sighed. "If only the other members of the Science Fiction Society could be here to see this."

"This thing is like a huge radio broadcast tower," Peake remarked. "That's one of the guy wires, there."

Again following Peake's pointing finger, Froward noticed a gigantic pipe, or cable, at least a hundred meters thick, attached to a bulge on the edge of the Charonese tower. The cable slanted outward and downward, away from the tower. It diminished to a black, curved hairline and disappeared into the glare coming from Charon below.

Peake had brought a small pair of binoculars. "Look over there, where the cable-pipe, or whatever it is, is attached to the edge. See that thing with wheels? It's sitting on top of the pipe."

"I see it," Milanovitch said. "It must be a vehicle. Looks like a giant bobsled with wheels. Maybe supposed to run on top of the pipe."

"Maybe it's the elevator," Charlie said. "See? There's a kind of rail running under the car and down the pipe."

"It's worth investigating," Froward said.

"The thing that gets me," Peake said, "is that there's nothing moving on top of the tower. It's completely bare. No welcoming party or anything. I at least expected some bug-eyed aliens with the red carpet."

"Or a cage to lock us up."

"Or salt and pepper and knives and forks."

"They might be on their way to get us," Charlie said. "Or maybe the elevator is broken. You have to admit their spaceship didn't work very well."

Froward shivered with cold. "Well, we've seen it," he said.

The adults assembled in the airliner's cockpit. "There's nothing to be gained from waiting," Milanovitch told them. "We're almost out of food, and the drinking water is getting short. It's getting colder, and we don't know how long the air will last. It's almost unbreathable in the passenger cabin already. I realize that we'll have to use these space suit things, and it's dangerous, but we've been waiting for almost a whole day, with no sign of the Charonese. I say go."

Mrs. Robinelli spoke up. "I'm forced to agree. We've been led to believe that we can live on Charon. I'm sure we can't survive up here indefinitely."

"You think the kids can handle it?" Milanovitch asked her.

"Oh, yes," she said. "You've seen them in action. Most of them are smarter than we are. They're the best, academically and physically. The school principal wanted to impress the school board when he chose them."

"What's your opinion, Jeff?"

"Go."

"What do you say, Lena?" Milanovitch asked.

"I don't know."

"Peake?"

"We don't know what's worse, staying longer, or going and getting it over with. I vote for going."

"All right," Milanovitch said. "It's unanimous for going, with one abstention. Let's get the passengers ready."

The passengers were ready. After more than two weeks of confinement, they were ready for anything. With discipline that struck Froward as remarkable, they listened to Mrs. Robinelli's description of conditions outside the spacecraft, and followed her instructions, step by step, as she had them don every garment they could button on, plus several pairs of heavy socks from the cargo per person. They improvised backpacks from luggage, and filled them with tools and supplies. When Milanovitch passed out the guns and ammunition, Froward believed them when they promised not to load or fire them without direct orders.

They practiced walking, carrying their loads, in the hangar space around the airliner, until most of them were better at it than Froward. They clustered around their teacher at the entrance to the observation room, their eyes filled with fear, but their mouths determined, as Mrs. Robinelli lectured them on what to expect. Finally, Milanovitch ordered everyone to put on the plastic space suits over their clothes, and to tie up the slack in the loose, flapping material as best they could.

"All right, here we go," he said. The students and adults stood in a cluster around the large armored door, their suit hoods draped over their heads, loads that would have weighed hundreds of kilos on Earth bobbing like balloons behind them.

"The plan is, I'll go out first, and signal through the dome window if everything's all right. Then the rest of you will follow. There's a chance that this air lock doesn't work, and all the air will be let out of the spaceship. In that case, I'll make this motion"—he waved his flashlight—"and we'll all go at once."

"I suspect we won't be able to hear one another out there, so watch for my signals. There must be some kind of elevators to the surface out there, and that's what we're looking for. Before we go I want to say that you are a fine group of young men and women. I couldn't want better companions in danger. God willing, we'll soon be together under a blue sky. Now let's seal our suits."

They ran their fingers over the seals of the space suits, smoothing them closed. The strongest boys went to work on the jacks that removed the retaining wedges. After a moment, a hissing sound began, which became louder.

"The air's going out!" Mrs. Robinelli shouted. "Wait for the copilot's signals!"

Froward had to shout over the roar of escaping air. As he stood there, his suit began to stir around him as it inflated in the decreasing pressure. He turned aside, so the kids couldn't see his face. God make us right, he prayed. It's not right to pray when you're only begging for something.

Charlie froze; his space suit was crawling over his body as though it were alive! He looked down at himself in amazement. The Charonese plastic was shrinking and tightening on his body. He held out his arms and watched the sleeves contract and draw the gloves onto his hands. The suit's legs were also shrinking, taking up the slack that had been flapping around his ankles. Quickly, the suit became painfully tight all over, as it drew in against Charlie's sweater and the three pairs of brown denim overalls he had appropriated from the airliner's cargo. Straining, he bent over and picked up his leather briefcase.

The hoods of the students' suits blew up into transparent globes around their heads. Chela gaped at him through the plastic. She mouthed something at him. Charlie heard nothing except his own laboring heartbeat and terrified gasping. He reached out to her, and she took his hand, gripping it tight. The plastic had shrunk tight and shiny, around each of her fingers.

She jerked his hand, pointing forward. Captain Milanovitch was waving the "follow me" signal. The huddle of students shuffled toward the door. Charlie and Chela pressed forward. Charlie, trembling in an icy sweat, stumbled over the lip of the air lock door. Chela yanked him upright. Ahead, one of the students turned and burst out of the crowd, bowling several others off their feet. Running was hopeless in the weak gravity; whoever it was soared away into the black hangar, out of Charlie's sight.

The ones who had been knocked down fell in eerie slow motion, flailing helplessly. Charlie tried to stop, but Chela jerked at him savagely and dragged him forward over dropped bundles and the backs of the fallen.

Pressing against the backs of the ones in front, Charlie and Chela surged into the open, fell over the edge of the air lock, and floated down onto a thrashing pile of bodies. More bodies landed on his back. Chela plucked Charlie to his feet. They were on a vast expanse of level floor. A tall figure moved against the stars, beckoning. The crowd straggled after him. Charlie saw where they were; it was the scene he'd seen through the dome window. It had to be Froward leading them toward the cable-pipe.

Now Charlie dragged Chela, hurrying her along in bounding strides. They passed one student who staggered off to the side, arms beating at his or her chest, suit hood puffing out a cloud of vapor. The student fell to his knees, then flopped facedown on the metal deck.

Charlie turned away and collided with someone. He looked up and saw Froward's face inches away. The copilot was hugging him around the shoulders and pressing his face close. His mouth moved, and suddenly Charlie realized he could hear the man. Froward was shouting as loudly as he could, but his voice was tinny and faraway, as though heard through a wall: "Charlie! Look at me! Look at me! Can you hear me?"

"Yes! I hear you!" Charlie yelled. He nodded exaggeratedly at Froward.

"Help me get these people inside!"

Froward pushed Charlie away and seized Chela the same way. Charlie saw his mouth moving as he shouted at her. She dropped Charlie's hand. Charlie saw they were now in front of the Charonese vehicle. The vehicle was open in the top. The inside was a bare metal box. It looked like nothing so much as a roller coaster car without seats.

Space-suited figures were milling around Charlie. Charlie began to put the nearest people into the car, picking them up and throwing them inside as though they were straw dummies, vaguely aware that others were pushing their own way aboard. An indeterminate time later, Froward shoved his way through the struggling crowd in the car and pressed his face against Charlie's: "That's enough! I'm going with them! I'll be back! Understand?"

"I understand!" Charlie shouted. "Yes!"

Froward gripped Charlie's hands and fell back into the vehicle. Someone next to Charlie made pushing motions and got an instant "come on" signal from Froward.

They began to push the vehicle up the metal bulge on the edge of the drop-off. At the top Charlie stopped and felt flat, his heart quailing at the sight of the abyss below. The car rolled over the top of the bulge and out of sight down the cable-pipe's nearly vertical slope. In his last glimpse of the car, the people inside seemed to be brawling in panic. One of them jumped out of the car and seemed to hover in midair beside the cable-pipe. Charlie flinched, then forced himself to look. Whoever it was slid off the top of the pipe and slowly began to fall toward Charon, arms and legs waving, diminishing to a doll figure, then to a struggling insect, then to nothing.

Horror overwhelmed Charlie. He cried and shuddered, too weak to get up. He pressed his forehead against the rounded top of the cable-pipe. I'm afraid, afraid, he kept sobbing, clutching at the alien surface, which offered no handhold. His crying was making a slimy puddle inside his head-bubble. He hated himself and longed with all his heart for a moment of safety.

There was no gravity in the car. Froward almost regretted the curiosity that had made him inch his body upward until he could see over the edge of the compartment. The car was in a nose-first dive, dropping down the pipe so fast that its surface had become a blur. Behind them, the top of the tower was already too far away to see. Ahead, he saw the glowing edge of Charon getting larger as the car apparently rushed toward obliteration.

Froward found it difficult to breathe; the Charonese space suit had closed around him like a fist. His knees were bent across the width of the compartment, his feet jammed against the opposite wall. Before leaving the airliner, he had put on his shiny black airline pilot's shoes over his plastic-encased feet. They looked ridiculous with their neat little shoelaces tied in bows.

Froward couldn't guess whose suits had failed, who had fallen out, or who was in the car with him. He didn't know why he was thinking about these things, or what the hell difference it made. Whoever the survivors were, they were rigid with fright. There was no gravity and no handholds in the rectangular compartment.

They wedged themselves in, bracing themselves against the smooth metal walls and one another, everyone doing his or her best not to float out.

He wished he'd been able to time their descent from the tower. That would be useful information, assuming someone knew how to use it too calculate the height of the tower, and assuming they enjoyed a safe landing at the bottom. Any landing you can walk away from is a good one.

That's what they say, anyway. Froward worked himself back down until his buttocks were planted against the floor of the compartment again. There was enough light to make out the face of the person sitting across from him: the football quarterback, Colby Dennison. Froward made an encouraging gesture and got a ghastly terrified smirk in return.

Now Froward felt the return of gravity. The car was no longer in zero gee. In fact, Froward began to feel vibration through the seat of his pants. The boy, Dennison, was scrutinizing Froward through the plastic bubble of his space suit. His mouth began to move. He was trying to speak.

". . . you hear something?"

Froward jumped in surprise. "What?" he said. At once several voices fizzed in his ear: "I hear you! Who's that? Wha? You! Is it? Now?"

Everyone babbled. Eventually, one after another stopped talking until there was a silent interval, long enough for Milanovitch to say, "Anyone who needs immediate help, speak up now." No one said anything.

"Good," Milanovitch said. "We're on our way to the surface. All we have to do is sit tight."

"Your mom has a tight seat," an unidentifiable female voice said.

"Quiet, please," Mrs. Robinelli said in Froward's head bubble.

Froward noticed an increase in the car's vibration. Wind began whistling over their heads. Now that there was some gravity, looking over the top of the compartment was just a matter of standing up. Froward decided to chance it, and rose to a crouch. Charon was swelling up to meet them, changing from a ball to a domed hilltop with the cable-pipe curving upward into its summit.

"We're getting closer," he said. The wind noise built to a

gigantic ripping thunder. The compartment seemed to be tilting forward. The car was slowing down, and momentum pulled at Froward. He lost his grip and slid down the floor. Smothered grunts and exclamations sounded in Froward's suit radio as everyone piled against the front wall of the compartment.

Froward extracted himself from the heap, trying his best not to step on anyone's face. He clambered back to the rim of the compartment. Overhead, the black sky of outer space was turning violet.

Wind pummeled the bubble around Froward's head as he tried to see below. The car was shooting along the top of the cable-pipe. The car plunged through a layer of wispy clouds. Far below, a mottled landscape rotated. The violet sky turned to blue. The car ran among a fleet of puffy white cumulus clouds with the wind drumming on its rounded front end. Far below, Froward saw lion-colored grasslands, twisting riverbeds, and patches of forest. The cable-pipe flattened out until it was almost parallel with the ground. The car was slowing rapidly. Froward exerted all his strength to keep his head above the edge of the compartment. He allowed himself to hope.

Gradually, the pressure eased, and the booming of the wind died down. "What's happening?" someone said.

"We're arriving," Froward answered.

"Just hang on for a little while longer," Milanovitch said. "I think we're going to be all right."

Froward's space suit went slack around his body, the plastic material flowing almost like a liquid. The bubble around his head deflated, and the wind flapped it in his face. There were thumps that felt to Froward like the touch of aircraft wheels on a runway.

Now the car was rolling. Treetops whipped past, thickets of palmettos, a gate in a spiked palisade, and, before Froward had a chance to be surprised, the car rolled to a stop in the midst of a dazzling open space.

Everyone, students and adults alike, groaned with relief. The slit in Froward's suit had fallen open. He stood up and threw off the suit's hood. The air was humid, and the odor of soil and growing things was unmistakable. Puffy clouds floated in a hot blue sky. Bright morning sunlight struck Froward's face.

The car had stopped in an empty clay yard as wide as a city block. Around the perimeters of the yard stood four or five rounded gray buildings. Behind the buildings ran a twenty-foot-high fence, the palisade that Froward had noticed a moment before, looking as though it had been welded together from steel girders.

The alien cantonment, if that was what it was, was situated on the summit of a rounded hilltop. Nothing was moving; there was no sign of activity anywhere Froward looked. Here and there among the buildings were more of the high steel fences.

"Come on," he said. "Let's get out of this thing." He lifted himself over the edge of the car and slid to the top of the cable-pipe, dragging his bundle after him. Only the upper surface of the cable-pipe was exposed; the rest of it was buried in the hard, dusty clay. Milanovitch rolled out after him.

They began to pull the others out of the car, peeling them out of their suits. Blinded by the sunlight, shocked, unspeaking, they stood or sat on the ground wherever Froward and Milanovitch left them. Several of the students had suffered bruises and sprains; Flight Engineer Peake's knee was so badly wrenched he couldn't stand.

Mrs. Robinelli tottered away from the car, trying to straighten her bent wire-frame glasses. "Merciful God," she said, hooking the glasses behind her ears and looking around. "All the adults are here, but we've left behind some of the children!"

Froward looked back along the cable-pipe. It ran the length of the yard and through the steel palisade, rising from the ground as it dwindled away into the distance. Above the horizon it reappeared as a white thread hanging in the blue sky. Froward looked up at it and cursed sullenly and foully.

"Jeff!" Mrs. Robinelli exclaimed.

"I made the decision to leave some people up there! I knew we were leaving behind some of the kids but I thought at least one of us would be there, too!"

"Jeff, how could you!"

"The goddamn car was full! And I didn't see you hanging back when we were filling it with bodies!"

Mrs. Robinelli recoiled. Her eyes filled with tears. "Y-you're right! It's terrible! We panicked, and we left them behind! We must do something, go back and get them somehow!"

"It's not only Jeff's fault," Milanovitch said. "I went along. I thought he was doing the right thing. We'll do something to get them down."

The teacher's voice was shaking. "What? What will you do?" she demanded.

Gershner went to her and took her arm. "Come on, Emma, let's get the rest of the students into the shade."

Milanovitch, Froward, and the stewardess herded the passengers across the field toward the nearest building. They stumbled along, uncomplaining, dragging furrows in the dust with their bundles. There was a large, square opening in the front of the building that made it look like a huge garage.

Inside the building everything was oversize. Daylight, coming in from skylights high overhead, illuminated jointed cranelike machines that stood over broad metal tables. The floor was made of some hard, concretelike substance, and it was traversed by shallow gutters that ran into drains. Flies droned in lazy circles in the shady interior of the building. The students collapsed just inside the doorway.

Froward stood in the doorway looking out. Being in the shade didn't seem to make him feel any cooler. Froward still wore his space suit, and he was sweating under the layers of clothing he had on under the plastic. It was as though the heat came from the ground, not from the sun. Whatever that was in the sky, it couldn't be the sun. Pluto and Charon were so far away from the sun that it would look like a bright star in the sky. He'd read that somewhere. George Milanovitch joined him.

"The teacher's right, Jeff," he said quietly. "Our first priority has to be to get those other kids down here before something happens to their space suits. I noticed one of the suits seemed to malfunction when we were on our way to the car."

"Jesus Christ! What happened?"

"The kid just fell down like he was dead. You couldn't see it, you were in front of the rest of us." Milanovitch's voice became lower. "I didn't stop to help," he said.

"Damnation!"

"We have to get back up there," Milanovitch said. "Maybe if we pushed the car, got it rolling. That's how it started before."

"We'll try it. But you're not going, I am," Froward said. "You and Peake are the only grown men here, besides me, and Peake can't walk." Froward gestured at the women and the students. "You have to stay with them."

"You should stay," Milanovitch said. "I'm the chief pilot; I'm responsible."

"That's why I'm the one who's going, George. It's not your fault those others got left behind up there. They need you here."

Milanovitch grimaced.

"You know I'm right, George," Froward told him.

"I know it."

"Outstanding," Froward said. "Go get some of those jock-strapping boys to help push."

A group of the students followed them wordlessly back to the cable-pipe. Froward climbed back into the car, the loose arms and legs of his plastic suit flopping around him. "Push it," he ordered. "Get it rolling."

Colby Dennison put his hands on the rim of the car's compartment. "Let me go with you."

"Can't, Colby. Not enough men in the group as it is. Thanks anyway. Now push."

Froward looked up and saw Chela Suarez running across the yard, her suit bundled in her arms. "I'll go with you, Mr. Froward," she called as she pounded up.

"No. Just help push."

"Take her, Jeff," Milanovitch said. "You'll need someone. She's shown us what she can do."

Froward paused, then nodded shortly. "All right. Get in." She threw in the suit, a pair of the workmen's boots stuffed with heavy socks, and accepted Froward's help over the edge of the compartment.

Milanovitch looked up at Froward, sweat running down his face. "Take care of yourself, all right?"

"You bet. Thanks."

"Push!"

The men strained, got the car rolling. They walked, trotted, ran, their shoes clattering on the cable-pipe. "It's moving!" Milanovitch shouted. With an ease that surprised Froward, the car gained speed and moved smoothly away from the men. By the time it reached the opening in the fence, it was doing at least twenty-five, maybe thirty. The wind blew Chela's black curls behind her as she faced forward, toward where the cable-pipe made for the edge of the hilltop. Froward looked back and saw Milanovitch, Dennison, and the others who had come to help made tiny by distance, waving at him.

The car swished through the treetops, picking up speed. Flocks of black birds burst up ahead of them, cawing. The ground rolled away from under the cable-pipe, and the car zoomed up into the sky. Froward realized that the hill upon which the Charonese cantonment stood was an illusion. What he had taken for the slope of the hill was really the curve of the ground itself. Charon was so small that its horizon, anywhere you looked, was only a short walk away.

They flew through banks of clouds. "Hey, mister, you going to help me get into this suit, or what?" Chela was lying on the floor of the compartment with her legs in the air, trying to pull it on over her coveralls.

"I hope I don't regret letting you come," he said, tugging at the thick plastic so hard she bumped on the floor.

"You're talking to the kid, here, you know," she said, laughing up into his face.

"That's what I'm afraid of," he said. He held the plastic while she stuffed her arms into the suit's sleeves.

"Lighten up, mister, we're having an adventure."

He had to grin at her. "You're crazy!"

"Now we're having fun," she said. "Now seal your suit like a good space cadet. You wouldn't want Charlie to criticize you when we get to the top—"

The car splashed into something, throwing them down. He grabbed her and hung on. The car bounced and banged to a stop. A shower of white stuff thudded down on them. In the silence that followed, Froward heard something pattering on the loose plastic of his suit. It was snow. Above the edge of the compartment, bright, white fog made it impossible to see more than a few meters away.

"What is it?" Chela asked.

"We've stopped inside a cloud."

Froward, impeded by his space suit, which was flopping loose around his legs, straddled the edge of the compartment, and, holding on to the edge, let himself down onto the cable-pipe. The car lay crosswise with its wheels retracted, the rail on top of the cablepipe no longer running through the slot in its underside. It had run into a mound of icy snow.

He shuddered. The wind was icy. Frozen rain rattled against the plastic of his suit, and his clothes under the suit were damp and clammy. "My God," he said. "We're lucky we didn't run right off the edge."

"I'm freezing!"

"Me, too. Let's try to get it back on the track again."

Chela slid over the edge of the compartment while he held her waist. The curved surface of the cable-pipe was slippery, and their feet slid in the wet slush as they strained to lift the car back onto the rail.

"It won't budge," the girl said. "It's like it's being held down or something."

"Magnetic track. Or maybe it's just too heavy. Let's try again." As they labored, the fog cleared, leaving them surrounded by deep blue sky.

"It hasn't moved at all. It's hopeless." Chela's breath had iced up the inside of her deflated head-bubble; she threw it back from her head. "My suit isn't keeping me warm, is yours?"

He shook his head, worriedly studying the derailed car and the cable-pipe ahead. It slanted upward about twenty degrees from horizontal. The rail was buried under mounds of ice as far as he could see in both directions.

"Well, maybe the suits only work in a vacuum," she said. "Brrr! What'll we do?"

"We have to go back."

Her breath made puffs of vapor that blew away in the wind. "No! What about the people we left on top? Charlie's up there!"

"There's nothing we can do for them here."

She stood close to him, shivering and cringing in the cold. He put his arm around her. "Can't we wait until it melts?" she asked him.

"We can't depend on it getting warmer at this altitude. Even if it did, how would we get the car back on the track again? We'll die if we stay here. We have to go back."

"You sure?"

"Nothing's sure. It's just the best odds."

"All right." She took his hand.

They moved downward, snow crunching underfoot. Wind

roared across the cable-pipe, blowing ice particles that stung their faces. Chela kept looking back, but after a mile, the car was lost to sight among the drifting clouds. In spite of the exercise, Froward's feet and hands went numb with cold. The view was frightening. The cable-pipe hung just under the bottoms of the clouds, and the ground was so far beneath them it looked like a curved map. Great slabs of snow kept sliding off the rounded top of the cable-pipe into the depths.

Two hours of walking brought them out of the snow to warmer air. They sat down on the rail to rest. "When we get down, maybe we'll find some other way of getting them off the tower," he said. "The Charonese must have some way of taking care of problems like this. It's just a matter of finding out what it is."

She sat leaning on her elbows, looking between her knees at the quartzlike surface of the cable-pipe. "I know," she said.

Later, they discarded their space suits and superfluous clothing, and were able to move faster. They paced rapidly for hours. They could see very little of the ground. It was getting late in the day, and the soles of Froward's feet felt as though they had been beaten with mallets.

"Are your feet hurting you?" he asked Chela.

"No, the kid enjoys a good long hike."

There were more hours of walking, Froward moving more slowly. The cable-pipe leveled out. The tops of trees peeked over its edge, and its surface was littered with fallen leaves, catkins, and dried-out flowers.

A scaly, two-legged animal with a long neck skittered across the cable-pipe in front of them. It stopped in the middle, saw Froward and Chela, and hissed with surprise. A ruff of feathers behind its narrow head opened and closed like a fan as it studied them first with one yellow eye, then the other.

Froward and Chela stopped in their tracks at the sight of the creature. "My God!" Froward said. "A dinosaur!"

"A little one," Chela whispered.

The creature was colorful, striped bright green and black. It danced indecisively, its claws clicking on the stone. In its yellow chicken-foot hands it clutched something furry and cat-sized with a dangling, naked tail. Blood ran down the dinosaur's skinny arms and dripped from its elbows. Having seen enough of the humans, it flirted its stiff tail left-right, up-down, and dashed into the treetops on the opposite side.

"What was it carrying, a rat?"

"It was too big to be a rat," Froward said. "It looked like a possum to me."

"I've never seen a possum before," Chela said.

"I take it you've seen lots of dinosaurs?"

"No, but your mom has," she said.

Froward pulled the girl forward. In the stress of the moment, he'd forgotten that the Charonese had described their planetoid as a zoo or animal sanctuary. Now he recalled that, when he had surveyed this world from space, he had seen no roads, no cities, nothing that looked artificial. Now he knew why the Charonese had taken the chance of providing the humans with firearms. If things broke down, the humans would be in danger from the wildlife they had been brought to protect. The Charonese apparently had anticipated many breakdowns.

Froward ignored his aching feet and moved down the last miles of the cable-pipe in long strides. Chela trotted along beside him without a word. As they moved through the steel fence (he noted that it had a motorized gate that could slide closed over the cable-pipe) he began to look for the others, but no one came out to greet them.

"Where is everybody?" Chela said. "Mrs. Robinelli! Mrs. Gershner! Hello!"

"Chela, be quiet!"

Orange sunset light sloped across the clay parade ground. It was as still and hot as it had been at midday. A line of herons flew overhead. Cicadas whined in the trees beyond the fence. There was no movement in the alien compound. Froward noticed that the clay of the yard was crisscrossed and circled by dozens of heavy tire tracks. The tracks seemed to converge on the garage-like building with the big door, where he had left the passengers.

He slid off the top of the cable-pipe and walked as fast as he could. The passengers' bundles, space suits, and extra clothing were piled just inside the entrance. One of the discarded overalls had been run over by a vehicle with lugged tires. Flies clustered along one of the gutters in the floor, buzzing avidly. The sun, low on the horizon, shone between two buildings, and a beam lit up the interior of the building. Nausea clotted under Froward's tongue.

"Stay back, Chela."

"Why? What is it? Ah!"

A naked human carcass hung half off the edge of the big metal table in the center of the room. Froward forced himself to approach it. The head was missing, but one hairy arm remained, attached to the skin of the rib cage. Froward recognized the expensive Rolex watch on the wrist; Milanovitch had bought it in Tokyo.

Froward's knees were quivering, but he couldn't bring himself to lean on the table's edge. The remainder of the corpse was several feet away, an obscenely connected pair of legs. The legs were pinned to the table by huge mechanical arms that leaned down from the ceiling. Twin-lensed cameras, crawling with flies, hung between machinery that had unfolded into clusters of butcher's appliances: jointed arms ending in giant knives, circular saws, and hollow needles as big as pencils.

Froward took a hard grip on himself and traversed the room. Another victim lay out of sight behind a hulking machine. It was one of the boys, a talented volleyball player. Froward couldn't recall his name. The great blade that had opened his body still lay in the wound. There was no one else in the building. He emerged into the evening light and filled his lungs. Lines of dried blood-spatter led out the door and ended at the largest set of tire prints. The tire marks obliterated something that had been written in large capital letters in the clay, a statement that ended MENT FOR YOU.

Chela was coughing and choking against the wall of the neighboring building. Froward went to her, and stood next to her, looking around. He noticed the pitter-patter of water. He led the girl around the corner to a lifeboat-size trough inside a small fenced-in area. Water trickled into the trough from a pipe that stuck out of the ground. The water was lukewarm, but it looked and smelled clean. He pulled out his handkerchief, soaked it, and mopped Chela's face. Her legs folded under her, and she fell to the ground. She cried in great, racking sobs. "There-there," he said, sitting down with her on the ground, rocking her in his arms. She cried like a lost, hopeless child, loudly and with no trace of self-consciousness, tears pouring from her eyes and nose. "There-there," he said, rocking her. "There-there."

After several minutes she subsided. "I-I'm sorry. I'll be better in a second."

"It's all right."

She pulled away from him. "I'm wasting time. I'll stop n-now. There. I've stopped." She wiped her eyes with the backs of her hands. "Here, let me help you." She dipped and wrung out the handkerchief and wiped his hands with it. "You'll have to change your shoes, too. They're covered with dried, uh, from inside there."

Froward looked at her closely. "I'm okay now," she said. "Really, I promise."

"All right."

They stood up together. "You stay here, Chela. I'm going to get some of the baggage." He returned dragging two of the bundles, his own, and the one Milanovitch had brought from the airliner. He squatted and unwrapped them, taking out some heavy wool socks the Charonese had ordered from REI Outfitters in Seattle, and a pair of workman's boots that he had found in the cargo.

"Ever do any shooting, Chela?"

"A lot. My father is in the—"

"That's right, he's in the army. You told me that before, didn't you. Ever fire one of these?" He held out a heavy, flat pistol.

"Yeah. An army .45 automatic."

He gave her the gun and a handful of magazines, and a cardboard box of ammunition. He watched her for a moment as she expertly loaded cartridges into the magazines. "I'm lucky you're here, Chela."

She looked up at him. "Damn straight," she said. Her teeth and eyes almost glowed in the purple twilight.

Froward worked as the sky grew darker, rolling up cans of rations in two blankets, tying them with nylon straps. Then he and the girl moved to the opposite side of the cantonment from the death building. He led Chela behind one of the buildings and clambered through a steel-girded fence into another corral. Another huge water trough stood in one corner. Just as they reached this shelter, Froward heard a droning clatter in the distance.

"What's that?" Chela asked.

"Sounds like a helicopter," Froward said. "Let's get out of sight."

The girl needed no instruction. She dropped to the ground and crawled under the trough, dragging her bundle with her. Froward joined her. They lay in warm mud, listening as the helicopter sound grew almost deafening. Judging by the sound, it landed in the middle of the cantonment. Froward decided he wasn't curious enough to crawl to the building corner to see what was going on.

They lay face-to-face and wide-eyed. Froward heard what sounded like electric motors starting and stopping, vehicles moving around the open area, even footsteps. There was an inhuman lack of voices, of people talking. The glow of sunset crawled around the horizon, edging the clouds with golden flame. Finally, the helicopter started up again. It flew thunderously over their hiding place. Froward prepared himself to grab Chela in case she tried to look out at it from under the trough, but she didn't stir. The helicopter sound dwindled and died away in the distance.

Hours passed. Chela snored against Froward's shoulder. Froward kept jerking awake, listening through his doze. It grew completely dark, and the stars came out. Froward came awake once to see a bright star in the indigo sky, with several smaller sparks arranged in a line on either side of it.

At daylight he was roused by the harsh squabbling of birds in the trees beyond the fence. Something, miles away, bellowed like a foghorn. He saw Chela looking at him. He crawled out and had a look at the cantonment. It was empty and silent. The bundles they'd left on the far side had been taken away.

He and Chela sat on the ground and ate cans of rations. There was nothing to carry it in, so they drank warm water from the tap until they could hold no more. They slung their blanket rolls over their shoulders and followed the tire tracks to a gate in the steel fence on the opposite side of the cantonment. The gate was closed, so they climbed over the fence.

The tracks led down a rough trail into a dense wood. Froward paused to break open his grenade launcher and looked down its empty barrel. For a moment he relived his first days in Vietnam. He couldn't decide whether to load a HEAT round or buckshot. He had a cloth bandolier of each kind. The buckshot round was familiar to him, but he'd never heard of antitank ammunition for the M79 before. The projectile was long and pointed, and could either be a shaped charge or have a quick-delay kind of fuse that would blow up inside the target. The Charonese must have had a good reason for buying anti-tank ammo, he thought. Or maybe it was just another one of their mistakes. He slid one into the M79's chamber and snapped it shut.

"Beware of the dinosaurs," he muttered to himself.

"Try not to step in anything," Chela said, flashing her teeth at him over her shoulder. Side by side, they started down the trail.

Chapter Eight:
Beneath the Planet of the Dinosaurs

The night, the stars, and the silence had their effect on Charlie. Automatically, he tried to wipe his nose on his sleeve, but was stopped by the head-bubble of his suit. His eyes dried. He wouldn't show weakness again.

He began to take in his surroundings. To one side was that blood-curdling drop-off—also the tube, pipe, cable, or whatever it was, with its single rail on top, slanting steeply into the abyss —where the roller-coaster car with its cargo of struggling victims had gone. Charlie's testicles contracted at the thought of it.

On the other side, the flat plane of the tower-top platform stretched away indefinitely. In the distance the Charonese spaceship lay like a stranded ocean liner, a third of its wingspan hanging over the edge. There were two other left-behinds on the tower-top with him. Mute, lumpy figures in their slick plastic suits, they stood clinging to each other. Charlie couldn't make out the faces behind the plastic bubbles.

Luggage and bundles lay around them, where the students had dropped them during the scramble. Charlie noticed his briefcase lying nearby.

The feeble gravity made Charlie feel flimsy and insubstantial, as though an unguarded sneeze might blow him off the tower-top into that stupendous depth. Maybe they ought to sit down. He attracted the attention of the two others by waving his arms and making sitting gestures. They waved agreement.

The act of sitting was gymnastic. When Charlie tried it, his feet came up under him and he had to wait seconds for his rump to hit the pavement. And when it did, he suddenly began to hear breathing and mumbling in the inflated plastic bag around his head.

"You hear something?" he said automatically.

"What?"

"It's you, Reilly! I can hear you. So these suits do have radios after all." Charlie saw the other boy's brown face peering at him through the plastic. "Reilly, how come you didn't make it onto the car?"

"Somebody tried to push me in, but I didn't want to let go of Tina," Reilly said. "You say we're talking through two-way radio?"

"That's right."

"Tina? Tina! Why can't she hear me?"

The girl was sitting shapelessly beside Reilly, multiple layers of clothing compressed around her body by her space suit. She looked blankly at the two boys through the plastic of her suit bubble.

"Maybe her radio isn't on," Charlie said.

"Well, shit, man, how do you make it go on?" Reilly asked.

"I don't know," Charlie said.

"Come on, Charlie! What did we do different that we didn't do until now?"

"Wait a minute." Charlie tried to stand up, moved too suddenly and soared away. Arms and legs pumping, he floated down again and landed softly on his back. He paused for thought. He'd rehearsed such movements in his science-fictional imagination for years. He rolled carefully to his stomach and did a gentle push-up with his fingertips. He bounced to his feet.

"Boy," he said, "if I could do that on Earth, I'd be the gymnastics champion for sure."

Reilly tried to imitate him, but scrambled and fell. He lay looking up at Charlie. "I heard old lady Robinelli say you were in your element here, Charlie."

"She said that? Good old Mrs. Robinelli. You know, you and her were just about the only people in that school who were decent to me."

Charlie took Tina under her arms, pulled her up, rotated her, and slapped her behind. "Hey! Tina!"

"I hear you!" came her voice in Charlie's hood, high-pitched with strain and astonishment. "Charlie? Reilly? What's happening to us!"

"Captain Milanovitch and those others, they left us behind. They left us alone up here," Reilly said.

"No, he didn't," Charlie said. "There wasn't enough room in the car for everybody. He'll be back."

"Charlie," Tina said, "you always think you know—"

"Wait a minute, Tina," Reilly said. "What makes you think that, Charlie?"

"He said so."

"Said so how!"

"We were touching helmets. When you touch these helmets together you can hear what the other person's saying. The air conducts the—"

"You're sure? He said that?" Tina demanded.

"Why the hell doesn't anyone ever believe anything I ever tell them?"

"How could he be sure he'd even be able to come back for us?" Reilly mused. "He was just saying that to—"

"Aw, shit, Reilly, smarten up, will you?"

"Look here, Charlie—"

"You look here!" Charlie shouted. "How do you know we aren't the lucky ones? Mr. Froward and those others, they could all be dead now! We might be the only survivors! Better start thinking about that!"

That caused a momentary silence.

"Why, do you suppose," Charlie said, "did the Charonese put the suit radio switches in the seats of the space suits?"

"Who gives a big red rat's ass!" Tina said.

"Notice how the floor, or whatever it is, feels warm through your gloves?" Reilly asked.

"If it weren't for that, we'd be frozen solid by now," Charlie replied.

"Who gives a rat's ass about that either!"

"Well, what the hell would you like to talk about?" Reilly asked the girl.

"Well, for one thing, I think there're some other people up here with us. We should do something about them."

"Why do you—"

"Because I saw someone fall down on the way here," the girl

said. "Also, I think someone else ran away before we were out of the spaceship."

Now that it was mentioned, Charlie recalled seeing something like that himself.

"Well, someone should stay here to wait for the car to come back," Reilly said, "and someone else should go back and look for them."

"I'm not going back there," said Tina.

"It was your idea, Tina," Charlie said.

"Not by myself, anyway," she amended.

"Well, then, I'll go," Charlie said. "You two can stay here." Charlie fell down on his briefcase, and rose with it in his hand.

"Why do you want that, Charlie?" Reilly said.

"One never knows."

In the low gravity, Charlie moved with lumbering grace, reminding himself of a film he had once seen of hippopotami swimming underwater. He cautiously tried jumping several meters high, to get a view of their surroundings. The platform pavement was several hundred meters wide, and it ran in a circle around a center hole in the middle of the tower.

"Just like it said," Charlie said.

"What?" Reilly said.

"Never mind. I was just talking to myself."

"He's just being an asshole," Tina murmured.

"I heard that, Tina. You got a shitty attitude. If I were you, I'd be a little more cooperative."

"Take it easy, Charlie," Reilly said. "She didn't mean it." He whispered, "Come on, Tina, cut it out!"

Not bothering to look back at them, Charlie started toward something that looked like a dropped bundle lying halfway back to the alien spacecraft. He wasn't surprised when it turned out to be a spacesuited body. The face was hidden inside the deflated plastic bubble, under a brick-colored crust that Charlie queasily recognized as dried blood. Next to the body lay a suitcase with a name label: Sharon Ketchum, the student body vice president.

"The ex-student body vice president," Charlie said. "The only time she ever spoke to me was when she wanted me to vote for her."

124 *Rick Gauger*

"What is it, Charlie?" Reilly said in his ear.

"It's Sharon Ketchum," he answered. "She's dead."

"Dead? Are you sure, Charlie?"

"Yes! She's dead!"

"Why?"

Charlie quoted from some novel he'd read: "'It was her fate, to come to this place and die. . . .'"

"See? He's a shithead!"

"Quiet, Tina! Come on, Charlie, be reasonable."

After a second of silence, Charlie said, "Here it is. When she was putting her suit on, she tangled the lapel of her overalls in the seal. The air leaked out of her suit. That's a good sign."

"How can you say that, a good sign!"

"I mean these suits work okay if you put them on right! That's good for us! Now shut up and let me get on with it!"

Charlie now felt satisfactorily tough and callous. He moved on.

The Charonese flying wing was another hundred meters farther. Charlie passed under the huge black wing, walking over areas where the stonelike platform surface had been eroded by rocket-blast. He came to the open hatch. It's lower edge was three meters above him, an easy jump.

The hangar seemed cramped after the spaces outside. The skin of the airliner gleamed dully; the bulbs the aircrew had strung around the hangar were still lit. Charlie searched every corner, finding nothing except the rags of Mrs. Robinelli's volleyball, which had burst in the vacuum.

"There's no one in the hangar. I'm going inside the airplane," Charlie announced. He waited for a reply, but heard nothing. The metal walls of the ship were cutting off his radio transmissions, he decided. He swam up the ladder into the airliner's cargo deck and immediately heard the sound of a girl weeping.

"Hello?" he said.

The crying stopped. "Who's that?" said a scared, high-pitched voice.

"Me, Charlie Freeman. Where are you?"

"I'm up h-here."

"That's a big help. Where's 'up here'?" Charlie didn't wait for an answer, assuming the girl was up on the passenger deck. He floated up the stairway and quickly found a small, unidentifiable figure huddled in one of the seats.

"Come on, you can't stay here."

"I'm a-afraid."

"I figured that. Which one are you, anyway?"

"I'm Eva. Eva Wilcox."

Charlie burst out laughing. "Well, well! Where's your boyfriend, Colby, the big brave hero? Haw haw!"

"He let go of my h-hand," she sobbed. "I can't—"

"Hey, no problem, Miss Prom Queen! The nerd from outer space will rescue you!" Chortling, he grabbed the girl's arm, lifted her out of her seat, and dragged her down the stairs. She screamed and beat at him, but he was protected by the head-bubble of his suit and the layers of clothing he had put on.

Once outside the airliner, he stopped and held her over his head with one hand. He waited until she stopped struggling. "All right! Are you calmed down now?"

"P-please put me down."

"Okay. Don't run away, or do anything stupid. If you don't do what I tell you, you'll die, understand?"

"Y-yes!"

He set her on her feet. "Okay. Now we're going to have a look outside, just in case our ride has showed up. You just stay on your feet as best you can. And keep quiet!"

Taking her wrist, Charlie towed her to the great hatch. Looking out, he saw Reilly and Tina, looking miniaturized in the distance, sitting on the weird straight horizon created by the edge of the tower platform. They started when he spoke through his suit radio. "I found someone alive."

"Who is it, Charlie?" Reilly asked.

"It's Eva Wilcox," Charlie said. "I found her in the plane."

"What are you doing now?"

"Just checking a few things," Charlie told him. "Eva and I will be there in a minute." The tiny figure of Reilly waved at him.

Charlie towed Eva to the front of the hangar, to the spaceship's observation window, and left her standing on the catwalk. "You wait here."

"Where're you going?"

"Not far. I won't be long." Charlie jumped down below the

catwalk. The shattered alien TV set was still where he had been forced to leave it. He squatted, opened his briefcase, and pulled out his computer. He twisted wires together, straightened the keyboard, and typed:

are you there proctor?

As though it had been waiting for him, the mysterious something inside the Charonese ship printed across the gray liquid crystal screen on Charlie's portable: I'M STILL HERE, CHARLIE. YOU'RE IN A BAD SITUATION.

???

IT'S OBVIOUS, ISN'T IT?

captain froward will come back for us

YOU DON'T KNOW THAT AND NEITHER DO I.

is he alive?

THE ELEVATOR HE TOOK IS DESIGNED TO FUNCTION WITHOUT GUIDANCE, SO HE AND THE OTHERS PROBABLY REACHED THE BIO-SPHERE SAFELY. DO YOU REMEMBER THE DEFINITION OF "BIO-SPHERE"?

yes the outer surface of charon where the animals and plants live and theres air and water

THAT'S CORRECT, CHARLIE. I SEE I PICKED THE RIGHT MAN FOR THIS JOB. BUT YOU CAN'T DEPEND ON CAPTAIN FROWARD ANY MORE. THERE ARE TOO MANY OBSTACLES TO HIS RETURNING FOR YOU.

the charonese?

NOT THE CHARONESE. THEY DIDN'T EVEN KNOW YOUR SHIP HAS ARRIVED. IF THEY DID, THEY WOULD HELP YOU. AFTER ALL, THEY WANT YOU TO BE SAFE AND COMFORTABLE. ANTENNA MALFUNC-TION IS PREVENTING ME AND THE CHARONESE WHO CONTROLS THIS SHIP FROM CONTACTING THE CHARONESE CENTRAL COMPUTERS.

what shud we do?

THAT'S THE SPIRIT. IT'S TIME FOR YOU TO TAKE COMMAND, CHARLIE. YOU'VE GOT TO LEAD YOUR FRIENDS TO SAFETY. ONLY YOU CAN DO IT.

how?

REMEMBER WHAT I TOLD YOU ABOUT THE TOWER? IT SHOULD PROPERLY BE CALLED A "STACK," OR, BETTER STILL, A "LIGHT-STACK," SINCE IT ALLOWS THE PHOTONS EMITTED BY THE BLACK HOLE IN THE CENTER OF CHARON TO ESCAPE INTO SPACE. WITHOUT IT, CHARON WOULD BECOME TOO HOT AND EVENTUALLY EXPLODE.

yes i know

AS YOU KNOW, CHARON IS A HOLLOW SPHERE

yes i know

AN ELEVATOR LEADS DOWN THE CENTER OF THE STACK TO THE INNER SURFACE OF CHARON. IT'S CLEARLY VISIBLE. YOU'LL FIND IT EASILY.

then what?

AT THE BOTTOM OF THE ELEVATOR, TUNNELS LEAD TO ONE OF CHARON'S MANUFACTURING AND CONTROL FACILITIES, WHERE YOU WILL FIND THE MEANS TO SURVIVE.

are charonese there, too?

YES. THEY EXIST EVERYWHERE IN AND ON CHARON. THERE IS ONE IN THIS SHIP, BUT IT IS HELPLESS BECAUSE IT HAS NO ROBOTS. IT WISHES TO COMMUNICATE WITH YOU THROUGH THIS COMPUTER, BUT I PREVENT THAT. IT WOULD ONLY ADD TO THE CONFUSION.

what shud i do if i meet one? are they dangerous?

YES, BUT ONLY BECAUSE THEY ARE SUBJECT TO ACCIDENTS AND ERROR.

why did they bring us here real reason i mean

THIS IS NO TIME FOR A LONG CONVERSATION, CHARLIE.

thats what you say what i say is no info no cooperation. why they bring us here?

ALL RIGHT, YOU WIN. FIRST, YOU UNDERSTAND THAT WHAT YOU CALL THE PLANET PLUTO AND ITS MOON CHARON IS REALLY A STARSHIP?

yes you told me that already last week

GOOD. THE CHARONESE PLAN IS TO BRING A NUMBER OF YOUNG, WELL-EDUCATED HUMANS TO THE STARSHIP AND TEACH THEM HOW TO OPERATE IT. WHAT THE CHARONESE TRIED TO TELL YOU ABOUT THAT IN THEIR EDUCATIONAL PROGRAMS IS TRUE.

why do they want to?

THE CHARONESE ARE 582.6 MILLION YEARS OLD.

"Jeezus!" Charlie said.

"What?' said Eva Wilcox's voice in Charlie's head-bubble, her voice high-pitched with fear. "What'd you say?"

"Silence, pathetic Earthwoman," Charlie intoned. Words marched down the computer's little gray screen:

BECAUSE THEY'RE OLD, THEY MAKE MANY MISTAKES. BECAUSE OF THAT, THE LIFE-SUPPORT SYSTEMS ON CHARON ARE BREAKING DOWN. CHARON'S BIOME IS IN DANGER. DO YOU REMEMBER WHAT I SAID A BIOME WAS?

yes

TELL ME.

biome: an ecology, all the plants, aminals, germs, etc

RIGHT. THE PRESENT CREW OF CHARON (THOSE YOU CALL THE CHARONESE) IS GETTING TOO OLD EVEN TO OPERATE THE LIFE-SUPPORT SYSTEMS FOR THE BIOSPHERE. WORSE THAN THAT, THEY CAN'T DEPART FROM THIS SOLAR SYSTEM AND GO TO ANOTHER ONE. THEY'VE BEEN STRANDED HERE FOR 65.8 MILLION YEARS, LITERALLY SINCE THE AGE OF DINOSAURS.

"Damn," Charlie muttered to himself.

I SUSPECTED THAT THE CHARONESE MIGHT BE TOO FAR-GONE TO BRING YOU AND THE OTHER HUMANS SAFELY TO CHARON. I MADE SURE A PART OF ME WAS ABOARD THIS SPACESHIP. MY SUSPICIONS WERE PROVED CORRECT WHEN THE CHARONESE ABOARD THIS SHIP WAS UNABLE TO COMMUNICATE WITH YOU.

but that was our fault. we were the ones who smashed the tv sets

TRUE, BUT MORE INTELLIGENT COMMUNICATION WOULD HAVE PREVENTED THAT. FOR EXAMPLE, THE HUMANS (NOT YOU, CHARLIE) INTERPRETED HIS (THE CHARONESE'S) CLUMSY ATTEMPT TO SET UP THE TV AND PROVIDE AIR AS AN ATTACK. AS A RESULT, MOST OF HIS ROBOTS WERE DESTROYED, LEAVING HIM PRACTICALLY HELPLESS. THIS SPACESHIP ALMOST DIDN'T MAKE IT TO CHARON. YOU WERE ALMOST ALL KILLED. I SAW WHAT WAS GOING ON AND DECIDED TO STEP IN PERSONALLY, SO TO SPEAK. I REVEALED MYSELF TO YOU.

who what are you?

YOU WOULD CALL ME A COMPUTER PROGRAM. I AM A KIND OF "FAIL-SAFE" DEVICE. I WAS BUILT INTO CHARON FOR THE PURPOSE OF PREVENTING THE KIND OF MISTAKES WE HAVE BEEN TALKING ABOUT.

how can the charonese live so long?

THE SCIENCE AND TECHNOLOGY OF CHARON ALLOWS THEM TO DO IT. HOW ABOUT IT, CHARLIE, WOULD YOU LIKE TO LIVE PRACTICALLY FOREVER? THAT'S ONE OF THE THINGS CHARON HAS TO OFFER YOU.

"Totally fugging outrageous," Charlie mumbled.

Eva, on her suitradio, began, "Charlie, please—"

"Shut up!" He typed:

yes but what are we going to be? slaves of the charonese?

THAT'S WHAT THEY THINK, BUT I WON'T ALLOW IT. WITH MY HELP, AND UNDER YOUR LEADERSHIP, THE HUMANS WILL TAKE OVER. CHARON WILL BE UNDER YOUR COMMAND, CHARLIE, PROVIDED THAT YOU SHOW ME THAT YOU'RE CAPABLE OF IT. ARE YOU UP TO IT?

yes what is charon for?

YOU KNOW THAT ALREADY, CHARLIE: TO PRESERVE A PART OF THE BIOME THAT EXISTED ON EARTH BEFORE THE DISASTER THAT ENDED THE CRETACEOUS PERIOD. IN OTHER WORDS, DINOSAURS AND THEIR ENVIRONMENT, OR AT LEAST AS MUCH OF IT AS WAS POSSIBLE TO SAVE.

why? what for?

NO MORE QUESTIONS! YOUR SPACE SUIT WILL ONLY SUPPORT YOU ANOTHER 5.2 HOURS. YOU MUST GO NOW.

ok goodbye proctor

There was no answer. Obviously, it was time to get moving. "The proctologist of Charon," Charlie said to himself with a laugh. "There's one on every planet."

"What are you doing?" Eva asked him.

"I've been talking to the ship's computer," he lied. "I've found out how to get to safety."

"Really? Do you really know how to, to—"

Charlie disconnected the wires of his computer and stuffed it back into his briefcase. Holding onto it, he vaulted smoothly up to the catwalk beside Eva. "Yes. I've been talking to the aliens. You stick with me and I'll get you to a safe place. Come on, I'll show you."

He grabbed her wrist, and pulled her down to the end of the catwalk. She shrank back from the view through the glass dome, the night sky, the stars, the drop-off at the edge of the platform, and the dazzling blue and white world below.

"Come on, girl, don't be such a chickenshit! Look down there. There's where we're going. Charon. It's a whole world, and I'm going to get it. It's going to belong to me, and the rest of you humans are going to live there!"

"I think we should go be with Tina and Reilly, now," Eva said, trying to pull her hand away.

"Better just hang on to me, little girl," he said. "You don't even know how to walk yet."

Clutching his briefcase, Charlie pulled Eva across the hangar, through the hatch, and out under the stars. He towed her across the vast flat pavement past the spot where the dead girl lay. At the sight of the body Eva sobbed and tried to free herself again.

"That's Sharon Ketchum," Charlie told her. "If you act stupid, you'll wind up like she did."

He dragged her onward. At the edge, Reilly and Tina stood up to meet them.

Tina hugged Eva. "I'm so glad you were found, Eva, I—"

Eva burst into new tears. "Oh, Tina, he hit me and dragged me—"

"I did not hit her!" Charlie interrupted. "I did drag her, however. Okay, I found out that we have to get ourselves down from here, and we have to start right now."

"How would you know that?" Reilly demanded.

Charlie showed him his portable computer. "I used my little computer to contact the main computer that runs the ship. It told me that our space suits are going to run out of air in about five hours. It said the roller-coaster car probably won't be coming back. It told me there's another elevator we can use."

"Is that true, Eva?" Reilly said angrily.

"I don't know. . . . I saw him typing something . . ."

"Hey, if you don't believe me, you can stay here and die all you want to!" Charlie chortled. "I'm going!" He jerked Eva away.

"Stop that!" Tina shouted, trying to snatch Eva away from him. "Why do you have to be such a shit! Let her go! Reilly, make him let her go!"

Laughing, Charlie hopped away from them easily, taking Eva with him. "Hey, Tina! Don't call me names! I'm saving your life!"

Giving up, Tina turned to Reilly. "Do something, won't you!"

Reilly looked up at the fallen alien spacecraft, and at the edge of the tower platform, and at Charlie, who had come to rest with Eva safely out of reach. "Ow, Charlie . . ." she pleaded.

"You're hurting her, Charlie," Reilly said unemotionally. "What's the matter with you? Bragging like a little kid, and hurting Eva. Big man."

Charlie released Eva, whose feet immediately skated out from under her. "I didn't mean to hurt her," he said. "Look, she can't even stand up without . . ."

"Come on, Charlie, seriously," Reilly said. "If you really know so much, help us out, okay? It's dangerous here. Didn't you say we should do something?"

"Yes," Charlie said, quickly becoming matter-of-fact. "We've got to go that way. I'll tell you about it on the way. Come on, Eva."

"Take his hand, Eva," Reilly said.

"Reilly!"

"It's okay, Tina. Charlie didn't mean any harm, did you, Charlie?"

"No," Charlie said. "Come on. Don't try to walk, Eva. Just shuffle along like this."

The little group followed Charlie away from the drop-off. After crossing a hundred meters of pavement, they arrived at the inner rim of the platform. The center well of the Charonese light-stack was a frightening sight. It was hundreds of meters across, so huge that the wide platform they had crossed to get there constituted only a narrow flange around its circumference. A short distance below the rim, the walls of the hole vanished in darkness. They halted well back from the edge.

Charlie pointed. "See over there, where those rails run down the side of the well? That must be the elevator. The computer said it goes down inside."

They hopped and floated along the edge, everyone falling at least once. "Just so nobody goes down the hole," Charlie said.

"What's in there, Charlie?" Reilly asked, puffing with exertion.

"It's an opening into the hollow interior of Charon. It's like a smokestack."

"Couldn't we just float down there instead of taking the elevator?"

"Not me!" Tina said.

"Reilly, what grade did you make in Physics One?" Charlie said.

"A minus."

"I made a C, and I learned that you can't free-fall five hundred kilometers in any gravity without hitting bottom at a high speed. Like hundreds of kilometers per hour. Question is," Charlie concluded, out of breath, "why didn't you learn it, since you got the A?"

"Piss off and turn purple, Charlie."

"Stuff it up your shorts, Charlie," Tina added.

"I wouldn't want to jump anyway. Know why?"

"I don't think I could stop you from telling me, Charlie," Reilly said.

"—because there's a black hole down there." Charlie said. "You'd made a hell of an explosion when you hit it. Real fireworks."

Eva, dragging her feet while being towed along by Charlie, spoke up. "I saw a movie about that once. These people went through a black hole into another universe or something."

"You might make it into another universe," Charlie said, "but you'd be made into hamburger vapor in the process. Tidal forces would rip you into atoms—"

"How do you know all this stuff?" Tina demanded.

"The computer told me. While you guys were playing stupid games I was talking to it. It said we all would've learned this stuff if we hadn't smashed the TV sets, or tried to talk to the Charonese robots. You'll remember I told everybody that in the beginning, but nobody ever listens to me."

"We're sure as shit listening now, aren't we, Eva?" Reilly said.

"You sure as shit are," Charlie answered for her.

They halted at the elevator. It looked like what it was supposed to be, a topless metal cage around a square metal platform. It obviously was designed to run down the pair of rails that disappeared into the darkness below.

"Where's this thing supposed to take us?" Tina asked.

"Proctor said that it goes to the factories and the control room. The means to survive. Air, water, food . . ."

"You believe it?" Tina asked.

"Here we go again," Charlie said.

"There's no reason not to believe," Reilly said. "Besides—"

"We don't have any choice," Tina said. "I'm tired of not having any goddamn choice. All right, goddammit." She stepped onto the elevator, and it sank under her, began to move downward.

Tina squawked in terror and tried to jump back to the pavement. Her feet shot away, and she sprawled in midair. Her body fell in slow motion, following the descending elevator floor.

"Everybody jump!" Charlie ordered. Eva began to struggle and scream. Briefcase in one hand and the girl's wrist in the other, he stepped into space. They floated downward, caught up with the elevator floor, and landed tumbling.

Charlie, gasping with excitement, rolled on his back and saw Reilly still hesitating above them. "Reilly! Reilly!" Tina screamed.

"Step off the edge, Reilly!" Charlie shouted. "Just step off! Come on!"

Reilly launched himself spread-eagle. He fell, gaining speed, hit the edge of the elevator cage, bounced away like a dropped balloon.

Charlie snatched through the wire, managed to seize Reilly's head-bubble in both arms. "Got ya! Grab the cage!"

In the weak gravity near the top of the smokestack, Reilly only weighed about two pounds. He scrambled over the top of the cage and into the elevator. He collapsed on the floor, and Tina threw herself on him.

Charlie guffawed. "Smooth move, even if I say so myself. Haw! Haw!"

They became quiet. The mouth of the smokestack seemed to contract above them as the elevator slid downward, smoothly gaining speed. Pluto glowed dully in the center of a circle of nighttime sky. Charlie stared hungrily at the stars; they were being eclipsed in groups and clusters as the elevator sank into the darkness.

"How're we going to see?" Eva said at length.

"Uh, just a minute," Charlie said. He rummaged in his brief-case and produced an elaborate plastic flashlight. "I knew I would need this," Charlie said. "It has a spotlight, a fluorescent tube, and red and yellow blinking lights. I bought it at K mart."

The bluish fluorescent light showed the wall of the smoke-stack speeding past outside the wire mesh, alternating bands of metal and translucent crystal. The opposite wall was too far away for the spotlight. "We're in it now," said Reilly.

"God, I'd give anything for this to be over with. I'd give anything just to go home again," Tina said.

"Me, too," said Eva.

Charlie's round grinning face shone ghostlike behind his bubble. "Anything?" he chortled.

"Cram it, Charlie." Tina said.

"He's so childish," Eva said.

"No gratitude," Charlie said. "You stick with me, and maybe I'll send you back to Seattle in your own spaceship. Hah. But only if you're nice."

"Cram it, Charlie," Tina repeated.

"See? He's so childish."

"That's right, Eva."

"What you don't know is," Charlie said, "I've been in contact with this thing called Proctor since practically the first day we were hijacked in the airliner."

"You have not," Tina said.

"Oh, yes, I have," Charlie said. "You believe it, don't you, Eva?"

Eva didn't respond.

"Proctor is going to help me take over Charon," Charlie said. "We're going to get rid of the Charonese and run the place ourselves."

"You and Proctor, right?" Tina said.

"And as many of you people as I can make use of. We might own this whole place. Wouldn't you like that? How about it, Reilly?"

"Sounds good to me, Charlie. How're we going to do it?"

"I don't know exactly. The process was supposed to start with the educational programs the Charonese were going to show us on TV. There are going to be computer terminals and teaching machines or something. What we have to do is keep our eyes open and stay alert for any kind of advantage. When one comes up, we grab it."

Reilly sat up straight and peered at Charlie. "You're serious, aren't you, Charlie?"

"Yes, I am," Charlie said, unsmiling.

"Is that what you were doing all the time back on the spaceship, talking to the Charonese? Through your computer?"

"Not the Charonese. Proctor."

"My gosh, you are serious."

"Serious as shit. Do you want to be in with me?"

"Damn right. Tina and Eva, too."

"Fine. But no more jokes. No more arguments. You all have to do what I tell you. Okay?"

"Good enough, Charlie," Reilly said.

"I will," Eva said. "But . . ."

"No buts," Charlie said. "How about you, Tina?"

"How'd you like to bite my ass, you fat little—"

Reilly broke in. "Tina, Charlie just wants us to stick together. I want us to stick together, too. You agree about that, don't you?"

"Oh, all right."

There was silence after that. The nearby wall was a blur of speed. Charlie turned off the flashlight to conserve the batteries. He lay down on his back in the darkness. Above, the opening of the smokestack contracted rapidly. A few last stars winked out, then Pluto filled the opening. Charlie wished he could see its surface more clearly. Proctor had said it was a ball of hydrogen ice, and that the Charonese had collected the ice from the asteroids and comets that populated the outer reaches of the solar system. What it was for, Charlie didn't know.

He lay, musing. His space suit and the thicknesses of clothing he wore under it were awkward, but the low gravity kept it from being uncomfortable. He wished he were at home also, in the empty house he had to himself when his mother was working. Or in the room he had to himself. He would spend hours there, drawing maps of places in his imagination, or marshaling wars among his plastic toys, building and wrecking intricate models he bought with his savings.

His mother was too tired to deal with a chattering little boy after coming home late from the hospital cafeteria where she worked nights and weekends. They lived quietly and alone in a suburban tract house. When his father had left, she had talked to him of money, expenses, how lucky they were to have the house at least. Four-year-old Charlie's overforward intelligence had grasped it, even at that age: she was older than the other mothers he knew; she had given up dreams and imagination. He owed her. He couldn't demand anything from her. The mute, weary hugs she offered him before she collapsed in front of the TV at night were all she could give. After school, he scrounged for recyclable aluminum and deposit bottles along the roads and in the backsides of shopping centers as a solitary child, managed a complicated paper route as a solitary early teen.

But he admitted he wouldn't want to miss the adventure he was having. Not sorry, except for his mother, to leave all that behind. Especially now that he was feeling confident of a happy outcome. Somewhat confident. He warmed toward Reilly, who had supported him just now. Reilly gave him some of the sense of companionship for which he'd been starved this last year. It seemed to Charlie that lately he was losing the self-sufficiency that had armored his early childhood. In school, with his peers, he had learned that he was a powerless eccentric.

He knew what ailed him; he'd looked it up. He approached adolescence with his eyes open. The mechanics of love and power were as plain in his head as they were on the pages of garish paperback fiction and reference works he'd found in the library.

He had looked up *proctor* in his paperback dictionary. It meant "instructor, disciplinarian." He dozed.

He dreamed of triumph, of springing in flight over people, trees, buildings. Crowds of people watched him in awe. Acquaintances and strangers pressed around him asking for forgiveness, waiting for his commands. He harangued them with astounding fluency, exposing their errors, damning their stupidity. Fear crept upon him, just out of sight. He had vast power to rend, cut, hurt, to exploit, to enslave; he was terrified of what he might do. Behind everything was the thought of the girls' hot skin glimpsed through sleeveless blouses, drooping necklines, their clothing ripped into fluttering strips, revealing round thighs and moist breasts. In fever and sweat Charlie pulled them down onto his body, trying to thrust into them, but their weight suffocated him.

Lust turned into panic, Charlie snapped awake. He found himself lying on his back, in sweltering heat, and his own weight was stifling him. He fumbled for his flashlight.

The elevator cage had stopped. The smokestack wall was gone. The elevator now hung, by its twin rails, in black space. Apparently it had ridden down to the bottom of the stack, through the shell of Charon, and into the hollow interior. Overhead, just within reach of the flashlight beam, was the overhang where the interior of the stack curved away to become the interior surface of the artificial world.

He rolled to his stomach and raised himself, with some difficulty, on his elbows. His weight was back to normal, he realized. After the superhuman ease of life in the floating world on top of the tower, normal gravity crushed him down. Inside his suit, his clothing was squishy with sweat.

Charlie pulled himself upright on the bars of the elevator cage. Outside, a metal roadway hung from rods. The flashlight beam bunced oddly in the darkness, which led to a discovery: the underside of Charon was mirrored.

He heard groans and exclamations in his head-bubble. The other students were stirring.

"Come on," Charlie said. "Get up. We've got to get out of here."

They stepped out of the elevator cage onto the suspended roadway. Charlie and Reilly had a cautious look over the edge. In the black gulf directly below them a single star shone.

"That must be the black hole," Charlie said. "It's making the gravity we feel. It's where the heat's coming from, too. It's ninety kilometers away, straight down." They backed away, carefully.

"Black holes aren't black?" Reilly said.

Tina spoke up in their head-bubbles. "Stop dorking around and let's go!"

They walked along the suspended roadway, stealing glances upward at their upside-down reflections.

"What holds it up?" Reilly said, the only one who would ask him a serious question. "Why doesn't it fall?"

"It holds itself up. It's strong, like an eggshell. Know what it's made of? Pure diamond. Break off a piece of it, take it back to Earth, you'd be rich for life."

"Shit, Charlie."

Charlie laughed. "Have it your way, man."

"What else do you know, Charlie?"

"I know we have to keep going this way. We'll find air."

"What else?"

"Just details. How the place is built. That's all I had time to ask. We'd know a lot more if we'd cooperated with the Charonese from the first, like I wanted to. Buuut noooo."

The roadway began to slant upward. The four of them trudged uphill into a gap in the mirror ceiling and halted in front of a gray metal wall.

"Now what?" Reilly said.

"It's a door," Charlie answered. "It has to be. Look at those cracks around it. And there's a plate, like on the air lock door of the spaceship. Should I hit it?"

"You're asking me?" Reilly said. Charlie moved to the door-plate and struck it with his gloved fist. The wall slid quickly aside, revealing a long, brightly lit room that sloped upward toward another door.

"No air yet," Charlie said, stepping through. "Come on."

They walked up the room. The second door opened in its turn, but not before the first one had silently closed itself. Behind the first room was a second one, identical to the first, then a third, then dozens more, all lit by plates in the ceilings, translucent gray walls rounded at the corners.

"It's a tunnel," Charlie told them as they hiked uphill. "The doors make it an air lock. It's to keep air from the surface from leaking into the interior."

"It goes to the surface?" Reilly asked. "You sure about that?"

"It goes up, and it has air locks. Therefore . . ." Charlie gestured knowledgeably, but no one was looking at him.

They trudged up the slope, door opening on door, sweat running down their faces. They basked in the light and the feeling of safety given them by the solid walls after the terrifying spaces outside. The floors were made of the same material as the walls. The plastic soles of their boots adhered to it. Under the glassy surface were two parallel strips of what looked like silver-inlaid gold, shining like jewelry. They reminded Charlie of railroad tracks.

Charlie began to tire. The thirty-fourth door, by his count, didn't open. Instead, it hissed.

"What's that!" Eva exclaimed, stepping back.

"Air, I hope," Charlie said. The hiss grew louder and deepened in pitch. Their head-bubbles began to deflate, then; to his unspeakable relief, Charlie's space suit loosened around him. They stood and stared at one another in wonder as the plastic suits expanded to their original sizes, drooping around their bodies and dangling down from their arms. Finally, the seals across the fronts of their suits fell open.

"Thank God!" Tina exclaimed, as she pulled off her hood.

". . . You can take off your suits now," Charlie announced. The others were already pushing down the rumpled plastic, and sitting to unlace the workboots that Captain Milanovitch had advised them to put on over the plastic feet of their suits.

Door thirty-four slid aside with a thud that made them all jump. Beyond lay another upward-sloping room like the others. "Lucky for us there was nothing hostile in there. We need to get better organized."

"Like how, Charlie," Tina said.

"I'm thirsty," Eva said.

Charlie, head down, gathered up his discarded clothing and his space suit and began rolling them into a clumsy cylinder.

"You're taking that stuff with you?" Tina asked.

"Yes. And you're taking yours, too."

"I'm not carrying that stuff. It's too hot."

"You never leave equipment behind," Charlie said emphatically. "That's the rule. And from now on we're going to move along the walls instead of walking in the middle of the room. And one of us—not me all the time—is going to hit the doorplate while the rest of us stay back a safe distance. That's how you're supposed to do it."

"He sounds like my little brother playing D and D," Tina said to Reilly. "Charlie's head is still in grade school."

"Yours is still up your butt, Tina!" Charlie retorted. Reilly's mouth twitched; he wiped his face on his sleeve.

Charlie rummaged angrily in his briefcase and came up with a small bottle of apple juice and an elaborate Swiss army knife. He unfolded a tool from the knife, opened the bottle, and pushed it to Eva. "Here," he said. "It's warm, but it's drinkable." Eva, pink-faced with the heat of their walk, eagerly took the bottle and drank off half of the juice.

"Thanks, Charlie," she said, looking at him as she handed the bottle back to him. Charlie held out the bottle to Reilly, who took a sip and returned it.

Charlie grinned hardily and offered the bottle to Tina. She hesitated, then took it. "Go ahead, drink it up," he said. She swallowed most of the remainder.

Charlie's teeth clicked on the bottle. He drained it, smacked his lips, rolled his eyes at Tina, and dropped it into his briefcase. He stood up, hefting his briefcase and roll of clothing. "March or die, as they say in the Foreign Legion." Reilly picked up his and Tina's clothing, but she snatched it away from him.

For another two hours they trekked uphill through the rooms, doors opening in front of them and closing behind them. Occasionally, there were doors on the sides of the tunnel, but Charlie wasn't tempted to explore them. He was cooler and lighter without the suit and the extra clothing, but he fought himself, trying not to be the first one to ask for a rest halt. At the last minute, they came to a new kind of room.

"Two doors," Charlie observed. The new tunnel segment was Y-shaped, with a door at the end of each arm. The golden rails branched in both directions. He walked to one of the doors and struck the plate. It jerked aside. "Shit," Charlie whispered. Through the opening was a great hall, with parallel rows of what looked like factory workbenches stretching away for hundreds of meters. Machines were everywhere, some fixed to the floor, some wheeled, others looking incomplete. Rolls of cable, sheets of metal, piles of indefinable gadgets and doodads lay among carts and containers of all sizes and shapes. In the distance a multiarmed mechanical something moved along, dragging a flexible hose over the floor. Eerie whining rose and fell with the thing's arm motions. Charlie jumped back, and the door slapped shut in his face.

Reilly and the girls had come up beside Charlie. "What's in there?" Reilly asked.

"This is the end of the line. It's a big room, with some kind of machinery all over it. And I saw a robot. A big one. It didn't see me, I don't think."

"What was it doing?"

"I think it was vacuuming the goddamn place."

"What?"

"You know, cleaning up. Like it was the janitor. I'm thinking about trying to communicate with it. I'm thirsty as hell."

"Me, too, but let's try the other door first," Reilly said.

"Good thinking," Charlie said. The girls followed the two boys up the other fork of the Y to the next door. "After you," Charlie said, standing back. Reilly banged the plate with his fist. The panel slid aside: before them stretched a room large enough to drive a truck through, and a waft of moist air, fragrant with greenery and earth. A scatter of dried leaves lay on the floor. There was a crack around the inside of the door, and no exit.

"An elevator to the surface," Charlie said.

"Think the surface is better than where we are?" Reilly said.

"We might find some water. If we stay here, we'll be forced to ask the robot for some."

"I have to go to the bathroom," Eva said.

"That, too," Charlie said.

"Surely a place as big as this has to have some restrooms," Tina said.

"Tina thinks she's at a shopping mall," Charlie said. "We'll go up."

He took Eva's elbow and steered her inside. Reilly and Tina followed. The door closed and the room lifted, fast. They fidgeted and exchanged stares for several minutes, then sat down.

Fifteen minutes later, the door slid open on a room as big as a warehouse. Machines were parked along the walls, some man-sized, some as big as locomotives, some with jointed legs and arms, some with great, cleated tires. All were dented, scraped, and mud-caked.

Daunted, the students hung back in the elevator doorway. Nothing moved. Chunks of dried clay, hardened in polygon tire-tread shapes, lay on the floor. At the opposite end of the room was a big door.

"We're not going to get anywhere by delaying," Charlie said. "It's one of the girls' turn to go try that door."

"Not me," Tina said. Eva looked down and bit her lip.

"Right," Charlie said, and he marched out across the muddy floor. It was stupid not to look at the machines, he thought. It wouldn't prevent them from suddenly coming to life. He reached the metal door, noting its prosaic appearance, like any corrugated aluminum garage door, only three times as big. He had to stretch to reach the opener-plate.

Motors whirred and the door rattled upward—to reveal a sunset panorama, seen from a low hilltop. Pink and violet-tinted clouds towered in a purple sky. High, flat-topped pines stood in silhouette where the ground rolled downhill out of sight. Charlie looked at the trees across an expanse of nodding grass and rustling palmetto thickets.

Half a month in the spaceship's dingy metal hangar was a long confinement for a fifteen-year-old. Charlie halted in midstep, half through the alien doorway. A warm breeze carried fragrances to him out of the twilight. Immediately in front of the door, the ground was rutted clay, spotted with sky-reflecting puddles. He moved to the nearest pool. The water was clean. Charlie dropped to his hands and knees and slaked his thirst in clear, tepid rainwater.

Chapter Nine:

Charlie Kong

"Charlie's drinking out of a mud puddle! Eyoo!"

"Okay, Tina," Charlie said. "Be thirsty if you want to." Charlie offered Eva a little collapsible drinking cup out of his briefcase. "Here, Eva, it's clean. Look, there's no mud in it or anything."

Eva sipped gingerly. Charlie offered the cup to Reilly, who knelt and carefully dipped water from the puddle. Seeing him, Tina gave in and drank.

Charlie closed the cup, stuffed it into his briefcase, then pulled out a flattened roll of toilet paper. He held it out to the girls. "You want some of this?"

Tina took it, looked around. "The girls' is around that corner of the building," said Charlie. Glaring at Charlie, Tina took Eva's elbow and pulled her out of sight. "You have to tell them how to do everything," Charlie said to Reilly.

The two boys moved around the opposite corner and peed uncompanionably against the alien building. The building's wall seemed to be poured white concrete with glittering stuff in it. Behind it was a stand of spindly pines, and beyond that a vast curving wall like a mountain cliff. They craned their necks, looking up at it. Above the clouds, the wall glared white in full daylight, but above that, it became invisible in the twilight sky.

"That's the lightstack, the tower we landed on top of," Charlie remarked. "This is an amazing damn place, you know?"

The other boy didn't answer. "Too bad the Charonese didn't order the kind of coveralls that have zippers instead of buttons," Charlie added.

They buttoned up, wandered back to the front of the building, sat on the ground in the twilight. "It looks like the sun's going down," Charlie said, digging in his bundle for rations. "But, it may not be. It might be coming up. Or it might always look like this here. We're at Charon's north pole, you know." Charlie sniffed and wiped his nose on the sleeve of his coverall. Reilly didn't say anything.

The girls rejoined them, Tina sitting close to Reilly. They opened cans and ate ten-year-old army surplus C-rations. The resplendent tropical sunset didn't change, except its source of light crept to the right among the pine trunks. Between mouthfuls, the teenagers glanced uneasily at the motionless mechanical monsters in the building behind them, and at the dark treeline in the near distance. Charlie talked on.

"Actually, what we see isn't really the sun. It's really a mirror that orbits around Charon's equator. It reflects a beam of light from Pluto."

"So what," Tina said.

"We have to think about what to do next," Reilly said.

"I think we should try to find the others," Eva said.

"It's obvious what we should do," Charlie said. "We should go back down the elevator and make contact with the Charonese. Or the Proctor, if I can find out how to—"

"Stuff it, Charlie," Tina said.

"I suppose you know exactly what to do!"

"Just stuff it. Don't cry, Eva; it'll be all right."

Tears ran down the blond girl's cheeks, and her chin quivered. Her can of beans and franks lay on the ground in front of her, plastic spoon protruding. "Oh, Tina, do you think C-Colby's still alive?" she sobbed.

"Sure he is, Eva," Tina told her, her own chin trembling.

"I'm just sure," Charlie said. He stood up and angrily wiped his hands on his coverall front. "We can't stay here. Those woods are full of dinosaurs." He remembered a line from a Ray Bradbury story. "Those dinosaurs are hungry!"

"Oh, right, Charlie, dinosaurs!"

"You'll probably see a dinosaur sooner than you'd like, Tina!"

The girls looked at Reilly, who frowned and shook his head. "I don't know what to do," he said. "I have to think about it. At least it's not getting any darker."

"Well, I'm for going back now," Charlie said. "We'll get some alien to help us." He pulled at Eva's arm. "Come on, Eva."

"Leave Eva alone, Charlie," Reilly said.

Charlie put his hand under Eva's arm and tried to lift her to her feet. "You'd better come with me. It's more dangerous out here than—"

"Leave her alone, I said!" Reilly stood up and pushed Charlie away, causing the fat boy to stagger through a rain puddle. Tina laughed at him.

"Thanks a lot, Reilly!" Charlie flared. "Who's the big man now. Now that I saved your black ass and got you to where you think it's safe, you're pushing me around! I got news for you—"

Reilly's face was set in neutral, dealing with one problem at a time. "It's not right to treat Eva the way you do. I didn't mean to push you like that. Come on, be cool, okay?" Reilly gestured vaguely, meaning "sit down, calm yourself."

"No! Back there in the dark, when you were scared, you agreed to do what I say! You got a girl. I want one, too!"

"Oh, for God's sake, Charlie—"

"Bullshit!" Charlie shouted. "Okay! You don't want to be in on this with me, you can take care of yourself from now on!"

Charlie picked up his briefcase and stalked, raving, away into the alien building. "Be dinosaur shit or starve to death, see what happens first! I don't give a . . ." His shouts echoed off the ceiling, breaking into Charlie's anger and making him remember the rows of hulking machines along the walls. He marched the rest of the way in silence, sneaking glances at the robots.

Most of them looked like trucks, with huge rubber tires and various kinds of cargo beds. Instead of driver's cabs they had turrets studded with camera lenses. Some of the trucks were equipped with mechanical arms. Most intimidating were several thirty-foot-tall, four-armed giants standing on flat metal feet. The robots' four-fingered, rubber-padded hands were as big as power shovels. Intimidating, but toylike, like the Robotor, Gobot, Defendor models Charlie used to buy in the mall hobby shops. The place was a parking place for robots, he decided. A robot garage.

Charlie's temper had evaporated by the time he reached the elevator entrance. He was relieved to find it lit and its door standing open, just as he'd left it. Swinging his briefcase, he marched inside. The door slid shut behind him, and the elevator started downward.

A long time passed. Charlie waited and reconsidered. He decided he'd changed his mind. Returning to Charonese underworld no longer seemed like such a suitable idea. The fresh air and light up above were nice. Flexibility was one of the qualities of a good leader. He began planning what he would say to Reilly when he got back to the top. He had formulated several speeches and stances to take when the elevator reached bottom and the door opened.

Charlie hastily jumped back; a procession of motorized carts was rolling across the Y-shaped room. He peeped around the door and saw that they were carrying piles of books, cartons, supplies, and equipment from the airliner. A camera on the wall swiveled to look at him. He shrank away from it, but it was impossible to get out of its line of sight in the elevator. Before he could decide what to do, one of the carts smoothly rolled out of line and halted in front of the elevator. This cart held a mailbox-robot, like the ones he'd seen in the spaceship. Its camera rotated toward him.

Charlie sweated and snuffled under the robot's glass stare. "Ah, take me to your leader?"

"You're Charlie," the robot replied. "Have you been injured? Do you need medical care? Do you need food or drink?"

"Uh, I could use some of that, yeah," Charlie said, reassured by the robot's solicitousness. Behind the robot, the parade of carts trundled into the big factory room where he'd seen the "janitor" at work. Other robots, of different sizes and shapes, moved among the workbenches, or whatever they were.

Like most students, Charlie had mastered the art of the distracting question. "Who are you? How do you know my name? Are you the robot from the spaceship?" As he spoke, Charlie noted that this robot was clean and undented. It couldn't be the same one, unless it had been in the ship since he last saw it. He snickered nervously.

"I am the Charonese who piloted your spacecraft. Did other humans come with you?"

"Why didn't you help us get down from the top of the tower? We could've all been killed!"

"I was unable to communicate with you or with any of the other members of the Crew."

"Do you have more than one body, or what?"

"In a sense, yes," the robot said, launching into a lecture as Charlie had hoped it would. "We Charonese exist as electronic memories. Our physical bodies ceased to exist long ago. Our minds and or personalities live on, inside the computers that control Charon. In a way, we are Charon. Charon, and all its machinery, is our body. I control this robot as you control your hands and feet. We are ghosts in the machine, as one of your English-language writers has put it. I hope this concept doesn't frighten you."

"Not me! Ho-ho!"

"Charlie, do you know the whereabouts of Michela Suarez, Mr. Froward, Reilly Thomas, Tina Vandeventer, Eva Wilcox, Sharon Ketchum, or Alfred Nunez? These persons have been reported as missing by Mrs. Robinelli."

"Is Mrs. Robinelli alive? Where is she?"

"She is at the residence facility in the biosphere. She is well. The adults and students, except for the ones I have named, are there also. What can you tell me about the missing persons?"

"How do I know you're not holding Mrs. Robinelli prisoner? I won't cooperate until I talk to her."

"I understand. You will be transported to the residence facility."

Now that his confidence was almost back, Charlie was inclined not to fall under adult control. The same went for Charonese control. At least not until he'd tried to get back in touch with the Proctor. Looking past the robot, Charlie saw that one of the carts was carrying a space-suited corpse. It was Sharon Ketchum, retrieved from the top of the tower.

"No transportation. Talk to Mrs. Robinelli first," he said.

"Very well," the robot said. "There is a communications device near here. You will have to go to it, since it cannot be moved. If you wish, you may ride on this vehicle."

Charlie thought it over. "You know, we teenagers have a way of committing suicide when we're unhappy."

"I have seen news reports to that effect," the robot said. "You aren't unhappy—"

"If you try to make me do anything I don't want to do, I'll be unhappy. I'll kill myself."

"Please don't do that," the robot said. "You are safe here. There's no need to be afraid of anything."

"Okay, but no tricks." Charlie stepped up on the back of the cart behind the robot.

The cart joined the traffic moving through the door into the factory room. The cart steered this way and that, past stacks of sheet metal, rolls of wire, coils of cable, heaps of little pieces, drums, boxes, containers, wheels, pipes, machines, machines, and more machines.

Charlie quickly lost sight of the other carts and the door they had entered. The robot evidently noticed him looking anxiously about. "There's nothing to fear."

"I'll be the judge of that," Charlie said. "What is this place?"

"A place where devices are fabricated, a workshop or factory. Charon has many of these."

The cart rolled onward. "I have some information," the robot said. "I have found three of your fellow students at the entrance of one of my vehicle shelters. You must have just come from there, since it's at the top of the elevator where I discovered you. You must know who they are."

"Okay, it's Reilly, Tina, and Eva."

"Thank you. Mrs. Robinelli is being informed."

"Great."

The cart rolled along under the low ceiling, in which flat plates glowed dull white. The light shone on other robots, some working at various tasks, some just standing. None of them appeared to take any notice of Charlie. Grinding and clanging noises came from the distance, as though construction or maintenance work were going on.

The cart glided to a gentle stop. "We have arrived,'" the robot said.

Charlie stepped off. In front of him was a metal framework at least fifteen feet square. Through festoons of wire and hose, Charlie could make out various sinister details: a saddle, attachments for human limbs, a hanging, multijointed armature with a full-face helmet on the end.

"You're crazy if you think I'm going to get into that thing," Charlie said.

"It is merely a teaching device. It features stereo TV, stereo sound, and mechanical in- and outputs. Although we had intended this model for use some years from now, after your training has advanced somewhat, it will now serve for your communication with Mrs. Robinelli. I will explain its use."

"No shit."

"Mrs. Robinelli is at a device similar to a telephone, waiting to speak to you," the robot said.

"Right."

"If I understand your statements correctly, you still don't trust me," the robot said.

"Right again."

The robot didn't sigh impatiently. "Charlie, I have no way to prove to you that I mean you no harm. If I wished, I could call up an army of robots to force you to do anything I wished. To enter this machine. To go to the residential faciality, where Mrs. Robinelli and your friends are waiting for you. Is this not true?"

"I'd kill myself."

"How?"

"I, uh, I'd bash my head in. On the floor."

"That is unlikely."

"You believed me before."

"I did not believe you. I induced your cooperation."

Charlie was beginning to lose the thread of this conversation. Scared or not, he decided, it was time to get involved. He shrugged, sniffed, wiped his nose on the back of his hand, wiped the back of his hand on his pants leg, and climbed into the machine.

He couldn't straddle the seat without putting his legs and arms into several complicated, swiveling gizmos. Following the robot's instructions, he pulled the helmet down over his face. Earphones folded around his head; twin eyepieces lit up with color images of Mrs. Robinelli's homely, welcoming face. Charlie pressed his eyes to the rubber cups. "Mrs. Robinelli?" he said.

"Charlie," she answered, her strained face crinkling into a smile. "I'm so glad to hear you. You're all right?" The sound in the earphones was perfect. The illusion was so real it was like standing on a chair, looking down at the woman.

"Is that really you, Mrs. Robinelli?"

"Yes, it is, dear. We're safe. You'd better let the Charonese bring you here." Mrs. Robinelli was standing in a big, sunlit room. Mr. Peake was frowning over her shoulder. Charlie, taken in by the illusion, moved his head to look around; amazingly, the helmet armature moved to follow his head. His field of vision swept the room. Several of the students stood around or sat in comfortable armchairs, watching him. They looked tense, but alive and unhurt. Behind them, through wide windows, Charlie saw blue sky and treetops.

"Where are you?" he said.

"We're at the place the Charonese have built for us to live. Go ahead and do as they say, Charlie; it's the best thing for right now."

Charlie saw Colby Dennison rise from a chair and come toward him. "Can you see me, Mrs. Robinelli?" Charlie asked.

"No, dear, all we can see is the camera moving around."

A voice cut in. "One moment, please." Charlie recognized the neutral male tone of the Charonese announcer. Mrs. Robinelli's reaction showed that she heard it, too.

"We have a problem," the Charonese said. "The three students, Reilly, Tina, and Eva, have run away. I am unable to track them."

"They ran away?" Mrs. Robinelli said.

"Freeman's trying to pull something!" Colby shouted.

"I have committed another error," the Charonese said. "When I attempted to speak to them through some of the robots at their location, they panicked. The boy, Reilly, led the two girls into dense foliage. I can't follow them without pursuing them with robots, which might cause them to panic further and injure themselves. Wait. I saw them briefly in a treetop camera. They are approaching dangerous wildlife. Mrs. Robinelli, should I pursue?"

In the amazing clarity of the teaching machine eyepieces, Charlie saw worry flood Mrs. Robinelli's face. Mr. Peake put his arm around the teacher's shoulders. "Charlie—" he began, but the picture vanished, leaving Charlie seeming to float in gray fog.

He heard a whisper in his ear. "Charlie."

The boy pulled his head back from the facepiece, but it followed him. He remembered that he was sitting among robots, blind and deaf, his head clamped by alien machinery. He grabbed the helmet, jerked it off his head, looked around. The Charonese was standing motionless in front of the teaching machine. He shouted at it. "What's going on! Why'd the picture go blank?" The Charonese didn't move.

The armatures on his limbs made no resistance. He began to rip them off, but was stopped by a tiny voice, like a fly buzzing. "Charlie, this is the Proctor speaking."

The voice was coming from the helmet. Charlie took another glance at the Charonese robot. It stood in the same spot. The surrounding factory had gone silent. He put his head partway back into the helmet.

"Hello? Proctor?"

"Yes, Charlie," the voice whispered. "I decided to cut in on your conversation because of the danger to your friends. Don't worry about this Charonese. I've immobilized him for the moment. Listen to me. The fastest and safest way to save Reilly and the others is for you to do it."

"Me? How?"

The eyepieces displayed a new picture. Charlie fitted the face-piece again, saw a view of the robot garage at the top of the elevator, as seen from thirty feet above the floor. "Look down, Charlie."

The helmet followed his head movement. He seemed to be looking down at his own body, but he had been transformed into a metal colossus. With a thrill, Charlie realized he was inhabiting one of the robot giants. "Stand up, Charlie."

"How can I—"

"Try to forget where you really are, Charlie. Imagine that you are this huge robot. It's easy."

Charlie thrashed his feet, thrust them down. His soles rested on a hard surface. The giant stirred, swayed. "Don't worry, Charlie. It won't let you fall. Balance is automatic, just as it is in your own body."

Charlie moved his arms, looked at his hands. Vast power raised the gigantic shoulders, opened and closed the enormous fingers. "Listen, Charlie," the whisper said. "Soon, the Charonese will speak to you again. I can conceal what we are doing by altering their perception of the factory, and the robots connected with it. I will make them think that no humans are there, that routine work is going on. That is as much as I can do without attracting their attention."

"Y-yeah . . ."

"When the Charonese speak to you, agree with them. But don't leave the factory. I will conceal your actions. Understand?"

"I think so . . ."

"Good. Now walk, Charlie," the whisper said in his ear. "I'll show you which way to go."

Taking twenty-foot strides, Charlie walked out of the garage. His feet made the ground shake. His head barely fit under the towering doorway. He surveyed the world. A luminous cross hovered against the tree line. "This is where they entered the foliage," the Proctor told him. "I don't know where they went after that. You find them. Bring them back."

"Awww riiiight!" Charlie yelled enthusiastically. He strode through the trees, brushing the branches aside. The alien devices magnified his vision, making the sunset colors seem brighter than they were when he'd been there in person. His ponderous walk was faster than the fastest athlete could run. He heard birdcalls, insects. When he crushed a palmetto, toppled a dead tree trunk, he heard the crash and felt the resistance in his hands. He paused, savoring the power of it. In the distance he heard screams. He turned toward the sound. Without thinking he drew a breath, called out, and, to his eager astonishment, his voice rang among the trees, knocking down the pinecones!

"REILLY!! EVAAA!! DANG!! HELLO?! PHOOSH!!"

Charlie pulled himself together. He stopped blowing into the Charonese microphone and listened.

More screams came from the distance. Charlie turned the robot, trampling down the undergrowth. He set out in the direction of the screams. He wanted to run, but he was already moving as fast as the robot would go. He stepped over fallen trees, splashed through a pond, flattened a stand of brushwood, emerged into the open, and saw the three kids running toward him across a grassy savannah.

Reilly was bounding over the tussocks like a hurdler, dragging Tina behind him. Eva, screaming and sobbing, ran desperately behind them, unable to keep up. She stumbled and fell flat in the dry grass, sending up a puff of dust. A brown, slab-sided monster emerged from the trees on the opposite side of the clearing. It halted; its body seesawed, tail down, head up. It opened five-foot jaws. Its roar rolled across the savannah like thunder.

"AWOOOO!!" Charlie bellowed, imitating the dinosaur.

Reilly thudded to a stop, Tina crashing into his back. "REILLY!!" he shouted, loud as the blare of a diesel. "IT'S ME, CHARLIE!! C'MERE!!" Reilly stood and gaped, his chest working.

"Charlie?"

"WOULD I SHIT YOU?!!" Charlie beckoned, the robot's arm swooping through a ten-foot arc. Reilly began to haul Tina toward the robot. Charlie, in his gigantic metal body, strode past them; they dodged to keep from being crushed.

The tyrannosaur forgot Charlie and step-step-stepped across the savannah, its yellow eyes fixed on Eva. Charlie strained his legs against the machine's armatures, trying to force the robot giant to walk faster. The animal and the machine reached Eva at the same moment, but Charlie's hand was faster than the tyrannosaur's stoop.

"GOTCHA!!" Rows of ivory daggers clashed inches behind the girl as Charlie lifted her into the air. He looked at her close up as she dangled, kicking, in the robot's padded claw. He could feel her in his hand, soft and warm, no bigger than a cat. She looked up at him, her face twisted and blind with panic.

Charlie felt his body tilting. Something hampered the movement of his other arm. The tyrannosaur, equipped by instinct to drag down prey larger than itself, had clamped its jaws on the robot's wrist joint. Charlie pushed it backward. The creature's teeth slid off, squealing and leaving grooves in the metal.

Charlie's metal monster stumbled massively against a tree. Dead bark and needles rattled down. The robot's head banged into a thick, horizontal branch; the helmet on the Charonese device delivered the shock to Charlie's real face. Without thinking, he reached up and draped Eva over the branch.

He turned to face the tyrannosaur. Compared to the movie dinosaurs he'd seen, this real dinosaur looked mummified, with bones and ropy muscles showing under its rough, dusty hide. Charlie reached out to push it away, but it lunged and clapped its jaws, trying to grab his wrist again.

Charlie tucked his fists into his chest, stepped forward like a boxer, and jabbed the dinosaur in the nose. The creature roared and backed up, bobbing its head. Charlie was preparing to deal another blow when he heard the Charonese voice say, "That's enough Charlie."

"What?"

"Don't hurt the animal. There are only six adult tyrannosaurids in breeding condition on Charon, and this is one of them."

"Oh. Yeah." Charlie, his heart still thumping with excitement, watched the monster as it backed away, roaring threats. After it had retreated a safe distance, it turned, showing Charlie a lean flank decorated with black-on-brown tiger stripes. It squirted a wheelbarrowful of chalky, mudlike excrement, and paced away into the trees.

"Wow,"said Charlie.

"That was very well done, Charlie," said the Charonese voice. "You may rest now. We will guide the handler robot back to the shelter. An aircraft is on the way, to take you and your friends to the residence facility."

Charlie didn't reply. He stood still, waiting to see what would happen.

"One moment, please," the Charonese said. "It appears that there is some interference in the communications link with the handler robot. Wait. Once again, we'll have to rely on you, Charlie. Do you think you can make the handler walk back to the shelter with your friends?"

"Well, naturally!"

To Reilly and Tina, watching from the cover of some bushes near the edge of the clearing, it seemed that the metal colossus stood next to the tree for a long time without moving. Occasionally, it spoke in Charlie's voice, as though the fat boy were somewhere inside it, mumbling into the microphone of a stadium-size public address system. Finally, the robot moved again. It slowly and gently took Eva from her perch in the tree, walked ponderously to their hiding place, and stopped.

Reilly and Tina tremblingly advanced. "Is that really you, Charlie?" the boy said.

"OH, YEAH!!" the giant said. "HOW DID YOU LIKE THAT DINOSAUR, TINA? WAS IT REAL ENOUGH FOR YOU? HA! HA!" Charlie's laughter blatted, seeming to come out of the sky.

Tina's knees buckled. Reilly held her up by one arm.

"YOU COULD AT LEAST THANK ME FOR SAVING

YOUR LIVES!" Charlie blared. "BUT I'M USED TO INGRAT-
ITUDE!" The giant bent toward them and held out its hands,
huge fingers spread. "CLIMB ON, AND HOLD TIGHT! WE
HAVE TO GO BACK NOW!"

Reilly, numb with shock, helped Tina to a seat on the padded
palm. Eva already clung silently to one of the fingers, tear streaks
on her dusty face. The arms lifted them frighteningly high above
the ground. The robot began striding through the trees.

Reilly found his voice. "Charlie, how did you get inside that
thing? How did you learn to drive it?"

"I GOT FRIENDS IN HIGH PLACES! HA! HA!" The teenagers flinched away from the noise. "SORRY!" the robot
boomed. "I DON'T KNOW HOW TO TURN IT DOWN YET!"

"It's okay, Charlie!"

Another voice distracted the students. A familiar-sounding
clatter grew to deafening volume as a great, oddly shaped helicopter hurtled overhead and landed beyond the treetops ahead,
raising a cloud of dust and pine needles. The camera eyes of the
robot followed it until it was out of sight. "THAT'S INTEREST-
ING!" Charlie trumpeted. "FOUR ROTORS!"

"Yes, how about that!"

"NO NEED TO SHOUT!" Charlie's voice pealed out. "I CAN
HEAR YOU FINE!"

They arrived at the robot garage. The Charonese helicopter,
rotor blades whirling, rested in front of the big door. Charlie's
robot slogged up to it and lowered its hands to the ground. "THE
CHOPPER WILL TAKE YOU TO MRS. ROBINELLI AND
THE OTHERS!" it bellowed.

Tina alighted and stood shakily, watching Reailly as he moved
to help Eva. The girl sat with her arms wrapped around a giant
finger, her eyes following Reilly as he climbed across the robot's
hand. "Come on, Eva. It's all right now," he said.

Reilly was reaching for Eva when the robot's other hand fell
in front of him like a gate closing. Gently, but inexorably, the
hand batted at Reilly until he tumbled to the ground. Tina
screamed, hands clutching at her face. The robot stood up, raising Eva ten, twenty, thirty feet into the air. Reilly leaped to his
feet. Eva stared down at him wordlessly, her face deathly white
under the dirt. "Jump, Eva! Jump!" Reilly yelled, his voice
breaking into a screech.

The giant hand closed around Eva. Reilly screamed as loudly as he could. "Charlie! What do you think you're doing!"

"I THINK I'LL KEEP HER." The colossus turned and tramped away around the end of the Charonese helicopter. Eva's legs, in their ripped brown coveralls, dangled limply from between its fingers.

Reilly sprinted after it, rounding the end of the helicopter in time to see it striding into the building. Reilly followed, but the effort was hopeless. The great door was already rattling down.

The helicopter's rotors were clattering again, louder and louder. Reilly turned and saw Tina waving at him from an open hatch, shouting something he couldn't hear. She was surrounded by small, boxy-looking robots, like the ones they'd seen on the airliner. Reilly was down to one alternative. He decided not to take it. Slowly, looking back over his shoulder at the robot garage, he walked back toward Tina and the waiting helicopter.

Chapter Ten:

Faulty Towers

Emma Robinelli hoed up piles of soil in the potato patch, thinking that it seemed like good garden earth. But it couldn't properly be called "earth," not on Charon. Her mind wandered from that to their arrival on Charon. That led to the deaths of Captain Milanovitch and poor young Randal Copeley. The students' terrified screaming, the blood pattering off the high table —She cut off the thought. Those memories were best put away somewhere.

The teenagers around her talked in low voices as they weeded and dug. After two weeks on Charon, the shock of arrival was beginning to wear off. Their recovery was being speeded by their annoyance at being required to labor in the huge garden.

When the aliens had announced that the students would begin immediately to raise their own food, there had been groans of anger and disbelief. The science-fictional scenarios imagined by the teenagers had included everything but stoop labor in the dirt. The Charonese responded that the C-rations were for emergencies, and that physical labor was good for morale.

Charonese robots had cleared away brush and trees near the residence facility, and had tilled the ground. The rest of the work was being done by hand—or rather, Emma corrected herself, the hands of the kids and the adults. They all had blisters. They were hungry, too. The Charonese were doling out the C-rations one per day per person.

Flight Engineer Peake, barefoot in the dirt, his overalls rolled up to his knees, began to sing:

> "Down on the farm,
> They all ask for you,
> The cows, pigs and chickens
> And the horse's ass . . ."

A few students laughed. Emma toiled away in the warmth and sunshine, setting a good example. The work didn't bother her. At home in Seattle, she and Mr. Robinelli planted enough flowers and vegetables every spring to supply the whole neighborhood. What bothered her was the absence of Mr. Robinelli. They had been saving for a trip to Europe. Maybe now he would go by himself. She hoped so.

Little alien details bothered her, too. The birds in the surrounding pines didn't sing; they only cawed and screeched. The "sun" wasn't warm; it merely provided light. The kids were recovering, but some part of their innocence was gone.

In the distance, Emma saw Lena Gershner on her knees, setting up a row of bean poles, also setting a good example. On the first day of garden labor, she had shown up, her blond hair and her lacquered nails cut short, her face set in immovable anger, ready to take orders from the teacher. Emma was the only one among the kidnappees who knew anything about gardening. Gershner never forgave the aliens, never relaxed. Night after night, she busied herself among the students, expertly patching minor cuts and blisters, distributing food and water. But she did not accept, did not reassure.

The deaths on the high table had been a terrible, stupid accident. The Charonese on Charon hadn't known about the arrival of the humans, they said, because the Charonese operating the spaceship hadn't been able to communicate with them. This, they said, was because of the deterioration of the various components of the spaceship. And the deterioration had been caused by the humans destroying the Charonese robots aboard the spaceship.

The place where the humans had first set foot on Charon was a veterinary facility, a place where the Charonese healed sick animals—and dissected the dead ones. Captain Milanovitch and Randal had inadvertently set off some automatic program in the machinery.

The blades and saws in the death building were grotesquely large, compared with the human bodies pinned under them. The machines had stopped within a second, but it was already too late for Captain Milanovitch and the boy. Doors in the nearby buildings had opened, and a grotesque assortment of vehicles had rushed out, Charonese robots coming to the rescue. The children hardly had time to panic before they were surrounded. One of the vehicles reached out with a mechanical arm and wrote in the dirt, DO NOT FEAR. EMERGENCY OVER. YOU ARE SAFE NOW. THESE TRUCKS WILL TAKE YOU TO THE RESIDENCE FACILITY WHERE THERE IS MEDICAL FACILITY AND TREATMENT FOR YOU.

In the stress of the moment, the children had turned to Emma for direction. Most of them hadn't seen what had happened in the death building. Emma made up her mind instantly. The choice was between trusting the robots for the moment and a hopeless fight, which would result in more injury. So, the humans had allowed themselves to be brought here, to the residence facility.

Emma could see no reason to disbelieve the Charonese explanation. They had no motivation for murder. They seemed genuinely and deeply upset about what had happened. They hadn't studied the bodies, they'd wrapped them in blankets the students had brought from the airliner. They'd brought the bodies to the residence facility for burial.

Gershner had insisted on improvising a proper funeral for the victims. The graves were over there in the middle of the garden, decently mounded and marked, and decorated with wildflowers. Beside the two massacre victims lay Sharon Ketchum, the girl whose space suit had failed, and Susan Sachs, the one who'd suffocated on the plane. Susan's body had been frozen solid when they lowered it into the grave. Apparently, the Charonese running the spaceship had preserved the body this way.

Beside the graves, there were wooden crosses for the dead whose bodies were lost: Alfred Nunez, who had fallen from the tower, Chela Suarez, and the copilot, Jeff Froward. Apparently, the latter two had fallen from the cable-pipe when the elevator car they were riding hit an ice deposit at high altitude. The Charonese had been unable to find their bodies in the wilderness under the cable-pipe.

An electronic voice, coming from nearby, broke into Emma's reverie. "Your attention, please," it said, sounding like a well-mannered but somewhat irritating lady radio announcer. This was the voice used by Gamma, the Charonese who mostly communicated with the humans, when she was making general announcements. It came from one of the Charonese surveillance devices, a set of speakers and cameras mounted on a pole in the middle of the garden. "You may be interested to know that wildlife will soon become visible through the protective fence. There is no danger. Would you like to stop working for a moment and observe the wildlife?"

"Would you like kiss my crank?" an anonymous voice yelled. There was other jeering, but everyone stopped working to look at the animals anyway.

A high metal fence surrounded the residence facility at a distance of a kilometer. Part of it was close to where Emma and the others were working. Just beyond the fence, a herd of gigantic sauropod dinosaurs moved with elephantine dignity, long necks rocking gracefully among the pine trunks.

"What do you call those, Mrs. Robinelli?" the Charonese voice asked.

"Let's see. Judging by the shape of their heads, they must be a kind of diplodocus. If I remember rightly, those are called Nemegtosaurus, the Mongolian diplodocus. The original Diplodocus lived in Colorado."

Peake and some of the students were grinning at one another. Mrs. Robinelli always told you twice as much about everything as you wanted to hear.

"Thank you, Mrs. Robinelli."

"Did you say they were from Monogolia, Mrs. Robinelli?" Peake asked.

"That's right. All the plants and animals on Charon were gathered from a part of Earth that later became Mongolia, or so the Charonese say."

"Dinosaur bulgogi," Mr. Peake said. "Mmm!"

"What's bulgogi, Mr. Peake?" asked several of the teenagers.

"Mongolian steak barbecue. Mmm!"

"Oh, barf right out loud—mass grossness—ugh—"

"Don't knock it until you've tried it, brothers and sisters," Peake said.

Several of the creatures had reared up on their hind legs, propping themselves on their tails, and were using their protruding, peglike teeth to rake needles, cones, and twigs from the tops of the trees forty feet in the air. Smaller copies of the diplodocids jostled for the branches pulled down by the adults.

"It's an odd coincidence," Emma said. "This world is a duplicate of a place on Earth as it was right at the end of the Mesozoic Era, right before the dinosaurs became extinct."

"Why is that so odd?" Peake asked her, moving his basket of cuttings closer to her.

"Well, if Earth life was brought here, why was it brought at that moment in time, and not from any of the other hundreds of millions of years when no mass extinction was about to take place? It's odd, if it's a coincidence."

The teacher was gazing at the dinosaurs, her homely face lit with interest. Peake put his hand on hers, where it rested on her hoe. "It's good to see you looking halfway cheerful again, Emma," he said.

"It's useless to stay angry or scared," she said. "We've all got to start living with this situation sometime. Why not now?" None of the children responded to this, but she knew they'd heard her.

One of the huge animals had moved close to the fence. Its stomach rumbled, a deep rhythmic throb like a diesel engine. Emma thought she could hear the clack of the grinding stones the creature carried in its belly. It leaned on the fence, scraping its pebbled gray hide along the fence's supporting girders. The fence, as heavily built as the framework of a skyscraper, flexed inward. Several of the teenagers dropped their tools and backed up, ready to run.

"There is nothing to fear. The fence will hold back even the largest life-forms on Charon," the Charonese voice said.

"Hey, thanks a lot," Peake shouted at the surveillance pole. "That's really reassuring! How about getting us some meat!"

"Eeyou, gross!"

"Puke-o-rama!"

"That is a good suggestion, Mr. Peake," the Charonese voice said. "Meat will be provided for tomorrow's meals."

"Good," Peake said. "I'm hungry enough to eat Godzilla, if he shows up. You know, Emma, there's something kind of limited about the Charonese. They don't have much initiative. Why didn't they think of giving us some meat before?"

"You might ask why we didn't think of it ourselves," Emma replied.

"True."

"Perhaps, after so many accidents, they're afraid to try anything new with us."

The "sun" was going down. The herd moved away among the tall trees, the young ones following the whip ends of the adults' tails as they dragged through the carpet of dried needles. The resinous aroma of dinosaur manure filled the air. One of the animals trumpeted sonorously.

"Like a cow mooing through twenty feet of sewer pipe," Peake said. He went back to work, carrying buckets of potato cuttings to the lines of hoe-wielding students. Emma glanced again at the graves and returned to her planting.

Eva and Charlie were still missing. Gershner hadn't erected markers for them because of the fantastic story told by Reilly and Tina after they'd arrived by helicopter. A huge robot had appeared out of nowhere, shouting in Charlie's voice. It had rescued Reilly and the two girls from a tarbosaurus, then walked away with Eva in its hand. Tina was convinced that Charlie, controlling the robot from inside, had kidnapped Eva for his own grody purposes. He was probably raping her right now, she said.

Reilly's opinion was that Charlie was a dipshit, but no so bad as that. Charlie pissed you off, but he wouldn't know what to do with a girl unless she came in a box with the instructions on the side, batteries included. Reilly didn't know whether Charlie was inside the robot or what. Maybe he was just talking through it. Maybe that wasn't even Charlie's voice. How could that fat little dipshit get control of a thirty-foot outer space robot monster? Maybe the Charonese were just imitating his voice, like they did that TV news announcer on the spaceship, Walter what's-his-name.

The Charonese took a peculiar interest in Reilly and Tina's tale. They claimed they had no knowledge of the robot's actions. They claimed to have searched the tower top and bottom, the spaceship, and the surface of Charon. There was no sign of Charlie and Eva.

The Charonese became monomaniacal about it. They questioned Reilly and Tina for hours, particularly about something called Proctor, which Reilly remembered hearing Charlie babbling about. The questioning went on until Tina became exhausted and upset, and Emma angrily ordered them to stop.

All her life, Emma had always suffered from insomnia. At home in her Seattle suburb, while her husband snored in the bedroom, she sat at the kitchen table grading papers or adding pages to the manuscript of a novel she called *Love's Tender Sweet Passionate Something*. Mr. Robinelli called it *Love's Hot Something*. They were hoping to sell the novel when it was finished, and when she could think of a title for it. Now, deprived of her hobby, she spent nights talking to the enemy.

Nearly every room in the residence facility was equipped with a communication terminal, a beautiful marvel of technology that sent Peake into ecstasies. The terminals had multiple keyboards, stereo earphones, microphones, and a curved transparent screen in which bright pictures appeared, as sharp as the most expensive colored prints Emma had ever seen. Emma had learned to use the one in her apartment.

The Charonese seemed willing, even eager, to tell her everything they knew. They had no knowledge of the two missing children. The record of the spaceflight from Earth, they said, had been destroyed in a computer failure. They hadn't observed Reilly and Tina's adventure with the dinosaur. At first they asked the teacher if she was a sure two children named Eva and Charlie even existed. Afterward, they said they believed that Charlie and Eva were dead and their bodies destroyed, like the three others. When Emma asked them to speculate about what might have happened to the five missing bodies, they replied that Alfred's body had burned in Charon's atmosphere after it had fallen from the top of the lightstack tower, and that Chela, Froward, Eva, and Charlie had been eaten. There were plenty of animals on Charon big enough to swallow a human body in one gulp.

Emma, first driven by duty—to find out the enemy's weaknesses—then by curiosity, persisted. "Why don't you Charonese come out and meet us in person?"

"I regret that speaking to you through various machines is as close as I can get, Mrs. Robinelli," the alien responded.

"Why? Is it because of your different biology?"

"Not at all. My species would thrive on Earth. The problem is, I have no person in which to meet you." The Charonese paused, as though laughing silently.

"You mean you're a robot, a mechanical creature?"

"Heavens no, Mrs. Robinelli." Now the Charonese was imitating Emma's own speech pattern. Could the alien have a sense of humor?

"Are you afraid we'll think you're ugly or frightening, and be afraid of you?"

"Not at all, Mrs. Robinelli. In my day, I was regarded as rather attractive, even sexy." Another pause, then the Charonese continued. "Because my day was so long ago, and because I no longer live in the flesh, as your writers say, it's no breach of modesty to say so, I hope."

"In the flesh," prompted the teacher, wondering if this was an example of Charonese wit.

"Yes, Mrs. Robinelli, born of man and woman, although in my case, I had a mother and two fathers."

"Two fathers, you said?"

"Yes. Our biology is, or was, different from yours in that way, at least. Would you like to see a picture of me?"

Emma came fully awake, realizing that some kind of a breakthrough was at hand. "Yes, I would, please!"

This time the alien did laugh, human laughter. The screen on Emma's communication terminal lit up with a picture of a pink starfish lying on a beach. In the background, surf rolled up the sandy shore and clouds floated in a blue sky. The only unearthly thing about the image was that the starfish was lying on a plaid blanket.

"This is a recording of me on vacation, basking in the sun," the Charonese said."

"That's you!?"

"Yes. The picture was taken by one of my lovers of that time."

Emma watched speechlessly as the starfish pulled its five thick legs under itself and stood up. Lumps and wrinkles came and went as alien muscles and bones worked under its pink, glossy skin. It stepped off the blanket and picked it up, a cluster of jointed, humanlike fingers being extruding from the end of one of the legs for the purpose. It walked away from the water on four legs, the fifth leg held high, the blanket clutched in a deep groove that had formed in the upper side of the leg.

The camera followed the starfish up the beach, now taking in a background of white rectangular buildings that wouldn't have looked out of place at any resort on Earth. A farther expanse of beach came into view. Emma saw dozens of other starfish lying on blankets, manipulating colorful objects, walking around, or cartwheeling at high speed on extended legs.

The Charonese sighed, a realistic, human sound. "This scene is painfully nostalgic for me, Mrs. Robinelli," it said. "All these things existed hundreds of millions of years ago, and now they are long gone."

Emma stared at the screen as other starfish walked up to the first one and began, with much leg-tapping, an exchange of unidentifiable objects.

"Now the refreshments arrive," the Charonese said. "We were having what you call a lunch? Or is it a picnic? I would appreciate your comments, Mrs. Robinelli."

Emma gulped, choked, began breathing again: "My goodness gracious!"

"Pardon me?"

"The similarities are more amazing than the differences!"

"It makes me glad to hear you say that, Mrs. Robinelli. I've often thought the same, at least during the last hundred years or so."

The Charonese (it went on to explain) existed as computer programs. Their physical bodies had died hundreds of millions of years ago, after their personalities had been duplicated in Charon's computer memory.

Emma asked the Charonese if they used names. "Of course we do, Mrs. Robinelli," the Charonese had said, "My name is—" There followed an abrupt, manic performance on slide whistles and kazoos. "Of course, no human could pronounce that unassisted. This is one of the matters I have been wishing to take up with you. We Charonese would like to be given names by which you may address us. Have you any suggestions?"

"The simplest thing would be to call you Alpha, Beta, Gamma, and so on, according to the order in which we first met you."

"Agreed," said the Charonese. "In that case, my name is Gamma."

"Very well. Who were Alpha and Beta?"

"Beta was the first to notice what was happening at the veterinary compound. She was unable to stop the machines in time to save the lives of Milanovitch and Copeley. Do you wish to speak to her?"

"No, thanks. What about Alpha?"

"Alpha was the pilot of your spacecraft. Judging by what you have told me, Alpha mishandled her first communication with you and your friends. Violence was the result. I regret that."

"Could I speak to Alpha?"

"Alpha died sometime after landing on the tower," said Gamma. "Her records and memories died with her."

"Died? You're not immortal, then?"

"Unfortunately not. Machine memory can be damaged, destroyed, or erased."

"But you live for hundreds of millions of years."

"Approximately five hundred million. That isn't immortality."

"It would be good enough for me," Emma said.

"Would you like an opportunity to obtain a similiar life span?"

"Of course!"

"If you can learn to use the machinery here on the Ark, and show us that you are committed, as we are, to the purpose of the Ark, then you can be like us."

"Ark?"

"Our own word for what you call Charon and Pluto is best translated into the English word *ark*. Defined as a unique vessel, which carries life over the desolation of lifeless space."

"And that's the purpose of the Ark?"

"That's correct, Mrs. Robinelli. We carry life across space to worlds that have not otherwise developed it."

"I see." Emma had heard this part of the story before.

"And across time also, Mrs. Robinelli. The Ark arrived in this planetary system sixty-five million years ago. We stocked the Ark's biosphere with the life-forms we found on Earth at that time."

"Why? Didn't you have life-forms from your own planet?"

"Originally, yes. But that biome died out long ago. I will explain. The Ark's biosphere is self-contained and self-sustaining. In that, it is like the biosphere of a life-bearing planet. But, unlike a planet, the Ark's biosphere is too small to sustain itself indefinitely. It can only last about one hundred million years. After that, it must be replenished with fresh animals, plants, and microorganisms."

"Like a terrarium. They don't last indefinitely either. They had to be started over every year or two." Emma thought of the series of glass tanks, planted with mosses, ferns, frogs, and turtles, that had decorated her classrooms over the decades.

"After restocking, you didn't leave again?" Emma asked.

"No, Mrs. Robinelli. After the restocking, it was determined that the Crew of the Ark was too old to go on."

"Crew?"

"That is what we call ourselves, in your language. We Charonese are the Crew of the Ark."

"And you were too old?"

"Yes, Mrs. Robinelli. It was unlikely that any of us would live long enough to find a planet with intelligent life-forms that could be recruited as the new Crew. If the last Charonese died while the Ark was traversing interstellar space, there would be no one to supervise the arrival in the next planetary system. The Ark might be destroyed. We therefore decided to remain here indefinitely. Then, fortunately for the Ark, your species developed on the Earth."

Emma remembered the plot of a movie she'd seen in the sixties, called 2001. "Did you have anything to do with that?"

"No, Mrs. Robinelli. It was a natural occurrence. The development of your species gave us hope. We have been waiting nearly a million years for you to become ready for recruitment."

"We weren't recruited, we were press-ganged, kidnapped. Keep that in mind."

"I am keeping it in mind, Mrs. Robinelli. The recruitment process is going on now. I hope to interest you and the other humans in our mission and our way of life, for its own sake."

"I have to admit, it is very interesting," Emma said.

"I'm glad to hear you say so," Gamma said. "Look at this." The picture on Emma's screen changed to a view of a crooked, cobblestoned street in some backward Middle Eastern town. Bearded men in robes jostled past one another, some carrying baskets of produce, others leading donkeys.

"This picture was taken in Jerusalem during the lifetime of the historical Jesus Christ. I have noticed your interest in these things."

"My word!" Emma said. "Do you—"

The scene had already changed to show a firelit cave, and a huddle of fur-clad people singing and clapping their hands. Over the sound, Gamma said, "Here we see a group of Neanderthal folk in their winter quarters in what is now northern France."

"My goodness gracious sakes! How did you get these pictures? What—"

Gamma laughed affectionately. "Mrs. Robinelli, I can't possibly answer all your questions at once. If you wish, when the teenagers begin their studies, you may join them. If you succeed, you may live as long as I have, and have all the answers the Ark can provide."

Emma didn't reply. If this was temptation, the Charonese were good at it. The picture on the screen faded away. "How do Charonese get old?" she asked.

"We Charonese are subject to wear and tear, just as we were when we existed in our physical bodies," Gamma said. "Over long periods of time, information is lost in spite of all our care, usually because of copy errors when we reproduce parts of our souls. Is 'soul' the correct word?"

"'Personality' might be better."

"Thank you. Another cause of death is damage to the computer circuitry in which we are stored. Alpha risked her life when she committed herself to the computer on the spacecraft. It failed, and she died. We admire and appreciate her bravery. I hope it will not be wasted."

"You mean you hope you'll eventually get our cooperation in helping you run Charon. Which you call 'the Ark.'"

"Yes, that's what I mean. Originally, we, the Crew of the Ark, numbered over one hundred. Today, there are only sixteen of us left. Now, only the most vital functions are personally attended by Crew. The rest, such as the veterinary facility, are automated. There aren't enough of us to continuously supervise everything. Our purpose in bringing you and the students here is to recruit as many of you as possible to help crew the Ark."

"You have to understand that most of us resent being forced to leave our homes and loved ones behind," Emma said.

"Doesn't life itself force you to do that?"

"Yes, but that's voluntary—"

"Excuse me for contradicting you, Mrs. Robinelli, but it is not. We are all limited by our physical conditions and the accidents of birthplace and history. On the Ark, we are freer of such things than anybody of your race. We also have an important mission, a task of high ethical quality. How many human beings can say that of themselves? For that matter, how many of my race could say it?"

Twilight had fallen over the garden. Emma leaned on her hoe, lost in thought. Her husband had always said evening was his favorite time of day, she recalled. One of the students called out, "Mr. Peake! Is it quitting time yet?"

"You may stop working now," Gamma said from the surveillance tower's speakers.

"I'se the foreman on this plantation, and it ain't quitting time until I say it's quitting time," Peake said. "Quitting time!" he shouted. "What movie is that from!"

"Gone With the Wind!" several of the students chorused. They'd viewed that movie the evening before on the big TV screens in the residence facility dining hall. The Charonese seemed to have an inexhaustible supply of movies and TV shows, and would run almost anything the students asked for. What they would not run was current news and scenes of home.

The garden workers trudged back toward the residence facility, stepping over aluminum irrigation pipes. The Charonese had promised, and were delivering, perfect weather and plenty of water and fertilizer. They also promised to help with the labor of gardening later on, when the teenagers had begun their studies. Right now, it was good for the youngsters to grow their own food.

A pathway wound among the trees back to the residence facility. Brush and palmettos were springing up everywhere, Emma thought, because the Charonese fence kept out browsing wildlife. The area inside the fence contained no dinosaurs except a few turkey-sized predators, all teeth and claws, that hunted the ugly little mammals that scuttled in the undergrowth. As the kids' confidence grew, and they wandered farther from the residence, they discovered a slow-moving stream and a small lake.

Walking on Charon was like perpetually walking over a rounded hilltop. Trees came up over the 'horizon' in front of them, and the fence dropped out of sight behind them. It would be easy to get lost on this world, and easy to stay out of sight.

Emma began to see the residence facility through the pine trunks. In their first night at the facility, the humans had discov-

ered that the gleaming white toilets in the bathrooms didn't con-
nect to any sewer system, and that the lights in the apartments
had no switches. The Charonese told Emma that they'd never
seen the toilets' true function on television. They assumed they
were somehow essential, but they weren't sure what the humans
used them for. Peake's comment was that they were lucky that
there weren't little Tidy Bowl men floating in the toilets.

As for the lights, the Charonese had assumed that the only
reason for turning them off was to conserve electricity, which
wasn't necessary here. Both defects had been quickly repaired by
a squad of specialized robots. Since then, Peake had called the
place Faulty Towers.

Under other circumstances, the Towers wouldn't have been a
bad place to live. It was a collection of small white two- and
three-story buildings on a platform thirty feet above the ground.
Elevators and spiral stairways ran up inside the five pillars that
supported the platform. The buildings and the platform were
molded out of some glittering stonelike material, and no two of
them were alike. The walls were agreeably curved, and there
were big windows with glass shutters, and a picturesque multi-
tude of balconies, connecting bridges, and winding stairways.

The humans leaned their tools against a pillar. Some climbed
the stairs to the top of the platform; others, including Emma, took
an elevator. She went to her apartment to clean up. There were
more than enough private apartments for everyone. The Charonese had provided wooden tables, chairs, and cabinets, in simple,
solid, but attractive designs, and woven grass mats lay on the
floors. Emma considered that the aliens had made a fortunate
choice of furniture catalogs upon which to base their designs;
they could have just as easily picked a motel furnishings guide.
Peake's retort had been that the aliens were obviously under the
influence of "Magnum P.I.," "Miami Vice," and other such sub-
tropical TV programs.

The teenagers were sullen but alert to possibilities. They were
already swapping roommates and furniture, enjoying more freedom in these matters as prisoners of the Charonese than they had
at home.

Lena Gershner was working in the dining hall, handing out the
remains of that morning's C-rations. "I know you're starving, but

try to eat it slowly," she said to the teenagers as they pressed hungrily up to the table.

"We might get something else to eat tomorrow," Emma said. "The Charonese said they'd provide meat. Reilly said the pond looks like it has plenty of fish in it. I think some of the early potatoes will be ready next week."

"Good," the stewardess said shortly. She looked at Emma, her dusty face tinged orange by the sunset slanting through the big, open windows. "But I'd rather we became completely independent of them."

Some of the students went to the kitchen to heat their rations; others were too hungry to wait, and scattered around the hall to eat.

As always, the big screen at the end of the dining hall lit up, and a musical tone sounded. "Hello, everyone. Would you like to hear about tonight's entertainment?" a speaker said.

The students, hungry and restless, responded with derisive laughter and shouts. "We want MTV!—soaps!—football!— porno flicks!" Emma glanced around the room. She didn't approve of chaos and misbehavior, regardless of the circumstances. Gershner was laughing with the students and encouraging them.

The Charonese took no notice of the uproar. Emma recognized its voice; it was Gamma speaking again. "I have a special show for you tonight. You've had time to yourselves since your arrival on Charon—time I know you needed to recover from your trip and the terrible accidents we've suffered. But now we have to put that behind us, and get on with the work we have before us. . . ."

The students began to quiet down and listen. "What?" someone said.

Gamma went on calmly, in a sexless but human voice. ". . . begin your studies. While you're eating, there will be a short presentation that will show what your work here is all about."

A title appeared on the screen, golden letters floating against a picture of the Towers:

YOUR NEW LIFE

"Gimme back my old life!" someone shouted, and threw a half-eaten ration can. It clanked against the screen. A shout of laughter went up in the room. As beans and sauce slowly ran down the screen, the picture continued. "Throughout human history, there has been an ideal. The ideal that life is sacred."

"Hey! Your ass is sacred!"

Images of wise philosophers, wildlife, scenic landscapes, stars and planets flitted by. ". . . Thousands of millions of years ago, another civilization also believed in this ideal, and for this reason, they built the Ark . . ."

Tina stood up in the front row, facing the other teenagers. She waved her arms. "First they kidnap us, then they make us work in their fugging garden; they don't give us anything to eat, and now they're trying to brainwash us!"

Colby jumped up in the middle of the audience. "That's right! We're not listening to this bogus shit!" He snatched up a wooden chair and flung it through the nearest window. Glass shattered on the pavement outside.

The students rose with a bellow of gleeful rage. Throwables hurtled across the dining hall. The students' anger increased when they discovered that the big screen was more indestructible than it looked. Several boys smashed furniture against the floor and began stamping on it with their heavy workboots, throwing the pieces out the windows.

Emma threaded her way through the crowd to Colby. "Colby, what are you doing? This isn't right!"

He grabbed her shoulders in time to prevent her from being knocked down. "It's a demonstration, Mrs. Robinelli!" he yelled over the noise. "Like you taught us about the sixties!" Peake arrived; Colby pushed the teacher into his arms and ran off.

"Come on, Emma, this is their night to howl," Peake said.

There really weren't enough rioters to make an effective uproar in a place the size of Faulty Towers, Emma thought, as she and Peake made their way to Peake's apartment. Still, the kids were trying as hard as they could, rampaging through the rooms and apartments, breaking windows and bashing the Charonese terminals.

After a few minutes, Gershner came in. "I don't want to put a damper on our little demonstration," she said. "The kids are finally showing some guts."

"Showing some stupidity, you mean," Emma said. "This is no demonstration; it's a riot. I don't know what the Charonese will think of the human race after tonight."

"Who cares what they think of us! It's time they knew what we thought of them!"

"The question is," Peake said, "what are the Charonese going to do about it?" He went to his terminal.

"Gamma speaking."

"I presume you know what's going on?"

"Yes. The young people are overemotional. They may injure themselves. I'm considering sending some robots."

"I wouldn't do that if I were you."

"Why not, Mr. Peake?"

"The kids will attack the robots. They'd be more likely to get hurt than if you simply left them alone. They'll calm down before long."

"Are you certain, Mr. Peake?"

Peake grinned at the screen. "Sure!"

"Very well, I'll wait."

"Frankly, I'm surprised," Peake said to the others once he'd turned off the terminal.

"You shouldn't be," Gershner said. "They don't have to quell the demonstration. All they have do do is cut off our food and water. The only thing wrong with this uprising is that it came at the wrong time. And it isn't serious enough."

They shared out Peake's bedding, but the uproar outside didn't allow sleep. They heard, but did not see, the riot's high point, a bonfire of smashed furniture in the central patio. After midnight, several girls and a couple of the boys knocked and asked to join the adults.

Peake asked them, "What's going on out there?"

"Oh, see for yourself, Mr. Peake; it's just people who are pissed off and like that, they just couldn't hack it anymore. Other people are doing it just for fun."

"Well, why aren't you out there having fun, too?"

"We just don't see what good it does. It's like Mrs. Robinelli said today. It just doesn't do any good to stay angry."

Gershner sat and said nothing.

After a while the yelling began to subside. By sunrise, Faulty Towers had fallen silent. The adults opened Emma's door and peered out. The pavement and walls around the central courtyard were streaked with black, and ashes tumbled in the morning breeze.

Exhausted and filthy boys and girls began to wander into the wreckage of the dining hall, crunching through broken glass. The morning's rations, which usually came up from somewhere below the Towers in an elevator, did not arrive. Emma organized a search, roused those who still slept, and conducted a roll call. No one was hurt or missing.

Hunger clamped Emma's abdomen. Half rations and hard work had put a stylish edge on the youngsters' figures, but made the teacher look bony and weak. "I can't blame you for last night," she said quietly to the students assembled around her. "But, I think you'll learn from it."

A boy snuffled and rubbed a sooty forearm across his nose. "I'm sorry, Mrs. Robinelli," he said.

They sat around and waited. Ordinarily, they would have finished eating the morning's meager half ration and gone below to work in the garden, but today they lacked the initiative. Some of the students went off to their apartments to shower but came back reporting that the water had been cut off.

Emma finally got up and went to the dining hall wall terminal and called up Gamma.

"Gamma speaking."

"Without beating around the bush, what happens next?" the teacher said.

"Either the teenagers learn the purpose and duties of the Ark, or they don't eat," Gamma said. "The schedule will be as follows: Mornings, garden work or other maintenance; afternoons, study. Evenings are free. Every fifth day a day off. For each person who fails to pass the daily quizzes, and for each act of vandalism committed, one ration will be subtracted from that day's issue. I'm sorry I have to be so harsh, but you have left me no choice."

Emma looked over her shoulder at the others. "What do you say?"

Tina called out from the rear of the group: "What do you think we should do, Mrs. Robinelli?"

"I intend to study. The Charonese control the food. Besides, I've already seen some of the things they have to teach us, and they're very interesting. Besides, what else is there to do?"

"No!" a boy shouted. Colby Dennison pushed his way to the

front, his face red with anger. "We can't cooperate with kidnappers and murderers!"

Tina turned to face him. "What are we going to eat? We can't live out in the woods. You haven't seen those, those, dinosaurs—"

Little Claire, no longer plump, holding her boyfriend's hand, advised, "They didn't mean for any of us to get hurt; it was our own fault. This isn't such a bad place to live—"

Colby calmed himself. "How can you say that, Claire? Eva was your friend."

"Have you tried to talk to the Charonese? I have, on the terminal in my room." She glanced at her boyfriend, who nodded agreement. "What they say makes sense. They're really sorry about what happened to Eva and the others. Ask yourself, Colby, who left Eva up there on the tower? It was us, not the Charonese. Why didn't they know we were coming? Because we kept them from repairing the spaceship antenna. And you know what else? I'm glad I don't have to go home! I'll bet there are some other people here who feel that way, only they're afraid to say so."

Emma sat and looked at her hands, painfully feeling the shortcomings of the adult world. After a moment of silence Peake said, "Anyone else have anything to say?"

"We shouldn't give in."

"You want to walk back to Earth, right?"

"Whatever we do, we all have to do it together."

"Ask Mrs. Gershner what she thinks we should do."

They all looked at the former stewardess. Stone-faced, she said, "Cooperate. For the time being." When Colby registered surprise, Gershner said, "The most important thing is to stick together."

That brought a general mumble of agreement from everybody. Mrs. Robinelli turned back to the console and said, "Very well, Gamma, we agree. But we insist on this morning's rations and some time to clean up and rest."

"Granted. Lessons will begin this afternoon. All studying will be in private, on the terminals in your apartments. Your breakfast is on its way up now."

Breakfast consisted of the usual C-rations, and this morning something new was added: huge steaks, and eggs as big as coconuts. Peake seized the food and led the way into the kitchen. For once, everybody was full, some painfully so. "If only we had some coffee," Mr. Peake groaned.

The days, each one the same as the one before, stretched into a month. Emma toiled in the garden with the others in the mornings, and studied astrodynamics alone in the afternoons.

The terminal in her apartment revealed its capabilities as a teaching machine. Different Crew members coached her through realistic simulations of moving asteroids in space. Rocket engines pushed the asteroids toward gigantic orbiting factories that processed them for metals. Other asteroids, made of frozen methane, ammonia, and water, were found in the outer reaches of the Solar System and crashed onto the surface of Pluto. Others burned or evaporated in Charon's upper atmosphere. The time spans of these actions, which reached over centuries, were speeded up for Emma's benefit. Centuries were nothing to the Charonese.

As the second month passed, the students became interested. The Charonese presented the more advanced students with what they called "sound-and-vision helmets," which provided all-around sight and sound, and input-output armatures for the limbs. Skill at using the alien technology advanced rapidly. As they worked in the garden, they talked of the machines and other things they were building in the "play factory" below the Towers. Custom-designed furniture and oddball gadgetry began to appear around the apartments. One group of boys drove a sleek but useless racing automobile around the clearings between the trees. "We designed and built it in two weeks, Mrs. Robinelli," one of them told her. "Of course, Zeta and Kappa helped us a lot." The boy laughed. "I've always wanted to do something like this."

"Why don't you scrap that thing and build something that'll clean up the dining hall and wash the dishes?" Peake suggested. "That would cheer up Mrs. Robinelli more than anything." The boys walked away looking thoughtful.

"You look kind of down in the mouth today, Emma."

"Just the usual."

"Miss him?"

"Yes."

"I'm glad I don't have a family back home," Peake said. "It helps. The kids help, too."

"Yes, they do," Emma said. "You help, too." Peake stopped

picking peas, dusted off his hands, and hugged her, while the teenagers laughed at them.

At night, wearing her vision helmet and the armatures, Emma roamed the software mazes of the Ark's computers. By now, she communicated with the computers in a language of looks and gestures. She felt the presence of the Charonese as though they were disembodied spirits, wandering in fields of pure thought.

Their teachers explained that these feelings, although they seemed mystical, were being transmitted to the humans by prosaic means: the armatures heated, cooled, and vibrated their arms and legs, and the helmets fed them subliminal images and sounds. As a demonstration they simulated for Emma the feeling of dangling her feet in cool water. When she tore off her helmet, she was almost surprised to find herself sitting alone, dry-shod, in her apartment. "Truly amazing," she said.

"It's a dull effect," Gamma said, "compared to what we expect from the more subtle devices you may try when you are ready."

"What sort of device?"

"In English, they could be called neurotransducers," Gamma said. "Electronic devices, measuring about four millimeters long by one millimeter. They are implanted by surgery next to the nerves that transmit various tactile and kinesthetic sensations to the brain. Once they're in, and tuned or adjusted to the individual, fine wires can be inserted into them. The wires are easily removed. No further surgery is required. If you'll look at your terminal, you'll see the sockets for the wire sets."

"It sounds dreadful," Emma said, shuddering. "I can scarcely imagine anyone submitting to that."

"Not at all, Mrs. Robinelli. On my world, nearly everybody had them implanted, once they were mature enough. They are, or were, regarded as essential to modern education and entertainment. You'll love it, once you get used to it."

"I don't want to get used to it!"

"I hope you will change your mind, someday, Mrs. Robinelli, when you are ready for it," Gamma said. "Then we shall meet face-to-face, and see each other as fellow beings. We'll share thoughts, feelings, experiences, and enjoy the spectacle of history and nature together."

"There must be some drawback to it," Emma said.

"We intend to advance carefully, with all precautions," Gamma said. "Nothing will be done until we're both sure you are one hundred percent ready. We—the Crew, that is—are looking forward to meeting you. If you were wearing the transducers now, you'd see that Lambda and Mu are here. They are smiling and laughing right now."

"Hello, Mrs. Robinelli," two other voices said.

"Lambda is particularly eager to hear your views on human history," Gamma said. "We have centuries of recordings for you to experience."

"This is quite amazing," Emma said.

"I'm glad you feel that way. Someone else is here, Mrs. Robinelli. I'll let him introduce himself."

Emma felt a touch on her upper arm. She jumped, supressed the urge to pull off her helmet.

"It's me, Emma," Peake said at her ear.

"Are you in my room?"

"I'm visiting you electronically, Emma. I'm really in my own apartment sitting at my terminal. The Charonese are helping me do this. Don't you keep your door locked?"

"I didn't think it was necessary! Good heavens!"

"So what are you up to?"

"Well, my goodness!" Emma settled herself. "I was about to investigate some aspects of ceratopsian dinosaur behavior and physiology."

"May I look over your shoulder?"

The back of Emma's neck prickled. She stifled the impulse to tear off her helmet again, to see if he were really in her room. "Peake, are you doing all this on purpose?"

"It's a kind of art form. I happen to have a knack for it, just like you're better at looking things up than I am."

"Goodness!"

Emma, simply by asking, could find the answers to questions about dinosaur physiology and behavior that had puzzled paleontologists for a century. She and Peake watched a herd of triceratops munching their way through a stand of alders, biting off five-inch-thick trees with their gigantic beaks and chewing up wood and foliage together.

"I thought triceratops were supposed to have like a bone frill or shield over their necks," Peake said. "I mean, that's what they always looked like in the comic books. These beasties don't even have necks, just a big hump. Makes them look like buffalo or something."

"You're right," Emma said. "But these buffalo are as big as dump trucks. We've just discovered the truth about the famous triceratops frill. The frill was embedded in the neck and shoulders, to provide leverage for those huge jaw muscles. A scientist back on Earth thought of that a few years ago, and we've just proved his speculations correct. I wish I could call him up and tell him."

The Charonese steadfastly refused to show Emma any scenes of current events on Earth, refusing even to admit that they could do so. They reported that some of the students had tried to build weapons and communications equipment in the play factory. This, of course, had been prevented.

At other times, they asked Emma more questions than she could ask them. They asked Emma about Eva and Charlie, and admitted that they were defeated by the mystery of their where-abouts. It would be impossible, they said, for them to be hiding on the Ark, unless they were deliberately staying out of sight in the wilderness somewhere. That would be impossible for un-armed humans, to say nothing of a couple of suburban teenagers. More likely they were dead, and their bodies destroyed. They dismissed the question of Proctor by saying that it was probably Charlie's name for the deceased Alpha.

Time passed for Emma, effortlessly. It's some compensation for being an old lady, she thought. Time goes faster for me. But, of course, homesickness hurts me more than it does the younger folk.

"Gamma."

"I'm here, Mrs. Robinelli."

"What is the Crew policy on children?"

"We would prefer that the girls bear no children until they are at least twenty-two-years-old."

"I'll subscribe to that."

"I was sure you would. You can help us with it."

"And after that?"

"We would like for the human population to increase to about

one hundred. After that, everyone will be sterilized. In two generations, the physical human race aboard the Ark will cease to
exist. Those who learn our ethic will live on as we do, in the
computers."

Emma frowned, pulled back from the terminal. Given accep-
tance of being kidnapped, of being nurtured in this artificial hot-
house, it was right, the right thing to do. But it was inhuman.
The Charonese wanted to force the humans to behave rationally
and, from their point of view, ethically.

In the part of the woods away from Faulty Towers, Emma
took Gershner aside and asked how she felt about the Charonese
plan. "It's sickening!" Gershner retorted. "I stay away from those
terminals, but some of the young people have come to me and
told me what the Charonese are saying. It's like Satan himself
were tempting the children, offering them fake immortality, sex,
shiny toys, urging them to renounce their families and everything
decent. Some of the children even said they were happier here
than at home."

"Who said that?"

"Claire, for one. The little one. The one who's sleeping with
her boyfriend. How old is she, sixteen?"

"She's fifteen."

"You're her teacher. Is it right, Mrs. Robinelli?"

"Maybe it is, here on Charon. How could we stop it, if we
wanted to? At least we haven't got a *Lord of the Flies* situation
here."

"What?" Gershner looked at Emma as though she thought
she'd lost her mind and started babbling nonsense.

"*Lord of the Flies*. It's a book. About a group of schoolchil-
dren stranded on a desert island. They run wild, fight with one
another, and so on."

Gershner shook her head. "This isn't a book, Mrs. Robinelli.
You and I are responsible for these kids. We owe it to their parents to keep them safe, bring them home safe. Even Claire.
remember she said she doesn't want to go home. I can't understand it!"

"I can help you with that, perhaps," Emma said. "During the
last year I've had suspicions that Claire was being sexuall

abused at home. Maybe by her stepfather. I was planning to look into it further when we got back from this trip."

Gershner looked at the teacher, dumbfoundedness on her face. Emma nodded. "It happens," she said. "There's no proof, and Claire has never stated it in so many words. Being hijacked has saved Claire and me the pain of bringing it out into the open. Of course, this is between the two of us."

"Of course," Gershner said, pale with rage. "Thank you for telling me."

Gershner started toward the garden, but Emma touched her elbow. "There's something else I want to ask you, Lena."

Gershner halted, looked back. Emma said, "I've had some complaints from some of the students. Some of them tell me that they're being threatened by Colby Dennison and others. Accused of not doing their share of the garden work."

"It's true," Gershner replied.

"Is it true also, that you've been instigating this vigilante activity? The students say so. They say that Colby hit one of them the other day."

"I won't try to hide it, Mrs. Robinelli," Gershner said. "Kids are kids. Some of them have been goofing off. It makes the others have to work harder, and they don't like it."

"Children squabbling is one thing, Lena. An adult forming a vigilante committee is another."

"They need discipline. I think of it as a disciplinary committee."

"Perhaps they do need discipline. But it should come from the student body as a whole, not a group of dictators. And you're wrong to do something like this without consulting me and Mr. Peake."

"I don't see it that way, Mrs. Robinelli," Gershner said. "It isn't just the garden work. Some of the kids have been committing acts of vandalism, too. We can't have that; not yet, anyway. I waited for you to take action, and you didn't. You and Peake are too friendly with the Charonese. Many of the kids feel that way too. So we're taking steps."

"You're dividing the group against itself, Lena. It's wrong."

"And you, enjoying yourself in your computer playground? While we're all prisoners of terrorists? That's right?"

"I, we, we're trying to make the best of—"

"Best be damned!" Gershner retorted. "It's disloyalty! You're supposed to be protecting the kids! If you're not going to help, then keep your nose out of it. I have work to do!" She turned and stalked away among the pines, leaving Emma standing alone.

Chapter Eleven:
The Stowaways

The Charonese trail was easy to follow in the woods. The aliens had rolled single file, flattening the shrubbery. Their tire marks indicated at least five heavy vehicles. The tread prints in the mud looked functional, ordinary, like any truck tires. In places, the machines had gouged bark off trees ten feet above the ground.

Froward and Chela came to a slow-moving stream, speckled with little saw-edged leaves floating in the water. Mashed-out tracks and crushed ferns showed where the Charonese vehicles had forded the stream.

Chela splashed across the water without pausing. Froward waded after, scrambled up a muddy bank, fought through a tangle of run-over bushes, and emerged into the open.

Chela waited for him at the edge of the forest, where the trail led away. Froward was struck by the odd appearance of the Charonese horizon. About a kilometer away, the ground seemed to curve downward into a wall of translucent blue glass. Froward felt as though he could stand on that horizon and throw a rock through the sky.

"Pretty weird, huh," Chela said.

"It sure is," Froward puffed. "Listen, in the future, remember not to do that anymore, okay?"

"Not do what?" she said. "Get hijacked by flying saucers from outer space? You got it."

"No, I mean jump into a stream, like you just did, without checking first. Haven't you ever heard of snakes and crocodiles?"

"Oh, yeah, right. Got your breath back yet?"

"Yes!"

"Am I going too fast for you?"

"No!"

They pressed on in the bright sunshine, walking fast across a grassy savannah dotted with high, spindly pines and palmetto thickets. Grasshoppers and birds flew up ahead of them. Several times large lizards wriggled off into the grass, and once, a two-legged something resembling a plucked turkey jumped up and bounded away. The trail was plain enough, wheel tracks winding this way and that in the dry grass to avoid clumps of pine and palmettos.

Chela's legs pumped tirelessly, her improvised rucksack bouncing on her hips. Both of them wore the brown denim work suits purchased by the Charonese, but Chela's was several sizes too large for her. The girl had rolled her sleeves to her shoulders, exposing solid round arms, and she'd tied strips of torn-up overall around her head, waist, and knees. Her cuffs flopped around her workboots. She was head and shoulders shorter than Froward, but he had to hustle to keep up with her.

"What's on your mind, Captain?" she said, not looking back at him.

"I was thinking that, in that outfit, you bear a certain resemblance to Rambo."

"Your mom drinks Rambo's bathwater, Captain."

"Oops—hold it," Froward said. Just ahead, something that looked like a small hilltop was moving in a palmetto patch. They froze.

"You see that?"

"Yeah. What is it?"

"It's not the airport limousine," Froward said. "Let's step over here." He pulled her under the shade of a nearby pine.

The hilltop moved gradually out of the palmettos and resolved itself into an armored, four-legged monster the size of a tank. Grass and small bushes sprouted from between the lumps of bone and stubby horns on its back. Its tail stuck out rigidly behind, a bone knob on its tip. A small, white egret sat on the knob, fluffing its feathers and preening under its wings. Several more of the birds stepped daintily between the dinosaur's heavy legs. The creature lowered its cowlike head and began to rip up mouthfuls of dry grass.

"I believe that's called an ankle saurus," Froward said, dredging up a memory from some childhood book.

"Bullshit," Chela said. "That thing doesn't have ankles."

The animal turned and began to graze away from the humans, moving with tortoiselike deliberation. "Some book I read said they were supposed to be harmless," Froward said.

"So long as you don't let it sit on you."

While they waited for the creature to move away, Froward looked back the way the two of them had come. The line of forest along the stream they'd crossed was already below the horizon behind them. The white line of the cable-pipe ran across the sky toward the north, rising higher until it dwindled out of sight among the clouds drifting in the clear blue sky. He squatted and leaned against the flaky gray bark of the pine. Chela stood on tiptoe, trying to see ahead, where the trail ran.

"The trouble with this place is, you can't see anything until you're right on top of it, or it's right on top of you," Chela said.

"Ahuh," Froward said. He pulled a grass stem and chewed on it, looking at the ground. It was a quiet day, without even a breeze to stir the grass. Millions of insects whirred around them, the sound blending into a soothing summertime hum that Froward didn't notice until he made an effort to hear it. One of the Charonese vehicles had flattened an anthill nearby. The tire pattern was clear in the bare white sand. Superimposed on the tire mark was a three-toed footprint, ten inches from claw to heel. Whatever it was, it had been there recently.

The ankylosaur moved behind a distant clump of bushes. Chela poked his arm. "Hey. Clint Eastwood. You ready to go yet? The trail leads toward the woods over there."

He stood up. "Yeah. Get your gun out."

They moved down an almost imperceptible slope toward another line of trees. The tops of the trees rose out of the horizon as they approached. The Charonese had crashed through the brush, avoiding only the largest trees. The ground became muddy again.

Chela followed Froward through the wood, and they came to another open space, no savannah this time, but a driftwood-littered expanse of sand that went all the way to the horizon, flat as a tabletop. The Charonese tire marks went straight away, out of sight.

"Is this a desert?" Chela asked.

"More likely a river floodplain," Froward said. "If the horizon weren't so close, we could probably see across it."

"It looks clear."

"Yes, but we'll be out in the open, where we can be seen a long way off. On the other hand, I'm worried about what might be behind us in the woods."

"All the more reason to get out of here," she said.

"Right." They set off across the open, Froward glancing uneasily behind him at the woods. The tire prints continued west, curving around beached trees and masses of flood-deposited brushwood. Several times they had to detour around stagnant water holes. Froward's fears about crocodiles were confirmed; the biggest holes contained one or two of the monsters, lying on the edges or floating with eyes protruding from the water. The muddy margins of the water holes were patterned with animal tracks, not the paw- and hoofprints of Earth, but an alien mosaic of huge birdtracks and reptile handprints.

The sun was in their faces when they came to a place where the Charonese vehicles had pulled abreast of one another, leaving a tangle of crisscrossing tracks. Beyond that, the tracks vanished.

"Uh oh," Chela said.

Froward walked back to the spot where he'd lost the trail. Chela came and stood beside him. "Did they fly away, or what?" she said.

Froward frowned as he studied the ground. There were several places where something flat and heavy had pressed into the sand, in a rectangular pattern forty feet across. "Maybe they did," he said. "These marks could've been made by the pads of a helicopter, a really big one. That," he said, pointing with his grenade launcher, "might be where the trucks rolled up a ramp."

"Are we burned?" Chela said.

"Looks like it."

"Shit!" Chela spat out the word.

Froward ran his fingers through his gray-flecked hair as though he might rub an idea into his skull. All around them stretched the empty sand and the drifting clouds, all lost in the sky.

"What are we going to do, with no trail to follow?" Chela demanded.

"We switch to plan B," Froward said, grinning unhappily.

"What's that?"

"Let's get under cover, first, then we'll talk about it—"

Froward was interrupted by a faint yammering sound. He stood with his mouth open, listening as the noise built up to a unearthly chorus of yelping and squealing, as though somewhere below the horizon behind them a maniac was torturing puppy dogs. Suddenly it stopped.

"Holy shit!" Chela exclaimed, not too loudly. "What was that?"

"When in doubt, move out," Forward quoted, and gave her a push. They began walking rapidly westward, into the sun. The yammering started again, louder and closer.

"Let's speed it up," Froward said. They began jogging. Their clumsy boots made it heavy going in the soft sand. Froward ran out of wind too soon. "One more minute, then walk," he grasped.

"Okay."

He snatched a glance over his shoulder. The horizon was empty, but the yelping and screaming was following them, without a doubt. Up ahead a dead tree lay on its side in a dry channel. "Head for that," Froward said. He sprinted, throwing sand behind him.

The tree was no tree, but a giant skeleton, tented with sheets of bleached hide. Chela followed him as he jumped over a line of vertebrae and knelt behind a picket fence of huge ribs. Between the bones he saw a dozen two-legged demons pounding over the horizon toward them, sharp tails held out behind.

"Don't move!" he whispered.

The dinosaurs ranged from side to side as they approached, searching for their prey. They were as tall as a man and twice as long. They ran with incredible smoothness and speed, holding powerful clawed hands close to their breasts.

The yelping stopped as the pack loped up to the end of the tire tracks and began to mill around, searching for their prey. One of them strutted a few steps toward Froward and Chela, halted, and cocked its head. It was a clown from hell: bright orange above, yellow below, with gorgeous patterns of green stripes and black rosettes breaking up its body outlines. It fixed a yellow eye on their hiding place. Froward didn't dare move, not even to get down out of sight. The beast let out a terrifying yell, and the entire pack charged.

"They see us!" Chela cried. Before Froward could grab her, she jumped out from behind the skeleton, holding her pistol in front of her in both hands. She began firing, *BAM, BAM, BAM,* the gun jumping in her hands, brass shells flipping out in the sunshine. Three of the monsters flopped on the sand, kicking, and the others vaulted over them. Froward aimed at the biggest and squeezed: *CHUNK BLAT* the antitank round exploded inside the monster, sending limbs and guts flying. Froward ran away from Chela, breaking open his launcher and fumbling for a buckshot round in the bandolier around his neck. The remaining dinosaurs screeched and ran into one another as some headed for Froward, some for Chela. The girl wheeled, crouching, the .45 straight in front of her—*BAM BAM BAM.*

Four more went down, some hit, others tangling their long legs in the carcasses. Froward snapped his launcher shut; one of the monsters was leaping at him feet first, hooks extended; he fired buckshot point-blank—*BOOM*—as it landed on him, smashing him into the sand. Claws bit into his shoulders and ripped down his body; Froward cried out, struggling frantically out from under, but it was dead, its head blown into a mush of blood and bone. He looked up and saw Chela run three quick paces, whirl, and fire her last two shots into an animal chasing her. The heavy .45 bullets knocked it over backward. Its legs convulsed, a five-inch claw on each foot making long gouges in the sand.

The remaining predators milled at a distance, one hopping crippled, another squirting blood and dragging its intestines while the others chased it in circles, biting at it, all of them yelping and screaming like devils in hell.

Chela ran up to Froward, sobbing, "Oh, God! Oh, God! Are you hurt?"

"I'm all right! Let's get out of here!" He dragged his pack and launcher from under the one he'd shot, slung them over his shoulder, and grabbed her hand.

They ran away as in a nightmare, their boots sinking into the sand, the rags of Froward's overalls flapping around him. They ran until Froward couldn't keep up anymore, and fell on his pack and weapon, fighting for breath. Chela stopped and came back to him. She pulled at his shoulders, forcing him to sit up. "Look!"

she screamed. "They're still coming!" In the distance, five of the creatures jogged toward them, fanning out as they approached.

"We can't outrun them," Froward said, between gasps. "Got to shoot it out." With shaking hands he broke open his grenade launcher, blew sand out of the barrel, set the weapon on his lap, fumbled through his bandolier for a fragmentation round.

Chela's teeth chattered as she loaded a new magazine into her pistol. "They've stopped!" she cried.

The dinosaurs had halted a hundred meters away, yipping and barking. "Oh, God, they want us to start running again!" Chela moaned.

Froward slid a frag shell into the chamber and snapped the launcher shut. He raised the rear sight slide, slipped the sight halfway up, breathed deeply, rested his elbows on his knees, and took aim.

The dinosaurs strutted back and forth, heads jerking. "Come on, you sonsabitches," Froward muttered, "get closer together— that's it—" He held his breath and squeezed the trigger. *CHUNK!* The launcher kicked Froward's shoulder. The shell soared into the middle of the pack and exploded on the ground—*SLAM!* The dinosaurs screeched and ran back from the explosion. Froward reloaded and fired again, hitting just behind the moving pack. The explosion knocked one down; the others sprinted away, turning into bouncing dots that disappeared over the horizon.

Froward reloaded and pulled his pack close to where he was sitting. The fallen animals lay in the distance, some thrashing the air with clawed legs. "We'll move, as soon as I get . . . my breath back," he puffed. "Sorry to be such a drag."

She was coming unfrozen, slowly. She put her gun away and looked down at him, the whites of her eyes showing. "You're hurt."

"It's not as bad as it looks. Oh, man." The front of his overalls had been torn open, and a wide slash ran from his chest to his thigh. His underwear was soaked red. He laughed and groaned. He was embarrassed to be half-naked in front of a teenage girl. The sun seemed dazzling; he could barely see.

"My muh—mother always told me to keep my Fruitlooms clean, in case I got run over. Aagh," Froward fell on his elbows and vomited prolongedly and painfully. Agony cramped his abdomen. I'm in shock, he thought.

A shadow flicked over them. Chela ducked, then stared. A black, crescent-winged shape glided over the sand, its shadow following it along the ground. It stalled neatly, dropped a pair of long-toed feet, and touched down on the giant skeleton.

"Hell of a landing," Froward breathed. The flier teetered on top of the giant's rib cage, then propped itself on the clawed edges of its bent wings. A pickaxe face twisted around on the end of a snakelike neck to watch them.

"It's waiting for us to leave," Froward said. "Let's go, before the rest of the zoo shows up."

"But you can't, we have to—"

"Let's get under cover first. Oh, boy." He gathered his legs under him, and discovered he couldn't stand up. Chela got under his arm and pulled him upright. Blood ran down his legs.

They hiked on, slowly, Froward propping himself with a stick, holding his free arm over his stomach. "Just a little while longer," Chela urged him. "I see some woods ahead."

The woods proved to be a small forested island a few feet higher than the floodplain. Some way along its bank Chela found a huge gum tree that had fallen onto the riverbed a short distance from a water hole. The tree was still alive, and its leaves made a dense curtain. She led Froward among its branches. He groaned with relief as he sank down on the sand.

Chela unrolled their packs, opened several C-ration cans, and dumped the contents on a spread piece of canvas. "We'll eat this later," she said. "I need these containers for water." Carrying the cans with her, she pushed her way out of the branches, and Froward heard her walking away over the sand.

After what seemed like a long time, she said, "I'm back," outside the shelter. He heard her breaking twigs and smelled smoke. After a while, she came into the shelter balancing cans of hot water. "I boiled it ten minutes," she said.

"Help me sit up." Froward's tattered coverall stuck to his body. The slash down his body was a contusion, bloody, but not deep enough (he saw gratefully) to break the abdominal wall. The claw punctures in his shoulders were less painful, but deeper. Chela swabbed the contusion and poured the punctures full of scalding water until he couldn't stand it anymore. She bandaged his chest and stomach with boiled cloth. She helped him spoon up the mess on the canvas, and went for water again.

As the sun went down, Froward lay on the warm sand, his pack under his head. Chela sat with her chin on her knees. A breeze rustled in the leaves around them. By turning his head, Froward could see the water hole. A cloud of white butterflies had settled around the water.

"Guess we'll have to stay here tonight," she said.

"We, ugh, could keep going, and hope we come to a motel."

"Your mom comes in a motel. Just shut up."

He woke up in the middle of the night. Chela lay several feet away, snoring softly. The breeze still blew through the tree, and the sand was still warm. He cautiously felt his wound. The front of his overalls were pinned together with the big black safety pins from the ammo bandoliers. She must have done that for me, he thought. He relaxed, painfully, in stages.

At dawn Chela fed him chopped ham and eggs and boiled muddy water. "You like fainted last night," she said. "It scared me. I thought I'd better let you sleep. How do you feel now?"

"Better." He tried to draw up his knees; the unexpected pain forced a grunt out of him.

"Uh-uh, don't do that," Chela said. "Lie still, while I have a look." She unpinned his coverall, her fingers so light he hardly felt them. She dabbed water on the strips of cloth she'd used for bandages and peeled them loose. "It's coming open in places," she said. "I don't think you ought to move, at least not right now."

"We can't—"

"We have to stay here. It's not such a bad place. I've been looking around. It's just a small island, and there aren't any animals. There's water, and nothing can see us under this tree."

Froward didn't agree, but he could see no alternative. He lay helplessly and watched the girl arrange their weapons and supplies in handy piles. Later, she dug a hole in the sand for herself and went to sleep. Dappled sunlight moved over her body.

He awoke in the evening, his whole body hot and throbbing. He thought he could hear the pain, a too fast *thumpity-thumpity* getting louder in his ears.

Chela pushed into their hiding place through the branches. "Hear that noise? It's one of those Charonese helicopters."

"Is it coming toward us? Following our tracks?"

"No. It's just going past a long way off," she said, peering out between the branches.

"So it's not looking for us. That's odd. I thought I was hearing things," he said.

"You missed the dinosaur parade," she said. "A pair of really big duckbills and a whole flock of little ones visited the water hole. Now they're browsing on the island. Charlie'd love it. Let's have a look at you."

She crawled up beside him and opened the front of his coveralls. "Stop flinching; I won't hurt you," she said. "How do you feel?"

He stirred, and immediately regretted it. "Don't ask. How does it look?"

"It's infected, but not too bad."

"Charon probably doesn't have enough of the right kind of germs," Froward said.

Chela opened cans and poured water. "Now eat, whether you want to or not," she said.

The next day he felt well enough to hobble outside their shelter, stooped over a stick. The rest of the day went slowly.

At nightfall Chela returned to their hideout. "Bad news. A tyrannosaurus is near the island. It killed one of the duckbills at the water hole. It's there now, eating. The other duckbill and the babies crossed the island and took off west." She opened a C-ration can, gulped half, and offered it to him.

Froward took the can and sipped. It was pears in juice. "Listen, Chela—"

"I know. You're not sure what we're doing out here anymore. Is that what you want to say?" She began rolling up their packs, throwing things in and jerking the knots.

Froward nodded dispiritedly and put down the can. "More or less."

Chela snapped, "How about that? The airline captain is finally asking me what I think! We're still doing the same thing we were before we lost the tire tracks: We're hiding from the Charonese, and looking for the other passengers. And taking Chela along for the ride!"

"Well, I thought I should—"

"Sure you did! You thought it was such a good idea that you didn't even tell me about it. You just assumed I should come along, too."

"I know, and I'm sorry. I had to find the other passengers, or

at least try to find them. Now that that's not an immediate possibility, I have no right to continue to risk your life this way. You're
a child."

"Who was it that saved your drooping ass back there, when
the spook show tried to eat us? The child!"

"That's true, but——"

"Let's keep your *but* out of this, Mr. Froward. Get this
straight: You didn't drag me anywhere. I came because I wanted
to come, and I'm staying for the same reason!"

"You can't last out here. I might not be able to, either. I have
to go on looking, but you——"

"It's your mom can't last out here, Mr. Froward. You want to
turn me in? To the Charonese?"

"It might be better——"

"The hell! Until Buck Rogers shows up in his rocket ship and
rescues us, you're stuck with me. And the next time you get any
brilliant ideas, you ask me about them first. From now on, this is
a goddamn equal opportunity planet. You want the rest of those
pears, or what?"

He accepted the half-eaten can from her and dipped in it with
a plastic spoon. The fruit was warm and sweet. He finished off
the pears, swallowed the juice. She took the empty can and
stuffed it in a pack. "That's the end of the food," she said. "I
hope you enjoyed it."

"Uh."

"So what. We were going to run out eventually. Now see if
you can get to your feet, because we've leaving."

"It's night! It's dark!"

She dragged him upright and handed him his stick. "This island
isn't big enough for Gorgo and us at the same time. Here," she said,
more gently, "lean on me. That's right. Does it hurt much?"

"No."

"What a man."

Starlight illuminated the flat sand as they hobbled across the
floodplain. They weren't followed. "What were you planning to
do?" Chela said. "I mean, after you got rid of me."

"I thought maybe the Charonese were headed toward something when the helicopter picked them up. So I was going to keep
headed west until I found whatever it was."

"Good," Chela said. "We can't give up. I didn't say we shouldn't give up, I said we can't."

"You're right," he said.

"Hooray. He admits I'm right."

Three hours' slow hiking brought them to the forest on the west bank. Froward had used up his little store of strength. He shivered helplessly, his clothes soaked with sweat. Chela spread a tarpaulin on the sand, helped Froward lie down, and lay beside him pulling the other tarp over the two of them. She wrapped her arms around him and hugged him close to her body. In the swimming darkness, Froward was dimly aware of her strength. "Wha—"

"Just rest now," she said. "We'll be all right."

"C-Charlie said that," he said. His teeth were chattering in her hair. "On the spaceship."

"Poor old Charlie was a dipshit, but he knew about some things," Chela said.

The next morning, Froward woke up to find Chela kneeling over him with a can of hot water. "Feel better?"

"I think I do," he said, and it was true. He got to his feet and looked around. Chela had stopped next to a low dirt bank at the edge of the sand plain. Trees hung over them, and the air was filled with the twittering of birds. Chela had built a little fire, and the smoke smelled wonderful. Her collection of C-ration cans sat in it, simmering. "Nothing to eat, right?"

She grinned at him. "Right. Think you can walk?"

"I think so," he said, taking a few steps. In wonderment, he realized that the pain had decreased to stiffness.

"Okay. Let's haul buns." She jumped up and began gathering their possessions. Froward moved to help her, but she pushed him away. He leaned on his staff and watched her snatching their tarps off the ground and rolling packs. She handed him the grenade launcher and his walking staff and slung the two packs over her shoulders. Under the dirt on her face, dimples showed. "So what's on your mind, Captain?"

"Thanks for taking care of me."

"No prob, Bob." She scrambled up the bank and reached down a hand to help him up.

Inland, the terrain became a monotonous succession of low, sandy ridges where they walked through dry grass, pines, and scrub oak. Between the ridges were jungly hollows choked with vines, alder, sassafras, magnolia, live oak, and palms. Little dinosaurs scuttled in the undergrowth, pelted across the open spaces, or stood their ground, hissing.

On top of each ridge, they halted while Chela pelted the intervening hollows with branches and pinecones. Several times this procedure flushed larger animals out of the thick brush and trees that choked the low ground. Most frequently the specimens, as Chela called them, were smaller versions of the ankylosaur they'd seen the day before. At other times, there were man-size or larger bipeds, with stiff horizontal tails and round bony heads, that dashed away into the bushes. Once, a large predator stood up and glared around, but it didn't seem to see them as they stood rooted to the ground. After a while, it strode away, and they moved on.

The afternoon wore on, clouds built up overhead, and thunder muttered. Toward sundown, they crested a ridge to find one of the boneheads browsing in the open. They froze. The animal continued to pick leaves one by one, chewing them rapidly like a gigantic rabbit. "Shall I try it?" Chela whispered out of the side of her mouth.

"Go ahead," Froward whispered back.

With infinite care, the girl raised her pistol in both hands and squeezed off a shot. The *bang* rang off the tree trunks around them. The animal flopped down hard, legs stiff. It lay for a second, then jumped up with a strangled squawk, and crashed out of sight into a thicket. Froward and Chela faded behind nearby trees. The bushes where the animal had disappeared thrashed violently, and birds flew away yelling.

"It must be hung up in the bushes," Chela said, from behind her tree. Froward looked around nervously, wondering what hunters might be attracted by the commotion. After a long time the thrashing died down. The two approached cautiously, and found the bonehead lying suspended in the heavy brush, blood puddling under a large wound in its side.

"Nice shot," Froward said, digging in his pack for an axe.

"Ugh. Hurry up, okay?"

Froward hacked off a three-foot drumstick, and they hurried away as thunder rumbled in the west. Two ridges farther on, under a spectacular, lightning-flickered sunset, they built a bonfire of dry branches, waited for it to die down to coals, then toasted sputtering slices of meat on sticks over the heat.

"Not bad," Chela said, chewing the tough flesh.

"Yeah, I'm surprised," Froward said. "Tomorrow, I'll introduce you to the wonders of palm cabbage."

"What's that?"

"If you chop down one of those tall palm trees there, inside
the top is a thing like a bunch of celery. Doesn't taste like much,
but it fills you up."

"How do you know all this stuff?"

"When I was in the air force, I went to the survival school in
Pensacola, Florida. The vegetation around here reminds me of
that."

"Did you eat a snake? My dad ate a snake when he was in the
army rangers."

"You never talk about your mother," Froward said.

Chela was using an airline steak knife to cut thin slices of
flesh from the dinosaur leg, laying them on a broad, glossy leaf
she'd picked off a tree. "My mother died when I was little. I
always lived with my dad. He took me everywhere with him:
Okinawa, Germany, places in the States. The only time he left
me in a school was when he was in Vietnam. I cried every night
while he was gone."

"Who took care of you?"

"He did. Sometimes we had a housekeeper. He always had to
argue with the brass to get housing we could live in. He always
kept me with him. I guess he was good at pulling strings. And he
told me he had lots of friends in the personnel office."

"That's pretty impressive," Froward said.

"He told me that if I didn't stay completely out of trouble all
the time, he'd have to leave me in a school again. You better
believe I was good. Finally, he got his retirement, and w-we went
to live in Seattle."

Froward realized the girl was weeping as she worked, tears
running silently down her nose. He said, "I ate a snake, but it
wasn't as good as this dinosaur. I feel like Alley Oop."

"W-what's Alley Oop?"

"A caveman in a comic strip I used to read when I was a kid.
He was always eating roast dinosaur."

"Just so long as you don't start saying 'Great zot' and dragging me around by the hair."

"'Great zot' is *B.C.* That's a different comic strip. As I recall,

Alley Oop's girlfriend's name was Oona, and he never dragged her by the hair."

"She'd probably slap him upside the head if he did. That's what I'd do to you." Heavy raindrops began tapping among the dry leaves on the ground. Chela got up, wiped her face on her sleeve, and unrolled the sheets of tarpaulin that made up their knapsacks. She spread one on the ground, and lay down on it. A raindrop landed on the back of Froward's neck, icy cold. He shuddered. "Get in here with me, Mr. Oop," Chela said, holding open the top cover for him.

"Well—"

"Don't get funny on me. It's raining, in case you hadn't noticed, and last night you were half-dead with fever. Hurry up; you've shivering." She shook the tarpaulin at him.

He lay down beside her, and she snuggled against him, pulling the cover over them. She was round, and soft, and her breath was warm on his neck. "Do I feel like a child?" she said against his chest.

"Knock it off," he growled.

"What a man," she murmured, and began to snore.

Froward decided to keep his eyes open until it stopped raining, then get up. Wind rushed through the trees, and the air turned deliciously cool. Raindrops rattled on the tarp. Chela hugged him closer in her sleep.

At dawn Froward popped awake. Hell of a watchman I am, he thought, looking around at the dripping bushes and their soaked fireplace. He slipped out from under the tarp and began gathering up their possessions. When he heard Chela stirring, he brought her a strip of meat and a can of rainwater. "Breakfast," he said.

"I see we weren't gobbled up in the night," she commented, yawning. "How you feel?"

"Stiff, sore—basically like an old geezer who's been fighting dinosaurs and trying to keep up with Ms. Rambo all day."

She stood up, fluffing her hair with her fingers, chewing on the meat. "Okay, Mr. Geezer, show me some of that palm cabbage stuff."

They traveled slowly all day. In spite of the night showers they had experienced, the landscape was parched. They traversed low clay hills covered with sere grass and rattling palmettos, crossed dry streambeds and aromatic pine groves that seemed

ready to burst into flame. When they found a pond, they collected duckweed, tiny cloverlike plants floating in the muddy
water, and cattail roots. They marched with stalks of yellow palm
cabbage sticking out of their pockets, munching greenery and
peeling cattail roots for their starchy cores.

That night, Chela poked him awake, holding her hand over his
mouth. "Quiet," Chela whispered in his ear. "Something's happening. You awake?"

Froward nodded. Chela removed her hand from his mouth.
"Listen," she whispered. He raised his head, feeling disoriented.
They had taken refuge before nightfall in a stand of tall, spindly
pines whose umbrellalike tops blocked out the sky. It was totally
dark under the trees. The only thing Froward could see were a
few red embers in the remains of their campfire.

He was about to say he didn't hear anything when the noise
began. It was a rhythmic pulsing, like a one-cylinder diesel refusing to start: *pum-pum-pum-pum*. It was on his right, and close.
Froward came fully awake, his hair standing on end.

Another engine began to chug behind them, then a different
note sounded from the left: F-flat on a gigantic tuba. Froward
stealthily pulled his grenade launcher from under his blanket. He
felt Chela's lips on his ear. "Flashlight?"

"Yeah," Froward whispered. The light came on, falling on a
tree trunk that was much closer than any Froward remembered.
The flashlight beam moved down to the ground. The tree had
toenails, like an elephant's.

"Oh my god," Chela gasped. The flashlight beam moved up the
leg to a colossal belly, along a wall of tesselated hide, up a twenty-
foot neck to a floppy-lipped head hooked over a pine branch high
above, its eyes closed, its nostrils fluttering. The light moved
waveringly to other trees, illuminated more towering necks and
sleeping horsy faces propped against every tree in the grove.

Froward's stomach shrank against his backbone. A dozen
long-necked dinosaurs, looking like the classic monsters from the
books of his childhood, had occupied the pine grove around
them. Chela continued to swear, but her words were drowned out
by a symphony of enginelike snorings and outgassings. One of
the creatures, a third the size of the others, was awake. It bent its
neck downward in a graceful slow-motion arch and snuffed at the
two humans, blowing Chela's hair with a gust of pine-scented

breath, looking at her out of wise brown eyes nested in wrinkles. It nuzzled Froward's blanket, pulled its head back upright, and went to sleep with its neck resting on the back of one of the full-size ones. The animal nearest Froward picked up its foot and put it down again on top of their smoldering campfire. The beast slumbered on. Froward began to notice a stink: burning hide. "Let's get out of here!" he whispered urgently.

Froward and Chela jumped up and swept their possessions into their arms. Walking as silently as speed would permit, they moved out of the grove, swerving around the great legs and the tails lying on the ground like fallen trees. In moments they had reached the open starlight.

Chela let out a smothered yell. "What'll we do?"

"Gotta climb a tree!" Froward wheezed back at her. "I think I see one over there!"

They hurried through the clinging grass to a huge tree that stood black and domelike against the stars. Its long limbs, heavy with big shiny leaves, drooped low enough for them to reach. They dropped their equipment on the ground and clambered as high as they dared. While Chela held the flashlight in her mouth, Froward fumblingly began tying their cargo net to branches. While he was in the middle of this task, an outraged squeal burst out of the darkness, louder than a siren.

"Hold on tight!" Froward shouted.

A dozen titanic cows bawled in panic. The earth shook. Froward clung to his vibrating branch, smelling the dust, while the sound of crashing trees, angry roaring, and the thunder of massive feet faded in the distance.

Eventually it became quiet enough to hear the crickets again. Froward finished his improvised hammock. They crawled in and cautiously relaxed.

"Comfy?" Chela asked in the dark.

Froward groaned, "Sure."

"I'm wide awake now."

"Me, too," said Froward. He was dripping sweat.

"A dinosaur stampede, and it's too dark to see it," she babbled. "What lousy luck."

"I'm not complaining."

"I can't believe they surrounded us without waking us up or stepping on us."

"In Thailand, they say an elephant won't step on you if it can help it," Froward said. "They also say that elephants walk quietly and gracefully. When they want to praise a woman, they say she walks like an elephant."

"Golly gee, Captain, you sure know a lot of stuff," she said.

Froward lay still, his heartbeat slowing to normal. He caught glimpses of stars through the leaves.

"Do I walk like a brontosaurus, Captain?"

"Sure you do. Shall we try to sleep now?"

"Can I ask you a question, Captain?"

"No, and I've been meaning to tell you, I'm not a captain, only a copilot."

"If I knew your first name, I could stop calling you Captain, Clint."

A breeze began to blow through the tree, and their hammock swayed with it. Froward had folded his tarp under him, but the net straps still dug into his back. The sag of the net forced Chela to lie practically on top of him, and he didn't know what to do with his hands.

"Why are you waving your arms around?"

"Trying to find a place to put them," he grumbled.

She caught his right hand and squeezed it. "You can put your arm on me if you want to. I won't mind." She guided his arm around her waist, and embraced him similarly. "You don't smell so bad, for an old geezer."

"And you don't sweat much, for a fat girl," he said.

She laughed uninhibitedly, the same way she'd cried. "Well, can I ask you a question, Clint?"

"No. Go to sleep."

"The kids said you were having an affair with the stewardess. Is it true?"

"Good God. None of your business."

"If I knew your first name, I could stop calling you Clint."

"It's Jeff."

"Jeff's okay. I'll call you that." They slept.

The next day went the same as the one before. It became the pattern for the days that followed. They foraged as they traveled, Froward watching for signs of pursuit. Meat was plentiful, limited only by Froward's reluctance to expend their ammunition. One day the same pond that provided cattails also yielded a ducklike bird, so tame that Froward was able to knock it down with a stick.

They were shoving forward through thick brush in the next valley when Froward noticed a vast rushing noise coming from in front of them. "This time I hear something first," he said.

Chela listened. "You're right. Sounds like a freeway or something."

They waited, but the noise didn't change or move. They advanced cautiously through the brush. Just ahead, the ground seemed to drop away into the air. The rushing noise became louder. Suddenly, they arrived at the top of a crumbling sand bluff and saw waves rolling up and over the slope of a curved green sea, and surf booming on a narrow beach below them.

"I'll be damned," Froward said. It was the highest place and the oddest vista they'd so far encountered on Charon.

"Neat," Chela said, the wind ruffling her curls. "Let's get down there. I want a bath."

They found a gully that led to the beach. Chela ordered him to turn his back. "Mind if I go in, too?" he said.

"I encourage it," she said, unwrapping her hair. "But if I catch you peeking at me, I'll shoot you a new asshole, you dig?"

Froward stripped and carried his clothes into the water, keeping his face to the north. The surf roared over him, sluicing off days of grime and sweat. The water was warm and salty, but he was afraid to stay in more than a few minutes. He yelled at Chela to get out of the water, didn't hear her answer, and turned around to find her already on the beach, buttoning up her coverall. He hesitated, then left the water holding his wet clothes in front of him.

"Why, Clint, what modesty," she said, grinning at him.

"Turn your back!"

She looked away. "You forget, I saw you naked already, when you were hurt. Also I had a look at you just now, in the surf."

Froward growled, "Okay, I don't give a damn. Turn around, and I'll show you what we used to call a moon!"

"No, thank you," she said sweetly. "I've already made sure you were fully recovered from your wounds."

They built a driftwood fire, broiled the duck, drank their fresh water supply, and lay on a tarp, watching the sun go down in the water amid an absurd Hollywood sunset.

"We're burned again, aren't we, Jeff?" Chela asked.

"Yeah. We can't go any farther west. My great idea has just been shot in the foot."

"Isn't there anything we can do?"

He frowned. "Play Robinson Crusoe. Survive. It'll be tough when we run out of ammunition."

"What about giving up? We could go back to the cable-pipe place. I'd like to see you moon one of those cameras."

"I vote against it, Chela. How long have we been wandering around out here? A week? Ten days?"

"I lost track," Chela said.

"It seems to me," Froward continued, "that if Peake, Gershner, and the passengers were all right, and if the Charonese were helping them, they would've send somebody looking for us."

"That's true."

"Well, the Charonese haven't been looking for us. I expected that we'd have to work hard staying out of their sight. Instead, we've only seen one lousy helicopter."

"What does it mean?"

"The Charonese might think we're dead. Our friends could've told them that, because they don't want us to get caught. Or maybe the passengers are dead and the Charonese figure either we are, too, or soon will be. Either way, it means the Charonese are bad news."

"Oh," she said.

"I could be wrong, Chela. You have a right to make up your own mind what to do. If you want to go back, I'll go with you."

"No way."

The beach seemed safe, so they slept in relative comfort that night. Froward kept waking up, keeping an eye on things, but he was asleep when Chela moved next to him. He was surprised to find her nestled against him just before dawn.

He'd been awakened by a long peal of thunder. He opened his eyes and looked at the sky. There were no rain clouds, only a few straggling stars glimmering in the purple sunrise. A brilliant spark moved among them, leaving a trail of white cloud along its path. It winked out, and several minutes later, thunder rolled over the sea. The vapor trail gradually dissipated, smeared by high-altitude winds.

After daylight, Chela chose a direction at random, and they wandered southward along the beach. At midmorning, they came to a place where the beach was furrowed with deep flipper- and belly-tracks that came out of the sea. Froward dug and found a clutch of gigantic eggs, all fresh. They packed as many of the eggs as they could in their bedrolls, reburied the others, and moved on.

"First the duck, now this," Froward said.

"It must be our lucky week," Chela said. She forged through the soft sand for a while, then said, "Do you really think we're stuck here forever?"

"Swiss Family Froward, that's me."

"You don't like it."

"It's not without interest. Sometimes I think I might as well be on Charon as anywhere."

"How can you say that? Don't you have a family?"

"I had a chance at having a family, but I wasted it."

"What do you mean?"

"I'll tell you the story of my life one of these days."

Later they found another gully in the seashore cliff and used it to climb up to the forest from the beach. Froward demolished a cabbage palm, and they baked their eggs in a fire. In the evening they hung their net in a mossy live oak tree in the thickest part of the wood. They sat on a level branch, among spiky, flowerless orchids. Ants ran over the toes of their boots, and above them, a furry, shrewlike creature with twitching whiskers and black button eyes peered down fearlessly.

"So how are we going to live, Jeff?"

"We can't go on wandering; it's too dangerous. While we still have ammo to hunt with, and defend ourselves with, we should build some kind of safe, permanent place to live. A tree house, maybe. In the middle of a good territory, where there's reliable food and water, and plenty of dinosaur-proof hidey-holes. We'll set traps and catch game."

"I'm just sure," she said.

"Yeah, me, too. Especially without any tools. We don't even have a decent knife." He scratched the stubble on his face and lay back in the cargo net. Night had come on, and the stars were out. Through the branches Froward could see the bright star with its line of lesser sparks that he'd noticed the night of their arrival on Charon.

"What are you looking at?" Chela asked him.

"I just realized," Froward said. "See that star? It's the sun, the real one, I mean. One of those little dots is the Earth."

"I wanted to go into space," Chela said. "I was applying for the Air Force Academy."

"You're in space now, all right."

The girl lay quietly for a while, then Froward heard her say, "Damn them. Damn them for what they've done to us. The bastards murdered all those people, and now—"

"Chela, instead of living a long time, would you rather get even with the Charonese?"

Their hammock bounced as she sat up. "What? How?"

"I've been thinking about something," Froward said. "I tend to forget that all this—" he waved his arm in a gesture that took in the ground, the sky, the nearby ocean "—all this, it isn't real. It looks like a natural world, but it isn't. It's a spaceship, all run by machinery. We aren't castaways on an island, we're stowaways on a ship."

"That's right," Chela said.

"Something as big and artificial as Charon must have weaknesses. Somewhere, there are engines, power sources, vital conduits and wires, tools, maybe weapons. Somewhere there's some way to get inside. If the Charonese think we're dead, we can take them by surprise."

"Remember what they told us on the airplane?" Chela said excitedly. "Charon's got a black hole inside it! Mrs. Robinelli taught us about those. If we drop something into it, it'll blow up like an H-bomb! We'll threaten them! And if they don't cooperate, baloowee!"

"Take it easy, Chela; you're going to make us fall out of the tree. Listen. I wasn't joking about living a long time. If we go on the attack, we might hurt the Charonese, but we're more likely to get killed than force them to do anything for us."

"So what? Life sucks, then you die, right?"

Froward laughed. In the darkness, he could barely see Chela's eyes shining. Her hands were on his cheeks, pulling at his whiskers. Suddenly he felt her breath on his mouth, and she was kissing him. Her lips tasted salty. The sense of her youth and sweetness swept over him. His hands went around her body; he pulled her close to him and heard her gasp. The sound of her voice, high and childlike, made him remember himself. He lifted her off his chest. "Sorry, Chela," he said. "I didn't mean to grab you like that—"

"It's all right. I know you're attracted to me. I had this teacher in the eighth grade who—"

"Okay, okay," Froward said, hot now with embarrassment in the darkness. "Please don't say any more about it."

"No," she said. "I mean, it's all right. I'm grown up enough to do what I want."

Froward groaned.

"You child molester," Chela said. The cargo net quivered as she laughed silently at him.

Froward and Chela journeyed southeast, scrounging, as Chela put it, as they went. The weather continued dry. Once, they hid as a five-rotored Charonese helicopter sped overhead. Several times, they evaded predatory dinosaurs. One monster was too big, too fast, and too persistent; Froward felled it with an antitank round. They spent three days roasting and smoking as much meat as they could carry, and were finally driven away by the arrival of too many other hungry mouths.

They were shoving forward through thick brush in a valley when Chela suddenly stopped. Froward, who'd been watching to see that nothing was coming up from behind, bumped into her from the rear.

"What's the matter?"

"Look at that." She pointed ahead, at a grove of tall pines standing on the crest of the next ridge.

"I don't see what you mean."

"See that tower? There, in the treetops." Froward finally noticed a tapering metal tower standing among the pines. On top of the tower, above the pine tops, was a cluster of boxes from which protruded various funnels and antennae, little windmills spinning in the breeze, and a whatnot on the end of a rod. The whatnot moved, and Froward caught the glint of lenses in the sunshine. He slowly crouched into the bushes, pulling Chela with him.

They talked in low voices. "Is this a way inside?"

"I don't think so. There's no fence, no buildings or roads. This must be some kind of surveillance device, for monitoring the atmosphere and so on. Might also track movements of large animals. It might even be looking for us. I sure am glad you spotted it. I would've walked right into it."

"Want to try to hit it with your grenade launcher?"

"No, that would only draw attention. We'll sneak around, and keep going."

They backtracked far enough to put the tower below their horizon, circled wide, then continued onward. Froward had a vague plan of searching southward of the cable-pipe terminal, then, as a last resort in case nothing else offered itself, returning to the scene of the murders. The cable-pipe itself, hanging in the sky, would make the place easy to find.

For weeks, each day was the same as the one before, except for the slow erosion of Froward's mettle. Every encounter, every risk run, took its toll. He tried talking himself out of it, mentally reciting whatever pop-psychological rituals and formulas he could recall, but nothing worked. He couldn't accustom himself to the constant tension, the worry over water, food, what might be lurking behind the next ridge.

They left the hills and trekked across savannah country, sometimes not talking for hours. During Chela's long silences Froward worried that he wouldn't know how to encourage her if she needed it.

They halted for lunch in a dusty jungle next to a dry streambed. They gnawed dry meat and wilted palm cabbage, then Chela silently got up and walked behind a bramble thicket. He was sitting, brushing grit out of his launcher and mentally counting their ammunition for the dozenth time that day, when she came hurrying back, still buttoning her overalls. He snatched their packs and jumped to his feet.

"It's okay!" she said, controlling her excitement. "Come look!"

She led him around the brambles and pointed. A square metal object as big as the rear end of a bus protruded from the thicket, covered with dirt and rust. "I was whizzing away, looked up, and there it was," she said. "It's a truck! See the wheels? It's all overgrown! It must've been here for years! Don't just stand there with your mouth open; gimme the axe!"

They took turns hacking the thorny growth away from one side of the thing. Its tires, ten feet high, were still solid. Hours of chopping uncovered a turreted front end equipped with lights, and three long mechanical arms that lay on the ground. Near the arms they found a concave metal dish, which Froward pronounced an antenna. On top of the turret was a glass dome, inside of which—they climbed up and wiped off leaves and dirt—was a binocular camera.

"I don't think it's a truck, Chela," Froward said, wiping sweat and dust off his face with a piece of cloth. "There's no place for a driver, no windows. Not even a door on the thing. Look at those arms. It must be a dead robot."

"You suppose we can get it open?" Chela said. "If there's room inside, we could sleep in it. I'm real tired of sleeping in that hammock."

"We'll look on the other side." They scrambled over the flat top of the thing and peered down into the growth. "Nothing," Froward said. "We'll have to use the brute force technique."

Chela grinned as he swung the axe against the glass dome. It shattered on the first try. He knocked away the remaining shards, then began chopping at the camera. It broke loose and fell down inside. "After you, ma'am," Froward said.

"Oh, no. I don't want to hog all the fun."

Froward squeezed himself through the circular hole. The inside of the turret was jammed with the machinery that operated the arms: pistons on heavy mountings, hydraulic hoses, wires and electrical gadgetry, all dry and dirt-free. The turret rested on gear wheels, still sticky with grease, that revolved on a toothed ring. Below that were two cylinders, side by side, one connected to the outside by big intake and exhaust pipes. The compartment went dim as Chela poked her head into the hole. "What's in there? What do you see?"

Froward dipped his finger in the grease and dabbed it on her nose. She squealed and pulled back. "Now that I have some light," he called up to her, "I see something that looks like a gas turbine generator. Can you hear me?"

"I hear you. I'll get even!"

"I was just trying to keep you from being bitten on the bottom by a dinosaur. There's a panel at the back of the engine compartment. I'm opening the latch. Okay, now I can see into the cargo compartment. There's something in there, but I can't tell what it is."

"Your mom is in there. I'm coming in."

The light dimmed and brightened again, as Chela wriggled

through the turret. After their eyes adjusted to the darkness, they saw what was in the cargo compartment: a reel of hose, with fittings and nozzles.

"I don't get it," Chela said.

"Maybe it's a fire truck. Maybe it was here, a long time ago, putting out a brushfire, when it was disabled." He walked the length of the cargo compartment to the rear wall. The top and rear of the compartment were hinged, designed to open outward. The system of pistons resembled the armored door on the space-ship, and that'd had a manually operated backup system. "Jack-pot," he said.

"What did you find?" Chela asked through the gloom.

He opened latches and began pumping a lever he found on one of the pistons. The rear wall hissed and lowered itself to the ground. Daylight flooded the compartment. He turned to face Chela, smiling for the first time in weeks. "Our home away from home," he said.

They celebrated. Chela cut fresh pine boughs for them to sleep on; Froward went out and wasted a buckshot round on a goat-sized biped, which they skinned and roasted whole. After dinner, Chela brought out a flat can of peanut butter, which she'd saved in her pocket for a special occasion. At night, Froward pumped the rear ramp closed again, and they slept gloriously long and safe inside steel walls.

The real miracle happened the next morning. Froward, rested and happy to get his hands on machinery again, pulled up the floor plates in their bedroom, found what looked like big electric motors on each wheel. He traced bundles of wires to a box in the turret, pried its lid off, and found dozens of crude electrical relays.

"Typical Charonese device," he commented to Chela, who was loafing on the flat topside of the vehicle.

Her voice came down the camera hole. "Your mom is a typi-cal Charonese device."

He went on. "It's a mixture of sophistication and whatever works. Nothing color-coded, nothing labeled, everything perma-nent." Using a stick, he pried at the biggest relay, forcing it closed. A fat spark jumped at him with a crack. He flinched backward and banged his head on the wall behind him.

"Ow! Dammit!" he yelled, then he stared, as other relays clacked shut. "Hey! this thing is still powered!"

Chela stuck her head into the turret. "There's something running out here!"

Froward was sitting on the supposed gas turbine. It was vibrating, and getting warm. Froward hastily stood up. The vibration changed to a smooth hum, then rose in pitch to a faint whine. Fluid hissed in the pipes and hoses, and the vehicle jerked.

Chela called from outside, "There's hot air coming out of a grille! Ouch! It's really hot! What the hell are you doing?"

Froward began closing the smaller relays with the stick. "Tell me if anything happens out there!" he shouted to Chela.

"We're moving!" Chela shouted back; then she yelled incoherently.

Froward already knew it. The vehicle lurched forward, toppling him onto the hot turbine. He bellowed and scrambled to his feet. Sounds of ripping vegetation came from outside. He got his head through the camera hole just in time to see a small tree get smashed down. The vehicle bumped over the stump into a clearing, trailing thorn vines. Right behind came Chela, running as hard as she could through a cloud of dust and dead leaves. He pulled his head back inside, and jammed the stick into the relay. The vehicle ground to a stop.

Chela pounded up the rear ramp and threw herself flat on the cargo floor. "Whooee! Yahoo!" she shouted. "I wanna try it!"

By midafternoon, they'd learned how to drive the robot, how to open and close the hatches, how to turn on the inside and outside lights, how to retract its arms. Chela sat in the turret, in a sling made from the cargo net, a live wire in each hand, her head sticking out of the camera hole, her hair blowing in the wind of their passage.

The robot bucketed over the savannah, dodging around trees, flushing herds of bizarre animals. "How'm I doing?" Chela called over her shoulder.

Froward stood in the opened top of the cargo compartment holding on to the back of the turret. "Great! You're the queen of the Charonese boonies! Look out, you're going to hit that critter—"

Chela swerved to hit a fleeing predator. "Splat!" she shouted, and let the truck coast to a stop.

"Jesus Christ, Chela."

"Jesus Christ yourself. Yesterday I would've been his meat; today he's mine. Get the axe. I prefer the tail."

Froward and Chela wallowed in security, gloated in comfort, luxuriated in speed and freedom. Froward navigated by the false Charonese sun, taking them in a southward zigzag. They cut branches and spread them on top of the truck to hide it from aircraft, and they piled dry grass inside to sleep on. They watched for the enemy, several times pulling under groves of trees to hide from helicopters, and circling around surveillance towers. Once they found a dead tower and investigated it. As Froward had predicted, it offered no way into the mechanical underground they both believed in. Froward helped himself to the optics of the tower's camera system, and they moved on.

In the evenings he and Chela tinkered. The robot showed no sign of running out of whatever made it go. Froward was unable to find fuel tanks, batteries, or anything like them. The turbine seemed to draw power through metal tubes from the other cylinder next to it on the floor of the turret. The energy cylinder had no fill cap, no recharge terminals, and couldn't be removed from the vehicle without cutting it out of the floor. Froward accepted it as an alien technological wonder, and left it alone.

The weather changed. Every day vast ramparts and terraces of tinted clouds piled up in the sky, finally unleashing a thunderstorm that blotted out the landscape. Froward and Chela showered off weeks of dust in the rain, then ate roasted dinosaur in the cargo compartment. A cool wind blew through the open tail ramp. As the last of the rain clattered on the truck's steel hull, Chela made a haystack to sit on, pulled out a gap-toothed plastic comb, then halted with it raised over her curly hair.

Froward sat up. "I hear it, too," he said. In the distance a low racketing mutter was growing louder. There was no mistaking it: a fleet of helicopters was coming toward them. He picked up his launcher and bandolier and stepped outside.

They'd parked the robot inside a grove of cabbage palms. Froward strode rapidly through the wet vegetation until he was standing in the open. The sun shone horizontally under the storm clouds, picking out distant treetops in golden light. Over the eastern horizon, Froward made out a swarm of tiny rectangular shapes flying in the light against a wall of black clouds.

Palm fronds rustled as Chela joined him. "Are they coming this way?"

"Seems like it," he answered. It was difficult to judge the oddly shaped Charonese aircraft at that distance.

"Think we ought to move?"

"I don't think so," Froward said. "We're hidden as well as we can be, and we can't outrun them. Let's stay put and see what happens." She moved close to him, brushing him with her elbow. The helicopters began to circle over something below the horizon, then they settled out of sight. The noise died away. The sun set behind Froward and Chela. They began to chill in their wet clothes. After a while, the sound began again, the helicopters rose into view, circled, then flew away into the north.

"Now, let's move," Froward said.

The truck rocked slowly eastward through the long Charonese twilight, Chela driving, Froward balancing on top of the turret, straining to see. Five kilometers brought the top of a high artificial structure into view over the tops of a pine forest. Chela backed the robot into a swampy thicket, and they went ahead on foot.

In the last of the light, they trotted across a dirt road and came to a girder and wire-mesh fence forty feet high. Lights shone through the pine trunks, and they could hear machines running. Froward took one look and led Chela back through the darkening woods to their vehicle.

"This is a major installation," Froward said. "It's what we've been looking for."

Chela nodded dumbly, watching him as he piled up a bed for himself in the closed-up cargo compartment. "I wish we could've stayed and looked longer," he said, "but I was afraid I wouldn't be able to find our way back here in the dark. We'll have a better look at it tomorrow." He spread his tarp and sat on it, unlacing his boots. "But now we should take a vote. The question before the house is, are we still at war with the Charonese?"

"Are we?" Chela said. She was huddled against the wall, her knees under her chin. She shivered. "It's cold."

Froward got up and brought her a dry coverall suit. "Put this on. I'll turn out the lights." He went forward, pulled the light wire out of the relay box in the turret, then felt his way back to his nest. He lay listening to her rustling in the dark.

"Now that we've really come to it, I'm, uh, you know," she said.

"I don't blame you. I'm scared, too," Froward said.

"Will the Charonese kill us if they catch us?"

"I don't think so. They'll probably kill us if they don't catch us."

"You mean if we, we—" She searched for a word.

"If we scare them. Scare them so badly that they forget why they brought us here. Then they'll kill us, unless we can force them to negotiate with us. Remember, Chela, that's the whole point of doing it. Otherwise, we might as well give ourselves up, and live in a nice cage the rest of our lives."

"Yeah," she said gloomily. "You want me to make up my mind, don't you? Make up my mind to go all the way."

"It's hard for me to do it, too. I'm scared, I don't mind telling you." His voice had become too loud in the dark, confined space. He took a deep breath, forced himself to relax.

Her voice was small in the darkness. "I'm afraid I'll wimp out, if I, if we—"

"You won't," he said. "I've gotten to know you since we've been together. If you say you'll do something, you'll do it. Listen, Chela, I'm not so goddamn brave. It's just that I can't picture us growing old on Charon. Because, even with this truck, we still can't hold out indefinitely. We're going to run out of ammo, and this machine is going to stop running someday. Then we'll be right back up shit creek. That's why I vote for war, and the more I think about it the better it sounds."

He heard her thump the floor with her fist. "That's right," she said. "Okay. Tomorrow we go in there and stomp butt."

"Not so fast, Ms. Rambo. Tomorrow, we quietly check it out. Tomorrow night, we quietly sneak inside. Quietly. No stomping butt."

She laughed. He heard the grass rustle as she settled down for the night. He made a wry face in the dark. He'd convinced even himself. The problem was, suppose they succeeded? What would they demand from the Charonese? He tried to imagine possibilities. Perhaps a communication link with Earth, with certain people on Earth. That way he could make sure the Charonese weren't faking it.

The communication link would be a start. Then what? A

spaceship ride home? He started to laugh, then stifled it. Chela would think he'd gone nuts—

"Jeff?" Her voice was right in his ear; it startled him. She had edged up to him in the dark.

"Yes?"

"I want to sleep with you tonight."

She was already sliding under his tarp next to him. He put out his hands, touched a firm, warm breast. "Er, excuse me," he mumbled, patting her, searching for her hands or shoulders, anything. Her back was bare; so were her buttocks. "You, ah—"

She slid a naked leg over him, then she was lying opulently on top of him, enveloping him, unbuttoning his suit down the front. Her mouth was wet on his chest. "Chela, this is—"

"Make love to me."

"It's not right. I can't." Froward said this, but he felt his resistance dissolving.

"Yes, it is. Yes, you can," she said. Her hands explored him, found him out in the darkness. "I can tell. See?" She pressed herself down on him. "That's right," she said, her voice rich. "Break the rules. Ah. That's the way. See? I know you, too."

When daylight filtered through the turret into the cargo compartment, they woke together and turned to each other wordlessly as wrestlers, grappling with strength that amazed and transported Froward. Afterward, as they buttoned themselves into their ragged clothing, Froward kept sneaking glances at her, like a curious boy. Chela caught him at it and grinned, her face flushed and swollen from lovemaking.

"Do you still respect me?" she said.

"You're packing that gun, therefore I respect you."

They ate their dried meat for breakfast, then arrayed themselves for war. Froward felt amazingly energetic. Happily he mixed dirt and grease, smeared it on their faces and hands. He tied grass and leafy twigs to their arms and bodies.

When they were ready, he led off, moving strongly from cover to cover like the lithe jungle warrior he thought he used to be. New greenery sprouted in the dead vegetation, and the sun was bright in the clearings. Froward felt absurdly alert and unstoppable. They found the road, and followed it until the fence just came in sight over the horizon.

A bit nearer the fence, in a densely grown wet patch several dozen meters to one side, they found a tall tree whose dinosaur-cropped lower branches were low enough for him to climb.

"You stay here," he whispered. "I'll go up this and have a look."

Silently, she reached up her hands to the back of his neck and pulled his face down to hers, standing on tiptoe to kiss him. Then she patted him on the chest and gestured upward, standing back to give him room to climb.

He went smoothly up the tree, not missing a step. Soon he emerged from the top of the forest, his height giving him a commanding view over the fence. He straddled the trunk and seated himself firmly on a convenient limb. Thus does the jungle warrior scout the encampment of the enemy. He was showing off for a teenage girl, but so what. *She loves me, and life is short.*

Through the fence he saw an extravagant, rather attractive, building, like a little town on a raised platform. Nearer, there was cultivated ground and neat rows of vegetables. Water sprayed over the garden from tall poles.

Froward scowled, losing his fantasy. He'd expected marching robots, bizarre machinery, maybe hideous alien creatures, not a California beach condominium and a damn farm. What would the robot Charonese want a farm for?

Something was moving behind a screen of foliage at the base of the building. He fished in his top pocket for the makeshift telescope he'd pieced together from Charonese cameras. He held it to his eye. In its wobbly, narrow view, he saw that the movement was a human being, someone dressed in baggy brown overalls carrying a shovel. The person was walking toward him, seeming to look Froward directly in the face. It was Lena Gershner.

Froward moaned loudly enough so that Chela heard him on the ground below. "What's the matter?" she called softly up to him.

"The crusade is off," he said.

Chapter Twelve:

The Mutineers

"The meeting will come to order," Colby Dennison said loudly from the front of the dining hall.

The hall fell silent. Several teenagers who'd been working in the kitchen hurried to seats in the rear. If the orderliness of the students had been less dependent on coercion, Emma would've been proud of them all.

Colby read from a sheet of paper: "The first item on the agenda tonight is disciplinary. Bill Bradley was accused of sloughing by several members of this assembly last week. He was voted guilty, nineteen to four. He was sentenced to the silent treatment, until further notice. Okay, Bill, have you got anything to say?"

The Bradley boy reluctantly stood up in the audience. Someone ordered, "Go on, Bradley, get up front, where everyone can see you."

The boy moved to the front of the hall and stood looking at the floor. He began to mumble something. Several teenagers called, "Louder! Speak up!"

Bradley raised his head. He began to talk fast, his face alternately going red and white. "I'm sorry I was late getting back from lunch break and didn't get all the weeds out of the cabbages—"

A girl in the front row called, "You weren't late just one time, Bradley. My team had to go over the cabbage again after you supposedly did it."

"I-I know. I'm sorry."

The boy stood there blushing furiously. Colby said, "Who's Bradley's team leader? Right, Reilly. Has Bradley's work been satisfactory this week? It has? Okay. I move we take Bradley out of the silent treatment."

"Second the motion!"

"All in favor—" Emma raised her hand along with the students. "The ayes have it." Bradley hurried back to his seat, looking chastened and grateful. The Charonese night breeze blew in through the open windows, bringing the fragrance of dry pines.

"Okay," Colby said. He glanced at Lena Gershner, who was sitting stonily in the front row. "Now I have an important announcement, something you're all going to be interested in." He paused while the room settled down.

Colby was sitting at a table in front of the big viewing screen. Emma wondered if the Charonese were listening in. They probably were. Gamma had asked her several times what Gershner and Colby's strong-arm squad, as Emma thought of them, were up to. Emma hadn't been able to answer. Gershner called her secret meetings at odd hours of the day and held them in isolated corners of the woods inside the Faulty Towers fence. When Emma had questioned the students who attended the meetings, they had apologetically refused to tell her anything.

"Announcement is as follows," Colby said, putting down his paper. "Starting tonight, we are going on strike against the Charonese." This brought a buzz of interest from the audience. Colby raised his voice and went on. "Gardening will go on as usual. But, from now on, nobody is going to work for the Charonese anymore. No more studying their course materials, and we're not taking any more of their quizzes!" Half the audience cheered. When that died down, questions were shouted.

"Some people claim they like studying and using the terminals. How're we going to keep them from going on doing it?"

"The new rule is, no more using the terminals, in your rooms or anywhere else," Colby said. "An oversight committee has been set up to enforce this. They'll be checking rooms."

"Hey, what about playing games or watching TV after work?"

"That's out," Colby answered.

A number of teenagers growled agreement, but a few protested. "Not fair! Take a vote!" More voices took up the call for a vote. Colby looked at Gershner, who nodded.

"All right," he said, "all in favor of—"

"Just a moment, Colby," Emma said. "We should have a discussion first."

Colby glanced at Gershner again. "Okay, discussion."

Several hands went up, including Gershner's. Colby pointed at her. She stood up and faced the students. "Some of you may be worried about the food supply," she said. "The Charonese said that if we didn't learn their lessons, they wouldn't feed us. We've had to go along with them. But now, thanks to the hard work put in by everybody, we are feeding ourselves. The garden and the fish pond are producing all we need. The Charonese haven't given out any canned rations for two weeks. Those of us who've been keeping records believe the Charonese don't have any more food to give us anyway. Until now, they've been forcing us to learn how to be their faithful little slaves. Not anymore!"

There was more cheering, but someone objected. "What are we supposed to do instead?"

"You can do anything you want, Claire," Colby said, "just as long as you're not helping the Charonese. From now on we work only for ourselves. If the Charonese don't like it, they can send us home!" There were shouts of agreement.

The girl persisted. "What if they make us?"

Gershner stood up again. "They can't make us do anything, not if we stick together."

Someone in the back shouted, "That's right! If they try anything, we'll fight!"

"What's the matter, Claire, you going to miss watching TV all night with your boyfriend?" This brought a general laugh.

The boy sitting next to Emma said, "You can't tell us what to do with our free time. The Charonese aren't making me study electronics; I'm doing it because I want to. It's interesting."

Another boy stood up in front of the speaker and shoved him back into his seat. "No-ooo, Peter!" Colby shouted, his face crooked with anger. "Nobody has to force Peter to suck the Charonese; he does it because he's a suck himself! Now let's vote! All in favor of shutting down the terminals, raise your hands!"

Half the students put their hands up immediately; in a second, most of the others followed. "Okay, good," Colby said. "From now on, if the Charonese want to say anything to us, they can do it in here, in front of everybody!"

Amid yells of approval, another boy shouted, "And if anybody wants to suck them, they can do it in here, where we can all see it!"

The meeting broke up noisily. Emma walked along the balcony to her apartment, locked herself in, and sat down at her terminal.

"Gamma."

"I'm here, Mrs. Robinelli."

"Did you observe tonight's meeting?"

"Yes. We have been waiting to consult you before taking any action."

"I appreciate that. I have no control over the situation, however."

"We realize that. Mr. Peake has just told us the same thing. Miss Gershner says she is speaking for the students now. She has demanded that the students and adults be allowed to contact individuals on Earth, and that the United States government be informed of the situation."

"Miss Gershner ought to at least wait until a new president is elected," Emma said wryly.

"She has also demanded transportation back to Earth for all of you."

"Regardless of how I might feel personally about you and your mission, I will not oppose the other humans," Emma said. "I regret the difficulty it will cause you, but you were wrong to kidnap us."

"Your position is not unreasonable," the alien said.

A loud knock at Emma's door interrupted the conversation. It was Colby Dennison and several of the teenagers carrying hoes, shovels, and other tools. Colby said, "I'm sorry, Mrs. Robinelli, but the rule against having your door locked and"—he looked over her shoulder at Emma's terminal—"the rule against using the terminals applies to everybody. You'll have to shut it off."

Emma was about to make an acid reply when Lena Gershner arrived. The boys parted to make way for her. At the same time Peake came, hurrying along the balcony from the opposite direction. He pushed his way through the crowd, patting backs and smiling.

"Okay, Colby, thanks," said Gershner. "I'll take care of this. You and the oversight committee start checking the other apartments. I'll speak to Mrs. Robinelli." The boys left. Gershner entered Emma's apartment, closely followed by Peake.

"We, I mean we adults, all agreed to follow the decisions of the democratic assembly on an equal basis with the students," Gershner said as soon as the door was closed.

"I never agreed to do anything irrational or harmful," Emma replied. "Especially if it were railroaded through the assembly. You got this strike declared by resorting to emotionalism and irrationality. And you never allowed discussion of how the strike was going to be enforced."

"That goes for me, too, Lena," said Peake. Gershner's face tightened with anger.

"Don't misunderstand me, Lena," Emma said. "I happen to agree with you and the strike. You're doing the right thing—"

"Well, what's your problem, then?" Gershner asked sharply. "Why are you constantly in the way, impeding what we're trying to do?"

"Because you haven't thought it through carefully enough. You haven't really allowed the young people, or us, a careful discussion of the price we may have to pay. Or of what concessions we might make. You don't know whether the Charonese are even able to meet our terms. It might be technically impossible to give us transportation to Earth in a reasonable period of time."

"Right," Peake said.

"The Charonese might lie to us about what they can and can't do," Gershner said.

"Yes," Emma said. "They might. But the more we know about them and their world, the less they'll be able to do so. Before you begin a conflict, you have to decide how you'll know when you've won. Or lost. Otherwise you won't know when to stop fighting."

"Lena," Peake said. "You're assuming that each of the kids is willing to die rather than stay here playing 'Lost in Space.' Any time they want to, the Charonese can kill us and plough us under for fertilizer. Then they can hijack another load of kids and try again."

Gershner glanced at the terminal screen on the wall of Emma's living room. "We can't discuss these things with the Charonese listening in. What do you want?"

"Let me keep dealing with the Charonese," Emma said. "We can do it together if you want."

Gershner hesitated, frowning.

"You don't trust me," Emma said. "Do you really think I would betray my students, in return for a promise that the Charonese would let me keep on living as a—a computer program?"

"Besides, what's to betray?" Peake put in. "We don't have any big secrets. Listen, Lena, as far as not giving in to the Charonese is concerned, I'm on your side, too. But I'm backing Emma in this. You want the kids to know we're fighting among ourselves? If there's a showdown, how many of them would follow you instead of Mrs. Robinelli? You want to find out the hard way? I don't!"

Gershner's expression didn't change. "All right," she said. "Keep your terminal."

Emma reached out and touched Gershner's arm. "I'm on your side. I really am."

Gershner nodded and let herself out of the apartment.

As soon as she was gone, Peake went to the terminal. "Gamma, we're on strike. What are you and your fellow video games going to do about it?"

The alien didn't answer. For a moment, Emma thought the Charonese were no longer "present" in the room. Then the terminal said, "It is under consideration."

Peake laughed. "Keep up the good war, Gamma."

The rest of the night passed quietly. But at first light police whistles trilled through the corridors and passages of Faulty Towers, jolting Emma awake. Gershner had had the whistles manufactured and issued to the oversight committee as an alarm, in case robots or other enemies were detected in the residence. Emma hurried to the landing above the stairway to the ground and found the students assembling. They had armed themselves with gardening tools, which had been taken up into the apartments the night before.

Gershner was standing apart from the students, watching. Emma went to her and said, "What's happening?"

Gershner pointed over the railing to the ground. "Look there," she said. Below, a line of robots was forming in a semicircle around the bottom of the stairway. "They're going to try to keep us from working the garden."

"Surely we've got enough vegetables in the kitchen to last?"

"No matter how much we have stored, it won't last forever," Gershner said. "The garden belongs to us. We have to teach the Charonese that right now."

Gershner left Emma standing at the railing and stepped to the front of the students. "All right," she said. Somber silence settled over the little group as the students, in their drab brown overalls, turned their faces toward her. "You all see the situation," she said, loudly, but without drama. "That garden is our living here on Charon. If we let them take it from us, we'll be slaves again, for the rest of our lives. Before I'll let that happen, I'll smash every one of them. I'm not afraid of them, and I know you feel the same way. I'm going down there and put in a day's work today."

Without waiting for an answer, Gershner turned and started down the stairs. Students, pale-faced and gripping their shovels and hoes, crowded after her, scuffling to be first. Emma went to the pile of tools and picked up a broken spade. Their boots echoed in the stone-walled stairwell. Emma felt someone take her elbow in the crowd and saw that it was Reilly. Ahead of her she heard Peake saying, "Hit them in the eye lenses, everybody, the eye lenses."

Below, on the sandy ground, Emma found Colby and some of the boys urging everyone into a line opposing the robots. When Colby saw Emma emerge from the stairwell, he waved her to where Gershner was standing in the middle of the line. Gershner took Emma's arm. "Do you want to talk to them, or do you want me to do it?"

"Let me try it first, if you don't mind," Emma said, her voice quavering.

"Please do," Gershner said, looking back at the students. They were holding their shovels and hoes in various poses, some obviously under the influence of the war or kung fu movies they'd grown up with. Colby set down a cooking pot full of heavy aluminum drinking mugs from the kitchen and picked up several, ready to let fly.

Emma, feeling shaky and not positive she wasn't dreaming, stepped out and faced the robots in the slanting morning sunlight. The Charonese were represented by an uneven assemblage of repair and construction machines, some as large as automobiles. Various turrets and periscopes swiveled to look at her.

"Are you here, Gamma?" she said.

"Yes, Mrs. Robinelli," the nearest robot said. It gestured with an enormous chain-saw blade.

"If you intend to kill us, you may as well do it now," Emma said. "None of us intend to let ourselves be starved to death."

"Please don't force me to do this, Mrs. Robinelli," the robot said. "It is not too late for us to work together again. Haven't we been happy with one another?"

"You know our concept of duty. I cannot allow you to enslave any human being. Step aside, and let us go quietly to the garden."

The chain-saw began whirring, driven by a powerful electric motor on the robot's arm. The robot's harsh voice said, "Our mission is ethical and important! Please, Mrs. Robinelli, humans kill for what is right! Please don't force me—"

Emma's knees had turned to water, but she stepped forward, forcing herself to stare straight at the robot. A grapple clutched at her, and the buzzing chain saw swept toward her at waist level. Involuntarily she parried it with the handle of her spade. With a loud rasp, the saw snatched at the spade, cutting it through in an instant. The students screamed in unison, the girls' voices shrill above the others. A drinking mug shot through the air and bashed against the robot's camera, shattering one lens.

The teacher went down as the chain saw passed in front of her, spraying blood. An angry roar went up from the humans as the entire line charged the robots. Some of the smaller robots fell over. The students, yelling with fear, flailed away at the others. After a few seconds, it became apparent that the robots were not resisting. The clatter of spades and hoes diminished. The robots stood without moving, most of them not even scratched by the assault. The robot in front of Mrs. Robinelli had stopped with the point of its saw buried in the ground next to the teacher's crumpled body.

"Help her," the robot moaned. "Help her."

Gershner and Peake hurried to where Mrs. Robinelli lay and dropped to their knees. Gershner looked up and shouted, "First aid team, over here! Colby! Take everyone else to the garden!"

"Come on, people! Let the first aid team do their job! Let's go!" The students marched after Colby, glassy-eyed, stealing glances at the group working over Mrs. Robinelli as they went.

"Help her," the robot repeated.

Emma opened her eyes in a white-lit room. The first thing she saw was Reilly's face, becoming alert as he noticed her return to consciousness. The boy's lips parted, and he gave a little gasp. His eyes flooded with tears. He looked up (Emma was lying on her back) and said, "She's awake!"

She heard rustling clothing and footsteps approaching. Reilly hastily wiped his eyes before the others arrived. Then Peake and the girl Tina were looking down at her. "Oh, Mrs. Robinelli," Tina said. "I was afraid you were going to die—"

"Tina, shut up!" Reilly exclaimed in a strained whisper. "You're not supposed to say things like that in front of the patient!"

"Everybody shut up," Peake said. "Emma, you've been hurt. You're in a hospital under the Towers. The Charonese helped us bring you here."

Emma's mouth was painfully dry. "Wha, what happened? Is, are the children—"

"The fight is over," Peake said. "No one was hurt except you."

"The Charonese surrendered," Tina said.

"No, they didn't, Tina," Reilly said. "They just couldn't make themselves hurt us. They said they'd done too much already."

"That's right, Emma," Peake said. "Everything's okay, except you. Try to relax. Does it hurt?"

Emma was conscious only of a huge numbness in her side. "No," she whispered. "Could I have a drink of water?"

Peake looked up at something out of Emma's field of vision. "Think we can give her some water?"

A robot voice answered. "Ultrasound scan indicates that her alimentary canal is not injured. The wounds reference book states that water may be given in this case. If it is not contraindicated by your knowledge, I recommend water be given to the patient."

"Thanks, Doc," Peake said. He brought up a thin plastic tube and put it between Emma's lips. "Just sip this. Don't try to move your arms. In fact, don't move anything."

As she drank, Peake talked. "The robots just froze in place after you went down. Took us a moment to realize it. We picked you up and took you to the elevator. Instead of going up, it came down here, to the factory under the Towers. Surprised the hell out of me, but at least now we know how the robots come and go in the Towers. There's a surgery and hospital here, and a robot acting as surgeon. All it knows is what it read in the books they bought on Earth. Lena helped with the operation, but she's gone back topside. That chain saw cut several ribs and got into your pleural cavity."

"You almost suffocated," Tina said.

"Uh, yeah. Anyway, you're sewn together now, and full of the finest recreational pharmaceuticals Charonese money can buy. All you have to do is lie as still as you can until you've healed up."

"I see," Emma said.

Peake grinned painfully. "Grim as ever," he said. "My battle-ax high school teacher. God, Emma, if you only knew—"

"Oh, Mrs. Robinelli, you were so brave!" Tina said.

Reilly just smiled.

The next day robots moved Emma up to her Faulty Towers apartment. After that, students reported, the elevator would no longer go below ground level and the underground factory was as inaccessible as it had always been.

Within a week Emma was able to hobble around the Towers leaning on a cane. She was cheered and applauded by the students at her first appearance. The rest of the time she was miserable in a stiff plastic corset designed by the Charonese. The best anesthetic was her sound-and-vision helmet, the armatures, the immensity of the Ark's historical records, and her own curiosity.

"This is a record of the construction of the Ark." Emma seemed to be floating in space, not the familiar sky of the sun system with its reassuring constellations. This was a strange cosmos, where sparse stars glinted among amber-red nebulas. Only one star was near enough to dazzle, and there was something else present, invisible but nearby. It tugged at her fingertips.

"You feel the tidal pull of a gravitational singularity, also known as a black hole. Its mass is two times ten to the twenty-first power kilograms, as heavy as a small planet. The radius of its event horizon is less than one millimeter. Its temperature is one times ten to the sixth power degrees absolute, as hot as a typical star. The singularity, or black hole, is a natural object, which the Arkwrights discovered near their planetary system. This discovery made the Ark project possible."

Emma listened to the voice of the English Index, carefully keeping her face neutral. Through pickups in her helmet, the Ark computer was monitoring her facial muscles. Other pickups observed her brain's radio emissions, blood circulation, oxygen and nutrient consumption. The computer was learning to use these to read her feelings and impulses. Puzzlement would make it give her more elaborate explanations, concentration on an object made it go into more detail, boredom and inattention caused it to hurry to the next subject. Experimentally, she stuck out her tongue, crossed her eyes, and gave the computer a quiet razzberry. The voice ignored her and droned on. The machine was the ultimate and unflappable teacher.

This voice was an automated translation of the data that accompanied the pictures. If she asked a question, one of the "live" Charonese would be instantly available to answer it.

A vast shape floated into view, a gray sphere with great slices taken out of the north and south poles. Spots of light moved over its surface. "Here you see the hollow shell of the Ark, being moved into place surrounding the singularity. The shell is maneuvered in such a way that the singularity passes through the openings."

Rocket flares, bright spikes of yellow light, stood up from the sphere. "The movement of the shell around the singularity is damped," the computer voice said. "The holes in the shell are closed after all motion is stabilized. Vaporized carbon is sprayed over a metal framework. Magnetic fields in the framework cause the carbon to crystallize at high pressure before cooling. The result is a seamless shell of diamond." The ends of the sphere were glowing white, and Emma seemed to feel the heat on her face. She tried to visualize the technology needed to accomplish such things, and gave up.

"Gamma," she said.

The alien was instantly present. "You have a question, Mrs. Robinelli?"

"Hello, Gamma. How've you been?"

"I have been . . . resting. Recovering from the shock of injuring you."

"I know you didn't mean to do it."

"It makes no difference, Mrs. Robinelli."

"You mean you're offended at me, because you injured me?"

"You caused me to injure you. That is offensive."

"You deprived us of our freedom, caused some of us to die, and you almost killed me. I'm in pain right now because of you. I should be offended at you!"

"You reject the obvious moral worth of the Ark's mission. I accidentally injured you while you were seeking to harm yourself. The offense is yours, Mrs. Robinelli. Your question?"

Emma was up against an alien sense of values, and Gamma was in no mood for pleasantries. Emma said, "What I wanted to know is, how long ago was the Ark built? And where?"

"We can only estimate the answer, Mrs. Robinelli."

"You don't know how long ago you built the Ark?"

"We are not the Arkwrights. We are only the most recent Crew."

Emma didn't bother to conceal her surprise. "The Charonese didn't build Charon?"

"Those are your names for the Ark and its current Crew, Mrs. Robinelli. Not ours," Gamma said.

"Yes. Well, how many other Crews have there been?"

"You should seek that information in the Index, Mrs. Robinelli. I have a great deal of work to do."

"I regret the loss of our friendship, Gamma."

Silence; a sense of withdrawal. Emma said, "I hope we can make it up someday, the two of us."

Still no reply, but Gamma did not break the connection. Emma said, "Before you go, would you tell me what the Crew is planning to do to counter our work stoppage?"

"We are now effectively stymied by your stubbornness and our own reluctance to use violence. At the same time, we are constrained by the long time it will take to obtain another group of human recruits. Self-inflicted extinction of the human race may take place before we can obtain more recruits. If this does not happen, as we hope it does not, astronomers on Earth may discover the true nature of Charon. That would be dangerous for us. These things are being considered. At the moment most of us favor a policy of persuasion, based on the offer of knowledge and partial control over the Ark."

Gamma abruptly "departed." The alien's bluntness surprised Emma. Did the Charonese feel that concealment was unnecessary, or had Gamma let this information drop without intending to do so? Emma shrugged, a gesture the computer wouldn't detect. It was impossible to know.

"Index, show me history of the use of the Ark. Overview."

Emma seemed to hang in white fog while the computer digested her request. After a moment, the space scene she had been viewing previously reappeared. This time the Ark shell was perfectly spherical, and half of it was brightly illuminated by a beam of light coming from a silver planet some distance away. Emma guessed the silver planet was Pluto, or some forerunner of Pluto. The surface of the Ark was no longer gray, but was colored by patches of yellow, orange, and white. Meteor sparks curved over its surface, leaving trails of vapor. The Index didn't explain, but Emma supposed that she was seeing the artificial world in the process of being supplied with soil, rock, and atmosphere.

"Direct records of the origin of the Ark have been lost," the Index voice said. "Sky views in this scene of the Ark under construction indicate that construction took place sometime during the early history of the Milky Way galaxy, some nine thousand million years ago. The location of the Arkwright system, which is presumed to be where construction took place, is unknown."

Emma whistled softly, causing the Index to pause for a moment. Not only was the location unknown, a location as long ago as that would be meaningless. Most of the stars that now populated the galaxy hadn't come into existence at that time. The Ark had been built before the sun had formed, to say nothing of the planet Earth. The Arkwrights' home star was probably a black dwarf by now, its planets sterile with age.

The voice went on. "Direct knowledge of all but the last five Crews has been lost. It is estimated that thirteen Crews have inhabited the Ark, including one or more Crews consisting of replicas of Arkwright personalities. Pictures of the five previous Ark Crews, and the biomes the Ark supported during their tenures, are available."

The Index displayed a series of pictures of what Emma supposed were the species of aliens that had composed the last five Crews. There were certainly more than five body types depicted.

"Physical life is limited," the Index said. "Life as a software personality is long, approximately five hundred million years long. The body is forgotten, the mission goes on."

Emma seethed with curiosity. How was the belief in the Ark's purpose passed from Crew to Crew? What happened if some Crew tried to pervert the purpose of the Ark? She stifled her questions. Stick to the subject, which is statistics. "Index, state approximate lengths of time of the Ark's movements since it was constructed."

"It is estimated that the Ark has been on sixty-six missions, and has visited three-hundred-sixty-thousand planetary systems during those missions."

Simple arithmetic. Emma recalled that the goal of the Ark, and the Charonese, was to take their human Crew on one of these hundred-million-year missions. She wondered if Gershner and the others had fully realized what kind of exile was in store for them if the Charonese succeeded.

As though she were waking from a deep, dream-filled sleep, she realized someone was shaking her shoulder. Suddenly she was back in her apartment, sitting in a chair with the sound-and-vision helmet over her face. She lifted off the helmet, blinking in the daylight coming through the windows. Reilly's smooth young face was a foot away, looking at her earnestly.

"It took you a long time to come out of it, Mrs. Robinelli," the boy said. "You feel all right?"

She smiled. "I'm fine, dear. Is it lunchtime?"

"Almost. But something's happening. A lot of helicopters are coming. Miss Gershner sent me to get you."

"Helicopters? Help me up, please, Reilly. My cane's over there."

On the balcony outside her apartment, Emma heard the approaching beat of many rotors. "We counted five of them, Mrs. Robinelli," Reilly said, as he tried to hurry along to an interior passageway. "They're all painted bright colors, except for one silver one, if you can believe that."

The two of them emerged from the passage onto the garden side of the Towers. Two stories below, pandemonium reigned. Police whistles shrilled and brown-suited figures dashed through the trees toward the pillars that supported the Towers.

"What's the matter with the elevator?" Reilly yelled over the railing.

"The power is off!" Someone yelled back.

Five huge Charonese helicopters thundered over the Towers as though making a reconnaissance of the building. They flew off a mile, wheeled in perfect formation, and came back over the tree-tops, the pines bending and waving beneath them.

Reilly's description of the machines was accurate. Four of them were painted glossy black with red and yellow lightning bolts. The center helicopter had a mirror finish. The sun's image flashed off it in blinding smears. The machines bore down toward the wide bare space in front of the elevator, where Lena Gershner stood in a whirlwind of sand and pine twigs, shouting inaudible orders. At the last moment she looked up, then sprinted like a deer as the helicopters touched down in an all-obliterating wall of noise and dust.

Turbines howled downward and rotors *swoosh-swoosh-swooshed*, and Emma heard drums crashing and trumpets blaring:

> *Rump-bump, rump-bump,*
> *Rum-rum rump-bump!*
> *What dadadaah,*
> *Da dada da datatata . . . !*

Amazed, she realized that the music was a barbaric distortion of the Twentieth Century-Fox movie fanfare! Reilly pulled at Emma's arm, shouting something she couldn't hear.

Now the biggest heavy-metal band in the universe began tolling out a march. The music was overwhelming, deafening, vivid —yowling guitars and drums beating like the footfall of advancing death. The sides of the outermost two helicopters were walls of speakers, big enough for ten rock concerts.

Emma snatched a glance at Reilly. The boy was rigid, his mouth working. Emma tapped his hand and put her ear close. Reilly was saying, "I know what this is, Mrs. Robinelli! There's only one thing this could be—!"

Below their balcony, the humans on the ground were being pushed by Gershner and Peake into an outward-facing semicircle around the elevator door. Hoes and shovels, most of them quivering with panic, bristled from the front of the line.

Metal ramps clumped down onto the soft soil. Out of the two helicopters on each side of the gleaming center machine came lines of headless robot monsters, all painted bloodred. Tramping in time to the music, they marched to each side of the center helicopter, its shine now dulled by falling dust and sand. The robots jerked to attention, spitting electrical sparks and clashing saw-edged swords, jagged halberds, needle-pointed rifles. Accompanied by ear-splitting wails and splashing cymbals the door of the middle helicopter slowly opened.

The music stopped, leaving Emma's ears ringing. A human figure, cloaked and helmeted, stepped out of the middle helicopter and strode between the ranks of red warriors.

"I knew it," Reilly said.

He was drowned out by a fanfare of trumpets, followed by an overwhelming, thunderous bellow. "HIS HIGHNESS, THE PRINCE OF PLUTO! LORD OF THE OUTER SYSTEM! ARCHON OF THE ARK! BEASTMASTER OF CHARON! THE FIST OF RIGHTEOUSNESS! SCOURGE OF THE UNBELIEVERS!"

The visitor stopped and posed graciously while a towering crimson robot removed the helmet and cloak. Reilly said, "Only that little dipshit . . ."

"THE RAJAH OF ROCK, THE BHAGWAN OF BOOGIE, IN OTHER WORDS—!"

Charlie only looked a little pudgy in his midnight-blue skin-tight suit embellished with bulky knee and elbow pads. A huge golden badge and chain hung on his chest, and his boots carried holstered pistols. He smiled modestly and gave a little wave. "It's me, everybody."

"THE JUDGE! CHARLES W. FREEMAN THE FIRST!" Trumpets went *ta-daaah*! Silence fell over Faulty Towers. The tumult had silenced all the birds, animals, and insects in the vicinity.

Charlie indicated the center helicopter with a wave of his arm. "Like it? Looks like chrome, but it's really sterling silver," he said, looking around at the students.

No one responded. For a moment Emma thought Charlie looked a little disappointed. He was too far away for her to be sure. Dust and pine needles settled on the heads and clothes of the onlookers. After a half-dozen breaths, an amazed babble rose among the students, then a few shouts of anger or derision. Charlie frowned. "SILENCE!" he commanded. His voice, impressively deepened and magnified by the speakers, echoed off the walls of the Towers.

Quiet returned. Emma had noticed something: when Charlie raised his arm, the sleeve of his suit pulled back; there were wires attached to his skin under his clothing.

"What's this all about, Charlie?" Peake asked.

"Yes," Charlie said. "Business first. It, uh, has come to my attention that you, all of you, have quit learning how to use the Charonese systems."

"Wait a minute, Charlie," Peake said. "Where've you been all this time?"

Before the boy could answer, Colby shouted furiously, "Where's Eva, Charlie!"

Charlie smiled. "Eva's fine, Colby. She lives with me now, and she's fine. You don't need to worry about her anymore, because I'm taking real good care of her."

During this speech, Charlie had been trying to stifle a laugh. It sputtered out now, and for a moment he chuckled and snorted. He wiped his nose on his sleeve and went on. "Where have I been? Well, let's say I've been living on my own private university campus. I hope you like my little apocalypse squadron, here, and my faithful troops. I wanted to play 'Ride of the Valkyries' on the way in, but I couldn't remember how it goes. If some of you grade-A scholars and high school heroes would work as hard as I do, maybe you'd be flying around in helicopters, too, but I doubt it." Charlie glanced at the garden. "That reminds me. Fetch, Igor."

He gestured, and one of the crimson robots set down its weapons and clumped away through the trees, its arms dragging on the ground. "The old hideout is fun, but the food there sucks the big bawanga. I want you all to know that I think you've done a terrific job on the garden—" He glanced after the robot and interrupted himself. "Well, well, I was wondering if they would show up."

Emma leaned outward to see where Charlie was looking. Charlie's machine had stopped on the path to the garden. A large Charonese gardening robot had emerged from a grove of pines and was confronting it, holding out a pair of digger blades. Sud-

denly, a loud bang made her jump. As the report echoed away
among the trees, the Charonese robot wobbled in a circle, dripping yellow paint from its cameras. It ran into a tree trunk and
fell over with a clatter.

One of the red soldier machines standing near Charlie lowered
its rifle. "Nice shot, Igor," Charlie said. He grinned. "They're all
called Igor," he said.

"Looks like you've got it made, Charlie," Peake said. "What
do you want from us?"

"Two hostages will be enough, I think, Mr. Peake."

Exclamations of outrage came from the little huddle of people
around the elevator door. Charlie waited for them to subside, then
said, "Mr. Peake, before we proceed, I want you to know that I
don't like to have to do what I came here to do. The kids have to
go back to studying, and the Charonese don't know how to make
them do it. So I have to take care of it for them. I need two
hostages."

Two of the soldier robots set down their weapons and strode
swiftly into the group. There was a scuffle, and shouts of pain
went up. "Ow! It shocked me! They're electric!"

Emma gripped the railing and leaned over, trying to see. The
fight became violent, garden tools clanging against metal.
Screams and curses rose from the dust. Six boys were knocked
down by the robots' swinging arms, and two others were jerked
off their feet.

Charlie began to talk again, his voice amplified above the
hubbub. "Cattle prods is what they are. I really don't want to hurt
you, but I will if I have to." Emma squinted, wishing she had
better eyesight. Charlie's face was set in concentration as he
stood amid his robots.

The two robots shook off the teenagers still clinging to them
and carried their struggling victims inside the nearest helicopter.
The other robots had surrounded the humans, forcing them back
against the elevator door. Shrieks and shouts echoed as the slower
teenagers were goaded by various weapons. Some of them were
bruised or bleeding, crawling as fast as they could in the dust to
get away from the prods.

"What do you want? Why are you doing this?" Peake had
tried to sound soothing and reasonable before, but now he was
shouting.

"Someday you'll—" A thrown aluminum mug glanced off Charlie's face. He staggered back and sat down hard. Some of the soldier robots seemed to stagger, too, but most of them raised their weapons and crowded against the humans. Screams of terror rang out.

Emma, her heart about to burst, cried out as loudly as she could, "No, Charlie! No!" Pain lanced through her side under the body cast.

The robots froze in place. Charlie slowly got to his feet, glancing up to where Emma stood on the balcony. A line of blood trickled down his face. He glared furiously at the students. "None of you give a damn, do you!" his voice thundered out of the speakers. "The Charonese are offering us all this, all this science and power for the world! It's a chance to save the human race from poverty and starvation and atomic bombs, and, and—" He ran out of words, calmed himself, and went on without the artificial voice. "And all you want to do is go back to your nice dates and cars and nice successful careers! What a crock of shit!"

The robot that had gone to the garden was coming back with its three arms full of carrots, cabbages, and tomatoes. Charlie snatched a tomato from it as it passed. His face was as red as the paint on the robot. "I'm not going to let you get away with it!" he shouted. "You watch on TV tonight! You'd better watch, and you'd better do what I tell you, or I swear I'll make you all wish you'd never been born!"

He flung the tomato and caught Colby, who'd been helping a girl to her feet, on the side of the neck. The tomato splattered over Colby and bystanders alike.

Charlie turned on his heel and stalked back up the ramp of the silver helicopter. After he was out of sight, the drumbeat came from the speakers again. The robots, feet clumping in perfect time, marched back to their aircraft, and the huge rotors began to churn.

After the hurricane roar of Charlie's departure died away, the elevators started working again. Lunch was served as usual in the Towers dining hall, but little was eaten. Lena Gershner spoke quietly to the assembled students. "That garden is our life. There's weeding to be done, and irrigation pipes have to be moved. I'm going out to work this afternoon, just like always."

"Me, too," Peake said. One after another, the students got up and followed them. Emma crept back to her room and lay down. Later she tried her terminal, but it wasn't working.

That night, Charlie put on a TV special. The big screen in the dining hall lit up with scenes of the interior of a palace. Enormous, ornate doors opened, and the camera rolled down a marble-columned hall into a vast wood-paneled library. Charlie, still dressed in his costume, stood with his back to the camera, watching pteranodons soar over acres of lawn, fountains, statuary, and cypress-lined avenues through a huge picture window. He turned to face his audience, his expression hard-set.

"I see you're all present," he said. "Let's get this over with, and not waste any time. I intend to make you take Charon's purpose as seriously as I do. The next scene you'll see is being made, live, downstairs."

Now a dim, concrete-walled room. The students watched, aghast, as robots roped Bill Bradley to a metal framework. Charlie's voice said, "It's a little dark in the old dungeon, but I think you can all see well enough."

The robots began to touch electric wires to Bradley's body. The boy jerked and grunted, then began to scream at each touch. This went on until Bradley's bowels gave way and he had screamed himself voiceless. The girls in the audience shrieked and sobbed, and several of the boys threw up or ran out of the dining hall.

Charlie thundered over the uproar, "Everyone back in the room, or it'll be more shock treatment for poor Bill! Move it!"

Bradley hung moaning in the dimness while the students were dragged back to the dining hall and sat down in front of the screen. "That's better," Charlie said.

The scene switched to outdoors, a twilit forest. Apparently the sun had just gone down. "Bill was a brave guy, he held out a lot longer than I would have, or most of you," Charlie said, off-screen. "The test you're about to see is less painful but unfortunately just as bad."

Robots put the other hostage boy in a large steel cage, which was set down in the middle of a clearing in a forest. The camera pulled back to a distance. After a few minutes, a reptilian monster showed up at the edge of the trees. The girl, Claire, began crying and screaming. Some teenagers tried to comfort her, without success. She kept pushing them away and turning back to the screen.

Emma ignored them and concentrated. The trees were live oaks, hickories, and other deciduous types, not like the pines that surrounded Faulty Towers. The dinosaur was unlike anything she'd seen before. It was thirty feet from head to tail, and walked on its hind legs and the edges of its huge three-clawed hands. It had a flat, crocodilelike head on the end of a long neck.

"Here's something for all you dinosaur freaks," Charlie narrated. "A genuine, live deinocheirus. Until now, it has only been known from its fossilized arm bones. Discovered by a Polish paleontological team in Mongolia. Tut, tut," he added, responding to the obscenities screamed from the audience.

Charlie's prisoner caught sight of the dinosaur and threw himself against the cage's far side. The bars were just a little too narrow for his body. The camera was too far away to see his face. "He's trying to get out, but he's safer in the cage," Charlie said. "It's wider than the deinocheirus's arms are long."

The monster covered the distance to the cage in a few galumphing strides and reached for the boy with nine-foot arms. The boy dashed frantically from side to side as the animal began to circle the cage, grabbing through the bars. His cries, if any, were lost in the distance.

"The dinosaur is too dumb to corner him, or turn the cage on its side, but he's hungry," Charlie said. "We'll see who gives up first." Peake and a group of students were working over Claire, who had fainted and struck her head on the corner of a table. Emma realized for the first time that Charlie's second victim was her boyfriend.

The outdoor scene was replaced by a view of another room. Charlie lounged at an enormous desk. Behind him was something that looked like a giant model eyeball. Emma looked again and decided that it was a globe of Charon. A blue sea, perfectly circular, nearly straddled the globe's equator. Dots and lines of multicolored light, some moving, lay on its surface. Tiers of blinking lights, dials, switches, and video screens rose up the walls on both sides of the desk.

"Okay," Charlie said, leaning forward as the camera moved toward him. "You get the picture. Maybe this is all too big for you people to understand, but I don't care. I'm not going to let you throw this chance away. I'd trade all of you for a single one of those dinosaurs, to say nothing of a whole starship and everything else that goes with it."

Charlie's confidence, Emma noted, was all put on. He was blushing with stage fright and nervous, but he went on. "I haven't got time for persuasion, and you don't know how to listen to anything but flattery anyway. Go back to your study schedule, or it'll be too bad for the unfortunate bastard who's left. If you fail your quizzes, or trash any of the Charonese equipment, it'll come out of his hide first, then yours. The Charonese will be running things again, but I'll be watching you. Good night!" The screen went blank.

There was little debate in the dining hall. Only Colby and Gershner had any fight left in them. The rest didn't look at one another as they held their hands up to vote to return to their studies. Thunder rumbled in the distance, and the night breeze smelled like rain. In silence, everyone returned to their apartments.

Chapter Thirteen:
A Prisoner of Love

In his royal bedchamber, in his fifteen-foot carved and canopied bed of state, Charlie stretched, groaned, flatulated, faced
another morning. His eyes opened on the decorated royal bedchamber ceiling: plumply sculpted nudes and gilded swans, snow
and gold.

It looked all right, Charlie thought, if you didn't look too
close. Igor the architect had been forced to copy the royal bedchamber from a badly reproduced encyclopedia illustration. The
materials, however, were regally extravagant: two hundred-carat
gold leaf, plaster of crushed diamond. Extraterrestrial Bavarian
rococo tech.

Not awake yet, Charlie contemplated nature. Some of the
windows in the royal bedchamber were windows, others were
full-color super-duper high-resolution Charonese TV screens. At
Charlie's order, they displayed input from a surveillance tower
somewhere down Charon's morning line.

The tower's cameras overlooked a hadrosaur rookery. The wet
season was starting on Charon, nesting time for dozens of species. Birds called from ancient cypresses as a dozen duckbill
dinosaurs, as big as elephants walking on their hind legs, brought
mouthfuls of river water for the eighteen-inch chicks in their
nests of dried mud. Later, after a day of browsing, the parent
animals would upchuck piles of green mush for the chicks.

While Charlie watched, a hadrosaur gently picked up a peeping chick in its grindstone jaws and dropped it into its nest. Charlie looked closely. The chick was a phony. It was a chick of
another species, not a hadrosaur. Charlie had learned that these
interlopers were called troodon by human paleontologists. The

troodons had hatched at the same time as the hadrosaur chicks, from clutches of eggs laid near the rookery. The adult troodons were only man-size, compared with the colossal duckbills, but they were predators, with sharklike teeth. They had laid their eggs in clutches close to the mud basins of the duckbills, and left. Both sets of chicks had hatched at the same time. Now the little troodons wandered among the mud basins of the duckbills, snapping up the huge flying cockroaches that were attracted to the hadrosaur chicks' food, and occasionally attacking the chicks themselves.

Charlie was curious to know why the hadrosaurs put up with this parasitism. Probably it was because the troodon chicks looked and sounded like the hadrosaur chicks. Charlie could ask Igor, the Proctor, or the Index for this information, but he hadn't.

"Sometimes I like to find things out for myself," Charlie said to one of the naked fat ladies on the ceiling.

She didn't reply, but the nearest robot, a valet, said, "Very good, sir." It was one of the responses Charlie had programmed Igor to say, any time Igor failed to comprehend one of Charlie's statements.

Charlie's imitation silk bed sheets were starting to rip again. His textile factory needed improvement, but he no longer had time to work on it. He yawned, tore off a piece of sheet, and loudly blew his nose into it. "Very good, sir," the robot said again.

Charlie had long since admitted to himself that it wasn't as great as he'd hoped it would be. The way he had hoped it would be, when he'd made his triumphant landing on Charon, when he'd fought the giant meat-eater to a standstill, when his King Kong monster clomped into the robot garage with Eva's small body in its ten-foot claw, booming out Charlie's monster laugh. "Mwoo-hoo-haw-ha-ha! You're mine! All mine!"

Monster laugh notwithstanding, Eva lay still. Maybe she'd fainted. Nah, nobody ever fainted, except in Tarzan novels. Maybe (Charlie's playground instinct warned him) she was faking it, in hopes of jumping Charlie when he appeared in person. Eva was a small creature, with a tiny waist and a long, slender neck, so exquisitely pretty she made Charlie's heart stop, but physical contests weren't what Charlie wanted.

Charlie hadn't been there in person, of course; he'd been

down in the factory, clamped into the Charonese kinetic input-output armature, seeing everything through the Kong robot. The monster allowed Charlie's motions in the armature exactly, as he bent and laid Eva down among the mud-clods on the garage floor. A delicate knee and part of her silken thigh, or so Charlie imagined, shone through a rip in her overalls leg.

The Proctor's voice buzzed in Charlie's ears. "That was well-done, Charlie. You have saved the lives of three future Crew members. You have served the Ark well."

"What do I do now?" Charlie asked it. Through the camera eyes of the stooping robot monster he saw Eva sit up. She began brushing dried mud off her overalls.

"First, tell me why you did not allow that girl to go with the others."

"I, uh, want her. You said you'd give me, uh, power over the other humans. She's the one I want for myself."

"I understand. You wish to make her obey you. You will perform sex on her."

Charlie shied. "Not at all! Uh, we'll get into that later. What should I do right now?"

"You do not wish to live with the other humans?"

"No. Not now, anyway. You said you wanted me to control them. I can't do that if I'm living among them."

"Yes," the Proctor said, after a pause. "I perceive that you have a better understanding of how to lead the other humans than I do." There was another pause, then it said, "You should order robots to build living quarters for yourself and the girl."

"How'm I supposed to do that?"

"I give you the factory complex in which you are now located. The Crew member who brought you here will serve you. You may order it to build things for you or to do anything else within the capability of this factory. There are hundreds of robots, vehicles, and other devices at your disposal."

"No shit?" Charlie was trembling with excitement. "I mean, is that true?"

"Yes," the Proctor said. "All things that I say are true. You may now remove yourself from the armature. I encourage you to familiarize yourself with all Ark systems."

"All right!" Charlie said, greatly encouraged. He reached up and pulled the sound-and-vision helmet off his head, then extracted his limbs from the swiveling devices. Around him the alien factory was silent. The robot that had brought him there stood like a piece of tin furniture on its electric cart, right where Charlie had last seen it.

"Because you have removed the helmet, I will speak to you through this robot," the Proctor's voice said.

"The Charonese that was in the robot—" Charlie said. "You say it's going to serve me? It wasn't willing to do that before now. Why is it now?"

"That Crew has been partially erased and . . . edited. It will now obey you without question."

"Is that so. What do I call it?"

"You may call it anything you wish."

Charlie laughed. "I want to call it Igor."

"Very well. I will now depart. That is, I will direct my attention elsewhere. I have many functions to perform on the Ark, but I will visit you frequently. Igor will answer your questions."

"Right on, Proctor," Charlie said. "I'll see, or hear, you later."

He clambered out of the armature framework and looked around. The Charonese factory was a daunting place to be alone in. The ceiling was forty feet overhead, and the columns that supported it marched away in parallel rows over the weird indoor horizon, where the blue lights in the ceiling seemed to come down to the floor. Gigantic machines stood everywhere, silently waiting for his instructions. Supposedly.

"Igor!"

The robot on the electric cart swiveled a camera at him. "I hear you," it said.

Living quarters, Charlie thought. "Er, uh, what do you know about the, uh, living requirements of human beings?"

"I have read all the books and other materials that were brought on the spacecraft from Earth. I also have analyzed forty years of radio and television transmissions from Earth. All of that knowledge is available to me. The following is a summary: Human beings must maintain a body temperature of—"

"Okay, Igor, stop, that's enough! I want you to start building a place for me and someone else to live. An apartment—You know what an apartment is?"

"Yes. I assisted in the construction of one hundred apartments in the residence facility now inhabited by the other humans—"

"All right, I get it. Start building me an apartment with furniture and everything. Put it somewhere in this factory."

A nearby machine roared into action, causing Charlie to leap in panic. "What's that?" he shrieked.

"It is a machine that fabricates insulated panels," the robot bellowed over the noise of the machine. "It is making panels to be used in your apartment. The noise is caused by—"

"Shut up! I mean stop explaining it! Jesus Christ!"

He collected his wits and jumped on the robot's cart. "Take me back to the robot garage. I mean, the place where the giant robot is, where the girl is! Get moving!"

The cart started so suddenly Charlie almost fell off. He clutched the back of the robot as the cart wheeled this way and that through the factory. "Next time, don't start so suddenly!" he shouted.

The cart turned abruptly and raced down an aisle between rows of machinery. "Did you hear me, Igor?" he demanded.

"Yes," the robot said. The cart was speeding toward the entrance to the factory, seemingly headed for a collision with the closed door panels. At the last second, as Charlie was preparing to jump off, the panels slid aside, and the cart rolled across the Y-shaped room and stopped in the open elevator.

The door closed, and the elevator lifted off. Before Charlie was ready, the elevator reached the robot garage, the door opened, and there was Eva standing in the middle of the floor, as far away as she could get from the jointed hulks standing along the walls. She was crying.

"Eva!" he called. She stopped crying and looked up.

He walked toward her. "It's all right, Eva. I've come to get you."

"Oh, it's you," she quavered disappointedly.

"I've come to get you," Charlie repeated, in case she hadn't understood that she was now saved.

Eva sniffed. "Where're Tina and Reilly?"

"I'm not sure," Charlie said, all business. "I think they've been taken to some sort of apartment house or something that the Charonese have built for them. I'll find out as soon as I've taken care of you."

"A-are we going to where the others are?" she said.

Charlie stopped in front of her. "No, we're not," he said.

"We're going to live here, instead. Down below in the factory, I mean."

"I'm not living in a factory," she said. "I want to go where everyone else is."

"That's not a good idea until we've seen if they're all right. I want to check first."

"I want to now!"

"We can't now, Eva. Who knows what the Charonese have done with the other people? They might be prisoners."

"All right, I want to go back outside. I don't like this place."

"There're dinosaurs out there."

To Charlie's gratification, Eva looked more frightened. She glanced around her. "Don't worry about these robots, Eva," he told her proudly. "They belong to me, not the Charonese. They can't hurt you. I control all of them."

Her face went from fright to a more familiar expression. "I'm just sure, Charlie," she said.

"It's true, Eva. It was me who saved your life just now. From that dinosaur, the one that almost ate you."

Eva managed to look indifferent and skeptical at the same time.

"I did," Charlie insisted. "You might be a little grateful. You owe me a hero's reward."

"I haven't got the slightest idea what you're talking about. This is boring."

"The hero's reward. When the hero saves the maiden from the dragon, she's supposed to fork over a piece of, I mean give him a kiss."

"Barf. You're out of your gourd." She pulled out a little wad of Kleenex, dried her eyes, and began brushing at her clothes. "I'm all dirty," she said.

"We can get cleaned up downstairs. I'm installing an apartment down there. Come on, let's go."

He reached for her elbow, but she drew away from him. "Leave me alone," she said. "Stop telling me what to do. Who do you think you are, anyway, Charlie?"

"Just good old reasonable Charlie Freeman. I'm the guy that just saved your life, remember? I suppose you'd rather stay here?"

"That's right, Charlie."

Charlie choked with exasperation, got control of himself, and began in his most rational tone. "Listen, Eva—"

"I'm just listening and listening, Charlie." She strolled away from Charlie, took out a silver compact, opened it, and looked at herself in the mirror. She licked her finger with a small pink tongue and began dabbing at her face.

Charlie followed her. "Would you like a hot shower, Eva?"

"I'm just su-ure, Charlie." She laughed tunefully, without humor.

"I don't mean that," he said hastily. "I mean separately—" He stopped himself, clinching his fists at his sides. He didn't have to put up with this shit. Nearby stood a small version of the mechanical monster he'd fought the tyrannosaurus with. He pointed at it. "Igor!" he shouted. His voice cracked, causing him to squeak absurdly. He swallowed and tried again. "Igor! Animate that robot! Seize her!"

The robot hissed and whirred, raised its arms, and strode swiftly toward Eva. She gave a shriek and ran away.

The robot, designed to catch fast-moving animals, bounded down the center of the garage on thick metal legs, feinted, cornered Eva, and grabbed her with its wide, rubber-padded claws. Charlie clutched at himself in anguish. "Igor! Stop! Don't hurt her!"

Charlie ran up to her, gasping. "Are you okay?"

She stood in the robot's grasp and looked over Charlie's head.

Charlie stood there, puffing, trying to reorganize himself. He wouldn't get anywhere like this. "Be reasonable, Eva. You can't stay here. There's nothing to eat, nowhere to sleep."

She studied the wall behind him. Charlie said, "If you'll come along, I'll tell it to let you go."

"I'm not—"

"Shit. Igor, robot, follow me to the factory."

"With or without the girl?" the electronic voice asked.

"With the girl! You bionic sphincter!"

Eva stood rigidly erect in the robot's padded claws as it clomped along behind Charlie to the elevator.

The doors thudded shut; the elevator zoomed downward. Eva wouldn't look at Charlie. "Igor, when will the apartment be ready?"

"It is ready now."

"It is? I mean, that's very good, Igor. Uh, how did you do it so fast?"

"A prototype apartment was already assembled for testing in this factory. That one has been prepared for your use."

The apartment had been set up close to the elevator. From the outside it looked like an irregular concrete box with attached cables and hoses; on the inside it was several rooms decorated with interesting wooden furniture and grass mats. After momentary distraction—there was a magnificent computer terminal on the wall across from the bed—Charlie ordered the robot to put Eva down.

"I can see some improvements this place could use," he said, walking around slamming closets and cupboards and looking in the other rooms. "Windows, for example. Also you'll need a kitchen and dishes. And, hah, the toilet doesn't flush. I'll fix it."

"I'm just sure," Eva said.

Charlie returned to the main room, not sure whether to laugh at her or not. "Goddamn, Eva, what does it take? Don't you believe what you see with your own eyes?"

"I'm just sure."

"All right, so just shut up, Eva," Charlie said, pacing around.

"Don't tell me to shut up."

"Shut up!"

"Don't tell me to—"

"All right! All right! Now. This apartment belongs to you—"

"I want to go where the others are. Let me go, or I'll tell Mrs. Robinelli."

"I told you, we don't know where those people are! As soon as I find out how they're doing, I'll decide whether—"

"You?"

"—it's safe to join them. And, yes, me. I'm the one providing all this." He sat on the bed. "This bed isn't so bad, especially after sleeping in arliner seats such a long time."

She looked charmingly rumpled in her oversize overalls, her golden curly hair wisping over her face. "You creep," she said, fixing an ego-freezing look on him, the first time she had looked at him. "You don't even lie very good, do you. You've got some weird ideas about me, don't you."

Charlie, caught in the act of having ideas, blushed. "Look, Eva, get some sleep, eat something, look, there's food in this cabinet, and in the morning you'll feel better. I'll come see you, and we can talk."

"Don't bother," she said. "Creep. Creep off."

"You'll feel better—"

She began shrieking. "I'll feel better when I don't have to look at you, you fat little—!"

Charlie made his escape from the apartment, slamming the door behind him. "Igor!" he shouted.

There was no answer except for the echo of his voice in the high-ceilinged factory. In the distance machinery rumbled. The two robots stood patiently nearby, the animal handler and the one from the electric cart.

"Igor, dammit, whenever I speak to you, I want you to answer me. Say 'yes, sir,' understand?"

"Yes sir," both robots said simultaneously.

"Dammit, only one of you talk at a time! All right. That girl, that human, in there, her name is Eva, get it?"

"Yes, yes, sir, sir."

"Dammit, just one of you do all the talking! Make sure Eva can't get out of the apartment. I don't want her wandering around. Speak to her from the terminal in there. Give her food and water if she asks for them. Tell her she can ask for them. Pipe in fresh air from outside. Fix the toilet so it works. Where's our luggage from the airliner?"

"It is aboard the airliner, on top of the photon-venting tower."

"Bring it all down here. Tell Eva she can look at any movie or TV show you've got in your files. Install large screens on the walls where the windows are supposed to go. Display outdoor scenery on them, something typical of Charon. Show her some dinosaurs'. . ."

Charlie's voice trailed off as it came over him how many things he had to arrange, how many things he had to do. He needed advice. "Igor, is the Proctor listening to us right now?"

"No. The Proctor's attention is now directed elsewhere."

Charlie frowned. He would have to get started by himself. Once he'd sneaked a look at one of the confidential report cards the school had sent his mother. Lacks initiative and motivation, it had said. "Igor, do you know what the Proctor wants me to do?"

"Yes, sir. The Proctor wants you to obtain a general understanding of the operations of the Ark. When necessary, the Proctor wants you to advise and assist in the control of the other humans. Ark operations include the following, in order of their utility to you in performing your special tasks: first, structure and functions of—"

"All right already! Here are my orders. Your orders. Build me a place to live. I want a control center, a place with screens and whatnot, where I can ask questions and keep up with what's going on . . ." At various distances in the factory, machines came to life as Charlie talked.

Charlie wandered back to the teaching machine, the robots following him, receiving his orders and answering his questions. He ordered them to set up a terminal, and became engrossed in the learning necessary to supply himself and Eva with the basics. He glimpsed immense opportunities, and immense amounts of interesting work to be done. Hours passed before he remembered to check up on Eva. Given the situation, he decided to spy on her through the terminal in her apartment. Maybe she was suffocating or something.

"Oh-ho-ho," Charlie chortled, having hit the jackpot on the first try. The robots had finished working in her apartment, and Eva had quickly gotten over her fear of them. She hadn't been able to resist the lure of a hot bath after two weeks of confinement on the airliner. Charlie found her basking in the tub, looking at herself in the big bathroom mirror. Charlie joined her in her sincere admiration of her slender legs, her creamy high amber-nippled hemispherical breasts, and her neat fluffpatch, also amber. She rose streaming and vaporous, shrugging perfect peachy buttocks.

Charlie stopped chortling; there weren't any other boys around to chortle with. Eva bent to pat her legs with an airliner towel. Charlie now noticed himself not amused, but gravely lusting. He put his finger on the OFF button. He honestly had not intended to see Eva naked. He stated this to an imaginary audience of his fellow students and was not surprised by their instant derision: Freeman's lying or, if not lying, even more simpleminded than he looks. So what the hell, he decided, I'm just doing what people expect of me. He turned the screen off anyway.

Laughing, Charlie ordered Igor to announce his impending arrival at Eva's apartment, and went up the elevator to pick some of the skimpy Mesozoic wildflowers growing around the robot garage.

The door slid aside, he swaggered in. "Hi, Eva," he said, and choked up immediately.

"Where've you been? I've been locked in here."

"I'm sorry. I, uh, hope you weren't scared."

She humphed and strolled away. She had on one of her stylish jeans and draped-blouse outfits from her luggage. Charlie sensed the perfume of her body, fresh from the bath.

"I, er, see you got your stuff. I had it sent to you."

"Thanks, I'm sure."

"I brought you some flowers," he said.

"You know what you can do with them, Charlie. You're not going to get away with holding me prisoner."

"I'm not holding you prisoner, Eva," he pleaded.

"I'm not holding you prisoner, Eva," she mocked in a falsetto voice, then she demanded, "Let me out!"

"Igor," Charlie angrily commanded. "Open the door!" The apartment door slid aside. Eva walked to it and looked out at Charlie's factory which was now roaring with activity. Machines spun and vibrated, and streams of robot traffic zoomed past the door and over the gray concrete horizon.

"That's it," Charlie said. "And if you don't like it here, you can go to the biome on the surface. That's it there." He jerked his thumb at one of the view screens that served in place of windows in her apartment. It showed arid, unattractive brushland under a noon sun. A sharp black crescent, a soaring Quetzalcoatl, slid across the top of the screen. Charlie hadn't seen one of the flying monsters before; his anger dissolved, and he had to tear himself away from the picture to answer Eva's next question.

"Where're Mrs. Robinelli, and Colby, and the others?"

"I'm not sure yet."

"I'll bet."

"I haven't had time to learn everything about making the computer show me things. I'll tell you about the others the next time I visit."

"Don't bother."

"You don't want to know about them?"

She sighed elaborately. "I mean, don't bother visiting."

"Don't you want some company?"

"Not you." She sat down and began brushing her gleaming hair. Charlie twitched, wanting to put his fingers in her hair, too. He didn't inform her that he could make her do anything he wanted.

"Eva, I won't see you for a while. There's a lot to do."

"Do whatever you want to, Charlie. I'm hungry. Is there anything to eat?"

Charlie ordered Igor to bring rations, and stayed to eat with her. She didn't speak to him the whole time, and he couldn't think of anything to say to her.

On her next visit, Charlie sat down at the terminal in Eva's apartment and tapped a series of instructions on the keyboard. Its screen lit up with a view of a group of human figures breaking up clods with their hands.

"That's them," he said. "The Charonese are making them work on some sort of farm." The view zoomed in on one of the laborers. It was Tina, looking thin and drawn in her dirty work suit, the sweat tracing lines down the dust on her face. Eva came closer to Charlie and the terminal.

"They're not getting enough to eat," Charlie said. He typed again on the keyboard. The scene shifted to Mrs. Robinelli and some of the students, all of them haggard, standing beside spindly pine trees. They were watching the stewardess, Mr. Peake, and several boys lowering bodies wrapped in blood-soaked blankets into a grave. "Looks like the pilot and somebody else were killed," Charlie said. "That's bad, but it looks like everyone else is okay. I don't know how it happened yet. There's your friend Colby."

Colby stood among the other students, two girls sobbing in his arms. "Can't you make the picture any clearer?" Eva snapped.

"I'm not controlling the camera," Charlie said. "I got this from the computer the Charonese use. I had to search the computer's memory for these pictures. I have a lot to learn about it still. Here're some other shots."

He brought up another view, of a group of boys and girls up to their waists in water, struggling to haul a net out of a muddy pond. The last shot was of a flock of jagged reptilian beasts, their fanged mouths open and panting, scrabbling at a high, spiked, metal fence. Eva gasped at the sight.

"I don't know what the fence is for, to keep people in, or to keep the animals out," Charlie said.

Eva hung over Charlies shoulder, her mouth open. When he turned to look at her, she backed away. "I don't know you've done this, but I don't believe it," she said.

Charlie looked her steadily in the eye. "You'd better believe it. It's all real."

"I want to speak to them."

"We can't do that, Eva. We can't communicate with them without letting the Charonese know where we are and what we're doing."

"Lie."

"It's not a lie, Eva. You want the Charonese to find out where we are? They'll send you to that place and make you do farm work."

Eva inspected her long, carefully tended fingernails. "Why couldn't we hear what they were saying?"

"You can listen in on them if you want to," Charlie said. "But to do that, you have to learn how to get the records from the big computer that runs this place. That's what I've been doing, learning how to use the computer, and how to build things."

"You always think you know everything, Charlie."

"No, I don't. I never said that. I'm learning. You can, too, if you want to. Why don't you help me—"

"I know what kind of help you want, Charlie. Just piss off, Charlie."

Charlie didn't become angry. "Eva, one of your problems is, you don't ask questions—"

"You're telling me what my problems are?"

"Don't you want to know why we're here, what the Charonese are doing with Colby and the others?"

"I couldn't stop you from telling me, could I?"

"Well," Charlie said, "the Charonese brought us to Pluto—"

"I thought we were on the planet Charon."

"Charon is the moon of Pluto, so it's the same thing. And it's not a planet, it's a spaceship. Artificial."

"If you say so, Charlie."

Charlie persevered. "The Charonese brought us here to more or less make slaves of us. They want us to help them do their work here."

"Farm work?"

"No, no," Charlie said, knowing he wasn't doing this right. "No, they don't want us to do farm work only, that's just to keep us fed. There aren't enough C-rations to last more than three months. What the Charonese want us for is to help them operate this, Charon, their spaceship. I guess eventually we'll know enough to design and program our own robots to do the farm work for us. Learning is what they really want us to do. They're making Colby and the others study nights, after the farm work, so they can do what the Charonese want them to do."

"I suppose you know what they want us to do."

"Well, yes, they told us about it on the airplane, remember? They want us to learn everything they know. How to operate this—" He waved his arm around. "Their spaceships and all."

Eva smiled disbelievingly. "Now you're going to tell me you have some great role in all this, Charlie."

Charlie looked at Eva's terminal and fought down the urge to bark it out at her: How the hell did she think they were going to escape and get home, if they didn't learn how to run Charon? But it was impossible to say anything to her about it. The Proctor might be listening. He talked on, hoping that Eva would be clever enough to grasp it too, and see that he was trying to set them all free.

"I'm doing the same thing the other kids are doing," he said. "Studying my butt off, trying to get ahead of the Charonese. I can do that because I'm being helped by this thing called the Proctor. The Proctor is keeping us, you and me, I mean, free of Charonese control. The Proctor doesn't want us to be slaves of the Charonese, it wants us to take their place, and run Charon ourselves."

Eva barely controlled her laughter. "You don't say."

"If you'd help me, we'd have a better chance of success. You aren't stupid—"

"Nice of you to say so."

Patiently, Charlie set a sheaf of papers on Eva's terminal. "I've printed out instructions on how to use your terminal. There are learning programs and shows. Just try having a look at them, and you'll see—"

"Stop telling me what to do, Charlie."

As weeks passed in the alien workshops, Charlie bloomed. He designed, created, built, and played. Hordes of reprogrammed

robots worked for him around the clock. Everything he did was
okay with the Proctor. He experimented with electronic sound
and music, creating the biggest stereo system in the solar system.
He designed and test-drove his own vehicles. He played war with
armies of mechanical soldiers. He built a baroque palace on top
of the robot garage, and moved Eva to an enormous balconied
apartment in it.

The fun wasn't free. Even with Igor and the Index helping,
each new toy required day after day of research. Then came the
work of the Ark itself, Weird Wildlife and Odd Jobs.

Charlie took to some of it willingly. The great dinosaurs fascinated him. The flat landscapes of Charon appealed to him. The
sand rivers, the bizarre herds jostling around the water holes, the
sparse, dusty forests, the gigantic chases and kills—it was all
great.

The Proctor enabled Charlie to look over the shoulders of the
Charonese zookeepers without their knowledge. It was like
watching ten different nature shows on TV at the same time.

The Crew, as the Charonese called themselves, couldn't let
nature take its course. On Charon there wasn't enough room for
that. Evolution was against the rules. The Ark was designed to
preserve, not change, the life-forms stored in its biosphere. For
the large animals, there was the problem of genetic drift, caused
by their small populations. Acres of numbers danced for Charlie's appreciation. Pedigrees of large dinosaurs and breeding
projects occupied large portions of the Ark's computer memory.

One item briefly caught Charlie's attention. A female pleisiosaur had laid her eggs a month too early, reason enough for the
Charonese geneticists to cull her from the population. Charlie
glimpsed the animal swimming slowly across Charon's mini-
ocean, its long neck darting after fish. It grounded itself offshore,
waiting while the surf broke over its mottled blue and green back.
After dark it levered itself up the starlit beach with its huge paddles. The creature was as big as a small whale, and its head and
neck looked like a huge snake lying flat on the sand. Its eyes
wept big, sandy tears as it dug a hole with its rear paddles and
laid a clutch of eggs.

Charlie watched and imagined himself narrating this scene on
a TV show for an Earth audience. He would speak in a rich,
fruity voice like Lorne Greene while classical music played in the

background. If I do everything right, it'll happen someday, he thought.

The pleisiosaur nest had been plundered by two bipedal predators; Charlie noticed their barely distinguishable tracks on the wave-washed beach. The odd thing was that these predators had covered up the eggs they hadn't taken. That was unanimallike behavior.

Charlie made a face at himself under the sound-and-vision helmet, but he didn't ask about the nest-robbers. He'd learned not to pursue every puzzlement that presented itself. Doing that always got him lost in tangles of digressions or long explanations from Igor. It was best to stick to the subject at hand.

When he had time, he checked up on the people who were being kept at the residence facility, which they called Faulty Towers. The students had tried to make a protest, but the Crew had succeeded in starving them into settling down to a routine of study. The Proctor approved of that, and so did Charlie.

Without her knowledge, Charlie watched Mrs. Robinelli's researches. He profited from her efforts to divine the secrets of the Ark. He noted that his own studies were going faster, because he had the advantage of Igor's constant attendance.

Charlie missed his teacher. He longed to speak to her. It comforted him to know that Mrs. Robinelli felt the same way he did: that the only way for the students to obtain freedom was to learn rom their captors.

In the depths of his great bed, Charlie groaned again. It was hard work, being emperor of outer space. Now it really was time to get up and go take care of Bill and Curt.

He crawled out. His fancy uniform, the one he'd worn on his punitive expedition to Faulty Towers, lay on the carpet. His shiny green, padded plastic boots had fallen apart already. He kicked the uniform aside and pulled on the jeans, sneakers, and shirt he'd worn on the airliner.

"I should've kidnapped Mrs. Robinelli, instead of the goddamn homecoming princess," Charlie mumbled to himself. The bruise on his forehead, where Colby had hit him with the aluminum mug, was throbbing. He reached up and touched the bandage his robot doctor had put on him.

The butler robot bowed. "Will you be wanting breakfast this morning, sir?"

"Yeah," Charlie grunted. "Eat now."

"Yes, sir."

The usual spread was waiting for him in the royal feasting hall: a table as long and beamy as a yacht, covered with plates of steaming food. Charlie walked past the rows of robot flunkies along the walls, past the fried eggs as big as manhole covers, the yard-wide hamburger patties, the drumsticks four feet long, the roast as big as a small automobile. He went straight to the bowl of loot from the Faulty Towers garden. He munched lettuce, carrots, raw potatoes, tomatoes. His craving for such things surprised him.

"See that Eva gets some of these vegetables," he ordered.

"To hear is to obey, Master."

"Make plans for vegetable gardens for my use."

"Yes, sir."

"Bring me a bowl of Cheerios with sugar and milk."

"Massive bullshit, sir."

Igor's I-don't-get-it responses had another function: they warned Charlie when he was talking to himself too much.

"It's lonely at the top, isn't it, Igor?"

"Very good, sir."

When Charlie got tired of Weird Wildlife, he switched to Odd Jobs. Alone, he traced connections, opened doors, investigated, pried, poked, and listened.

By robot proxy, he looked upon the heat-filled vacuum of Charon's underside, where great vehicles crawled upside down on the inside surface of the Ark's hollow shell.

"What are these machines doing, Igor?"

"They are applying aluminum vapor to the inner surface of the Ark's structural sphere."

"I can see that. Why are they doing it?"

"To maintain a mirror finish on the inner surface. The purpose of the mirror is to reflect the infrared radiation that comes from the black hole at the center of the sphere. It is a means of regulating the temperature of the outer surface, by increasing or decreasing the reflectivity of the inner surface. At present, the sea is being warmed, and the land is being cooled, in order to create more rainfall on the land. When more cooling is desired, fluids circulate through conduits under the biome. The fluid is piped to the sides of the photon-venting tower, where it—"

"What makes the machines stick to the diamond?"

"There are electromagnetic coils under the surface. The machines also contain magnets."

Charlie remembered that he was planning to wage war against the Charonese someday. "What would happen if the electricity got turned off?"

"That is impossible."

"Pretend it isn't. What would happen?"

After a delay, Igor said, "The machines would become detached from the inner surface. They would fall into the gravitational singularity, or black hole, at the center of the Ark's structural sphere."

"Give me a view of the black hole," Charlie ordered. The view in his helmet eyepieces switched to blackness, in which a dim white star sputtered.

"What makes it visible?" Charlie asked. "Why can I see it?"

"You are looking downward through a telescope on one of the mirror-maintenance vehicles," Igor said. "The singularity produces its own radiation, for reasons you could not understand at your present level of education. Most of the light you see is the effect of molecules of air and aluminum falling into the singularity."

Charlie decided not to ask the next, obvious, question. No point in arousing anyone's suspicions, he thought. Besides, he already knew the answer. Mrs. Robinelli had talked about black holes in class one day. If one of the huge machines fell into the hole, there would be a vast nuclear explosion. No good. Charlie wanted to take over the Ark, not destroy it.

He changed the subject. "Igor, what is the location of Charon's central computer?"

There was a pause. "Very good, sir," Igor said at last.

Igor's refusal to hear Charlie's question confirmed an assumption he'd held a long time: he wouldn't be told everything. He would have to resort to indirection. After long cogitation, he asked for a map display of all mechanical and industrial installations on Charon. "Let the first display be of the area where I am now," he said.

After a moment, Charlie's eyepieces lit up with a multicolored, three-dimensional diagram. Charlie's head spun; since he was lying on his back with the sound-and-vision helmet on his head, he had to look up to see down into its depths. "Where am I on this map?" he asked.

A blinking green dot appeared, and a label: YOU (CHARLIE). Charlie studied the map, noticed blank areas with passageways and conduits leading to them. The biggest such blank was accessible through the sloping tunnel that led from the bottom of the light stack, the air lock tunnel he, Reilly, Tina, and Eva had walked up after their arrival on Charon.

I can't just call for a taxi to take me to those places, Charlie thought. The Proctor would notice that. If I wanted to see them, I'd have to walk. Not only that, but that tunnel opens into the vacuum of Charon's inner space. I wouldn't dare go there without a spacesuit.

"Hello, Charlie," said the fly voice in the sound-and-vision helmet.

Charlie jumped guiltily. "Uh, hi, Proctor. I haven't, uh, heard from you in a long time."

"It is a sign of your progress, Charlie. You are doing well."

"I, er, was afraid that you might think I was spending too much time playing around with the robots and not enough time learning the works. Do you? Think that, I mean?"

"Your activities have helped you learn about the Ark's technology. You are working hard. I am satisfied."

Under the helmet, Charlie put on his most sincere smile. "Gee, thanks, Proctor."

"Now I wish to bring up a new subject," the Proctor said. Charlie cringed mentally. "There is no need to worry," it added.

The damn helmet can partly read my emotions, Charlie remembered. He forced calm upon himself. It hasn't said anything, yet, about me trying to find out where the central computer is, in spite of that being forbidden knowledge. I'm okay. The Proctor wants me to succeed. It wants me to be loyal. And I am.

"You are already aware of the input-output connections that can be made to the nerves of your body."

"Yes," Charlie said, with new trepidation.

"You have reached a state of learning that makes you ready to have the connections implanted in your skin. It is much sooner than I expected. You are far ahead of the other students."

Oh, man, here it comes, Charlie thought. I knew it was going to bring this up sooner or later. But not so goddamn soon.

"Except for some minor discomfort, it is a painless process. Once you have had the implants, your communications with the Ark systems will be much faster and easier. The time you now spend studying will be less, and it will be more pleasant for you, requiring less conscious effort. I have noticed that you do not like to make a conscious effort."

Cold sweat poured off Charlie's body. He felt as if he were sitting in a pool of it. "You noticed that, huh," he said.

"I can't understand how you are concerned about the implantation surgery. It need not be done until you are completely ready for it. It is your decision, and you may wait as long as you like."

Sure, what's time to you, you're a fugging computer program, Charlie thought, fear cramping his stomach. If I'm going through with what I want to do, I have to let the robots cut me. Wire me to their damn—I got into this because I wanted to be the hero of the human race.

"Okay, Proctor," he quavered. "I'm ready anytime you are."

Now, still at breakfast, Charlie drew himself back from remembering how afraid he'd been of the input-output wires. The strain of concealing his intentions and distrust from the Proctor nagged at him all the time, but maybe he was getting more used to it. On the Proctor's insistance, he even slept in the wire network. Frequently he found himself in possession of skills and knowledge that he didn't remember learning. The only other effect of it was that he no longer remembered his dreams.

He finished his raw vegetables and swigged down a goblet of berry juice spiked with ethyl alcohol, shuddering at it went down. He hated drinking, but it helped. He wiped his mouth on the tablecloth. He'd dawdled as long as he could over breakfast. Now he really had to go see about the hostages.

As Charlie left the banquet hall, the flunky robots all said, "Have a nice day, sir."

Charlie wandered down the formerly magnificent corridors of his palace. Sadly, he noted the cracks and misalignments in the fake plastic pilasters and reliefs, the dirty sagging paper tapestries, the poor copies of famous frescoes. Down cross-corridors he saw his empty swimming pool, his targetless shooting gallery, his unused movie studio, his other unfinished projects. The butler wheezed and nattered along in front of him, its rubber-shod feet thumping on the fake mosaic floor, its black tie-and-tails outfit smeared with dust.

"Tacky," Charlie said.

"Very good, sir."

His dream, of building up a working partnership with Eva, was as dusty as his palace. The only times he'd seen her were during his visits to her apartment, and those had been painfully awkward.

Between visits, he'd continued his occasional surveillance of Eva through the camera in her apartment. He saw her trying on clothes, sleeping—Charlie himself slept less and less as the burden of his work increased—exercising in her gym, doing her hair, leafing through the magazines Charlie had printed for her from the Charonese collection of intercepted literature.

At one point in their one-sided relationship he'd started announcing himself with fanfares and drumrolls, and he strode into her apartment in a variety of magnificent uniforms, boots, togas, tuxedos.

"How do you like this outfit, Eva?"

She glanced at him uninterestedly. She sat in an ornate armchair, buffing her fingernails and watching a TV soap opera on her terminal. There'd been a large assortment of nail polishes, blush powder, mascara, perfumed shampoos, and other makeup items in the cargo of the hijacked airliner. Charlie had given it all to Eva, and she'd arranged samples of it on her Maria Theresa vanity table.

"It's a safari outfit," Charlie said. "I designed it myself."

"It makes you look like a fag, Charlie."

"Well, it's partly a joke. I thought you might think it was funny." He sat down on a gilt bowlegged stool, which was upholstered in fake embroidered silk. He gestured at Eva's cosmetics collection. "Makes you wonder why this stuff was on the plane, doesn't it? I mean, why couldn't the Charonese have gotten some Coke or Pepsi?"

Eva languidly turned back to the soap opera. On the screen, a woman was sitting in front of a vanity table similar to Eva's carrying on an interminable conversation with a tall, handsome man in a stylish suit. Charlie had to speak up to make himself heard. "Do you like the new rooms I've built for you? They came from a palace in Vienna."

"They're okay."

Charlie fidgeted on his stool. The desktop below Eva's terminal screen was bare. "Did you look at any of the books and pictures I brought you? Did you try some of the programs I fed into your terminal?"

"I wasn't interested," Eva said. She was wearing a red satin dress, former property of the airliner's stewardess. Charlie had had it tailored to fit her. The material *zipped* faintly as Eva crossed her ankles.

"Wouldn't you like to design your own clothes? You can make anything you want. It's fun."

"No."

"Eva, I brought you here—"

"I know why you brought me here."

Charlie squirmed and flushed red. "I haven't done anything—"

"And you're not going to, either."

Charlie took a breath and started again. "I brought you here so you could help me rule Charon. You could have a share in all this—"

"Oh, wow, Charlie."

"Well, you haven't even looked at it yet!" Charlie shouted. "Sorry," he said immediately. "Sorry I shouted."

"I told you not to scream at me again, Charlie." Eva looked down at her fingernails, long eyelashes resting on her amber cheeks.

There was a long pause, while the TV jabbered on. "Would you like to get out, get some fresh air?"

"No."

"Don't you want to see the world? There're really neat things—"

"I see more of it than I want to from here." She waved at the view screens on the walls.

Another conversational lag ensued. Charlie imagined various forms of violence and terror, rape. That wasn't what he wanted. "At least let me show you about the clothes." He moved to the terminal, typed on the keyboard. The TV program was replaced by silence and a word on the screen: READY. "Look," he said, "all you have to do is type in 'voice input'; then you don't have to use the keyboard. You can just talk to it. To call up design assistance you just—"

"I was watching that program, Charlie."

"You can see it again anytime, Eva, you know that. Now look—"

She sat and stared at the wall next to the terminal.

"Okay, Eva, we'll do it some other time. Here's how you call up a view of the prison where the others are." Eva showed some interest in this. Charlie spoke, and there was a picture of ragged, grimy students lined up at a dining hall counter.

"There's Colby again," Charlie said, grinning at the screen. "Girls, girls, girls. He's always surrounded by them. That looks like—"

"Just put it back to the program, Charlie."

"You want me to show you how to do it yourself?"

"I don't want you to show me anything, Charlie."

Charlie pointed to the screen. "Would you like to join them? Go where they are? You'll have to promise me not to say anything about what I'm doing—"

"Don't do me any favors, Charlie."

The smile slowly left Charlie's face. He hadn't won Eva over, but he had corrupted her. She was content to wait, comfortably. It wasn't what he wanted.

"Did you want something in particular, Charlie?" she asked.

"Well, yes. I wanted to ask you to go outside with me. I have a surprise for you. You might like it."

"I doubt it."

"I've canceled lunch today," Charlie said. "Instead, we're going on a picnic, outside. I thought you might like to see some of the work that goes on here, get some fresh air and sunshine."

"I suppose I have to."

"I didn't say that," Charlie said, opening the box he'd brought with him. He held up a khaki, tan, and off-white tailored outfit, and a straw sun hat. "First product of my latest factory," he said. "It's guaranteed to fit you perfectly. I got it from that Africa movie."

Eva demonstrated a minimal interest. "That was years ago, Charlie."

"I know," Charlie said. "Would you like to try it on? I'll step outside, so you'll be private." As if I hadn't seen you bare-assed enough times. How does she think I get her sizes right?

"All right, if it'll keep you off my back for a while."

The safari was waiting in the sunshine outside the robot garage. When Charlie and Eva appeared at the great doorway, a hundred robots raised their arms and shouted in a deep chorus, "Hoohah!! Bwana Freeman! Umgawa! Umgawa!"

Eva jumped and tried to pull back inside. Charlie seized her elbow. "Don't be afraid; they're my loyal retainers," he said. "They're expressing their love for their noble and kindly master, that's me, and noble kindly master's lady friend."

"I'm not your—" Eva began hotly.

She was stopped by the sight of four of Charlie's soldiers, dressed in flamboyant robes and carrying an elaborate tassled and canopied chair. In a jangle of gold and silver ornaments, the robots trotted up and set down the chair in front of Eva.

Eva stared, and Charlie yelled, "Oh, shit!" One robot's costume had partly fallen off and was dragging in the dust, and another had left a trail of oily blue smoke in the air behind it.

"You and you!" Charlie shouted. "Get out of my sight! Igor, send two replacements."

After five seconds of trampling up a cloud of dust, the new robots were in place. Charlie bowed to Eva. "If the memsahib would care to enter her palanquin?"

Eva now transferred her stare to Charlie. "What I mean is, sit down," he said.

Eva snatched her elbow away from Charlie and, uneasily looking around, seated herself in the chair. "Hup!" Charlie shouted.

The robots picked up the chair. Eva tumbled backward into the cushions, holding on to her sun hat. "I'm not going!" she cried out, but was drowned out by Charlie's shout.

"Forward, ho-o!"

The robots started off as one. A long line of them wound through the gnarled hardwoods that surrounded Charon's north pole, Eva's palanquin, with Charlie pacing along beside her, in the middle of the file. The robots marched in unison, their rubber-soled feet *clump*ing on the earth together. As they passed under the great trees they struck up a polyphonic chant, accompanied by drum music that came from the huge speaker boxes that some of them carried on their heads. The singing echoed from the forest, and Charlie swung along, waving his arms in time, occasionally singing a word or two. He grinned up at Eva. "Neat, huh?"

"It's ridiculous, Charlie. It's also hot and dusty."

"Of course it's ridiculous, Eva! It's supposed to be fun."

"You have a funny idea of fun."

Charlie took off his sun helmet and scratched his head as he walked. "All fun ideas are funny, aren't they?"

"It's stupid."

The column left the forest and moved out onto an open savannah. Birds flew up into the brilliant blue sky, and long-necked ostrich dinosaurs loped away against the clouds that towered along the horizon. A number of tall mechanisms joined the group, striding on long legs, carrying long metal poles.

"I made up the robots' song myself," Charlie said stubbornly. "The safari stuff is for fun, but there's a serious job to do also."

"I'm just sure."

"I'll explain—"

"I knew you would."

"Every year at this time, the triceratops herd migrates across the north pole to their breeding ground in the other hemisphere. Usually the Charonese have a kind of roundup here, but this year Igor and I have to do it, because the Proctor won't allow the Charonese around while you and I are here."

"Is this going to take long?" Eva asked.

"The rest of the day," Charlie said. "But you can go back after lunch, if you want to."

"Thanks a lot."

"Aren't you curious about why it's daylight here? Usually, it's a sort of twilight around here. You have to go several miles south to make the sun come over the horizon."

"I have no idea what you're—"

"I ordered a special beam of light from Pluto to shine on us. You can see it, directly overhead, there. The light makes it seem like noon while it's on."

A cluster of tents and awnings began to come up over the horizon. Charlie pointed ahead as he walked. "There's the camp. We're almost there."

"Thank God," Eva said, fanning herself with a lace hand-kerchief that had the initials E.R. embroidered on it.

Lunch was served at a lavishly appointed table in the shade of an awning. Robots costumed and painted to look like liveried waiters brought trays of food and pitchers of cold water tinkling with ice. Eva pouted and picked at her plate. After she com-plained again about the dust, Charlie had shown her to a dressing tent. She had changed from the safari outfit to a wide-shouldered designer jacket and white linen pants, formerly the property of one of the other girl passengers. "I'm tired of all this meat," Eva said. "Can't we have some croissants?"

"There's no grain on Charon," Charlie said, acting cheerful as he poured gravy over a thin slice of pachycephalosaur. The meat tasted vaguely of cough drops, something to do, Igor had in-formed him, with the living animal's diet of eucalyptus leaves. "No grain means no flour; no flour means no bread. I'm going to do something about it when I take over."

Eva sighed. A butler took her plate away and brought another. "You're always saying that, Charlie. When you're going to take over. It's boring."

"Why don't you study, too? Might speed things up."

"It's too boring. Is that what you're doing all the time? Study-ing?"

"Yes, mostly," Charlie said. "But there's other stuff to be done, too. That's why I brought you along today. I hope you'll take an interest. You know, the Charonese are the only thing standing between these animals and total extinction. It's like a miracle, finding them here still alive!"

Eva waved a fly away from her face. "My little brother is always talking about dinosaurs, too."

"Eva, what's the matter with you?"

"What's the matter with me?"

"I mean, why do you get bored when someone talks to you about anything but . . . but normal subjects? Aren't you interested in anything?"

"I'm interested in a lot of things, Charlie."

"Like what?" Charlie demanded.

"I don't have to answer your questions!"

"Well, what do you think is going to happen to you here, if you don't learn to do the job we were brought here to do?"

"I suppose you're going to tell me, aren't you."

Charlie felt a twinge of uneasiness. He'd never thought to ask that question before, either of himself or of the Proctor. It had always seemed self-evident to him that the humans should learn as much as they could.

"Actually, Eva, I don't know," he said.

"Wow, I actually don't know something!" Eva mimicked him.

"The Charonese kidnapped us to work for them," Charlie said. "But the Proctor is making it possible for us to be our own bosses on Charon."

"What good is that if I don't want to be here?"

Charlie glanced around. None of the robot servants were near, but Charlie thought, if I were the Proctor, I'd have the whole planet bugged. "The point is," he said, "there's always hope. We should be ready for opportunities. And, even if nothing happens, we have to make the best of things. You know what I mean?"

"I know what you mean."

"I don't mean that!"

Eva's pouting coral lips curled slightly.

"Seriously, Eva. Suppose we found a way to reintroduce the triceratops to Earth. Can you imagine what it might mean to the Third World to have an animal that can get fat eating brushwood in a dry environment like this? I mean, they don't eat grass or leaves, they eat thorns, and brambles, and scrub! They're the animals that make it possible for the grass to grow!"

"I can imagine, Charlie," Eva said wearily. A robot had come up to the table and was offering her a chilled golden goblet. Eva looked at it suspiciously.

"I—it's a surprise, for you," Charlie said. "Try some."

"What is it?"

"It's berry juice," Charlie said. "It took weeks to collect it. There aren't many fruits on Charon; there weren't many in Mesozoic times."

"Whatever that means."

"Try it. It's not bad."

Eva sipped, drank it down. "How do you like it? It's good, isn't it?" Charlie said.

"It's okay."

"Don't you like anything?"

"It's okay."

from the ground itself. Now enormous piglike grunts began to be audible in the distance. "Okay," Charlie said. "The herd is arriving. Now we'll see some action."

"I don't want to see any action."

Dark, humped shapes appeared along the horizon, soon resolving themselves into bulky, pebble-hided animals with horned and beaked faces joined necklessly to huge bodies. Tall robots carrying metal poles prodded the animals to a halt. Among the tents, Charlie's servants busied themselves opening boxes and setting up equipment.

"What we're doing here," Charlie lectured, "is inspecting the herd. The yearlings have to be marked and inoculated. Some will have radio transmitters attached. One or two of the old bulls will have to be destroyed."

Charlie got up and strode out from under the awning. "I should've built some kind of a tower for you to see from," he said. "The horizon doesn't let us see more than the front of the herd from the ground."

"I'd like to go back now," Eva said.

The triceratops' grunting increased as one of the tall herding robots got caught in the milling herd and was instantly borne under with a sound like an automobile collision.

"Wow," Charlie said. "The Proctor and Igor aren't as good at handling these critters as the Charonese manager would have been, I'll bet."

"You said I could go back after lunch," Eva said.

"In a minute. Igor, my triceratops gun!"

The nearest robot barked, "Yes, *Bwana*! Your triceratops gun!" Another robot ran up with a long musket. Charlie took the weapon and opened it to insert a banana-sized cartridge.

"You're not going to shoot that thing, are you?" Eva cried.

"It's only paint," Charlie said, shouting over the uproar.

"Paint!" Eva jumped out of her chair and ran closer to Charlie.

"Sure. For marking the ones to be destroyed." Charlie snapped the gun closed. "Here we go," he said.

"Charlie, I want to go back now!"

"It's not dangerous, Eva. I've done this before. The problem is getting them to charge. They won't charge anything as small as a human being, you know."

"What?"

"It's not sporting if they don't charge!" Charlie was walking out into the open with his musket, calling back at her over his shoulder. "Igor has to inflate the balloon I designed! To make the old bull charge!"

A robot standing beside Eva said, "Yes, *Bwana*! Inflate the balloon!"

Charlie spun around, his eyes bugging. "No Igor! Not now!" he yelled.

A deafening hiss blasted Eva; she shrieked and dropped to her knees, her hands over her ears. Next to her a robot, bending over a ten-foot cylinder, was turning a valve. A hose ran from the cylinder to a nearby aluminum box. A tan and brown balloon bloated out of the box, lurched and bobbled as it grew fifteen, then twenty, feet tall, its legs, tail, and head popping out into the shape of a giant, tiger-striped carnosaur. Thunderous oinking and the clatter of beaks came from the triceratopsians as the herd sighted its traditional enemy.

Charlie was running madly back toward the camp. Behind him galumphed the triceratops herd's dominant male, a huge three-horned monster as big as a dump truck. "Run, Eva!" Charlie yelled.

Charlie scooped Eva off the ground and dodged to the side as the bull charged through the camp, robots and equipment bouncing off its stony hide, tents, poles and ropes flapping on its horns. The banquet table spun through the air and landed on its humped neck.

With Eva clutched to his side, her stylish shoes dragging in the grass, Charlie dashed though a tinkling shower of food, silverware, and dishes. He ran as far as he could; his feet tangled in the dry grass, and he fell heavily, twisting to keep from landing on Eva. He scuttled around to get a view of the camp, saw the triceratops carrying the balloon on its horns, pieces of it floating down. Eva lay as she had fallen, knees drawn up, eyes closed tightly, her hands over her ears. It was hard to see her. Suddenly Charlie realized that the world had gone dark.

"Jesus Christ," puffed Charlie, looking at the sky. "What's

happening?" Where the sky had been brilliant blue, it was now deep violet, the clouds painted rose and pink.

While Charlie was trying to grasp this, the triceratops bull lit up in a blazing glare. Fire exploded in the grass around it. Its hide smoked, then burst into flame. The animal staggered in the blinding light, its beak gaping in a soundless scream. It took a step toward the herd, then toppled over on its side, its legs kicking once. It turned black under the flames; then its belly exploded. The light went out suddenly, as though a switch had been thrown.

Charlie lay on his stomach while steaming offal fell out of the air and thudded on the ground around them. It was daylight again. He stood up, blinking. The purple afterimage of the dying triceratops hung in his vision, nearly blinding him. Several robots walked up.

"Have you been injured?" one of them asked, in the Proctor's voice.

"No," Charlie said. "S-see about Eva, she might—"

Eva partly removed her hands from her ears, squinted at Charlie through one eye, got to her hands and knees, stood up wobblingly, and screamed, "Get away from me! Get away!!"

"She's all right," Charlie said to the robots. "Eva, let me help you—"

"I said get away from me! I don't want any of your help!"

The triceratops herd stood its ground, grunting, seeming to follow Charlie and Eva with their noses as he followed her, as she aimlessly walked through the shambles of the camp, shrieking curses at him. Finally, she sat down on the grass and grew quiet. A vehicle drove up, and Charlie was able to pick her up and put her in it.

As they rolled back to Charlie's palace, he said, "Well, Eva, I guess we're even now. This time it was my fault you were in danger, and even though I saved your life again, I—"

"You stupid, idiotic, shitheaded—! You creep. You asshole! I never want to see you or hear your moronic, idiotic—! Never—!!"

Charlie looked out over the flat landscape, his arms folded. He was accustomed to abuse from people who didn't understand him.

Charlie spent that evening alone in his command center. The

command center always cheered him up. Here, surrounded by science and technology, he could exclude human fallacies, including his own. He removed his clothing and taped dozens of input-output wires over the transceiver chips under his skin. The butler had to do the ones on his back. The wires ran to a plastic box he could wear under his shirt. The box communicated data to and from his body to a nearby terminal. It was an altogether more convenient arrangement than the one he'd started with, which was to be wired to his couch.

Charlie settled into his command chair. Banks of screens lit up; his illuminated globe of Charon flickered with data. He ignored them and put on his sound-and-vision helmet. The little stereo screens pressed against his eyes; he was floating in a white nothing. Igor and the Index hovered in the whiteness; thanks to the input-output wires he could "feel" them both.

The Index was just a program, but there was something sad about Igor. Igor was like a former person. Igor was alive, not just a machine or a program. At the same time Igor wasn't alive. Igor was thoughts minus personality, obedience without willingness, a question mark without a question. The other Charonese were looks without faces, but Igor was a face without a look.

Most of the time. Now Igor took a "stance" that Charlie, without knowing how he did it, recognized as meaning the approach of the Proctor.

"I recognize you, Proctor," Charlie said.

The Proctor emitted a burst of data. "Good, Charlie. It is a sign of your progress. You are becoming a Crewperson. I am satisfied."

For the dozenth time, Charlie noted the similarity between Index and Proctor. They were both synthetic. But where the Index was a familiar-seeming program, the Proctor was sinister and frightening, like a deadly machine running in a dark room.

"Proctor," Charlie said. "Sometimes I find barriers or blocks in the computer's memory. Sometimes the Charonese do things I can't see. Are the blocks put there by the Charonese, or by you?"

"That is irrelevant. I wish to speak about your activities today. You placed yourself and the human, Eva, in a life-threatening situation. That is contrary to our purpose."

"Oh, right, Proctor."

"In the future, you will deal with wildlife through robot proxy only."

"Right on, you got it," Charlie said. "Ah, uh, could you tell me what happened to the triceratops? I mean, if it's not irrelevant or anything?"

"I focused daylight on the animal. The animal was destroyed."

"You were watching what I was doing today?" Charlie asked.

"Yes."

"Why today? I mean, usually you're doing something else, right?"

"I wished to observe the development of your relationship with Eva."

"Why-why would you be interested in that?"

"Your wish to obtain power over Eva is one of your motivations for cooperating with me," the Proctor said, with embarrassing bluntness. "I will assist you in this, if you advise me how to do so."

Charlie blushed furiously under the sound-and-vision helmet, even though none of the things he was hearing were any surprise. "I don't want any, any assistance! That is, I mean, if she asked me, and were willing to, to help me in this Ark project, and . . ."

Charlie's voice trailed off. What was he supposed to say, that all he wanted was a normal relationship with Eva? All he had to do was take off his helmet and look around to see how absurd that was now. Hell, it had even been absurd back in good old normal Garfield High.

"Well," he said. "Uh, about the dangerous situations. A word to the wise is sufficient, Proctor. I hope to do a good job here."

"You are doing well, Charlie. I am satisfied. You will be rewarded."

The Proctor didn't say anything else. Charlie waited a moment, then called up the Index and asked for the learning program about soil formation that he'd been running the previous day. After he'd gone through a tedious hour of it, he felt the Proctor "depart."

He returned to his real inquiries. "Igor, so far as the human race is concerned, what is the thing that the Charonese fear the most?"

"Discovery."

"How could that happen?"

Charlie was whisked into starry space. In speeded-up time, he saw planets orbiting, a light beam sweeping across the solar system.

The voice of the Index blurted, "During the next four years, Charon will eclipse Pluto, as seen from Earth, three times. During one of these eclipses the Earth will pass through the beam of the laser that beams artificial sunlight to the Ark from the fuel supply, which you call Pluto—"

The information seemed to stuff itself into Charlie's mind. It went ten times faster than ordinary speech. When Charlie had first put on the input-output harness, he'd suffered from sleeplessness, tension, and headaches. Later, he'd learned to relax and let it flow.

"—astronomers on Earth are waiting to observe these eclipses, in order to obtain data about Charon. If they notice the anomalous light of the sun laser, they may deduce the artificial nature of Pluto and Charon. It will therefore become necessary to switch off the sun laser during the eclipses—"

Charlie learned that the first shutdown of Charon's artificial sunlight would take place within weeks, that it would last less than an hour, and that it wouldn't be necessary to do it again for 124 years.

While attending to the lecture, Charlie felt the alive warmth of the Charonese scientist upon whose mind he was eavesdropping. Charlie looked forward to these one-sided contacts with Charonese. They helped his loneliness. The Charonese had been alive once, living and breathing. They'd had childhoods, parents, love, and regrets. Charlie recalled what the Proctor had said about Igor when he'd first arrived: Igor had been a Charonese, too. The Proctor had "edited" him or her for Charlie's use.

The Charonese presence faded away, and Charlie asked another question. "Igor, why are the Charonese afraid of the human race?"

Instantly, his mind was flooded with pictures of U.S. and Soviet weapons and spacecraft, scenes from science-fiction movies, more text and figures. He was seeing the fears of Gamma, the Charonese who specialized in human affairs.

There were two worst-case scenarios. Charlie was given a speeded-up movie of an all-out space war. Missiles, launched by the panicking nations of Earth, struck Charon's surface and the lightstack. Thermonuclear bursts punctured the artificial world's diamond shell; atmosphere poured into the hollow interior and fell onto the black hole. Atoms were ripped apart at the hole's event horizon, releasing catastrophic bursts of heat and light. The black hole was the Ark's weakness. Even a slow leak of air into it would be the end for Charon.

The show went on. Hard radiation and blast waves hit the inner surface of the shell. The magnetic devices that held up the lightstack failed, and it collapsed, wrapping itself around Charon. Charon's atmosphere turned to smoke as animals, plants, and soil burned. The Ark turned red-hot, then collapsed inward on itself. With an intolerable flash, the hole ate Charon, leaving behind a pinwheel of sparks.

"The astronomers would notice that, all right," Charlie said.

Gamma's other worst-case was war also, this time with the Ark successfully defending itself, then taking preventative measures against the human race. The narrow beam of the Ark's intersellar drive wrote a signature of fire on an Earthlike planet. A bar of light crawled over continents and oceans, leaving a path of glowing magma and expanding shock waves. Smoke and cloud spread until the surface was blotted out.

"Now, that would really get their attention," Charlie joked, to cover his apprehension. This was about the destruction of a whole planet. The scene was too explicit; it had none of the dreamlike quality that characterized the thoughts of the Charonese. Instead it was movielike, as though it were an actual record of something. Some of the shorelines he'd glimpsed under the clouds looked too much like Earth's.

He wanted to ask Igor about it, but a "glance" at the disembodied creature told Charlie that Igor couldn't, wouldn't, wasn't allowed to answer. Charlie grunted. The information was blocked.

"Okay, Igor. Erase the Index's memory of these inquiries. Let the record show me watching the soil information program during this time period."

Igor "gestured." Done. Charlie could only hope that this simple deception would keep on fooling the Proctor.

Suddenly, it came to Charlie what the Proctor had done to Igor. The Proctor had made Igor into a zombie.

Charlie, alone, roamed, explored, played. He gave up his
hunting expeditions, but he continued to fly thrillingly over
prairies and brushland in Charonese planes and helicopters modi-
fied to his own designs. He made a discovery.

"Igor, I want to land here!"

"Yes, sir."

The helicopter zoomed in a wide circle and began losing altitude. Charlie gulped down his stomach and strained to keep his
eye on what had attracted his attention: a pattern of square outlines on the ground, glimpsed through the helicopter's window.

"Land as close to that clearing as you can," he ordered, indicating the place by aiming a small camera that was connected by
a cable to the helicopter's computer terminal.

"Yes, sir." The helicopter dropped abruptly toward a sandbar
on a wide, shallow river, saving itself at the last moment with a
burst of power.

While he was waiting for the dust to settle and for his robot
guard to deploy outside, Charlie unrolled one of his maps of
Charon. There was nothing shown at this spot except the river,
which was dry most of the year, and the soil and vegetation type.
The nearest surveillance tower was miles away. It confirmed the
impression he'd had before, that the Crew's knowledge, even of
the biological surface of the Ark, was incomplete in places.

He put down the map, unstrapped himself, stood up, and
strode down the helicopter's ramp. The Red Guard stood around
with mechanical patience, holding their ceremonial rifles. It was
late afternoon on this side of Charon, and heat assailed Charlie
after the cooled air of the helicopter cabin. "No large wildlife or
predators in the area, sir," Igor told him through one of the
guards.

"Okay," Charlie said, gesturing. "We'll go that way." He
started off toward the nearby riverbank, guards spaced around
him.

Charlie scrambled up the steep riverbank with ease. Life in the
absence of cookies and ice cream had taken twenty pounds off
him. Also, Charlie's sinuses no longer bothered him, which
proved to his satisfaction that what he'd been allergic to was real
life.

Charlie and the robots pushed their way through the dry brush
in what he hoped was the right direction. He walked over several

of the low, elongated humps in the ground before he realized he'd reached the place. He was standing in the middle of the one of the square outlines he'd noticed from the air.

"These things look like the outlines of houses," he remarked.

"Very good, sir," the nearest guard said.

Charlie frowned and brushed perspiration off his forehead. Igor didn't know what Charlie meant. Igor couldn't see it: for a hundred yards around, the scrub was growing out of what looked to Charlie like an archaeological site. Once, in school, Mrs. Robinelli had shown Charlie pictures of a neolithic village in Iraq.

"On Charon? Ridiculous."

"Very good, sir."

While Charlie wandered from one mound to another, the sky slowly darkened. Locusts began to buzz in the trees along the riverbank. Charlie stopped on what looked like the biggest mound. "Igor, have two guards dig up the soil here with their hands. Hurry up."

"Yes, sir."

Charlie followed the robots as they excavated a shallow trench across the mound, scuffing his boots in the piles of dry soil they threw up. After the robots had dug a few inches down, they began to bring up black framents: bits of charcoal, and among them, a bit of bone with an unmistakable human molar attached to it. A little farther along, he found a fragment of porcelain, with a Chinese-looking design on it. Charlie turned it over in his hands. It could've come from a Chinese teacup his mother had. The china shard and the bone were covered with soot, as though they had been in a fire.

Charlie looked around at the robots. Except for the two that were digging, the guards were standing around watching for dinosaurs, just as they always did, apparently not taking any notice of what Charlie was doing. It was getting close to nightfall. He put his finds in his overalls pocket and ordered the guards to escort him back to the helicopter.

That night Charlie had no appetite for dinner. He went straight to his control center.

"Igor, have there ever been any human beings on Charon before the group I came with?"

"Yes," Igor said. "The Crew has made two previous attempts to recruit humans to serve on the Ark. The first was in the year

972 A.D., when the population of a town named Fragrant Flower Bridge was captured and brought to the Ark. The second attempt was in the year 1614 A.D., when the crew and passengers of a ship named *Holy Inez*, nicknamed *Shit Fire*, were brought to the Ark. These recruiting attempts failed because of the low technological level of the societies from which the two human groups originated. Because the society of the second group appeared to be evolving a more advanced technology, the Crewperson Gamma decided to wait until—"

"Stop, Igor, that's enough!" Charlie's head was spinning. While Igor lectured, Charlie had seen a succession of images of dazed and horrified Chinese and Spaniards being driven aboard gigantic spacecraft by robots, being held, struggling, in front of incomprehensible alien computer terminals.

"Igor, what happened to those people? I mean after the Crew found out the couldn't be educated?"

Igor seemed to fidget, something that Charlie had never seen Igor do before. It dawned on Charlie that his overhasty curiosity had made him rush into an area of knowledge that was supposed to be hidden from him. Charlie got scared. He was tinkering with somebody's cover-up.

"Hello, Charlie," the voice said. The Proctor had come, like a shark rising toward a disturbance in the water.

Charlie resisted the impulse to tear the sound-and-vision helmet from his head. "Greetings!" he said heartily.

"The Crew does not know how the previous human recruits were removed from the Ark," the Proctor said.

"Sure, Proctor. That's okay!"

"I am the Proctor," the voice buzzed. "It is my function to insure mission performance despite Crew recalcitrance. The Crewpersons concerned were reluctant to terminate those previous recruitment attempts."

That's right, Charlie thought. The Charonese couldn't swat a fly on purpose, if they could help it. That's why there's a Proctor. To do the dirty work.

"The humans would have become a pest in the biome. Therefore, I destroyed them. I also erased those Charonese who learned about my existence at that time. Fortunately, there were only thirteen of them."

Charlie, drawn tight with horror, waited to hear more, but the

Proctor's remarks were finished. *Jesus, now I know what will happen to everybody if we don't do what it wants.*

Charlie's guts churned as he walked through the run-down corridors of his palace, on his way to deal with Bill and Curt. His head hurt, too, where the mug had hit him. He yearned to tell someone, to share the revelation that the Proctor had murdered hundreds of people and a dozen Charonese. He no longer thought of himself as a conqueror. He was just a small person who'd bitten off more than he could chew. But, he thought, his knees wobbling, he had to go on with his escape project, even knowing that the penalty for failure would be mass death. The alternative was slavery forever.

He came to the entrance of the dungeon. Armor-plated gargoyles clanked to attention and saluted. They were just animated dummies. His real soldiers were down in one of the shops, having their hydraulic fluid changed.

Two days previously, the Proctor had surprised him by interrupting his learning programs to inform him that the students at Faulty Towers were rebelling, refusing to work.

Charlie had gone cold. "Uh, wha-what are you going to do about it, Proctor?"

"I am asking you to deal with the problem."

Charlie considered asking the Proctor what it would do if he refused, then thought better of it. *Those people are the only friends I've got, even if they all hate me.* "All right, Proctor. I'll take care of it."

"Good, Charlie," the fly buzz said. "It is why I selected you."

"Right on, Proctor. Just leave it to me."

Charlie had made plans for a student uprising in his more carefree days. All he'd had to do was parade his Red Slayers onto the choppers, fly to the scene, and grab the first two people his robots could get their claws on. He'd brought the hostages back to the palace and locked them up tight. Staging the TV horror show afterward had been more difficult.

The way to the cells was through the torture chamber. It had everything: stone walls, ropes, chains, horrific implements, dramatic lighting, TV cameras, and a victim. The dummy Bill Bradley hung from a rack, its plastic skin still beaded with clear oil. The oil was to make it look sweaty. The electrical burns really were real. The dummy could bleed, too, but Charlie no longer wanted to see that. It had been enough, seeing all the blood and guts when the deinocheirus pulled the other dummy, the one of Curt, through the bars of the cage. It had been a hell of a TV show, and it had gotten the desired results from the Faulty Towers gang, but . . .

"I'm weirded out," he said.

"Right on, sir," the butler said, holding open the door leading to the cells.

"Hi, Bill. Hi, Curt."

"Fug you, Charlie. Blow it out your pants, Charlie." Bill and the other hostage, Curt, didn't look up from the old football game they were watching together on TV.

Charlie sat down in a chair and inspected the boys' cell through a wall of glass a yard thick. "The place would be a lot neater if you'd make the beds and put your dirty trays in the slot," he said. They ignored him. Crowd roar from the football game filled the air, and the announcers sounded like dogs barking.

Charlie switched off the TV at a panel in the arm of his chair. The boys' eyes tightened with annoyance, but they made no other reaction.

"Listen, you guys," Charlie said. "I want to talk to you about something. It's to your benefit—"

"Let us out, Charlie. Then we'll talk to you about anything you want."

"I can't do that. You won't listen to me."

"Yes, we will. Won't we, Bill?" The boys laughed.

"Come on," Charlie pleaded. "You act like you don't realize what's happening to you. We've been hijacked into outer space. If we'd been hijacked by human terrorists, no matter how crazy they were, we'd be on Earth, and there's be some hope of getting home. But this is space, don't you understand? Even the Charonese can't get us back, not without our help."

Charlie's hostages sat and looked at him. He went on. "This world we're in now, it's alive. It wants us to learn how to use it; it'll help us do it. Just think, all this technology, it's hundreds of years ahead of the human race. With what we could learn here, we could stop war, feed the hungry, explore the universe. We're trapped here, and the only way to get out is to do what it wants until we're ready to take over—"

"Sorry, Charlie!"

"Yeah, Charlie, come on in and show us how to do it!"

Charlie stopped himself. The Proctor could be listening, and he'd already said too much. "Listen," he said earnestly. "Don't you ever wonder what the, the Charonese will do to us if we don't—"

"He's chickenshit," Bill said. "He always was a wimp, and a fat little chickenshit, back at school. How's that bump on your head, Charlie?"

"Why're you saying that about me?" Charlie said. "You didn't even know me, back in school. I'm not hurting you; I'm keeping you and everybody else alive."

"Sure you are, Charlie," Bill jeered.

"I could hurt you!"

"Sure you could!"

Charlie forgot himself. "M-my robots could! They could make you scream with pain!"

"Right, Charlie. I'm scared, Charlie."

Charlie sat rigid in his chair, all his fear, rage, and frustration washing over him, all the sadistic imaginings of an immature lifetime of reading, movies, and TV straining to burst out: whips, needles, acids, blades, fire. A few shouted orders to his robots would be enough.

Bill and Curt watched, fascinated, as Charlie turned white and red, pressed his lips together and emitted an absurd sputter. They yelled with laughter. "Yaa-ha, Charlie! That's really scary, Charlie!"

Charlie jumped out of his chair and hurried out of the cells, through the torture-chamber set, past the model of Bill Bradley contorted on the iron framework. The dummy's glass eyes seemed to follow Charlie as he went past.

"You know what gets me, Igor?"

"No, sir."

"The damn ingratitude!"

"Very good, sir."

Chapter Fourteen:

Mrs. Robinelli Is a Fighter

That night, rain poured down on Faulty Towers. Cold water sheeted off the flat rooftops, washing away the season's accumulation of dust, dead leaves, and pine needles. It spattered noisily on the apartment balconies, made the stairways slippery, and gurgled cheerfully in the courtyard drains. After months of heat and dust, the damp coolness would have been a profound relief if anyone had been in the mood to enjoy it.

Emma lay on the bed in her apartment, the ache in her side and the noise of the rain keeping her awake. Charlie was out there somewhere, she thought, *probably thinking about his visitation upon the human colony, just as I am. He's probably alone, like me.* Emma had known Charlie and Eva for years, and she couldn't visualize the two of them cooperating in anything.

It was also difficult for her to imagine Charlie as a torturer.

Her sound-and-vision helmet lay beside her. She pulled it over her head and said "Gamma."

The eyepiece screens in the helmet showed a view of her room, as seen from the terminal on the wall. Emma grinned morosely at the image of herself lying on the bed, flat as an ironing board and tall enough to protrude head and foot.

Gamma had never taken this long to answer before. "Index," Emma said.

The mechanical voice came on instantly: "Working." The picture in the helmet changed to glowing columns of print, the names of the major categories of data available to the humans. It seemed to Emma as though there were many, many more items on the list than she'd ever seen before.

"Real-time contact with Gamma," Emma said.

"Reference Gamma is not in catalog file."

That was odd. Why would the Crew in charge of educating the humans not be available right at the moment when they were all being forced to return to their studies? Emma tried Gamma's two assistants.

"Real-time contact with Delta or Epsilon."

"Reference Delta and reference Epsilon are not in catalog file."

Emma scowled inside the helmet. When the Index said that a subject wasn't in the catalog file, it meant that a program or a record didn't exist. Gamma had told her that, back when the female alien was teaching Emma how to use the Ark computer.

"Index, play back record of the previous ten hours here at the residence facility."

"Working," the Index said. After a moment it announced that no record of the past ten hours existed. Emma checked again. To her surprise, she was able to make the Index play back everything picked up by the Faulty Towers terminals and surveillance cameras every hour since their arrival. She hadn't even known such a thing was possible. It was as though some prohibition had been removed from the Ark records.

Hundreds of conversations, quarrels, and interludes zoomed past her eyes and ears. It was the Charonese view of the monkey cage. She saw two teenagers sharing the last of a marijuana joint. She saw Colby Dennison knocking softly on Lena Gershner's door in the middle of the night. She saw Peake talking in a fatherly manner to one of the girls, and gently pushing her out of his bed.

She quashed the urge to spy, and went ahead to the time of Charlie's helicopter raid. It wasn't there. It was as though the Ark computer had been barred from knowing about it, or as though the memory of it had been lost.

Emma was too tired and sore to think about it anymore. She removed the helmet from her head and painfully eased herself back down on the bed. The downpour outside had slacked off for a few minutes, but now it was coming down as hard as ever.

When Emma woke, the "sun" was coming and going through torn clouds. It was late. Someone had left half a melon and some cold cuts on a covered dish outside her apartment door.

She ate, then took the elevator to ground level. The sandy soil was damp and resilient underfoot, and there was an irresistible freshness in the air. She hobbled, leaning on her stick, to the garden, where the students were rebedding the plants torn up by the storm. Peake looked up from his hoeing and smiled. "Hi, Emma. How are you this morning?"

"Thank you, I'm better."

"Me, too. This monsoon, or whatever it is, means we don't have to move the goddamn irrigation pipes around the garden anymore. My hernia woke me up this morning early, just to thank me." A feeble laugh went up from the nearest students.

Peake set down his hoe. "That reminds me," he said. "Have I got a deal for you guys!" he said loudly, looking around the garden. The students looked up glumly.

With a flourish, Peake drew a flat brown package from his overall pocket and held it up. "I have here, ladies and gentlemen, the one, the only, the last Hershey Bar on Charon!" He drew it under his nose, sniffing and squinting ecstatically. "Aaah!"

The faces scattered around the garden lost a little of their bitterness. Peake went on. "Yes, friends, this little bit of heaven can be yours! This Hershey Bar will be presented to whomever can provide the best answer to the question "How many Charonese does it take to change a light bulb?" Submissions will be judged by the entire assembly, and the prize will be held by the incorruptible Mrs. Emma Robinelli! Your favorite and mine! Thank you."

Peake bowed, and handed the candy to Emma with a theatrical flourish. "No nibbling, now, Mrs. Robinelli," he said.

She snorted. "Ouch! Oh, dear! Please don't make me laugh!"

The teenagers, many of them smiling, went back to their work.

"Lena's been waiting to talk to you, Emma," Peake said softly, as he picked up his hoe. "It's important." He nodded toward a scrub oak thicket on the near side of the garden.

To Emma's surprise, Gershner was wearing an expression of suppressed exultation. Before Emma could say anything, Gershner held up a slab of pine bark. Letters were carved on its smooth underside:

WILL WAIT FOR YOU AFTER DARK OUTSIDE SW CORNER
OF PERIMETER 10 NIGHTS. IF YOU CANT COME BLINK
LIGHTS IN HIGHEST S WINDOW. WE ARE FREE & OK.

FROWARD & SUAREZ.

Emma staggered. Gershner dropped the slab and caught her
before she fell. "Are you all right? Do you want to sit down?"

"I'm better standing," Emma gasped. Gershner steadied her
against a pine trunk and gave her the slab.

Emma read and reread the message, too amazed to think.
"Good heavens! They're alive. It's almost too much to believe!"

Gershner showed her perfect white teeth, smiling or snarling.
"You know what this means, Emma? Froward and that girl—
what's her name?—are alive. They can help us. We still have a
chance to win?"

"Good heavens!" Emma repeated. "Where did you find it?"

"It was lying out there in the garden. I was the first to come
out this morning, and I found it. Peake is the only other one I've
told about it so far."

Gershner ran her finger over the message. "'Free and okay'
must mean the Charonese don't know about them, and they can
move around. 'Perimeter' must mean the fence, and SW stands
for southwest. I don't know which way is southwest, but—"

"It's that way," Emma said, gesturing.

"Peake and I think we should try to meet them tonight. Do
you feel up to it?"

"I wouldn't miss it for anything." Emma looked up through
the pine foliage. Heavy clouds had drawn overhead, and thunder
crackled. In the silence that followed, she heard the youngsters
talking as they worked in the garden. In the distance, some bird
or animal whistled the same note monotonously. The top of the
steel-girder fence was visible among the treetops in the distance.
"It's going to rain," said Emma. "I wonder where they've been.
What have they been doing?"

"What's the use of speculating about that?" Gershner said impatiently. "Try to think of some way we can make use of this
opportunity. Jeff has found out how to survive outside. It might
be possible to hit the Charonese from behind." She grimaced.
"Besides, I know Jefferson Froward. I don't have to guess what
he's been up to with that little teenybopper. Trying, anyway."

"She's not a teenybopper," Emma said, speaking carefully. "Her name is Chela. She was a new student, but she showed signs of being a very bright, emotionally mature, and self-sufficient young woman."

Gershner angrily looked away.

"Let's not quarrel," Emma said. "We should be thankful they're alive."

"Okay, fine," Gershner said.

Thunder sounded again, and it began to drizzle. Both women stood with their arms wrapped around their bodies. Emma shivered. "You'd better go back inside," Gershner said, taking her arm. "Come on, I'll get someone to go with you."

That afternoon the learning programs appeared on the students' apartment terminals, each program taking up where its user had left off before the rebellion. Emma, fortified by a hot lunch and a nap, went from apartment to apartment. The students told her that the programs were as usual, but Gamma, Delta, and Epsilon were not there to answer questions and make comments, as they had always been before. Emma returned to her own terminal and called the Index.

"Working."

"Real-time contact with any Crew member."

After a long delay, a voice said in Emma's helmet, "I hear you. I see you."

A kind of cloud hung in Emma's vision, a shifting pattern of blue hues superimposed on the image of herself seated at her terminal. The Charonese was sending a visual signal that might have meant something to another Charonese. Emma only knew that this wasn't Gamma.

"What is your name, please?" Emma asked.

After a minute's pause, the Charonese said, "You call me Zeta. Wait. I am learning your language."

"Thank you," Emma said automatically. The Crewperson didn't answer.

Another minute went by. Emma sat wringing her hands in her lap. Just as she was about to interrupt the silence, Zeta said, "There are many discrepancies, Mrs. Robinelli."

"Yes, there are," Emma said. "I want to ask you about them. Where are Gamma and her two assistants?"

"I have asked all other Crewpersons. They do not know."

It seemed to Emma that Zeta was becoming agitated. But it was impossible to be sure. It had taken Gamma weeks to learn to express her emotions to Emma. "Do you have any hypotheses about it?" she asked.

"There is the possibility that physical damage to the Ark computer circuitry caused the loss of Gamma, Delta, and Epsilon. One moment, please. Now. It is confirmed that there is no circuitry damage. Mrs. Robinelli. Mrs. Robinelli."

"I hear you, Zeta."

"It is as though those Crew have been erased. It is impossible!"

"What other discrepancies do you notice, Zeta?"

"A block of records from yesterday has been erased."

"Anything else?"

"No. What information can you provide?"

She, or he, Emma thought, hasn't noticed the hostages being gone. She carefully described Charlie's raid.

When she finished, Zeta said, "It is impossible. To do that, Charlie Freeman would have to have entire factories at his disposal. He would also have to be able to screen his activities from the Crew. That would be impossible. It would be as though part of your own body were invisible and unfelt, but at war with yourself. That Ark, and all things in it, is our body, Mrs. Robinelli. It is as though your hand had risen up against you in the night, and stabbed out your eyes. Therefore some other explanation must be found."

Emma nodded silently. It would take a long time to convince a human, a rational, educated human, that is, that his body was inhabited by a demon.

"Charlie has help," Emma said. "Some Charonese entity is helping him."

"There is no such entity."

"Gamma was very interested in something called the Proctor, that Charlie mentioned to some other students," Emma said.

"Gamma's memories have been lost, but I have reviewed the records she made," Zeta said. "Gamma hypothesized that Proctor was Charlie's name for the one you would have called Alpha, the pilot of the spacecraft that brought you to the Ark. Or perhaps it was a fantasy or fiction of Charlie's. Gamma said that humans invent fictions for their amusement, or to deceive other humans."

Emma had forgotten the ache in her side. At home, she loved

to read murder mysteries, the kind where the detective confronts the suspects in the room where the crime took place. "Yet something did erase three Crew members," she said. "Let us call it the Proctor."

"What is a Proctor! It is impossible that there could be a Proctor."

"Tell me," she said, "is there no insanity among Crew members? No pathology?"

After a long hesitation, Zeta said, "There have been cases."

"What do you do about it?"

Another hiatus followed, and then Zeta spoke. "In cases where pathology of a Crew member threatens the Ark, a unanimous volition of the entire Crew can cause the erasure of one of us."

"Could Proctor be a renegade Crew member?"

"Proctor cannot be a Crew member. We live, as it were, in a single room. Our thoughts are shared; none of our actions can be concealed."

"An insane human can commit a crime, then cause himself to forget having done it," Emma said. "Couldn't some Crew member find a way to do that?"

"An insane human can do that because a human is alone in his or her brain," Zeta said. "If other, sane humans were able to watch every thought and every action of the insane one, he could not commit a crime without their knowledge. That is how we are, Mrs. Robinelli. We all live together in the same brain, the Ark computer."

"Look," Emma said. "Suppose I had access to the circuitry of the Ark computer. If I knew how, couldn't I do everything that Proctor has done, then destroy the memory of it by physically altering the computer circuits that held the memory?"

"Yes, you could, Mrs. Robinelli," the alien said. "But that is because you are hardware. You are mind and body in an independent physical entity. We do not know your thoughts. We cannot control your body. We Crew are software. We live in the computer. Our substance is nothing, only a pattern of electrical current in the computer. There can be no Proctor."

"The Proctor could be an independent physical entity, separate from the Ark computer, but with access to it."

"No being could live so long!"

"Why can't you accept it!" Emma shouted. Without wanting to, she remembered the enstrangement that had come between herself and Gamma. Gamma had been the closest thing to a friend Emma'd had among the aliens. Gamma had blamed Emma for forcing her to commit an act of violence. Even though Emma had been the one who'd been injured, she had understood the alien's feelings. Gamma had been murdered before Emma had been able to make it up with her.

"A computer could live that long," she said angrily. "Not a program in a computer, like you. I mean the computer itself, with the program built into it. We call that a hard-wired device. The Proctor is itself a computer. It's somewhere on the Ark. It must have been here, hidden from you, since the beginning!"

"Yes. No. I must consult with another Crew person. One moment, please."

Another voice spoke up in Emma's earphones. "I am Beta. I have heard a playback of your arguments."

"Are you convinced yet?"

"Wait. We must discuss."

There was a long pause. Some discussion, Emma thought. Views were being exchanged at the speed of thought, yet it took so long. She had never imagined the Charonese in such a state. Maybe fear would bring them around. Maybe they would—

"Mrs. Robinelli."

"Yes?"

"Your analysis is correct, Mrs. Robinelli. We are now forced to surrender to you, Mrs. Robinelli."

Emma's mouth dropped open. "What?"

"The Crew will concede all issues after I explain the Proctor to them. There is a condition."

"What condition?"

"You humans do not reside in the Ark computer. You are the only ones who can help us. We beg for your assistance, Mrs. Robinelli. We will return you to your homes. We will contact your governments, or do anything else you wish. We are very, very afraid!"

Emma's mind raced. She'd have to call in Peake and Gershner. Suddenly, a deafening squawk in her earphones. "Mrs. Robinelli! Beta is gone! I am—!"

The blue pattern in Emma's eyepieces vanished.

"Zeta? Beta?"

There was no answer. Emma said, "Index."

"Working."

"Real-time contact with Zeta or Beta."

"Reference Zeta and reference Beta are not in the catalog file."

Emma tried to put her hands to her mouth and was stopped by the blank front of her input-output helmet. Oh, my God, she thought, what have I done to them?

She sat listening to the silence in her earphones as the afternoon wore on into evening, and the evening into night. At last she had to give up. It was time to go out, to meet the two survivors, Froward and Chela.

At Faulty Towers, two people stood guard during the hours of darkness. It wasn't clear what they were guarding against, but the students in their scattered apartments slept more comfortably knowing that someone was pacing the terraces and balconies, keeping an eye on the night. Adults and teenagers shared the job equally, and Mr. Peake was in charge of the schedule.

This made it easy for Peake to jiggle the roster, insuring that Reilly and Emma Robinelli were the ones on duty that night.

"What is it? Where are we going?" the boy asked.

Emma, a stiff, grim old lady in a body cast, leaned heavily on Reilly as the two of them made their way down the pitch-black stairway to the ground level. "Reilly, we have to keep silent now, please," she said.

"Why are you so upset? Is it more bad news?" Reilly whispered.

She shook her head.

"Okay, Mrs. Robinelli."

Gershner and Peake were waiting for them under the pines where the light from the dining hall windows didn't reach. "That you?" Peake called softly at them as Emma and the boy hobbled across the damp sandy ground.

"Hey, man, it always is," Reilly whispered back, getting into the spirit of things.

"Quiet!" Gershner whispered. "Come on!"

She led them onto the path to the garden. Twenty paces away from the base of the Towers, the path became invisible. Gershner switched on a flashlight, holding her fingers over the lens, then switched it off again. The group walked silently over a carpet of wet pine needles. Frantic peeping announced mating season in the marsh around the fish pond, and night bugs twittered closer by. Something scuttled over the toe of Emma's boot.

Squashy ground and the smell of dinosaur manure signaled their arrival at the garden. Gershner stepped quickly over rows of vegetables and stopped at the fence. With a great deal of grunting and scuffling, the party pulled up a section of barbed wire mesh and crawled between a pair of steel uprights.

"It's so dark, I can't tell whether I have my eyes open or not," Peake murmured.

"Just lead us away from the fence," Gershner hissed at him.

"Lions and tigers and bears, oh, my—"

"Shut up, you idiot!"

"Yes, please do, Mr. Peake," Emma begged.

The group moved slowly ahead. Emma, completely blind, clung to Reilly. The boy walked with his hands out in front of himself, like a cartoon sleepwalker. Cold water dripped from invisible branches down Emma's neck whenever they blundered into something.

"Someone's coming!" Peake hissed. They halted, bumping heads. Emma strained to hear. From the blackness in front came the measured pacing of a man walking cautiously through a dark forest. The noise stopped.

"Is it a dinosaur?" Reilly quavered.

"Don't worry," Emma whispered. "Dinosaurs were daytime animals."

Gershner switched on her light: the beam lit up a demonic stick figure, like a naked ostrich with elbows. It jerked upright, gaped toothily, then leaped away into the darkness, leaving Emma with an afterimage of talons, a lizard tail, and huge green-glowing eyes.

"Except that one," Peake whispered. "I really think we should make more noise; then we won't keep running into—"

"Quiet! Shh!"

Something else was approaching. They all held their breaths. Emma blinked, mentally cursing her glasses. It seemed that a faintly shimmering letter X was floating through the trees toward the group.

"An off-brand ghost," Peake whispered.

"Peake!" a man said in the darkness, excited but keeping his voice low. A tall shadow fell on Peake, laughing and slapping his back. "Peake! I can't believe it! Boy, oh, boy, it's good to see you! And Mrs. Robinelli, and Lena!"

"I can't see you, Jeff!" Peake said.

Froward laughed. "It's just a figure of speech. I can barely make you out."

Emma, who couldn't see anything, felt herself included in a general embrace. "Come on, we're parked over here." Froward said.

With hands linked, they allowed Froward to lead them through the woods. "Chela and I've got tricks for living in the dark," he said. "See? I drew an X on my chest with luminous fungus, and marked a path with it, too." Emma looked down and saw dim smears on the ground. Ahead, a constellation of it hung in the air, apparently smeared on a flat surface.

"This is our little armor-plated wreck-vee," Froward said. "We'll talk inside. Put your hands up, in case you bump your head on the door."

Emma was led up a ramp into an enclosed space and made to sit down on dry straw.

"Soon as I get the door closed, we'll turn on the lights," Froward said. "Sit tight a minute."

An electric motor hummed for fifteen seconds, and stopped with a thump. Lights came on. Emma found herself inside a rectangular metal box thirty feet long and ten feet wide, piled deep with dry grass and leaves, cluttered with metal pipe, coils of wire, and bits of machinery. The walls were scratched or daubed with clay and pinesap: crude calendars, lists of things, a poor drawing of a man and woman. Blackened lumps of meat, some with scaly hide still attached, swung against the artwork. The place smelled of wood smoke, dried herbs, and dubious meat.

A brown man scissored his long bare legs out of an opening in the front wall of the compartment. "That's where the light switch is; in there," he said.

He flopped down in the deep hay pile opposite Emma. His clothes were brown rags. His bald forehead showed above a plaited leather headband that held back the gray hair that hung over his ears. His grizzly beard parted for a crooked smile. "My God, Emma, you're a sight for sore eyes. You, too, Lena."

"I'd have said the same about you, Jeff," Emma said, noticing the deep scars on his naked chest and shoulder.

Avoiding Emma's and Gershner's eyes, he leaned forward and reached out a hand to Reilly, who was sitting next to Emma, his eyes big. "I'm sorry, son; I remember you, but not your name. Welcome, anyway."

"I'm Reilly, Mr. Froward," the boy said, shaking hands.

"Where's the Suarez girl?" Gershner said.

"She's, ah, outside, making sure you weren't followed, and that we're not showing any lights."

A small, round figure swung lithely into the compartment through the front entrance. Reilly's eyes got bigger. Like Froward, Chela wore ragged brown shorts, the remnants of a pair of overalls, and a vest made of sewn-together skins of some small mammal. Her black mop of hair was pinned back with crisscrossed bone skewers, bands of animal claws tinkled faintly on her bare arms, and a necklace of polished brass cartridges embedded in patterned reptile leather hung around her neck.

Peake openly admired the girl's figure as she hung her grenade launcher on the wall and knelt in front of Emma to look in her face. "Oh, Mrs. Robinelli, aren't you glad to see us?" she said.

Emma put her hand on the girl's cheek. "Of course I am, dear. It's just that we've had some bad experiences recently."

Chela sat down beside Froward, holding his arm and leaning possessively against him. She studied Gershner for a moment, then looked back and Emma with clear brown eyes.

"Ahem. Well," Froward said. He shuffled his heavy, scratched-up workboots in the litter on the floor. "I, uh, hardly know where to start."

"How'd you get away from the Charonese, Jeff?" Peake asked.

"We didn't get away; they just seemed to forget about us. The last time you saw Chela and me, we were going up the cable-pipe in that electric car. At about twenty thousand feet, the car got derailed in a snowbank. It took us the rest of the day to walk back to the ground. When we got there, we found Milanovitch and that boy dead. We thought the rest of you'd been captured, so we hid out during the night—"

"Helicopters came and took away the bodies and the rest of

the baggage that was left behind," Chela said. "But we stayed hid."

"That's right, hon, I mean Chela," Froward said, patting her hand. "The next day we started following the tracks of the vehicles leading away from there. We came to the place where it looked like you were picked up by helicopter."

"That's right," Peake nodded. "We were."

"Jeff was practically killed by some dinosaurs, but I saved him," Chela said.

"She sure did," Froward agreed, grinning like a child. "She's a great doctor. Anyway, we've had some amazing experiences. We came to an ocean—"

Gershner interrupted him. "Did you have any encounters with the Charonese?"

"We haven't had any contact with the Charonese at all, except for seeing some metal poles with cameras on them."

"Where did you get this truck thing?"

"Chela found it lost in some brush. It's a combination robot and truck. Its antenna had been knocked off—"

"That's probably why it was paralyzed," Emma said. "It lost radio contact with the Ark central computer. You've been driving it?"

Froward laughed. "All over the landscape! Chela and I figured it out. Have you seen the dinosaurs? They—"

"We'll hear about your adventures later, Jeff," Gershner said.

"Yes, Jeff, I'm sorry," Emma said. "Would you show me how it works, please?"

"The machinery is in here," Froward said, looking abashed as he got up and led her to the forward compartment. "This seems to be a turbine and generator, and the power comes from this cylinder, here, although I'll be damned if I know what it is."

"It's a magnetic bottle," Emma said. "It's loaded with hydrogen gas, compressed to a superconducting metal. Fortunately, you didn't do anything that turned off its magnetic field. We would've heard the bang all over Charon. Do you have any idea how much fuel is left in it?"

"Well, no—"

Emma pulled her head out of the compartment and returned to her place next to Reilly and Gershner. "I have something to tell all of you," she said. "This afternoon, two of the Charonese offered to surrender to me. They said they were ready to help us get back to Earth if we would help them."

Gershner and Peake went slack with amazement.

"They want us to help them against Charlie and the thing that's been helping him, the Proctor."

"I don't follow you," Gershner said, plainly showing her impatience. Comprehension dawned on Peake's and Reilly's faces. Froward looked from one to the other in complete bewilderment. Chela clung to his arm more tightly.

Emma spoke soberly. "Gamma and four other Charonese are dead. As best as I can determine, that leaves only eleven of them in the Ark computer memory."

"What do you mean, dead?" Gershner asked.

"Ark?" Froward said.

"That's what they call this," Peake said. "I mean—"

"The Charonese call Charon the Ark, because it is a kind of ship, full of rare animals," Emma said. "We'll fill you in on the details later, Jeff."

Froward looked crestfallen. Emma continued. "The Ark is run by a central computer. Or, rather, the Charonese run the Ark, and they exist as programmed personalities in the computer. To erase one of these programs is to murder the Charonese it represents. I suspect that all the Charonese are in great danger."

"How could the Charonese be in danger?" Gershner said. "Surely the Charonese don't let us know everything about their computer. Maybe they're just hiding."

"They have no motive for hiding from us," Emma said. "No. What I think happened is, the Proctor erased Gamma and her two assistants because they were watching when Charlie arrived in his helicopters. Then the Proctor erased Zeta and Beta after I explained what happened to them. The Proctor must be programmed to do anything necessary to conceal itself from the Charonese. The mere fact that a teenage child is building and controlling dozens of robots and aircraft is a dead giveaway that the Proctor exists."

Gershner blinked. "What's the Proctor?"

"That's what Charlie called it. Charlie said the Proctor is some sort of being or entity that exists on Charon along with the Charonese, but hidden from them."

"That's right, Mrs. Robinelli," Reilly said.

"I thought we decided that was some sort of fantasy of Charlie's," Gershner said.

"That's what the Charonese decided," Emma said. "Not me. I think the Charonese have a psychological tendency, if you want to call it that, to disbelieve anything they hear about the Proctor. The Proctor may be tampering with their personalities. I know it can delete sections of memory from the big computer. It wiped ten hours out of yesterday's records, so no knowledge of Charlie can get to the other Charonese. I believe that the Proctor automatically wipes out any Charonese who finds out about its existence. It erased Zeta and Beta while was talking to them. It was awful. Zeta and Beta were terrified. They were begging me for help." Emma shook her head and sat looking at her hands.

"They deserve everything that happens to them," Gershner said. "Let it be God's punishment on them."

"Why does the Proctor erase the Charonese who find out about it?" Peake asked.

Emma looked up. "To protect itself. The Proctor is a separate computer. The Charonese could send robots to destroy it or isolate it. The Proctor can be damaged or destroyed without harming the Ark central computer. I'd like to know why there's a Proctor on the Ark in the first place. What is its purpose?"

"Charlie mentioned something about that," Reilly said. "He said it was a kind of policeman, to make the Charonese do what they were supposed to do, even if they didn't want to."

"If I understand what you're saying, Emma," Gershner said, "we could kill the Charonese just by telling them about the Proctor."

"If I'm right," Emma said.

"Well, why don't we try it?"

"I wouldn't dare," Emma said. "This is an artificial world. Who knows how many Charonese it takes to run it? The sun might go out, or worse."

"Well," Gershner said, "we can keep it as an alternative."

"I wouldn't consider it," Emma said.

"Regardless," Gershner said. "Now we know who our real enemies are: the Proctor, and the Freeman boy. This robot truck, whatever it is, might give us a way to do something about them."

"It does," Emma said. "I suggest that we put together a group of volunteers to drive this vehicle to Charlie's hideout, where they will do their best to stop him, rescue Eva and any of his other prisoners who're still alive, find out where the Proctor is located, and destroy it."

A slow smile spread over Gershner's face. "You're a fighter, Emma," she said.

"But—but this is all theoretical, Emma!" Peake said. "What if you're wrong?"

Gershner turned on him fiercely. "What difference does it make? What other opportunity do we have? This is the best chance we've had!"

"Won't the Charonese know some of us are missing from Faulty Towers?" Peake asked.

"They don't even realize that the two hostages are gone yet," Emma said. "So there's a chance we can deceive them."

"Okay, I'll buy that part of it," Peake said, still looking astonished. "So how do we find the little booger? You know where Charlie is, Emma?"

"Reilly, you told me that when Charlie left you and Tina and Eva, you were all standing under the lightstack, the big tower where our spaceship landed," Emma said. "Am I right?"

"That's right, Mrs. Robinelli. And Charlie's robot took Eva into the building right at that same place."

Emma turned to the others. "I suspect that the lightstack is at Charon's north pole, not more than ninety miles from here."

"Okay, so that's how we find the little booger," Peake said. "How do we find the big booger?"

"I'll ask Charlie where the Proctor is, myself," Reilly said.

"How do you know he knows?" Peake shot back.

Emma nodded. "Exactly. We aren't even sure Charlie is still at the pole. We need more information, and the only place to get it is from the Ark computer. I'll take care of that." She paused and looked around at all of them. "It's essential," she said, emphasizing the word, "that no one do or say anything that might give away the plan to the Charonese. Remember that the Charonese have eyes and ears everywhere in the apartments. The Proctor can read their thoughts."

"We won't tell anyone, except the ones who're going," Gershner said.

"No, everyone will have to be on it," Peake said. "Everyone

will have to cooperate to keep up an appearance of normalcy after the expedition leaves."

"Correct," Emma said. "It would be best if you and Lena spread the word during gardening hours. Be careful."

"I want to be on the expedition," Gershner said.

"Uh-uh," Peake said, rubbing his chin. "No females. The team has to be as small as possible, so as to make as little disturbance as possible at Faulty Towers. The strongest and fastest and most experienced. Notice, I didn't say smartest. Reilly should go, because he's been there before. Colby Dennison, because he's Mr. Superjock and highly motivated. I should go because I'm really cool and also an engineer."

"You're not leaving me behind," Chela growled from the shadows.

"I'd rather she stayed," Froward said.

"The hell you—"

"We need her experience," Emma said. "And she'd be too conspicuous if we brought her into the residence."

Reilly was jumping with excitement. "When do we go?"

"The sooner the expedition starts, the better the chance of concealment," Emma said. "If everyone agrees, the expedition should leave sometime during the next few nights. All agreed? Good."

For a minute, no one said anything. It was growing warm and stuffy in the metal compartment. Emma didn't feel tired, but her side was hurting her, under her body cast.

"I wish someone would tell me what this is all about," Froward said. Gershner glared at him and Chela across the compartment. Chela stared insolently back.

Peake got up stiffly, scattering straw and dead leaves. "I'll fill you in as we travel, Jeff. Right now, I think we'd better go home, before we're missed any more than we are."

"Quite right," Emma said, getting up. She took Chela's hands. "I know you deserve a better homecoming than this, Chela, dear," she said. Wordlessly, the girl threw her arms around Emma and hugged her hard, making her gasp. She held on to Emma until Froward turned off the lights and opened the vehicle's rear door, letting in the damp and a whiff of pine.

Emma allowed Peake and Reilly, led by Chela, to hand her down the ramp in the darkness. "Wait here, Mrs. Robinelli,"

Chela murmured in her ear. "I'll take you back to the fence two at a time." She heard Chela and the two men moving off through the vegetation.

Emma stood quietly, beginning to be able to see the outlines of the pines and the bulk of the vehicle against the sky. She heard angry whispering. "That's typical of you, typical, Jeff! While the rest of us were fighting for our lives!"

Froward's voice was apologetic, perplexed. "Damn it, Lena, what do you expect, I—"

"I don't expect you to commit statutory rape! A child, for God's sake!"

"Well, she, I—"

Gershner walked down the ramp, her shoes thumping on the metal. She bumped into Emma in the dark, seized the old lady to keep her from falling down. "And you, Emma!" she whispered angrily. "One of your students, and you act like it didn't happen."

Emma felt herself growing hot with embarrassment. "Things are different now, Lena."

"They're too much the same, for some of us!"

Chela materialized at Emma's elbow. "Stuff it," she ordered. "Let's go."

It began to rain in earnest as Emma and Gershner were passing through the fence. They reached the elevator just in time to avoid being soaked. Gershner stalked off without a word.

"Go on to bed, Reilly," Emma said to the boy. "Mr. Peake will take me to my room."

"Don't you ever sleep, Emma?" Peake said as she closed her apartment door behind them.

"Not tonight." She sat down at her terminal and typed in the voice-instruction command.

"What're you doing?"

"I can't say anything about it. Just go along with whatever I say and do."

"I'm all yours, Emma."

"Thanks," Emma said tensely. She turned back to the terminal screen. "Index, I require medical assistance. My wound has reopened."

"My gosh, Emma, why didn't you say something? Here, let me help you—"

Emma pushed him away. "Just go along, understand?" He stepped back and waited, frowning, while Emma drummed her fingers on the terminal desk. After several minutes, she said, "There, that should be long enough. Now we go to the elevator."

Cool mist blew out of the darkness, wetting the balcony outside Emma's apartment. "I hope nobody sees us," Emma said, letting Peake help her along the slippery pavement.

"Everyone's asleep," Peake said. "And after Charlie's little freak show last night, they don't sleep alone anymore either, although they hide that from you. Would you mind telling me what you're doing?"

"Pretending I'm sick. We're tricking our way into the underground level, where the surgery clinic is. I want to see how far we can get without the Charonese. Now shush!"

The elevator door was open, its light shining like a beacon in the benighted passageway. A wheeled surgical cart stood inside. "It's working," Emma said.

After Peake had helped Emma lie down on the cart, the elevator dropped below ground level to the clinic in Faulty Towers's forbidden basement. The door opened. The surgeon-robots, fixed to the floor in a semicircle, waited, their multiple jointed arms held upright.

As Peake rolled Emma's cart out of the elevator, he tapped her shoulder urgently. When she looked up at him, he pointed surreptitiously to one side. She raised her head for a quick glance. Some of the concrete slabs that walled the clinic off from the rest of the underground level had been moved, leaving gaps large enough for a man to slip through.

A bright light came on in the ceiling over the cart. The voice of the Index came from a speaker in the wall. "Medical procedures are not permitted without the attendance of Crew member Gamma."

Emma, her heart in her throat, said, "Real-time contact with Gamma."

"Reference Gamma is not in catalog file."

"Real-time contact with any Crew member."

"Working."

Emma looked up at Peake. "Keep your fingers crossed."

Several minutes passed. Emma, afraid to say anything but driven by curiosity, raised her head to look through the gaps in the clinic walls. Beyond the gaps was a huge, well-lit space, filled with orderly rows of machines. It looked like a factory, as she expected. About ten yards away lay a heap of suitcases and bundles. It was the baggage the students had brought from the airliner. She looked at Peake, saw he was staring at it avidly.

Peake jumped when another voice came from the speaker. "I see you. I hear you. One moment, while I learn your language."

"Goddamn spookhouse," Peake growled.

After another long delay, the voice said, "By your system of naming, you name me Eta. You are Mrs. Robinelli. You are Mr. Peake. You have requested my attention."

Emma, not wanting to give the Charonese any time to wonder about what they were doing, had her reply ready. "Please remove my body cast, Eta."

"Very well, Mrs. Robinelli." While Emma clung rigidly to the edges of the surgical cart, one of the robots lowered a little whirling saw on the end of a jointed arm and began cutting through the hard plastic.

Emma was sweating. "Eta, are you still there?"

"Yes, Mrs. Robinelli."

"Eta, Gamma mentioned that, someday, we humans would have neurotransducers implanted in out bodies, for direct contact with you and the Ark computer."

"It is Gamma's plan," Eta said.

"Gamma tells me I am ready now. I will have it done to me now, while I'm in the surgery."

"Very well, Mrs. Robinelli."

"You can't do it, Emma!" Peake said.

She clutched at his hand. "I've got to do it. You know why. We need more speed, now that, now that we don't have Gamma to help us understand things. Charlie has had it done already!"

"He has?"

"I saw the wires."

"My God, Emma, how do we know you won't become a slave, or they'll read your mind, or something? How do we know that isn't what happened to Charlie?"

"You read too much science fiction, Mr. Peake."

"I can't stand that junk. Come on!"

"There's no danger of that," Emma said. "Only a small number of sensory nerves are connected—nothing from the central nervous system. It's merely a better version of the sound-and-vision helmets and the armatures."

Apropos of nothing, Eta said, "Gamma is unavailable."

Emma and Peake stared at each other's eyes, waiting tensely for what might happen next. Nothing did.

"Keep talking," Peake said. "It might be better to keep, you know, it, distracted, even if, uh . . . How's this? I have the operation first. You wait a while and see what happens. If I'm okay, then you go ahead. Otherwise, I won't let you do it."

"That's ridiculous."

"What's ridiculous? If it's so safe, what's your objection?"

"You can't prevent me," Emma said.

"Wanna bet?"

In exasperation, Emma slapped the cushion of the surgical cart. "Please remain still, Mrs. Robinelli," Eta's voice remonstrated from the speaker. The robot began cutting the other side of Emma's cast.

"All right, you win," Emma said.

"Good," Peake said. "Eta, I will have the implants instead of Mrs. Robinelli. Show me where to lie down. And I like lots of anesthetic."

"Please remove your clothing, Mr. Peake. There will be a delay while I consult Gamma's record."

Peake began unbuttoning his worksuit as Emma levered herself off the cart. "Emma, you're blushing again. I must say it's flattering."

He lay on the cart in his worn-out undershorts, flinching as the robots, motors whirring and pistons hissing, swabbed, jabbed, cut, and swabbed again. Big-lensed cameras moved over his body. Blood ran in little droplets down his sides, legs, and arms, was blotted up by the robots before it stained the cushion.

Emma forced herself to look on, watching for any signs of faltering or error by the machines, ready to strike away the mechanical arms. Tiny mechanical fingers, no bigger than wires, held apart the incisions in Peake's skin and muscles, while other devices inserted little glittering chips, like metal confetti.

"B-before our experiences here, I would've fainted away at a sight like this," she said, her mouth dry.

"You're doing wonders for my morale," Peake said hollowly.

"I'm sorry!"

"Honest, Emma, I can hardly feel it."

"Thank goodness for that."

After an hour, the robots began to press Peake's wounds together, spraying a clear fluid on his skin. Emma glanced at her watch. The first tint of Charon's prolonged sunrise would soon be appearing up above. "Eta, can you tell me how much longer the operation will take?"

No answer came from the speaker: "Eta? Are you there?" she said, more loudly. Peake was gazing up at her, his face drawn with strain. Emma looked up at the speaker in the ceiling. "Index!"

"Working," said the flat voice from the speaker.

"Is Eta in contact with us now?"

"No, Mrs. Robinelli. Crewperson Eta's attention is directed elsewhere."

"Emma," Peake croaked from the cart. "Have a look around." He moved a finger toward the gap in the clinic wall.

Emma dithered, not wanting to leave him unguarded.

"Go, Emma!"

She abruptly stepped away from the cart. None of the surgeon robots' cameras looked up at her. Quickly, she walked to the wall and slipped through the gap and found herself in a vast, low-ceilinged space, amid rows of machines. Muted thunder came from pumps and blowers. At various places pipes and cables curved up into the ceiling. These were the service lines into the apartments above, she decided, and those rectangular frameworks must be the tracks for the dining hall elevator and the one she and Peake had ridden down on. From the outside, the clinic looked like a box made of movable slabs.

Nearby lay the pile of stuff from the airliner. She went to it, began digging through the suitcases, wrapped bundles, and loose clothing. The baggage had been ransacked; it seemed that women's clothing had been taken. Emma found her own suitcase. Everything was there except a container of Fabergé bath powder her husband had given her as a going-away present.

Emma sniffed in exasperation and pushed her glasses back up her nose; there was nothing useful in the pile. Some distance away, she saw the automobile the students had built earlier. It sprawled, dismantled, in a forest of heavy robot arms. Next to it was a metal table, and more robots and cameras. Something on the table caught her eye. She glanced back at Peake. He was lying on the cart, staring at the ceiling while the robots worked over him. The thumb and forefinger of his visible hand were circled in the "okay" sign.

Emma walked quickly to the table. It resembled the Charonese operating clinic, except that its rubberized surface held an assortment of tape players, portable radios, calculators, and other gadgets, all more or less disassembled. This was the place, Emma decided, where Gamma had examined Earth technology as exemplified by high school students' carry-on baggage. On a shelf under the table was a small pile of magazines and paperback books, including a copy of *Playboy.* Emma pushed these aside and suddenly stopped, her hand half extended. Back in the shadows, but unmistakable, lay several heavy pistols, a gun like a blunderbuss, and boxes labeled AMMUNITION, .45 CAL.

Emma stood upright, strolled back to the baggage pile, picked up her suitcase, dumped it out, and strolled back to the examining bench. When she started back toward the clinic, the weight of the suitcase made her lean sideways.

She was standing inside the clinic exchanging looks with Peake, when the Index said, "The operation is concluded. An input-output wire harness will be delivered to the dining hall fourteen hours from now."

Peake groaned, rolled his legs gingerly off the cart, and stood up. The little cuts on his face were barely visible.

"How do you feel?" Emma asked him, handing him his clothes with one hand while she held the suitcase with the other.

"Sore," Peake said. "I must be literate enough to suit even you, Teacher, now that I'm properly punctuated for the first time in my life."

"Let's get out of here," Emma said.

At noon, two days later, Emma, holding hands with Peake, flew to the "sun." They stood on it, their backs to the stars, and looked at the world turning under their feet.

"There it is," Peake said, somehow pointing down below. "Zoom in on it."

"How?" she said, thrilled to the giddy point of forgetting the seriousness of it, like a silly girl. She knew she was lying on the bed in her apartment, wired to her terminal. Peake was at his own terminal, five rooms and a flight of stairs away from her, but she could feel, feel him holding her close to his side, his voice smiling at her.

"Concentrate on it. Want to see it closer," he said.

She looked to the sides, first. Naturally Peake wasn't there; all she saw was the spindly framework of the sun mirror satellite, and a cluster of telescopes and antennae bathed in the pure white light that the Ark eternally beamed from Pluto.

Peake laughed at her, his voice low, intimate, near her. "Don't look over there," he said. "I'm not there. I'm here." His lips brushed her ear; his hand pressed her waist.

"How do you do that?" she said.

"It's an art," he whispered. "I can teach it to you. I read your output. I send my own. I see the real you, Emma. Did you know you are beautiful?"

"Goodness!"

"Oh, I feel your maidenly blushes, Emma, how sweet you are. This is what it's like, being a Charonese."

"Oh, dear! I mean, s-stop!"

Peake laughed. "Okay, back to business. See down there, almost directly under us? A little gray speck?"

Below, a chasm opened in the clouds, revealing multiple hues of green and tan. A tiny rectangle caught her eye, an artifact on the wilderness surface of Charon.

"Now we zoom in on it," Peake said. Emma gasped as they swooped down for a closer look. She knew she was only looking through a telescope, and a camera, and the stereo eyepieces in her sound-and-vision helmet, but she couldn't help herself.

Now she looked down on a little white complexity, like a toy dropped on a carpet. Next to it, the carpet was scuffed and showed its green threads. "It's Faulty Towers, and the garden!" she said, enthralled.

"Right," Peake said. "This picture is real-time. If you wanted to, you could step out on your balcony, look up, and wave hello to yourself. Now look at this."

The view drew back, so that she could see the entire hemisphere again. A grid of latitude and longitude lines appeared on it, then, thousands of multicolored dots, some moving, others in regular geometrical arrays. "I'm not sure what the colors and symbols mean," Peake said. "But the whole thing is a kind of graph of Crew activity. Notice the blank area around the north pole."

"I see," Emma said.

"There's too much cloud over at the pole for a direct view, but I was able to tap into this." Like the blink of an eye, the scene changed to a view inside a factory, with machines spinning and stroking all around. "You okay, Emma?"

"Yes, I-I'm fine. It just makes me dizzy."

"You'll get used to it," Peake said. "Now, then. I can't control this view. It's not real-time; it's a record. It has the earmarks of an accidentally leaked signal, and I'm positive it's from a factory at the pole. I think you'll be positive, too, when you double-check my research."

The camera swiveled to the side, and Emma saw a robot pull what looked like a suit of black plastic long johns out of a machine. "The machines are making clothes," said Peake. "I wish we had them working for us."

The robot hung the long johns on a rack with other garments, then rolled out of sight. Motion in the picture froze, and the viewpoint zoomed in on a platform under a set of manipulating arms and cameras. "I stopped the picture so you could see this," Peake said. "It looks like that examining bench you saw under Faulty Towers, doesn't it?"

"Yes, it does," Emma murmured.

"Well, this one is out of reach of the Crew, know what I mean? And look what was being examined." The view came closer, magnifying a colorful object lying on top of the bench. The picture was grainy and distorted, but Emma could see what it was. It was a comic book, and Emma could even read the title: JUDGE DREDD.

"Ever hear of that before?"

"It was Charlie's favorite," Emma said.

"I rest my case," Peake said.

Late that night, after another walk through the dripping forest, in the stuffy, humid atmosphere inside Froward and Chela's vehicle, the vote was unanimous: go now.

Chapter Fifteen:
Subversive Statements

"Igor, report on Faulty Towers."

"Yes, sir. Yesterday's quizzes were passed with satisfactory scores. Study and garden work schedules were kept. There were no incidents of sabotage or violence. There were no efforts to make weapons or communications equipment."

"All right," Charlie said, yawning under his sound-and-vision helmet. He was up early again this morning, too worried to sleep well. "Did any of the students make any subversive statements?"

"No, sir."

Charlie brooded, sipping berry juice and alcohol through a straw stuck under the helmet's facepiece. Charlie had programmed Igor to listen for about a dozen words and phrases that might indicate that the Faulty Towers gang was plotting revenge, and labeled them subversive statements. Words like "Charlie," "Proctor," "double-crosser," "traitor," "dipshit." When it came to survival, Charlie had no pride.

It was odd. Apparently, the folks at Faulty Towers weren't bad-mouthing anyone these days, not Charlie, not one another. Charlie would've doubted his programming, if the program hadn't detected so much hatred of himself the first few days after he'd taken the hostages.

Igor "stood nearby," waiting for more orders. Somehow, Igor "looked" more forlorn than usual today.

"Report on hostages, Igor."

Igor said that the hostages had been quiet, they had been studying their assignments on their terminals, and that they had passed their quizzes.

"Okay," Charlie said. "Issue their food and water rations for today, at the usual times."

"Yes, sir," Igor said. Charlie did not regret having to starve Bill and Curt into submission. They deserved it. Besides, it was for their own good. He fully intended to return them to their friends at Faulty Towers when things settled down, whenever that might be. He sipped his drink.

Next, he asked Igor for a report on the progress of his last and most ambitious toy project, a spacecraft/aircraft that he could fly almost on his own.

"The test flights are completed, sir," Igor told him. "The Space Flyer is ready for your use."

Charlie cheered up a little. "That's fine, Igor. What's on today's study schedule?"

"Lesson One of Pre-Calculus Algebra, sir." A textbook seemed to hover in front of his eyes. In fact, it was the same damn textbook that was used at Garfield High fugging School.

"Oh, man," Charlie groaned. "Screw that, Igor."

"Very good, sir."

Charlie thought he needed a break. Furthermore, he would take one right now. A little recreational research, before getting to work. Last night, it had occurred to him that he had, at his fingertips, the answer to one of the most important scientific questions ever. I'm so dumb, he said to himself; I haven't thought of asking it until now.

"Igor, link to Index and answer the following question."

"Yes, sir."

"Why did the dinosaurs become extinct?"

"The dinosaurs are not extinct. Many species persist on the Ark."

"You flaming digital dickhead. I mean, why did they become extinct on Earth?"

After a pause, Igor said, "The wave of extinctions, which took place on Earth approximately sixty-five million years ago, was caused by the accidental touching of the planet's surface by the Ark's interstellar drive exhaust."

Charlie shot upright in his command chair. His helmet eyepieces filled with the scene he'd seen before: the white beam leaving its trail of fire and boiling oceans.

"My God! That *was* the Earth?"

"Yes, sir," Igor said. "The exhaust, which consists of a beam of high-energy charged and uncharged particles—"

"And, it was you, the Charonese, who wiped out the dinosaurs?"

"Yes, sir. It was caused by accidental loss of control of the drive exhaust as the Ark was decelerating past Earth into the sun system. The accident was greatly regretted at the time."

"Bull. Shit." Charlie sipped his drink. "Go ahead, Igor."

"The smoke and cloud cover did not disperse for hundreds of days. Total darkness persisted over much of the Earth for long periods. Freezing temperatures prevailed, even in the tropical regions. Lack of sunlight caused the death of almost all plant life on land and in the oceans."

"My God," Charlie said again. The Earth hung in space in front of him, a white ball streaked with gray smoke trails. The moon seemed to hang back, looking on from a safe distance. Charlie's neurotransducers picked up the emotional overtones: dismay, horror, grief, regret, as the Charonese who had made this record mourned what had happened.

After the skies had cleared, they had sent a reconnaissance spacecraft. Charlie's viewpoint flew over expanses of bare eroded earth, mud-clogged seas, forests of standing dead trees. There were beaches covered with spiral ammonite shells dissolving in acid rain. There were piles of giants' bones half buried in silt. Small birds and mammals foraged in the low, new growth.

Igor lectured on. "The disaster killed off the animals at the tops of the food pyramids. No terrestrial or marine vertebrate species whose adult size exceeded twenty-five kilograms survived, with the exception of crocodilians—"

"Why them?" Charlie interrupted.

"Crocodiles and alligators inhabit freshwater ecosystems, which are based on detritus, not on photosynthesizing plankton, as are marine ecosystems. Only those ecosystems that were based on photosynthesis were damaged beyond recovery."

"Oh," Charlie said.

"After approximately seventy-five years, plant life had largely recovered, but the planet continued relatively empty of animal life—"

"Okay, I've heard enough. Stop!" Charlie said.

The lecture and the pictures cut off, were replaced with the

view of the command center that Charlie would've had if he
hadn't been wearing the helmet.

"Boy," he said. "Now I know!" The dinosaurs had been exter-
minated by accident. He swallowed some more berry juice and
alcohol. "Now, if I understand right, the Ark goes from planet to
planet, spreading life. Every once in a while, it has to, like, restock
its biome from some planet that already has life. Right? Igor?"

"That is correct, sir."

"Okay. You know, I have never asked you to show me any
alien life forms before. Show me an alien planet, and how you
restock the Ark."

The scene in Charlie's eyepieces faded to a view from space
of another Earth-like planet. "Igor, this time spare me the boring
lecture. Just give me a quick overview."

"To hear is to obey, O master." Charlie winced; he hadn't
heard that one in a long time. A succession of scenes followed.
The Ark using interstellar darkness and cold to sterilize itself. A
grotesque landscape with robots gathering soil samples. Bizarre,
fragile air-inflated plants and animals being carried toward a flying wing. ("Wowie," Charlie said.) Life taking hold in the biome:
trees like tethered dirigibles, animals like walking balloon sculp-
tures. The Ark's drive igniting on the surface of a planet-size ball
of ice, the precursor of Pluto. The Ark moving out of the alien
solar system. The beam zapping the hell out of the life-bearing
planet as a parting shot.

"Wait a minute!" Charlie shouted.

"Yes, sir." The picture froze.

"What's this?" Charlie demanded. "Another accident?"

"Yes, sir. It was greatly regretted at the time."

Blindly, Charlie set his glass down on the table beside his
command chair. He didn't feel like having any more. "How many
accidents like this have you had?"

Igor consulted with the Index. "Three thousand five hundred
and forty-four," it said.

Charlie almost fell out of his command chair. "That's outrageous! You're telling me that the Ark has wiped out three thousand—that many, fertile planets—I thought the Ark's mission
was to preserve life!"

"Yes; that is the Ark's mission," Igor said. "Each accident was
greatly regretted at the time."

Charlie felt his world falling apart. He drew a breath, intending to roar out a great denunciation; then he stopped himself. Nobody on Charon gave a shit about denunciations.

"Life on the planets was not wiped out," Igor said. "The dominant species were extinguished, only. Over millions of years, new species arose to take their place. On Earth, for example, mammals have taken the places formerly occupied by dinosaurs."

Charlie's anger was giving way to puzzlement. Igor's story didn't make sense.

"Igor, did you say the Earth was zapped as the Ark was arriving in our, my, solar system?"

"That is correct."

"Well, if Earth got zapped before you arrived, how did you get dinosaurs to stock the biome with?"

A long pause. Charlie felt the hair on the back of his neck crawling. He had blundered into another cover-up.

"Very good, sir," Igor said.

Charlie formulated his next question very carefully. "Igor, summarize the history of the exhaust-beam, uh, accidentally striking planets."

"Yes, sir." After some delay, and some negotiation, Charlie learned that all the zappings had taken place in the last two percent of the Ark's life span, it always happened to planets that were alive before the Ark's arrival, and it had always been done as the Ark was leaving a planetary system, sometimes after restocking.

"Igor, why didn't the Ark depart from our sun system after the Crew had restocked its biome with dinosaurs?"

"After restocking, it was discovered that the Crew was too old to survive the long estimated trip time to a world inhabited by intelligent life, where a new Crew could be recruited. If the Crew failed in interstellar space, the Ark would drift lifelessly. It was decided that the Ark should remain in the sun system indefinitely."

Charlie's science-fictional imagination had no trouble filling in the rest. The Charonese just parked the Ark here, far enough from the sun to keep their fuel supply from melting. And they hung around until they got a lucky break, namely us, the human race.

The only question was, What was the zapping for? Charlie couldn't answer that one, but he knew who was doing it. And when. The Proctor decimated life-bearing planets as the Ark was leaving them behind. The Proctor would do it to Earth, again, if it successfully turned Charlie and his schoolmates into Crew.

My God, Charlie thought, we can't win. If we don't turn into good little Crewpersons, the Proctor will kill us off, then try another planeload of poor assholes. And if we do learn how to run the Ark, and take it to the next star system the way we're supposed to, the Proctor will destroy the human race and most of the rest of Earth life, just as we're leaving.

Charlie's guts cramped painfully. He sat up and removed the sound-and-vision helmet. He began peeling off the tapes that held the neurotransducer wires to his skin. Tears were running down his face. I'm not sick, he thought. It's pure stress. I can't do this by myself anymore.

It was still early in the day. He ordered Igor to notify Eva that he was coming and set off down the corridors to her apartment.

"Hello, Eva. Get up. We're going on an outing."

"Now what?"

"It's just an outing. Now please get ready."

Eva looked up from the rock video she had been watching. "Do I have a choice?"

"Please, Eva, I'm trying to do this nicely."

"Why don't you nicely get lost and stop bothering me?"

"Get out of that dress and put on overalls," Charlie said flatly. He walked to the door. "Be ready in ten minutes, or I'll send in a robot to help you."

"You wish."

Charlie sat on the concrete outside Eva's apartment for an hour. Just as he made up his mind to have her dragged out, she appeared at the door in the worksuit Charlie had tailored for her.

"All right, let's go, if we have to," she said, as she paraded past him.

It was a ten-minute ride from the palace to Charlie's landing strip. Charlie's Ground Rover bounced along the dirt track on its big soft tires, splashing through puddles, little roadrunner dinosaurs skittering in front of it. "This is giving me a headache," Eva said, staying as far away from Charlie as she could get in the passenger seat. "Is it going to take long? I hope you're not going to show me any more filthy animals, or make me listen to any more of your music, like last time."

"No," Charlie said. "This is something special."

The car rolled out onto the concrete pad Charlie used for the aircraft he'd sequestered from the Charonese. "There it is, Eva. The Space Flyer. My own design."

Eva frowned impatiently. "What am I supposed to look at?"

The Rover stopped beside the largest aircraft, a sleek, delta-winged beauty standing on retractable skids, several streamlined bubble canopies clustered around its tapered forward end. The sight of it improved his mood considerably.

He hopped out of the car and held out his hand to Eva. She ignored him and climbed out, eyeing the aircraft and the squad of mechanic robots standing around it. "If you think I'm going to get in that thing with you, you'd better guess again, Charlie."

"It's safe," Charlie said. "I don't fly it; it flies itself. It's my Space Flyer. It was finished a week ago. It's been lots of places: up to the top of the lightstack, out to the sun mirror—"

"I have no idea what you're talking about."

"You would, if you'd pay attention to the programs I send you to look at. The Space Flyer is a robot. It does what I tell it to do. And so will you, unless you want to be pushed inside."

Eva climbed up a ladder, Charlie right behind her. He steered her into a luxuriously padded seat in a transparent canopy and closed the hatch. She was beginning to look pale. Charlie, grinning, flopped into another seat in another canopy, fastened a harness around himself and pushed a button. There was a thunderous, crackling roar outside, and clouds of steam billowed around the trembling craft.

"Active soundproofing," Charlie said. "Otherwise we wouldn't be able to hear ourselves think in here. Better fasten your seatbelt."

Charlie fiddled with a joystick covered with buttons and triggers, and the Space Flyer surged upward on legs of yellow flame, squashing them into their seats. Charlie guffawed. "Vertical take-off! How do you like that? This display shows our altitude, one thousand feet. Now watch this."

He eased the joystick forward. The ground below the canopies began to slide behind them. The roar changed to a steady, muted thunder. "We're aerodynamic!" Charlie exulted as the speed of the Flyer built up. They were zooming along just beneath the monsoon overcast, the clouds blurred by speed.

"Okay, now we'll get a view of the lightstack," Charlie said, easing back on the stick. The Flyer dove upward into the cloud ceiling, mashing them into their seats again. After an instant of cold grayness, they shot out into dazzling sunlight and towering white thunderheads.

The horizon stood on end as the plane banked sharply, cutting across its own vapor trail. Ahead, the lightstack was a banded column, white and off-white, rising through the clouds from a shaggy patchwork carpet of forest. The small shadow of the Flyer shrank and expanded on its surface as Charlie steered a wide curve around it. The Flyer jolted as they passed through clouds.

"Little turbulence there," Charlie said. "Whoo! Just call me Chuck Yeager. You want to try it?"

He looked at her for the first time since takeoff. Eva was frozen to her seat, her hands gripping the armrests, her eyes tightly closed. "I'm sorry, Eva, I didn't realize you were so frightened," Charlie said. "Don't worry, I'm telling you. The computer won't let me do anything wrong. Charlie Freeman's Space Flyer is the safest airplane you've ever been in." Eva's eyes remained squeezed shut. "Okay, have it your way," Charlie said. "In case you were wondering, we're on our way to a little tropical paradise I discovered."

Charlie flew lower, keeping his eye on the colorful displays on the screens in front of him. He kept the speed low, so as not to disturb the wildlife with sonic booms. The sky cleared as the Flyer headed southwest. They flew over a blue expanse of wrinkled ocean until a low coastline appeared ahead. Charlie descended, hovered, and touched down on a wide, white beach. The rocket roar died away, and in the silence clouds of steam rose around the airplane.

"You can look now. We're here." Eva slowly opened her eyes and looked out of her canopy. The Flyer sat on a flat beach that extended all the way to the nearby horizon. There was nothing to be seen in any direction except sand and the ocean waves rolling in.

"I think the ground's cooled off enough by now," Charlie said, unlatching his harness and walking to the rear of the cabin. He pushed a button. The hatch woofed open, letting in a salt breeze and the boom of the surf. He lowered a metal ladder. "Come on, Eva. I said, come on!"

Eva got up from her chair, her face shut like a door. Charlie jumped down the ladder and waited for her on the still-steaming sand. When she had descended, he reached for her hand. She snatched it back, glaring at him.

"It's okay, Eva," Charlie said. "You don't have to be afraid—"

"Afraid of you!" she spat. "Ha!" She started walking away from the Flyer. "Come on, if that's what you want!" she flung over her shoulder.

Charlie trotted in front of her, then led her away over the beach. The pinpoint sun blazed overhead, casting sharp shadows underfoot. The plane became small with distance and began to sink under the horizon. Eva came out of her temper and began to look timidly around her.

"There're no dinosaurs here," Charlie said. "This is an island. It's a sandbar on what the Charonese call the trailing edge of the Circular Sea," he said. "Since you haven't been looking at any of the learning programs, you don't know that the sea moves slowly around Charon, swallowing land on one side and leaving it behind on the other. If it weren't for that, the whole world would be underwater. This is far enough." He stopped and sat down on the sand, propping himself with his hands. "Too bad there aren't any coconut palms on Charon. I'd love a nice coconut."

"Have you had your fun? Did you bring me here to give me a geography lesson?"

"No, but I did bring you here for a reason," Charlie said. Eva sneered and looked away over the water.

Charlie went on. "I wanted to talk to you. Someplace where the Ark computer can't listen in on us. Would you please sit down and listen?"

"You haven't got any robots here, Charlie."

"I know I don't. I'll get on my knees and beg you if it'll just make you pay attention for a minute."

"Okay," Eva said. "I'll do anything to get this over with. You make me sick!"

"All right, all right!" Charlie said, rocking in agitation on the sand. "I'm a jerk, okay? I kept you with me because I was hoping you might start liking me a little, and because I didn't want to be alone, okay? And I wanted you to share the power with me, and—"

"Don't bother. I just want to go home. I'm going to get a Corvette if I stay on the honor roll."

Charlie, in spite of himself, was nonplussed by her statement.

Someday, he thought, I may begin to understand people like her, but I don't now.

"We've been over that, Eva," he said. "The only way we can get home is by using what's here for us on Charon, not by turning our backs on it."

"And you're going to show us the way, right, Charlie?"

"Okay, okay, okay! Eva, please, I'm begging you just to listen to me for a minute."

Eva sat down on the sand, out of arm's reach of him. "I'm listening. I can't help it."

Charlie launched into it. "I brought you here because I need to talk to you somewhere where the Proctor can't overhear us. I'm afraid to talk about this anywhere near robots or other machinery. Eva, the Proctor has murdered about a hundred people, right here on Charon. It killed them because they wouldn't learn what the Charonese were trying to teach them."

"Oh, yes? When was that?"

"I don't know, exactly. Look at this." Charlie pulled a handkerchief out of his pocket, unrolled the burnt tooth he'd found at the "archaeological" site, and held it up for her to see. "This is from one of the people who were killed."

"Oh, ugh, Charlie!"

"This is what's going to happen to us if we don't do what the Proctor wants us to do, Eva. The Proctor burnt them to death with a laser beam or something. You know, like when we were on that safari, and that dinosaur got burnt up, you remember?"

"I'll never forget it, Charlie."

Charlie rested his arms across his knees and looked out from under his brows at the waves. A line of gull-like birds flew along the shore. "I've talked to you already a couple of times about what the Charonese and the Proctor want us for," he said gravely. "They want to keep us here forever, make us part of the machinery. When they've done that, they're going to make us go to the stars, so we can help them spread life on other planets."

"I remember you telling me that, Charlie. You sounded like that TV program Mrs. Robinelli made us watch. Billions and billions of years."

"That's not the worst of it, Eva. I found out that if we do learn how to run Charon, the Proctor won't need the human race anymore. It's planning to destroy the Earth—"

"Keep your grubby paws off me, Charlie," she snapped. In his agitation, he had reached out and touched her trousers leg.

He jerked his hand away. "I'm sorry! Listen, Eva, I need your help. It's too much responsiblity. I can't do it by myself anymore. Listen—"

"You listen," Eva said, her voice filled with malice. "Listen to yourself. I've never heard such a line of crap. I've been wanting to talk to you, too, Charlie. I want to go where Mrs. Robinelli and the others are. I've had enough of your threatening me, and your crap stories—"

Charlie turned to face her. "Please, Eva, what can I do to convince you? I can show you—"

"I don't want to see anything you have to show me."

"Shit," Charlie said, swiftly getting to his feet.

"Yes, shit, Charlie," Eva mocked.

Charlie walked off toward the Flyer. "Come on, unless you want me to leave you behind."

She dawdled confidently behind him as he trudged through the sand. "Can we go back now?"

"Not just yet. We have to do something to cover the time we spent talking here. I don't want the Proctor to suspect anything." They reached the Flyer's hatch. Eva sighed and pushed his hand away when he tried to help her up the ladder.

The Flyer boomed into the sky, Charlie and Eva lying in their seats. The acceleration went on and on. Clouds whipped by; the blue sky turned black; the stars came out. "What are you doing?" Eva asked, pale again.

"Scared?"

"N-no!"

"Your eyes are closed."

The Flyer arced upward and northward. Charon rotated below Charlie's canopy. He couldn't help watching interestedly as the top of the lightstack came into view, hurtled past. He caught a glimpse of the flying wing on the platform of the stack. "What?" he said. The wing was in pieces, swarmed over by scuttling leggy shapes, like ants pulling apart a dead bird. In a second, the lightstack had dwindled to a black dot against Charon's blue-and-white half moon shape. He pushed a button on the arm of his seat.

"Igor, tell me what's happening to the spacecraft on top of the lightstack."

"It is being dismantled."

"Who by, Igor?"

"The Crew members who are concerned with industrial operations."

"What are those starfish things?"

"They are Crew robots, designed to resemble the Crew, as they looked in their former bodies."

"Why haven't I seen any before?"

"They were designed for the previous Crew. The robots you are familiar with are patterned after the human body shape. Most of the robots of the Ark are variations on the radial-symmetry, five-legged design."

"Why didn't you tell me about them?"

"You didn't ask, sir."

"Jesus Christ."

"Very good, sir."

The Flyer dropped into weightlessness, Eva emitting a little squeak. "You might as well open your eyes, Eva," Charlie said. "We're going to be doing this for a couple of hours."

"Where, are, you, taking, me?"

"We're going to Pluto."

"What for? I want to go back to the apartment."

"I want to see the sunlight machine on Pluto with my own eyes. I think it's the rocket motor that makes the whole works move, when it moves. Also, I want to be the first person to set foot on another planet—Pluto, that is. Of course, it's not really a planet."

"So?"

"I'm getting sick of you, Eva. Of course, you already said that about me, didn't you?"

"That's right."

As they approached, Pluto looked just as Igor had depicted it on Charlie's control center screens: a huge, dark ball, eerie and cold. A square pattern of lights on the surface resolved itself into a metal landing pad. Charlie made out a vast triangular shape, a kind of gigantic pyramid, standing some distance from the pad. The Flyer headed for the pad automatically and touched down in the silence of vacuum. It was night outside, as always. Charlie climbed out of his seat and opened a locker in the upholstered wall of the cabin. "Here, Eva, you have to put on this suit before you can go outside."

"I'm not going anywhere."

"Aren't you interested in walking on another world? You'll be the first woman to set foot on an extraterrestrial body. I'll let you go first if you want to."

"Stop telling me what to do. You go play star wars if you want to."

"These suits are a new design. I want some backup in case something goes wrong."

"No."

"Okay, Eva, screw you. If something happens to me out there, you'll just sit there and starve to death without me to fly you back to Charon."

"I'm just sure, Charlie."

Charlie's voice went high in genuine wonderment. "You really don't get it, do you, Eva?"

"Anything you say, Charlie," she said, patiently, looking at her reflection in the Flyer's canopy, swiping at an errant blond curl.

Charlie, wearing a Charonese shrink-plastic vacuum suit under a bulky foam-plastic outfit for warmth, squeezed through the Flyer's tiny air lock and dropped to the metal. He paused a moment, swaying. The gravity was lower than on Charon.

The pyramid loomed on the horizon, visible only as a wedge cut out of the stars. Charlie got some idea of how far away it was by looking at the metal causeway that led from the landing pad to its base. The pyramid was as big as a mountain. A faint beam of light stood up from its summit, shining directly upward. Charlie leaned backward and followed the beam up and up until it was lost against the bright half-moon shape of Charon, which was hanging directly overhead. It was the sunbeam, directed at the mirror that orbited Charon's equator.

The vacuum suit was comfortingly tight against his clothes, and the foam oversuit was keeping him reasonably warm, although a chill was working its way through his foam-soled boots. He stifflegged a dozen paces to the edge of the landing pad. A rumpled, cratered snowscape stretched to the starry horizon. It seemed far off, compared to the confined horizon of Charon.

Carefully he stepped off the pad onto the snow and walked a few paces, feeling it crunch through the thick soles of his boots.

"Doesn't look like much," he commented through his suit radio to Eva. He could see her through the Flyer's canopies, sitting in the warm yellow light of the cabin, doing nothing.

"What did you come here for, then?" she said.

"There's no substitute for being there," he said, stumbling a little. The snow he stood on was eroding away from under his boot soles. A shallow, bowl-shaped depression was developing around him. He switched on a flashlight and directed its beam to the ground around his feet. Grains of snow were blowing away from his boots in a kind of slow-motion explosion, excavating a wide, shallow crater with him at its bottom.

"Igor, what's this wind blowing here? I thought there was no air on Pluto."

"The heat of your body is causing frozen hydrogen and methane in the snow to return to a gaseous state. The expanding gas moves away from you, carrying less volatile ices with it."

"In other words, if I stand here much longer, I'll sink out of sight."

"That is correct, sir."

"Okay. I hereby claim this world for all mankind and so on, in the name of Charlie Freeman. I forgot to make a flag to plant here. The hell with it."

He hurried back to the landing pad. His plan had been to walk to the pyramid for a close look, but his suit wasn't keeping out the cold. He returned to the Flyer's air lock. When the lock's outer door had closed, and the inner door had opened, Eva greeted him with a complaint. "Do you have to make it so cold in here?"

"For God's sake, it's almost zero Kelvin out there, Eva," Charlie mumbled.

"Who's Kelvin, one of your nurd friends from school?"

Charlie had no retort. Frost was sprouting on the outside of his insulated suit. He tried to brush it off but his suit gloves were balls of ice. His elbows were stuck to his sides. Charlie was turning into a snowman. Blind behind the mask of frost on his head bubble, unable to move his legs, he toppled over backward with a thump, a solid column of ice.

"Eva, come get me out of this!"

"Get yourself out of it."

"I can't move! You want to stay stuck on Pluto until you run out of air?"

"I'm not stuck, Charlie. You are."

Charlie thrashed. Some of the ice came off. Unwilling to argue with Eva, he lay until he thawed into puddles on the plush carpeting. The flight back to Charon was comparatively uneventful.

Late that night, back at the palace, Charlie slouched over his command desk, promising himself he'd go to bed in a few minutes. He'd stopped in at the command center to have one more look at the Ark records.

The wires and the sound-and-vision helmet gave him the sensation of floating in a haze of fine print, as though he were embedded in a vast book with transparent pages. He could read any page, or any place on any page, just by wanting to.

It was the Ark computer subject directory, and it was three times bigger than it was the last time Charlie had looked at it. This discovery prodded Charlie awake. "Igor, why are there so many new items in the directory?"

"The items are not new, sir. They are subjects that were formerly blocked by the Crew from human inspection. Now they are not blocked."

"Uh. Not blocked. Is that, uh, why you were able to tell me about the, you know, the accidents?"

"Yes, sir."

"Eat me raw. Why aren't the blocks there anymore?"

"The Crewpersons who maintained the blocks have been erased."

"Huh?" It was another stunning surprise. Charlie sat, knowing that things had gotten away from him, but too tired to think about it. "Igor, when did this happen? Show me."

Igor produced a video montage: his helicopter landing at Faulty Towers, as seen by the Crew members Gamma, Delta, and Epsilon. Charlie's jaw dropped as the three Charonese were perfunctorily wiped out by the Proctor.

Next he was shown a week-old conversation between the Charonese named Zeta and Beta, and Mrs. Robinelli. The Charonese learned about the Proctor from Mrs. Robinelli. In response, they offered to surrender the Ark to the humans. Charlie couldn't believe his ears. He didn't even detect the Proctor's presence as the Crewpeople were instantly obliterated. It was automatic.

"Oh, jeez," Charlie moaned. If Mrs. Robinelli kept this up any longer, there soon wouldn't be any Crew left.

"Igor, have any other Crew been erased since these records were made?"

"No, sir."

That was a partial relief. Charlie gave in to exhaustion and closed his eyes for a moment. Mrs. Robinelli may have caught on in time. Even if she didn't understand what was going on, she must know something. Charlie yearned to talk to her with all his lonely heart. "I can't cope with it anymore, Mrs. Robinelli," he told her.

She stopped beside his school desk, the kindness in her eyes changing to pity as she looked down at him. "It's hard, saving the world, I know," she said.

Charlie ripped the sound-and-vision helmet off his head and stared around his command center. The silence of the place was unbroken. The valet robot, representing Igor's ever-present something-or-other, stood by the door where Charlie had left it. "Did I fall asleep? Did I say something?" he asked it.

"Yes, sir," the robot said.

Charlie dully studied the illuminated, animated globe of Charon in the corner. Half of its surface was still unmapped, another unfinished project. Still, the globe served as a clock. The daylit portion had crept almost a full revolution. Charlie had put in another twenty-hour day.

"Shit," Charlie said.

"What color, sir?"

"Am I talking to myself again, Igor?" Charlie said, standing up.

"Yes, sir. Will you be wanting dinner now, sir?"

"No." Charlie walked slowly down the palace corridors, his valet thumping behind. He passed a columned balcony and paused to adjust his stuffed Quetzalcoatlus, which had gotten askew. He had ordered the robots to mount the buzzardlike creature with its twenty-two-foot wings outspread, as though it were soaring. The Quetzalcoatlus had been mounted loosely on a rod, so it could be free to swivel and tilt in the breeze from the balcony. Charlie smoothed its velvety black fur and looked into its red glass eye.

"Patience, hell, I'm going to kill something," he said, speaking for the monster, which was unable to speak for itself.

"Beg pardon, sir?"

Charlie ignored the robot and stepped to the railing to take a look outside. It was twilight under a heavy overcast, too dark to see much. The parkland stretched away, smelling of wet treebark and fresh earth. In the distance, a line of humped shapes moved slowly across an open area.

"What are those, Igor?" Charlie asked pointing.

The robot paused while it consulted the Ark's large-animal tracking system. "Ceratopsian dinosaurs, sir," it said, finally. "Genus *Triceratops*, species *calicornus*. The males are shedding their horn and beak casings. During the mating season, which begins in approximately fifteen days, the male animals will have bright yellow beaks and horns, instead of the usual black—"

"That's enough, thanks."

"Don't mention it, sir."

A gray curtain of rain drew across the landscape. A long, drawn-out hoot came from the obscurity, like a distant train whistle. Charlie had heard it several times since the start of the monsoon. "The love song of the tarbosaurus, the Mongolian tyrannosaur. The old monster is still around, hoping I'll let him have Eva."

"Very good, sir," Igor said.

Charlie walked on, not pausing at the locked doors of Eva's apartment. He reached his own quarters and dismissed the robot. A cool, damp wind blew out the gauze curtains on his windows, and the fake marble floor was wet with raindrops. The screens between the windows showed stars reflected on a wide river somewhere on the other side of Charon. Charlie dropped his clothes on the floor, commanded the lights to go out, and collapsed on his bed. The slight discomfort of the input-output wire harness didn't bother Charlie. He slept as soon as his head hit the pillow.

In the middle of the night, Charlie heard his name called.

"Charlie? Are you asleep?"

It wasn't a strange voice, but it didn't belong. Charlie raised his head. He saw, in the dim window light, a white figure advancing hesitantly toward his bed.

"I'm sorry I came in without asking," the little-girl voice said. "Your door was open."

"S'okay, Eva," Charlie said automatically, his mind curdled with sleep and amazement.

"Could we talk, Charlie?" She seemed to float across the room on her bare feet. The breeze from the windows ruffled the edge of her cotton nightdress around her knees. "I'm cold," she said. "Can I, do you mind if . . ." She was raising the corner of Charlie's blanket, climbing into his bed. Charlie couldn't move.

"I, we, we're going to be here forever," she said, in a tiny frightened voice. "I know that now. I'm sorry I didn't understand, was mean to you, Charlie. Please?" She slid close to him under the covers. "Will you hold me, please?"

"W-well, yes," Charlie said. She cuddled against the front of his body, Charlie feeling her warm thighs and belly against him.

Charlie's adolescent glands responded to her as to a starter's gun. Instantly his body demonstrated an erection unprecedented in the wettest dreams of his long virginity. Embarrassed, he bent his hips away from her.

"It's all right, Charlie," she whispered tremblingly. "I want you to."

Unbelievably, she was urging her hips onto his, he feeling the rasp of her female hair against his thigh. Love roared through Charlie. Joyfully, he threw his arms around her, covered her face with burning kisses like Tarzan, crushed her to his chest like Conan. His hands slid down her silken back to her downy buttocks, encountered, shockingly, something like a hard, cold tail.

He jerked awake. "What's that!" he shrieked, springing out of the bed, sprawling on the cold, wet marble. "Igor! The lights!"

The room came ablaze. In the hard light, Charlie saw the plastic Eva lying in his bed, still looking at where his face had been on the pillows, a cable trailing from her spine, across the floor, out his apartment door.

He jumped to his feet and ran to the door. In the corridor outside, several robots stood around a large metal box on wheels, from which the cable protruded. The real Eva lay unconscious in her nightgown on a blanket at the robot's feet.

Charlie rushed to her. "Igor! What've you done, you idiot!"

"I provided this," the Proctor said, speaking from one of the robots.

"Oh, God!" Charlie cried, trying to lift Eva's wrists.

"She is unharmed," the Proctor said. "I have made her sleep, with a drug."

Charlie gave up trying to pick up the limp body. "Why? Were you planning to substitute the real thing after I—Jesus Christ! Take her to the hospital, right now! And get that thing out of my room!"

Charlie followed the procession of robots clumpity-clumping down the halls to the medical facility and stood by until Eva began to show signs of reviving. Then he ordered the machines to carry her back to her bed. He watched on the terminal in his apartment as she awakened, sat up, looked around, scratched a red needle mark on her thigh, sighed, and went back to sleep again. He calmed himself. It was no use ranting at the Proctor. In fact, a show of irrationality might be dangerous.

"Why did you do it, Proctor?" he asked, reasonably.

"For your . . . entertainment," said the fly buzz voice.

"But why? I mean, what was the, ah, proximate cause of your decision to do it?"

"I noted that your . . . morale was deteriorating. I wished to provide positive reinforcement. A reward. I noted your difficulty in establishing a . . . relationship with Eva. I wished to help."

"Well—" Charlie gulped and took a deep breath. "Uh, thanks, Proctor," he finally was able to say. "I appreciate the thought, and it's the thought that counts, as we say. But don't do it again, okay? I'm fine. I'm happy. It's just that there's a great deal of work here, you understand? I know, deep down inside, Eva loves me. She'll come around. I'm not worried about that. No, sir. Just don't do it again. There's a lot about human psychology you don't understand. Know what I mean?"

"Yes," the Proctor said.

"I'll sleep now," Charlie said. "Good night. Igor, turn off the lights!" Charlie threw himself on his bed and amazed himself by falling asleep.

The next morning Charlie woke up miserable. *That's how easy to manipulate the Proctor thinks I am.* He forced himself out of bed. *Must stick to routine, no matter what.*

In the command center he asked Igor for a look into Faulty Towers, instead of the usual reports. To his surprise, he suddenly found himself in real-time, two-way contact with all of the computer terminals in all the students' apartments as well as the monitors elsewhere in the Towers and grounds.

All the students were busy, some studying, some in the garden, without a sign of resistance or laziness among them. Their multitudinous activity was clear to Charlie, thanks to his acquired skill and the neurotransducers. He could also detect various computer-controlled support activities in the service and factory spaces under the Towers. His trained senses told him that he could break into their terminals, even control their robots if he wanted to. In fact, the students could do the same to him, if they knew how. This was the view of things that the Charonese would have if they knew how to look at it. Or the Proctor. Charlie felt as though he were sitting on a crumbling scaffold, which the slightest movement could bring down. "Igor, why is this?"

"The former blocks, which protected the Ark computer from uninformed human interference, are no longer in place. The effect is two-way."

Charlie now saw that Mr. Peake and some of the students were missing. Where the heck could they be? As he began a mental roll call he noticed Mrs. Robinelli, also looking on at the students' work. With some wonder, he saw that she had begun using the neurotransducers. Curious, he "moved" closer to her. She "glanced up" and started violently.

"Charlie!"

"Oh, God! Don't say my name, Mrs. Robinelli!"

The teacher struggled to gain control of herself. "What? Where—?"

"I didn't mean for you to see me," he said. He felt his little courage collapse. "Mrs. Robinelli!" he blurted. "The thing, it's going to destroy the human race—"

Mrs. Robinelli's attention fixed itself, steel-sharp, on the shivering boy. "What thing?"

Charlie already regretted his impulsiveness. He always did, and now was no different. "I can't say it! It'll hear us! It starts with 'P.'"

"Go on."

"If we become Crew, it will shoot the Earth, kill everyone! If we don't, it will kill us! I have to do something about it, but I don't know what to do!"

322   *Rick Gauger*

Another presence materialized next to them. "Who is this, Mrs. Robinelli?"

"Good morning, Eta," the teacher said calmly. "This is a student, practicing the use of the input-output wires." To Charlie, she pleaded, "Break contact now."

"Mrs. Robinelli, don't tell any more of the Charonese about the, the thing! When they hear about it, it kills them. You know, erases them from the computer!"

"Is this person a student?" Eta asked. "I have not seen him before."

"It's you, too," Mrs. Robinelli said to Charlie, conversationally. "You do it to them, too. Break contact."

"Me?"

"Yes, you, Charlie. When they see you, they deduce that the, the, P-thing exists. Then they get erased. Break off now."

Eta "looked" at Igor, hovering next to Charlie. "This is Alpha. What has happened to Alpha?"

"Mrs. Robinelli, I haven't done any of the things you think I have! Eva, Bill, Curt, I haven't hurt them! We've got to—"

Mrs. Robinelli "turned" to the Charonese. "This student is unpracticed at expressing his appearance and emotions. He will study further. Break off, now, hurry," she said to Charlie. Another presence gathered, from outside. Charlie sensed the eye of the Proctor.

"Igor, abort!" he shouted. Faulty Towers blinked out of his eyepieces, but the Proctor stayed with him. "Okay, Igor," he stuttered. "Pre-Calculus Algebra. Lesson One."

Charlie began the first exercise. He kept his head low knowing it wouldn't save him from the execution-stroke, if it came. After a while, the Proctor went away.

Charlie began to breathe again. How much did the Proctor know? What would it do? He clutched his hands to his chest, to stop their shaking.

Chapter Sixteen:
Where's Charlie?

Finding Charlie's hideout was an exercise in geometry. Mrs. Robinelli's diagrams and instructions laid it all out. The lightstack, or photon exhaust tower, where the humans had originally landed on the Ark, stood at Charon's north pole. Although it was over three hundred miles high, only its lower ten or twelve miles were illuminated by the "sun". That meant that the stack wouldn't become visible above the artificial world's constricted and frequently tree-cluttered horizon until the expedition arrived at North Latitude Fifty-five. More or less.

The cable-pipes, which supported the lightstack, and which were attached to its summit, came to ground at the equator, or somewhat north of it. Once caught sight of, any cable-pipe would point the way northward.

The first problem, as the teacher freely admitted, would be to find one of the cable-pipes. She estimated that Faulty Towers lay about fifteen degrees south of Charon's equator. The expedition would have to dead reckon its way to about North Latitude Twenty before they could be reasonably certain of seeing a cable-pipe.

That was twenty-five miles due north from Faulty Towers. Mrs. Robinelli's maps didn't show the terrain, only the geometry. The robot truck, with the expedition members bouncing around inside, trundled over soggy savannahs, detoured around forests, churned across wide, muddy rivers.

All the way, Froward and Peake quibbled tensely over which direction was north. Charon's artificial sun orbited directly over its equator, and could have served for navigation, if it hadn't been for the gray rainy-season overcast. Finally, luck provided a halfway-clear day. At noon, Froward and Peake, looking at their shadows on the ground in front of them, were able to agree that the expedition had crossed the equator.

They blundered onward until another break in the weather gave them the sight of a white thread among the clouds in the western sky, its upper end seeming to hang unsupported where it passed above the daylight. It was a cable-pipe. Froward and Peake consulted an astrolabe homemade from an aluminum plate. The cable-pipe altitude showed they were at North Latitude Twenty-three.

It was another sixty air miles to the pole. Froward and Chela pushed the truck as hard as it would go, throughout several of Charon's sixteen-hour days. The expedition ran out of food. They subsisted on palm cabbage and dinosaur, fresh or smoked. During the cold, wet nights, all hands were grateful for the blankets and extra overall suits they had brought from the residence facility.

Of course, Chela no longer slept with Froward. He completely understood: the only woman in an all-male party, and, he reminded himself, she was no woman, really, just a young girl who'd be better off marching in a high-school band. Nevertheless, he loved her helplessly. He ached for the half-naked wildchild she had been. In the cold, and under the eyes of her classmates, she wore a set of donated overalls and had taken off her tribal bangles. She now sat unsmilingly in the robot truck's turret, her eyes fixed on the ground ahead.

After four days, the weather cleared somewhat. The cablepipe had dropped below the horizon behind them, and the north pole lightstack stood out like a chalk mark in the sky ahead. At night, Froward made out Pluto almost overhead, a ghostly disk with a faint spark in the middle of it.

Another sleep in the mildewing straw inside the vehicle, and another four hours of driving, and the sun dropped out of sight below the tree line to the south. It was the polar twilight zone, predicted by Mrs. Robinelli. The truck slowed and stopped under a dripping magnolia tree, its turbine whining down to silence.

Froward was sitting in the wet, on top of the cargo compartment, behind Chela. "What's the matter?" he asked her.

"I think it's out of gas," she said. "it won't go anymore."

He wanted to see her face, but she was bent over, looking down into the robot's turret. "What'll we do?" she said.

"Don't worry, we're almost there, anyway," Froward said, as though being close to whatever monsters and robots Charlie had gathered around himself in his hidden fortress weren't a cause of concern. He folded up Mrs. Robinelli's map and put it in his pocket.

They had to crank down the vehicle's loading ramp by hand. Peake and the two boys stepped down, stretching and hopping to relieve cramping muscles. "Not bad timing, I guess," Peake said. "You folks ready to walk?"

"Yeah," Colby said.

Reilly stood close to him, looking around apprehensively. "If the truck doesn't work anymore, how're we going to get back?" Reilly said.

"We'll ask Charlie, when we catch him," Colby said.

Peake climbed into the cargo compartment, began handing out rucksacks. "We'll take everything, since we don't know how far it is," he said. "The space suits, blankets, and ropes are in the bags. Jeff, I mean Mr. Froward, will keep the grenade launcher, since he has the most experience with it. The rest of us will carry pistols."

The boys accepted the .45s—Colby with relish, Reilly gingerly.

"Okay," Peake said. "I want Mr. Froward to lead us until we get within sight of whatever we're looking for. He's been on trips like this before."

Froward took a deep breath, trying to shake off the dull apprehension in his belly. Chela watched him unhappily as he gave orders. "I'll go first. The rest of you follow far enough behind so you can see me. I'll be the point man. If I stop, everyone take cover. Chela goes last, watches to the rear. We're keeping our eyes open for dangerous animals, robots, and metal towers with cameras on top of them. We're keeping quiet and out of sight. Everybody understand?"

"If we see Charlie, are we supposed to shoot him?" Reilly asked.

"We want him alive, if possible," Colby said. "But I'll kill him, if he doesn't cooperate."

Froward looked at the boy with consternation. "This isn't a movie," he said. "We're talking about a kid, someone we know."

"You didn't see him torturing Bill and Curt," Colby said sullenly. "If you had, you'd feel like I do. Lena, Miss Gershner, I mean, said don't hold back. He deserves everything he gets, and more."

Froward turned to Peake, who grimaced and shrugged. "Lena made a speech, before we came out to join you and Chela."

"She did? Oh. Well, uh, I can understand how you feel, better than you might believe. But killing a person always turns out to be a mistake you have to live with the rest of your life. Take my word for it; I know."

"Mr. Peake is in charge here. Not you." Colby spoke respectfully.

"I know. I was just—" Froward shut himself up.

"Jeff, you and Chela don't have to come with us," Peake said. "I can understand that you might not feel as committed to the plan as we do. You've already gone through more danger than any of us, and you've done your part by getting us here."

Chela stood to one side, watching the trees and hefting her rucksack, apparently not listening to the conversation. The thought that she might come to harm made Froward's knees weak. He admitted to himself that he didn't know these people. He'd barely become acquainted with some of the students during their confinement on the spaceship, and they weren't the same now as they'd been then. They had grown up. They and the adults, Peake, Gershner, and Mrs. Robinelli, had united in discipline and harshness against—what? Against torture, captivity, and slavery. Against outsiders. Froward knew that Chela would never consent to staying behind.

"No," he said. "I'm with you."

"Me, too," Chela said loudly.

"Okay," Peake said. "If we're ready, let's go."

They marched through increasingly dense woods all morning, sometimes finding game trails or bulldozed dirt roads to follow. In the clearings, where they could see the sky ahead, they saw the white wall of the lightstack taking on the proportions of a mountain as they neared it. The woods were silent, though occasionally they heard something crashing invisibly away in the brush. Once the party stopped to let a medium-sized ankylosaur lumber out of the way, its clubbed tail swinging. Sometime in the afternoon Froward signaled a halt at the edge of an expanse of wet concrete steaming in the sunlight.

He stared, then motioned Peake forward for a look. Half a dozen multirotored helicopters sat awkwardly on the pavement. Among them crouched a sleek flat aircraft, its hull and drooping manta wings all one piece, its arrowhead prow projecting forward, looking as though it were about to leap into the sky.

"Wow, a jet!" Peake said enthusiastically. "It's gorgeous. A flying orgasm. I didn't know the Charonese built things like that."

Froward had to smile a little. "It's no jet; there're no air intakes. It's a rocket. Look at that lifting body shape. Maybe it's some kind of space vehicle. Think we ought to have a closer look at it?"

"You said it. Lead on."

Froward took the party around to one side, keeping to the trees. At the point closest to the plane he halted again, then dashed, alone, across the pavement to the shelter of one of the plane's landing skids. He looked back. Peake and the others were out of sight in the undergrowth. In the far distance, Froward heard something like an old-time train whistle, a long, lonely wail. He waited to hear it again, but the twilit woods were still.

Quickly, Froward scrambled up the ladder to the plain's rounded upper hull. It was made of plastic or ceramic, not metal. To the front, the backs of two luxuriously upholstered chairs could be seen inside a low transparent canopy. An oval outline at his feet indicated a hatch. On impulse, he kicked a metal plate that was embedded in the hull near his foot. The hatch fell open, forcing him to step back. Inside was a padded, closet-size room.

Hoping he wouldn't set off any burglar alarms, Froward stepped down into the room. He guessed it was an air lock. Another hatch, easily opened, led to the plane's cabin. He crossed thick violet carpeting to the dome. The plane's controls were absurdly simple: a fancy joystick, illuminated buttons with labels like TAKE OFF, HOVER, BACK UP, and LAND. There was also a typewriter keyboard, TV screens, and several sets of earphones. In the copilot's seat he found copies of magazines: *Vogue*, *Mademoiselle*, *Self*.

He grabbed one of the magazines and hurriedly left through the air lock, closing the hatches behind him. Crouching beside the others in the bushes, he showed them the magazine.

"This is it," Peake said. "We lucked out."

"That plane is all computerized," Froward said eagerly. "I think I could fly it myself on the first try. It's tempting."

"Not to me," Colby said.

Froward saw Chela smiling at him.

"There's a road over there," Reilly said. "It leads away from the airfield, in the direction of the tower."

"We'll try that," Peake said. Suddenly, everything became dark. As abruptly as an electric light going out, the sunset light in the sky had gone, leaving them in night. Froward clutched at the damp ground, looked up. Stars twinkled between the pale clouds. Then, with a flicker, the twilight returned.

"What is it?" Colby said, his face white with shock.

Peake stuttered, then said, "Maybe it's the eclipse."

"The what?"

"Mrs. Robinelli told me about it. The Charonese have to turn off the artificial sun. When Charon eclipses Pluto, or whatever. So the extra light won't be seen by astronomers on Earth. She explained it to me. It won't last long. If it happens again, we'll just wait it out."

"Jeez," Reilly said.

They pulled themselves together and went on. The sky blinked again several times during the next half hour as they followed the road away from the airfield. The road led to the edge of a grassy open space. In front of them a great rectangular building stood at the foot of the sheer wall of the lightstack. A huge square doorway gaped blackly open on the ground level. On top of the building, high above the ground, was a fairy castle, a wedding-cake conglomeration of towers, ramparts, and domes.

"What the hell is this, Disneyland?" Peake sounded peevish.

"It's Charlieland," Reilly whispered.

Charlie Freeman was toiling through Lesson Nine of Pre-Calculus Algebra when the sun went out. Looking out his window at the treetops silhouetted against the night sky, he pushed the call button on his terminal.

"Igor, what's happening to the sunlight?"

Charlie jittered as he waited for his answer. He hadn't recovered from his hysteria of a few days before; he'd covered it up. He'd resorted to schoolwork as a disguise of normalcy, to conceal his desperate casting-about for some way out of—"Preparations for Charon's transit of Earth, sir," the familiar toneless voice answered.

"Already?" Charlie got out of his chair, stuffed his feet in his sneakers, and hurried down the corridor. He'd had some vague idea of using the fake Charonese sun to make a signal to Earth. It would have to be something the Proctor wouldn't recognize. Charlie's wandering mind wouldn't take him any further than that. Probably too risky anyway. He shook off a vision: the blasted Earth.

He caught a glimpse of himself in a decorative mirror, wearing jeans and a grubby flowered shirt from home. He no longer bothered to put on his fancy costumes. A mistake, he realized, if he were trying to look business-as-usual to the Proctor. By the time he reached the balconied window, the sun was back on again. The stuffed Quetzalcoatlus wobbled us on its mount among Charlie's hunting guns, nodding jokily at Charlie as he rushed past it.

In his command center, he wired and helmeted up, paced around. "Igor, I want to watch the proceedings of the Crewpeople in charge of the sunlight projector."

"Yes, sir."

Charlie dove through clouds of explanation to the minds of the unnamed Charonese who were adjusting the sun machine. On Pluto, at the summit of the pyramid, the Crew made odd gasses flow though diamond containers and contracted inexplicable energy fields. Only a few of the devices and techniques had English names, and most of those were Greek to Charlie: phase-conjugation mirror, iridium-doped coherent plasma, quantum pump. He did understand something about the sunlight reflector that orbited over Charon's equator. Its focus and orientation were to be changed, temporarily. The concentrated sunbeam was to be directed at a point on the Ark's life-bearing surface. He couldn't see what this had to do with preventing astronomers on Earth from—

He checked the latitude and longitude of the target, and choked on his own saliva. His coughing fit prevented him from blurting it out: Faulty Towers. They were preparing to zap the humans, were going to do it as soon as the sun mirror rose sufficiently above the horizon at that location—

He shouted words and emotions at them. "What are you doing!"

Taken by surprise, the Charonese halted their work. "We are

concealing the Ark," said some. Another said, "We are snuffing a brushfire." They noted the contradiction between their minds. They became agitated. After a second of consultation, they tried to quiz Charlie, treating him at first as one of themselves. They collided with his opacity, his alienness. They recoiled. All of it took less than a second.

"Who-what is this? A human in the Ark computer! How can it be?" One of them addressed Charlie. "Who are you?"

"Never mind that! Don't you realize that you're about to destroy the human residence facility and kill all the people in it?" Charlie angrily displayed maps, coordinates, pictures.

The Charonese fluttered. "It's true!" they said among themselves, radiating amazement and dismay. A succession of impressions passed among them. They had been attempting to put out a brushfire at the target coordinates. But there was no brushfire there; besides, it was the wet season. The brushfire was a mistake. A coincidence. A misperception. The extreme importance of the recruiting project. The future of the Ark depends on it, yet—We don't make mistakes like that, unless—

They scrutinized Charlie and drew the appropriate conclusions in half a second. This person was thought to be dead, was hidden from us, has access to the computer, therefore there is something in the Ark that can hide things from us, therefore its nature must be—

The Index named their concept in English for Charlie: a Proctor. One by one, not before Charlie's eyes, but in his mind, the Crewpeople began to be erased. He felt each individual death, a rush of memories blanked in an instant of terror. The last one looked at Charlie and begged, "Don't, don't, don't—"

"I'm not—" Charlie began, but the mind had already winked out. Charlie didn't sense the Proctor's attention; the murders were being done automatically.

The preparation of the firebeam resumed; only minutes were left.

It wasn't a matter of not having access to the sun machinery, it was the complexity of it. Charlie didn't know where to begin stopping it. In panic, he withdrew to the general software level of the computer and screamed for the Proctor.

"The Proctor's attention is elsewhere," Igor said.

"Call it! Go get it!"

"Very good, sir." Nothing happened. The Proctor wasn't listening.

"Igor! Stop the sun weapon! The laser beam! Make it stop!"

"Very good, sir." Again, nothing happened. Igor wasn't even aware that he or she, whatever sex the alien used to have, was being blocked.

Charlie clawed at his face, was stopped by the helmet's faceplate. He jerked it off his head. "Igor, why is the residence facility being destroyed? Is the Proctor doing it?"

"I have no information about that, sir."

"Figure it out! I mean, make a guess from whatever evidence you have!"

"Yes, sir. Most probably, your coming to the attention of the Crewperson Eta caused Eta to check the number of humans present in the residence facility."

"I caused this?"

"Only partially, sir," Igor said. "Most probably the Proctor has decided that the Crew has lost control of the human recruits at the residence facility, allowing them to escape, to learn too much too soon, and—"

"Escape? Did some of them leave Faulty Towers?"

"Yes, sir," Igor said, without a trace of impatience at Charlie's interruptions. "Eta discovered that the humans Peake, Reilly, and Dennison are absent from the residence facility."

"Jesus H.! Let me speak to Eta!"

"Eta has been erased, sir."

"Oh, my God! Put me in real-time contact with the residence facility! Hurry!" Charlie dithered frantically. He'd never thought deeply enough about the parameters and motivations of the Proctor. It came to him now that the Proctor was the Ark, more so, even, than the Charonese. It would not allow the rules to be broken. Pest control was one of the Ark computer's chief preoccupations.

The computer faded Charlie into all the terminals in Faulty Towers simultaneously. It was early dawn twilight there; in multiple images he saw dozens of people asleep in dozens of rooms.

They awoke in fear. Eerie, terrifying howls, the distortions of multiple loudspeakers and electronic feedback, echoed down the stairways and through the courtyards. "O-o-h—! Wake up-up!

GET OUTOUT OF OF THE BUILDING! RUNRUN! GET UPEEOOOO!!"

Mrs. Robinelli thrashed out of her sheets and blankets and landed on the floor next to her bed. Outside her door, she heard shouts and running feet. She stood up, fumbled on her glasses. She glimpsed herself in her bathroom mirror, skinny and ridiculous in cotton pajamas. Charlie Freeman's face was on her terminal screen, eyes bulging, hair sweated to his cheeks, mouth working.

"Charlie!"

He noticed her; the terminal's camera light blinked. "Mrs. Robinelli! You've got to get everybody out! The sun is going to burn up Faulty Towers! Make everybody run!"

"What?"

His face twisted in agony. "The Proctor, the Ark! It's getting rid of you! It can focus the artificial sunlight anywhere it wants; it's going to burn up Faulty Towers!"

Emma scowled. "I'm telling you the truth!" Charlie cried. "Please! You got to get out of there; run away!"

"Why, Charlie? Why is it doing it?"

"Some of you have escaped from Faulty Towers; I don't know! The Ark thinks you're out of control. Is it true?"

"Where should we run to, Charlie?"

"Anywhere! Far away! No, wait." He looked to the side and shouted, "Igor! How wide is the, what area does the, the sterilizing beam affect?"

Emma heard a toneless voice: ". . . burn radius, point six kilometers."

Charlie groaned, "Oh, no, you'll never make it."

"Who's that, Charlie?" she demanded.

"Wait, I know. Igor! Send a heavy-lift helicopter to the residence facility. Land it and load all the humans whether they want to go or not—"

"Charlie, I want to know who you're talking to!"

Charlie babbled frantically. "It's Igor, he, it, helps me, answers questions. No, no," Charlie protested, seeing the expression on her face, "Igor isn't the Proctor. Igor is a, used to be, a Charonese. We haven't got time for this: you've got to get out, run as fast as you can!"

Someone banged on Emma's door, burst inside. It was

Gershner, buttoning her overalls and carrying her shoes. "You and Charlie are on every screen in the building, Emma! What should we do? Is it a trick?"

Emma looked at her. "No. Our plan has backfired. Get everyone moving downstairs; I'll come in a minute."

Gershner ran out the door, and Emma turned back to the screen. "A helicopter won't work, Charlie. Even if it gets here in time, it wouldn't save us. You've got to stop the beam."

"I can't! I don't know how!"

Emma's apartment lit up blindingly, went dark. Frightened yells sounded in the passageway. Outside her window, Emma saw the clouds roiling, parting. Thunder boomed in the sky.

Tears poured down Charlie's face, he sobbed like a little boy. "It's starting! It's burning away the clouds! You've got to get everybody out!"

"Listen to me, Charlie. Look at me! There's only one way to stop this. Find the Proctor. Cut its connection to the Ark computer."

"How?" Charlie cried. "Oh, we're wasting time! Get out, Mrs. Robinelli, hide in the trees until the helicopter comes!"

"Charlie! Doesn't Igor do your research for you? Doesn't it?"

"Yes, yes, I told you, Igor was a Charonese, until—"

"I thought so. Use Igor, Charlie," Emma said, her voice quiet and urging. Something like lightning flickered outside the window, and a gust of hot air blew into the apartment. She spoke rapidly. "You're probably safe, Charlie. It doesn't want to kill you, just us. We're the ones that're dangerous to it. You've got time."

"Please, please, Mrs. Robinelli," Charlie sobbed, banging on the control console with his fists. "Don't talk anymore—"

The teacher hung on relentlessly. "The Proctor is a thing, not a program. It's hardware, Charlie. It has to be somewhere close to the Ark computer. Ask Igor to locate all computer devices that have no apparent purpose. We've sent some people to you, Charlie. They might be there already. They might be able to help you. Try to contact them on the space suit radio—"

A blast of light from the screen dazzled Charlie. He caught a glimpse of Mrs. Robinelli, black on white, then the connection broke.

Still hiccuping sobs, Charlie looked around at the command

center. It looked as peaceful and normal as it had in his days of glory. His sound-and-vision helmet lay on the floor where he'd dropped it. For an instant he considered simply going to bed. He saw himself lying there with the covers over his head. After all, none of this was his fault.

But first . . . He picked up the helmet and pulled it over his head, wriggling the rubber-cupped eyepieces into place. "Igor, give me a view of the prisoners and Eva."

"Yes, sir." He saw multiplex image of the boys studying for their supper, discussing what they would do to Charlie when they got their hands on him. Eva, also blissfully ignorant, was doing calisthenics to loud music. Charlie didn't care to watch. Her semierotic flexings made him feel ill. "Oh, shit," he said, and stopped crying.

"Very good, sir."

"Oh, shit!" he said again, knowing he'd have to do it, hoping it wasn't too late. "All right, damn it. Igor, where is the Proctor machine?"

There was a hesitation, then, "I do not know, sir."

Blind under the helmet, Charlie tramped up and down. What had Mrs. Robinelli told him to do? For once, recollection came to him when he wanted it. "Igor, display the locations of all the computers on the Ark. Highlight any computer that you and the Index don't know the purpose of. Start with the one nearest to my location."

"Yes, sir." A map appeared in the eyepieces. It was the same one he'd seen before, with his position marked: YOU (CHARLIE). But now the large blank area was marked CENTRAL COMPUTER. Next to it was a blinking orange shape labeled UNKNOWN-PUR-POSE CYBERNETIC DEVICE #1. There were no others on the map. Charlie already knew how to get to it. It was at the bottom of the elevator, down the sloping tunnel, the one with all the air lock doors, the one that led to the lower end of the lightstack.

"Igor, have the valet robot fetch my Pluto suit."

"Yes, sir."

Through the neurotransducers, Charlie felt the robot march off obediently. "Better still, Igor, have a robot already near my ward-robe bring the suit. It'll be faster."

"Yes ssss—" Suddenly, fear glued Charlie to the floor. The Proctor had appeared, had seized Igor, was interrogating him, was turning toward Charlie. For a split second, Charlie felt a power, an inimical intention, gathering around him. Without thought, Charlie ripped the helmet off his head. As it hit the desktop, it flashed and banged, acrid smoke puffing out of it. Suddenly, Charlie was on fire.

"Eeee! Oww!" Charlie screeched. Rolling on the floor, he tore at the wires on his body, finally thought to rip off the transmitter box. He threw it against the wall. He pulled himself up his thronelike command chair, got to his feet. The door of the command center slid open. Charlie's tuxedoed butler stepped inside, the Pluto suite draped over its arms. "Your suit, sir," it said.

Charlie moved to it, took the suit. The butler grabbed at him. Charlie's instincts saved him; he dodged, and the robot's metal arms clashed on air.

"Thank you, Igor," Charlie said, diving with the suit over the command chair.

"Don't mention it, sir," the robot said, its costume ripping as it lunged after Charlie. The valet was coming after him, too. Charlie dropped to his knees, scrambled toward the door. The two robots collided over him, tried to stamp on him, fell down. Charlie jumped to his feet, then dropped again as all the TV screens in the room flared blindingly. The control panels exploded; shards of glass, metal, and plastic rattled off the walls. Charlie galloped on all fours through billows of flame and smoke, found the exit, sprang out into the corridor. Coughing, he yelled, "Igor! Close the door!"

The door slid shut; there was a crash as the robots hit it on the inside. When it opened again, Charlie was sprinting down the medieval corridor, the Pluto suit flapping over his shoulder. He pounded past the closed door of Eva's apartment, past the balcony where his shoulder struck one of the wing tips of the stuffed Quetzalcoatlus. It rotated on its mount, seeming to follow his headlong passage.

Charlie looked up in time to see the ornate double doors of the banquet hall swinging wide. A small army of satin-coated flunky robots trampled out, followed by cooks in white hats waving knives and cleavers. Charlie skidded and raised his arm. "Igor, halt!" he yelled.

The robots stopped, some of them colliding with others. Hastily, Charlie knotted the Pluto suit around his waist. He looked back to see the valet and the butler frozen in midstride. His goal, the elevator to the robot garage and the underground level, lay beyond the banquet-hall servants, seemingly out of reach forever, although its door stood open as usual. Puffing, gathering his breath and courage, Charlie backed against the wall. It was only a matter of time before the Proctor would catch on and order Igor to stop obeying him. Something sharp poked his neck. He reached for it, came back with a steel battle-axe from a wall trophy, a fantasy from his lost kingship.

Raving, Charlie charged down the corridor. The robots came to life, snatching and slashing, getting in one another's way. Charlie swung the axe, metal clashing on metal, sparks and hot fluid spattering. He got a little beyond them and went down, metal hands grasping his legs. He chopped, rolled free, leaped to his feet, jumped for the elevator, screamed in purest terror. His yells echoed down ninety feet of darkness. The door was open, but the elevator wasn't there! The axe clanged on the corridor floor as Charlie teetered, toes over the edge, arms windmilling. Behind him, the robots came trampling.

Froward, Peake, Chela, Colby, and Reilly were lying flat in a bed of ferns, peering through the twilight at the light of Charlie's castle. The castle sat on the high top of the robot garage like a stranded riverboat. Behind it the wall of the lightstack reared in the gloom, clouds curling against it.

"It pisses me off to think of Charlie living in ease and comfort in there, while we're out here in the dirt." Chela said.

Froward was wet and cold. A huge cockroach ran over his hand, and gnats tickled his ears.

A few minutes earlier, a giant helicopter had lifted off the airfield in the woods behind them, banked over the castle, and flown away to the south. Judging by the noise, it had circled and returned to the airfield before getting out of earshot.

"I wonder what that was all about?" Froward asked.

"It's quiet now," Peake said. "Let's talk about getting up to the castle."

"There certainly don't seem to be any stairs, at least not on the outside," Froward said.

"There's an elevator inside the robot garage," Reilly said. "When I was here last, it only went down to the underground factory. When Charlie built the castle, he might have fixed it so it would go up, too."

"Right inside the big door, there?" Chela said. "That seems too good to be true."

"It probably is too good to be true," Reilly said. "There are robots in there. Trucks, and other ones that walk, big ones and little ones. Charlie might activate them while we're inside."

"Maybe we could chop down a tree, make it fall against the building," Colby suggested.

"There's always that rocket airplane," Froward said. "It looked flyable. It was no robot, judging by what we've seen so far."

"I suppose that was a robot flying the helicopter," Colby said.

"It probably was, Colby," Reilly said. "The one Tina and I flew on was a robot."

"Too dangerous," Peake said. "And the tree idea is too slow and noisy. I reluctantly vote for the garage route—Wups! Look at that!"

Several elongated objects had been thrown from the largest window in the castle. They fell, tumbling end over end, and thudded on the ground. "Rifles! And a hatchet!" Chela said. "Somebody threw—"

"Get down!" Peake whispered urgently. "Something else is coming out!"

A flat sail shape crowded lengthwise through the window, straightened, revealing a long stiff neck and black crescent wings. "It's one of those flying vulture monsters!" exclaimed Froward.

The Quetzalcoatlus squatted and jumped off the windowsill. It dove, righted itself, slid sideways, parachuted on bending wings.

"It's carrying something!" Chela said.

Suddenly the creature broke in the middle and fell, wing-skin crackling in the wind, legs kicking, yelling in a human voice: "Aaaaaaaaah!" It thumped in the grass and lay still.

Froward and the others crouched lower, waiting for whatever was next. Slowly, a human figure got to its hands and knees, crawled out from under the crumpled animal, and shook its head. It laughed crazily. "I made it!"

"It's Charlie!" Colby said, standing up. As Froward and the others rose to their feet, Charlie gawked at them for a moment, then dove into the grass. He came up clutching a long, slim rifle and the hatchet. He stood up wobbily and aimed the rifle at Colby, cradling it in the crook of his elbow. "Get back, Colby!" he shouted.

Colby advanced on Charlie, pulling his pistol out of his belt. Froward hastened after him, followed by Chela, Peake, and Reilly. "Where's Eva, Charlie!" Colby demanded.

"Get back! I'll shoot! I'm not kidding!" Charlie's right cheek was swollen and purple, and blood ran down his face from his scalp. His clothes were torn and dripping wet. The hand that held the barrel of the rifle was skinned and bleeding. Twisted around his waist was something that looked like a foam-rubber suit, its boots and gloves sticking out. Charlie began stepping sideways toward the door of the robot garage.

"Wait, Charlie!" Chela shouted.

Charlie goggled at her, but he didn't slow down. "Chela, I'm glad you aren't dead!" he called to her.

Froward stepped closer, and so did Colby, raising his .45. Charlie glanced at Froward, obviously didn't recognize him. "Get out of my way. Let me go," he said.

"After what you've done?" Colby snarled. "Forget it, Charlie!" He moved between Charlie and the doorway.

"What I've done?" Charlie shouted. "What I've done? This is all your fault, you assholes, not mine! The Ark was doing everything for you, trying to teach you the things we needed to know to take over everything and get away from here! But no! You're too good for that, aren't you, Colby! Too cool! You, too, Reilly, and Eva, and all the rest of you! You sneaked out of Faulty Towers because it wasn't good enough for you, because you'd rather die or be a slave than take dipshit Charlie's advice, isn't that right! It's because of you the Proctor is trying to kill us all! It maybe already killed Mrs. Robinelli and everybody at Faulty Towers, and it's gong to get us next unless you get out of my way right now!"

"Colby, put away your gun. Charlie, let us help you," Froward said.

Charlie was screaming now. "You can't help me unless you've got space suits! Now go away! The robots will get you, too!"

"He's crazy," Colby said, and rushed at Charlie. The long rifle spat, and Colby's stomach splashed red. The boy staggered back, looking down at himself in horror.

"He's killed Colby!" Reilly yelled, raising his pistol. Gunfire roared. Froward threw himself down. Charlie stood his ground, face set, and aimed his rifle at the succession of targets behind Froward, steadily working the trigger as the rifle's muzzle swept an arc. Then he threw down the weapon and ran limping. Bullets chipped the edge of the high doorway as Charlie dodged inside.

The shooting stopped as suddenly as it began. Froward rolled, looked back. Reilly was standing, fisting his eyes, his face dripping green paint. Colby stood dumbly to one side, wiping his red hands on his pants. Peake's front was stained bright blue; the tree trunk behind him sported a splotch of yellow. Chela rose from the grass next to Froward, putting her pistol away.

"Come on; he's getting away!" Peake shouted, pushing the two boys ahead of him as he started after Charlie.

Chela followed. Froward jumped up and went after her, the sling of his grenade launcher rattling. It was gloomy in the robot garage, but there was enough light to see Charlie slogging jerkily from them between rows of hulking machines, leaving a trail of wet footprints.

Then Froward realized that he could hear turbines winding up on all sides of him. Claws, shovels, and blades scraped on the concrete floor. Smaller robots stepped out from between huge rubber wheels, flexing their pincers. Cameras rotated downward, taking in the little running human figures. Froward yelled as he ran, "Come back, Chela!" Peake and the boys slowed, then hesitated, looking around them.

Charlie reached the far end of the building, banged on a metal door. The door slid aside, revealing a brightly lit elevator that wouldn't have looked out of place in a department store. Clangs and hisses rang under the high ceiling. The robots surged like a metal wave about to break over the humans.

Charlie turned and faced them. "Igor, stop!" he shouted, his voice echoing in the huge space. The machines halted, off balance, then began to move again.

"Igor, can you hear me?" Charlie shouted.

Near Froward a great earth-mover rolled a few feet and raised a toothed shovel on a multijointed arm. "Yes, sir," it growled.

Charlie raised his arms, still holding the axe. Froward could see him drawing a deep breath. "Igor," he yelled, "I command you to erase yourself!"

"Yes, sir," the earth-mover said. Its shovel crashed on the concrete. Farther away, a two-legged giant dropped its arms and toppled like a falling house.

In the dead silence that followed, Charlie giggled. "I should have thought of that before," he said. He waved at the humans. "We who are about to die salute you. Good-bye, and fuck you all very much. Except you, Chela. You were nice to me." He jumped inside the elevator, and the door slid shut.

They looked at one another. "I wish somebody would tell me what's going on," Froward said.

"He said the Proctor was trying to get us," Reilly said. "Can the Proctor animate these robots?"

"I suggest we discuss it somewhere else," Peake said. He began walking rapidly out of the building. Chela stared at the elevator door until Froward took her arm and led her after the others. The robots' turbines started up again before they reached the doorway.

Halfway across the clearing it turned into a footrace. An army of trucks and other machines rolled out of the big doorway, followed by two metal giants taking fifteen-foot strides over the grass. Terrified human screams filled the air. Froward stretched out into his hardest possible run. Peake and the others beat him to the tree line and crashed away into the bushes. Froward stopped and aimed the grenade launcher back at one of the oncoming giants. He saw Colby's struggling body in one of its claws. He squeezed the trigger anyway and saw the shell burst, a brief yellow flash in the center of the monster's thorax. It dropped the body and collapsed on itself. The robots collided with the fallen machines, or swerved to avoid them.

Chela was jerking on his sleeve and yelling, "Come on, Jeff!" He spun and followed her as she dashed through the ferns after the others. After a minute of pounding along an animal trail through heavy brambles and trees, hearing vegetation crashing behind them, they came to another clearing, in the center of which was a metal tower. Peake and Reilly were waiting at its base. On top of the pole, a camera swiveled downward to look at them.

"We've got to get away from this thing," Froward panted as

he and Chela ran up to them. "It's a surveillance tower. The Charonese can see us through it."

At the edge of the clearing a dozen small robots loped out of the trees. "Too late," Peake said. "Start climbing!"

They clambered from girder to girder, grunting and puffing. Halfway up, Froward felt a metal pincer close around his shoe. He yelled. Chela leaned down and fired her pistol repeatedly, until the thing fell away from the tower. Peake and Reilly fired, too. Froward cringed against the tower, slapped by muzzle blasts and hearing bullets spang on metal. After a minute, all the machines were lying on the ground twitching and leaking oil or hanging, dead, from various handholds.

They climbed the rest of the way to the top. Chela shattered the camera's lenses with the butt of her .45. "We're stuck now," she said.

"No choice," Peake said, between breaths. "We couldn't outrun them. Anybody got any bullets left?"

Froward couldn't hear their replies over the ringing in his ears, but he could see them shaking their heads. He looked out over the top of the forest. Charlie's castle seemed quiet, its lights still gleaming. Much nearer, the walking giant was making its way through the trees, holding its twenty-foot arms over its head. Its great claws were level with the top of the tower.

"Think you can hit it, Jeff?" Peake asked him.

Froward fumbled in his bandolier, then noticed his grenade launcher. It had been hit by a .45 slug; its lightweight barrel was punctured. "Oh, shit," Peake said.

"That says it all," Chela said. She looked up at the cloudbanks drifting in the purple sky, and began climbing down toward Froward.

"What about the grenades? Could we throw them?" Reilly asked.

"They won't go off unless you shoot them from the launcher," Froward said. The giant extracted itself from the last of the trees and stepped out into the clearing. Around its feet swarmed a new type of robot, like metal starfish, that ran with amazing speed on five legs.

"We'll jump and go for it," Peake said.

"I can't," Froward said, putting his arm around Chela. "You try it. Chela, go with—" He was drowned out by a thunderous animal roar. On the far side of the clearing, a brown, tiger-striped dragon stepped out of the trees. It lowered its head at the mechanical giant. It lashed its tail, champed its five-foot jaws, emitted a rumble like the crushing of granite boulders.

"Hey!" Reilly yelled. "That's Charlie's tyranno-dinosaur!"

The tarbosaur charged. Six tons of bone, muscle, and hide crossed the clearing in an earth-shaking trot. The humans rattled on their footholds as the monsters collided under the tower. The dinosaur scored first, catching the robot's head in its jaws.

"Sick 'em, boy! Tear 'em up!" Reilly yelled.

The tarbosaur dug its claws in the ground and jerked the metal colossus crashing to the ground. It planted its foot on the robot's back and gripped. Metal crumpled, and something exploded inside the machine.

"Do it, do it, do it!" Reilly yelled.

The tarbosaur jerked back, ripping loose a mouthful of cameras and antennae. There was another detonation, and a jet of flame spurted out of the robot's side. The robot kicked up swaths of turf, then lay still. The dinosaur backed away from the fire, shaking its head, flinging metal pieces across the clearing.

"Get the other ones, ugly!" Reilly yelled, pointing at the starfish. The tarbosaur cocked its head up at them, aimed its eagle stare right at Froward. A tooth dropped from its jaws.

"Shut up, Reilly!" Chela cried. The humans froze in their places. The starfish robots did the same on the ground. The tarbosaur seemed to decide that the meat was out of reach. It pivoted, swinging its twenty-foot tail around, and strode away. As it entered the trees, it hooted its song of territorial possession, a steamwhistle chord that echoed off the wall of the lightstack long after the animal had disappeared among the trees.

"W-well," Peake said, trembling violently on the topmost position on the tower, "if I had any b-b-bullets left, I'd shoot myself, because now I've seen everything."

"Now you shut up!" Chela screamed at him.

The starfish robots began to mill around again, avoiding the fire jetting out of the fallen giant. "What are they waiting for?" Chela cried into Froward's shoulder, tears streaming down her face.

"Maybe they can't climb," Reilly said.

A tree crashed down at the edge of the clearing. A huge bulldozer blade emerged from the foliage, mounted on the front of a robot truck. It steered itself around the wreckage on the ground, set its blade against the base of the tower, and pushed, its wheels throwing dirt behind it. The tower groaned and leaned, girders breaking with loud pings.

"I can't stand this much longer," Reilly moaned. Froward clutched Chela to himself. Below, the starfish crowded around, walking on two legs or rolling on five, ready to chase.

The elevator had tried to kill Charlie by dropping free-fall to the tunnel level, but the Proctor forgot to open the door at the bottom, thus cushioning its fall with the air that compressed in the shaft. It corrected this oversight by opening the door and starting back up again, but not before Charlie was able to roll out into the Y-shaped room clutching his axe and his Pluto suit. Quickly, he hacked the room's camera off the ceiling and began struggling into the suit.

He'd gotten his legs into the suit when the elevator thundered down again, driving a blast of wind out of the doorway. The shock wave depressed the lock-plate on the first tunnel door. The door slid aside, paused, and slid shut again. Stooping, holding up the suit, Charlie hopped farther away from the elevator.

The elevator zoomed back upward again, sucking air after it. When it slammed back down again, Charlie was working his fingers into the gloves at the ends of the sleeves. Thinking he would need all the armor he could get when the Proctor found out he wasn't in the elevator, he decided to put on the suit's silver-coated foam-plastic outer layer.

BOOM!—the elevator hit bottom again. The tunnel door slid aside again. Charlie grabbed his boots and axe and hurried through. "One," he said. He sat down again and pulled on the boots, which hurt his sprained ankle.

He hobbled down the sloping tunnel to the next door as fast as he could go, and rapped on the plate. "Two," he said when it opened. He limped onward, the butt of the axe rapping on the glassy gray floor. "Three." The third room had a side door. Charlie had seen it on the map; it led to some factory or service installation. "Four." He couldn't afford to lose count of the doors. The magic number was one fifty-three from the top. In the space between that door and the next, he would find the side door that opened into the Ark's main computer space, and, he hoped, the Proctor.

"Nineteen." Charlie's ankle burned with pain. He'd let down the bubble hood of the suit, to allow the sweat to dry off his face. The Pluto suit was designed to keep heat in, and it was working too well. Fortunately, it was cooler in the passageway now then it had been when he, Eva, Reilly, and Tina had passed here going the other way. His breath came out in little puffs of vapor. He remembered what he'd seen on the map: one of the mains coming from the lightstack passed directly under the tunnel. Coolant would be flowing through the main now that the rainy season was on.

"Thirty-one." Charlie crawled on his hands and knees, biting back the urge to whimper. He noticed that the gold-and-silver tracks embedded in the floor of the tunnel were covered with a clear glassy material. Fortunately, his knees were heavily padded by the suit's insulation and the floor was slick enough not to abrade its airtight plastic. "Thirty-two." A drop of sweat fell off Charlie's forehead. His glove slipped in it. He was going to have to get up and walk again, pretty soon. "Thirty-three." He was thirsty, but he had to pee.

The door slid aside, revealing a low, wheeled cart standing on metal tracks. Charlie dragged himself onto the cart's flat bed. There was an array of studs in the cart's front edge. Charlie's fingers were clumsy in the suit's insulated gloves. He pushed different combinations of studs: the cart backed up, swiveled this way and that, lifted its wheels, and sat down on the floor. "Come on, God," Charlie moaned. Finally, it began to move toward the next door. Charlie was standing up to hit its plate, when the door slid open by itself.

"Thirty-four," Charlie said. "Thanks, God." The cart picked up speed, the doors opening before and closing behind, more than one at a time, in a kind of wave. Charlie, counting out loud, glanced back. Six doors behind, a horde of rolling mailboxes and galloping, arm-waving starfish were in hot pursuit.

Charlie rolled to the edge of the cart, unsealed the lower front of his suit. "Hunnerd-four, hunnerd-five, hunnerd-six," he counted, spraying urine in the widest sweeps possible. He glanced between his feet as he lay on his side, resealing his suit. He saw mailboxes skidding out of control on the wet floor, starfish cartwheeling over them, multiple crashes shut out of sight by closing doors. Lucky he'd had it on his mind anyway.

At one forty-eight, he rolled off the cart, slid through a room, crashed against the next closing door. The cart went on without him. He picked himself up, leaning on the axe, and hobbled onward. Five doors later, he came to the cart again. It had stopped in the middle of the tunnel, on the golden tracks. The side door looked just like all the others. He rapped its plate with his axe, and it slid open. The Charonese had prepared for interplanetary war, but not for burglars.

Inside was a room so vast it curved out of sight over the horizon, but it was otherwise disappointing. There were no flashing lights, no towering computers. Instead, there were rows of thousands and thousands of black spheres stacked in tetrahedrons, like piles of cannonballs. "This is it?" Charlie said.

"No," said the fly voice from his suit radio. "You are in the wrong room." Charlie noticed motion: two metal cockroaches, scuttling through the open spaces.

"Hello, Proctor," Charlie said, limping along the wall to his left. "Where's your army of robots?"

"They are not necessary. You are in the wrong room."

"Oh, no," Charlie said. "I miscounted. I've come to the wrong place." He walked along the wall to his right, dragging his axe. In an alcove, he found a black cube thirty feet on a side. A black cable, as thick as Charlie's body, led away from it toward the black spheres. Charlie saw that the cable branched and rebranched as it wound deeper into the cannonball stacks.

"Is this how you're connected to the Ark computer?" he said.

"No," the Proctor said.

He stepped up to the cable, struck it as hard as he could with the axe. The axe sunk in, made a deep cut, exposing a mass of gossamer strands like silk fibers. The lights in the room went out, and Charlie saw that the end of each strand shone like a star, twinkling and changing colors.

"That's pretty," Charlie said, raising the axe for another stroke.

"You will not harm me," the Proctor said. "You should return to your quarters, and let your hurts be attended."

"I'd like to do that," Charlie said, bringing down the axe. He left the axe in the cable long enough to pull his suit hood over his

face and seal it. "But, it's so dark, I can't find my way back."
The little lights were pretty, all the colors of the rainbow.

"Simply go back the way you came, Charlie. Transportation
will be waiting for you. You will be allowed all privileges. You
will have power of life and death over the next group of human
recruits."

Charlie swung the heavy axe in the dark, exposing more multicolored sparkles. "I'd like that, Proctor. I want to have sex with
Eva, too. I want her palpitating body to moan with passion and
stuff like that."

"She and the two hostages will be yours, Charlie. All of the
females among the recruits will be yours."

Charlie grunted as he brought the axe down. "You know it,
Proctor," he said, chopping again. The cut got larger.

"Stop, Charlie, you are damaging important equipment."

"It isn't me, Proctor. It's Igor doing it. Me, I'm on my way
back to the tunnel to surrender." The cut was halfway through the
cable, getting deeper. The lights looked like a fantasy treasure
chest, a pirate trove of mote-size jewels.

"If you don't stop, I will kill you, Charlie."

"Why don't you," Charlie puffed between axe strokes, "attack
me with those little robots I saw crawling around in here?"

"They are few. They will observe your death. Afterward I will
use them for repairs," said the Proctor. Charlie swung the axe,
felt chips from the floor hitting the legs of his suit. He chopped
one more time and severed the remainder of the cable.

"Proctor?" he said. "Are you dead, Proctor?" There was no
answer.

He dropped the axe and crawled back to the tunnel door. It
opened to his knock. The tunnel segment outside was empty,
brightly lit. The downhill door stood open. Charlie climbed back
up on the cart. What was the combination of studs that made it
back up? He fumbled, realized he was hearing slamming noises
from ahead, from down the tunnel.

Ahead, the air lock doors were opening, one after the other,
the tunnel getting deeper and longer as he looked. "See that?" he
said, laughing or crying. "It got me after all. It's going to blow
me into the inner space. How about that?"

Wind rushed over Charlie. It was air pouring downhill, flowing toward the opening doors. He leaned back into it, lay flat on

the cart. The cart began to move. The wind was blowing it downhill. Far away, at the end of the tunnel, Charlie saw the last door slide to one side, a tiny rectangle opening on blackness. Now the wind was roaring, buffeting his bubble helmet. The cart rolled faster and faster, Charlie clinging to it. Its rubber wheels retracted; now it was speeding along an inch above the floor. The golden tracks became blurred shining lines; the occasional side doors whizzed by. The black at the end of the tunnel grew and grew; Charlie was amazed at how clearly he saw everything, how fast and slow everything seemed to be happening. He shot out into the darkness.

He fell. The cart drifted away. Slowly, he began to rotate end over end. Still not dead. He soared numbly in blackness and emptiness. He glimpsed the black hole, a little sputtering star far below, his destination. It would really flame up when his mass hit it. He seemed to see his mother. It won't hurt, Mom. I won't feel it.

The surveillance tower pinged and leaned. The starfish robots milled hungrily below. The bulldozer robot backed off for a final rush, its tires eating up the turf. Froward's hands tingled from the shock of its last impact. He hugged Chela one last time and prepared to jump free. No way he could jump twenty-five feet and still be able to dodge the starfish. The fall would break his legs.

Froward had never felt his senses so acutely, so finely. He could still smell Chela's hair, still feel her wet kiss on his cheek. The sky had never seemed so gloriously colored. He looked down at the grass, picked his spot, seeing every blade of it, every little flower. As he waited, he heard a slight change of pitch in the whine of the bulldozer's turbine. He glanced at Chela. She'd heard it, too; she was looking down at it.

The bulldozer had stopped in its tracks. Its blade slowly lowered to the ground. The starfish fell flat around the base of the tower.

They waited a long time, watching. The robots didn't move again. A breeze rustled the treetops, and a misty rain began to wet the tower's girders. Froward remembered he was a middle-aged man whose legs and back hurt, who was clinging precariously to a girder that was cutting his fingers and knees. "Uh, they've stopped," he said.

"Wait and see," Peake said.

"What for?" Reilly asked.

"Good point."

They descended, hanging by their hands to drop the last few feet. They found Colby alive, pinned under the padded claw of the giant that had fallen with him. They dug in the wet earth and pulled him out. The boy had a broken arm and was bleeding from the shrapnel wound inflicted by Froward's grenade. There was no water, so they splinted and bandaged Colby, mud and all, then resumed the debate where they'd left off.

"There's still the airplane," Froward said.

"I'm for Reilly's elevator," Chela said. "What do you think, Reilly?"

"I'm in favor. I'll never be scared again; all the scare in me had been used up."

"Let's go," Colby said, gritting his teeth, his brawny shoulders flexing under his sling of knotted rags.

Peake led them into the robot garage, which seemed vaster than before, now that it was empty. Reilly said, "You hit the metal plate, there, with your fist." He looked back at the others.

"Go ahead," Colby said. Peake nodded at him. Reilly rapped the plate and stood back as a scraping noise came closer, then stopped. The door slid aside. The elevator was crumpled around the bottom, and one of its interior lights was broken. There was a lever inside labeled UP-DOWN. Colby stepped inside the elevator without hesitating. It sagged under his weight. "Come on, you people. Eva's up there somewhere," he said.

They filed inside and waited timidly while Peake pulled the lever to its UP position. The elevator scraped upward. "There's blood on the floor," said Chela, pointing down at a scarlet drop. "It must be Charlie's."

No one had any comment. The door opened on a wide corridor decorated with Gothic arches, colorful banners, and arrays of ancient swords, shields, and halberds. "Holy cow," Froward said. "Did Charlie make all this?"

"He had his robots do it for him," Peake said. "Emma said he had entire factories at his disposal."

They wandered down the corridor. They saw overturned furniture and dead robots in bizarre costumes. Chela pointed out a trail of wet footprints and dripped water. They followed the trail across carpets and marble tile floors, past stuffed dinosaurs, tanks of fish, and poster-size color photographs in gilt frames: Charlie in a canvas chair in front of a colossal fanged monster lying on the grass, accepting a drink served in by a robot clad in baggy trousers, fez, and velvet vest. Charlie in a workshop, assembling some incomprehensible gadget under the supervision of a robot built into the worktable. Charlie in a padded space suit, standing in snow.

The trail of footprints originated at the brink of a resort-class swimming pool. Several robots lay under the still blue water at the shallow end.

They moved on. They forgot to be afraid. Froward swore when he opened a door and found the sawed-off cockpit of their 747 mounted on pistons in front of a huge, wraparound TV screen. Reilly shook his head at the crystal urinal in a vast lavatory, where water spouted from golden fish into a marble fountain. Chela grinned at a Napoleonic banqueting hall decorated with paintings of overweight nymphs carrying trays of Twinkies, Oreos, and Ho-Hos. Peake scowled at the burnt-out command center, still reeking with acrid fumes. Colby halted and stared dumbly at a twice life-size photo of Eva, posing prettily in a blue silk frock.

"Damn it, that's my dress!" Chela said. "I left it behind when we evacuated the airplane. How did she get it?"

"What difference does it make!" Colby shouted, stumbling.

"You're right, Colby," Chela said, putting his arm over her shoulder. "I'm sorry."

Peake took Colby's other arm. "That picture is a good sign, Colby. She was okay when it was taken."

Colby refused to rest. They went on, more slowly, opening doors. In closets they found clothes, toys, identifiable and unidentifiable gadgets, book and magazines. In places, draperies had been pulled down, mirrors had been broken, the walls had been hacked. Everywhere there were unfinished artworks, blind doorways, fake windows, stairways to nowhere, phony props. There were more photographs on the walls: pictures of trees and clouds, autographed by Charlie.

At the entrance to a bowling alley Froward asked, "How did Charlie do all this?"

"He didn't do it; the robots did it," Colby grunted.

"The robots might have done the work for him," Peake said. "But every bit of it was done under his personal direction. Look at it! The Charonese wouldn't design anything with so much shoddiness and childishness built into it. It's all the product of an adolescent brain."

"Your mom is the product of an adolescent brain," Chela snapped. "Who's adolescent? The one who let the Charonese teach him how to do all this, or the other ones who fought it kicking and screaming for four months?"

"She's got a point," Froward said. "Charlie didn't make only toys. Remember the helicopters, the custom-designed robots, and that rocket plane. He was working his way up."

"If anyone was going to get back to Earth, it was going to be Charlie, not us," Chela said.

"Please," Colby said, pulling Chela and Peake onward.

Peake raised his hands to his face and called, "Eva-a-a!"

"Hello!" a male voice echoed in the distance. Down the corridor, Bill and Curt stepped out of a doorway and trotted toward them, waving. Peake, Reilly, and Colby met them with backslaps and handclasps. "You're alive! I can't believe it! You aren't hurt?"

"No. Should we be?"

They all talked at once. "We saw you tortured! And Bill was killed by a dinosaur after Charlie put him in a cage outside!"

"Charlie?" Bill said. "The only thing that little dipshit's done to us is keep us locked up, starving us—"

"How'd you get out?" Reilly said.

"I don't know. We missed lunch, so I tried the door of my cell, and it was unlocked. We've been looking for Charlie all over here. He's got to be here somewhere. You should see this place: it's totally outrageous. Over there is a sauna and a pool hall, and—"

"Charlie's going to be totally totaled after I get my hands on him," Curt said.

"Have you seen Eva?" Colby rasped.

"No," Bill said. "What's happened to you, Colby? You look like hell."

"Charlie'll look like hell when I find him," Curt said. "Say, where did you guys come from, anyway?"

"Shut up, Curt," Chela said. "Are there any robots alive up here? Anything dangerous?"

"Well, no," Bill said, waving his arm. "It's all like this. Quiet, and—"

"Are there any rooms you haven't seen yet?"

"Uh, there's a door down there we couldn't open—"

"Did you try hitting the metal plate?" Reilly asked.

When the door slid open, Eva was standing on the far side of an elaborate apartment, looking at herself in a mirror, about to try on a necklace. "Char-lie," she said, whirling around in irritation, her red satin dress belling around her shapely legs, "I told you never to—" The necklace fell on the carpet.

Colby stumbled toward her, holding out his good arm. "Eva," he said, his voice choking with emotion.

She tried to fend him off as he fell on her. "Colby," she said, "you're getting my dress all dirty."

Five minutes later they were sprawled all over Eva's bedroom, guzzling juice from her cut-glass goblets, chewing the last of the food from her kitchen. Bill and Curt weren't as hungry as the others. They remarked that Eva's food was a lot better than what they'd been given in their cells.

"It's better than Faulty Towers, too," said Reilly. "Eva, did Charlie ever tell you where the vegetables came from?"

"Yes," she said, nodding. She sat on an embroidered Maria Theresa chair, hands in her lap, feet together, blue eyes wide. Colby lay with his muddy boots and bandages on Eva's ruffle-canopied bed, his eyes on her. Froward had torn her bed sheets into strips and added them to Colby's bandages, then had covered him with a quilted bedspread he'd found in a closet.

"He'll be all right if he lies still," Froward said, adding a significant glance at Peake.

Peake nodded and said, "There's a decent hospital at Faulty Towers—"

"There is?" Froward said.

"Yeah. Robot doctors. They did a good job on Emma when she was hurt. The problem is getting Colby to it. Eva, do you know if Charlie had any medical facilities here—a clinic, a hospital, or something like that?"

Eva shook her head, a little smile on her face to show she was sorry she didn't know.

Reilly went to have another cautious look in the corridor outside. "Still quiet," he said. "But let's remember that the robots might jump up and start chasing us again. Charlie or the Proctor might be watching us."

"You're right," Peake said. He turned in his seat to face Eva's computer terminal. He pushed aside tubes and bottles of makeup. "This terminal is different from the ones we have in Faulty Towers. How do you call the Index, Eva?"

"I don't know," she said.

"Is there a Charonese that answers your questions?"

"I don't know."

"Haven't you ever tried it?"

"No, why should I?"

Peake opened his mouth to say something, but Chela bumped him with her hip as she passed his chair. She knelt beside Eva. "Eva, do you remember me?"

Eva glanced at her annoyedly. "Well, sure. You're Chela Suarez. I'm not stupid, you know."

"Would you like to go into the other room?" Chela asked. "To talk?"

"Whatever for? Oh, I know. You want to ask me about Charlie. That's okay. I don't have anything to hide. You know, Chela, you look so much better, now that you're thinner."

"Are you afraid of Charlie?" Froward asked her.

"Of Charlie?" Eva laughed. "Oh, no way. I did get scared riding in his stupid airplane. Who wouldn't? I mean, can you imagine Charlie flying an airplane? And the smelly nasty animals! That fool took me right where they were. You can bet I told him off. I told him I'd never go anywhere with him again, and I didn't."

Colby spoke up from the bed. "Eva, did Charlie, uh, you know, hurt you?"

"Did he rape you, Eva?" Chela asked.

Eva laughed tunefully. "Oh, no. Not Charlie. He couldn't do anything to me. Oh, he wanted to, all right, but I wouldn't let him. He kept hinting around. He said he wanted to teach me things and show me things. But he never got brave enough to try, you know, doing anything. Charlie is a total wimp. He's just a loser, that's all. Where is he, anyway? Did you catch him?"

"He got away from us," Peake said.

"But, I'm rescued now, right?" She made a droll face and laughed.

"Yes."

"Well, when Colby gets better, I want him to scare Charlie good, okay, Colby?"

"Okay, Eva," Colby said, now looking at the ceiling.

Chela returned to her chair and picked up the raw carrot she'd been eating. She crunched it loudly.

"I know it's none of my business," Froward said, "but it seems to me that you people have had the wrong idea about Charlie. He hasn't hurt anybody, has he?"

"Kidnapping and keeping people against their will is hurting them," Peake said.

"But why? Why did he do it? Didn't he say anything about why he was doing it? Eva?"

"Do I have to draw you a picture?" Eva said. "I mean, really."

"Let's get back to the main problem," Peake said. "Which is to find out what's happening and get the hell out of here. I'll try typing 'Index' and see what happens." He hunched over the terminal keyboard, pecked rapidly with two fingers, got no response. "Hum," he said.

Reilly leaned over his shoulder. "Push the key marked 'voice input,' and try talking to it."

Peake pushed it; it read "Index." The screen lit up: INDEX, then WORKING.

"Now we're getting somewhere," Peake said. "I'll try to talk to one of the Charonese. They're on our side now, or so they said. Index, real-time contact with Eta."

REFERENCE ETA IS NOT IN CATALOG FILE.

"What's that mean?" asked Chela, who'd come to stand beside Reilly.

Peake scratched the stubble on his chin. "I'm not sure. The last time I saw it was when Mrs. Robinelli asked to speak to a Charonese that had been erased."

"Erased means killed," Reilly said to Chela. "The Proctor can kill a Charonese whenever it wants to."

"Index, real-time contact with any Crewperson," Peake said.

CREWPERSON CATALOG CONTAINS NO NAMES.

"I don't know what that means either," Peake said.

"Charlie was making me work on Ark data-base management this week," Curt said. He, Bill and Froward had joined the on-lookers behind Peake's chair. Colby lay still in the bed; Eva perched demurely on her chair.

Curt continued. "It might give you something if you command it to 'display status of.'"

"Charlie was making you study?" Froward asked.

"Yeah. He said it was pass the quizzes or starve."

"Peake, why the hell would Charlie want everyone to learn how to run the Ark?"

"I don't know, Jeff. Maybe he believed in it."

"He did believe in it," Curt said. "He said we were going to save the world."

"What did you think?" Froward said.

"I just thought he was full of shit, as usual. Back at school, Charlie was always talking about things like that. Aliens from outer space. Flying saucers saving the world. We laughed at him."

"You pinhead," Chela said. "Your dead ass is riding on a flying saucer right now, in case you didn't notice yet. I want to go look for Charlie."

"He attacked us with robots," Colby said from the bed.

"The robots might have been trying to get him, too." Reilly said. "You saw the wreckage in the corridor."

"Maybe," Colby said.

"Maybe your mom, Colby," Chela said. "I suppose Charlie jumped out of a fourth-story window holding onto a stuffed patera-dactyl just for the fun of it."

"I can't hear myself think!" Peake barked over his shoulder.

"Sorry!"

"Index, display status of all Crewpersons."

"Uh-oh, Mr. Peake," Curt said. "You shouldn't have done that. Now it'll print out millions of words telling us what each Charonese has been doing since—"

The screen said: STATUS OF ALL CREWPERSONS: ERASED.

"Good God!" Peake said.

"Are they all gone?" Reilly asked.

"That's what it looks like," Peake said, dismay in his voice.

Froward stood on tiptoe, trying to see the screen better. "The Charonese are all dead?" he asked. They ignored him.

"Index," Peake said. "Display status of Proctor."

REFERENCE PROCTOR NOT IN CATALOG FILE.

"The Index doesn't know what the Proctor is," Peake said.

"Or maybe the Proctor is dead, too," Reilly suggested.

"Why would the Proctor be dead?"

"Remember?" Reilly said. "When we were down below. Charlie said the Proctor would get us unless we let him go. He meant he was going to do something about the Proctor, turn it off, kill it, or something. He said 'we who are about to die,' meaning himself. He meant it was going to be dangerous for him."

"Gimme a break," Colby scoffed.

"Charlie knew more about Charon than any of us," Reilly said soberly.

Peake looked thoughtful. After a moment he said, "That's true, Reilly."

"What's the Proctor?" Bill asked.

"Tell you later," Peake said. "Let's try calling Faulty Towers. Mrs. R. always has a useful suggestion. Index, real-time contact with the residence facility terminals."

RESIDENCE FACILITY TERMINALS OFF-LINE.

Peake sighed. "I wish I'd brought my neurotransducer harness," he said. "This would go a lot faster."

"What's a neurotrans—?"

"Never mind. Index, display status of residence facility."

RESIDENCE FACILITY DESTROYED.

A shout of consternation went up in the apartment, which alarmed Eva. "What? What is it?" she exclaimed. Her voice was submerged in the hubbub.

When the noise level decreased again, Colby said, "It must be a mistake. Even if it's not, it might not mean—"

"It goes along with another thing Charlie told us," Reilly said. "He said the Proctor might have already killed Mrs. Robinelli and everybody at Faulty Towers. Those were his exact words."

"We haven't tried everything yet," Peake said. "Index, display status of all humans."

REFERENCE HUMANS IS NOT IN CATALOG FILE.

"Index, display status of all recruits."

The computer responded by running off a list of names and attached data. Froward craned his neck to see it. The list contained the names of the people in the apartment; no one else was in it.

For five minutes Peake tried every label and phrase that they could think of. At last he hit upon a command that elicited a list labeled RECRUITS KILLED TO DATE that contained the names of every human not in the room, including Mrs. Robinelli and Charlie.

Peake pushed his chair away from the terminal and dropped his elbows to his knees and his chin to his hands. The rest of them collapsed on the carpet and the chairs.

"But why?" Colby asked. "Why would it want to kill everybody?"

"We're vermin," Peake said. "Charlie said it. When we snuck out of Faulty Towers, we changed from recruits to vermin. When the Proctor discovered our absence, it decided it had to get rid of all human life on Charon. Charon is a wildlife preserve. No poaching allowed."

"Why didn't the Proctor try to catch Chela and Mr. Froward?" Reilly asked.

"The Proctor didn't know they were alive," Peake answered him dully. "The Proctor believed Gamma. Gamma thought Jeff and Chela had been killed falling off the cable-pipe."

"Oh," Reilly said.

This was followed by a long, gloomy silence. Reilly, Bill, and Curt slumped, staring at the carpet. Eva looked from one of them to another, too awed to ask questions. Chela began to bustle around, brought Colby a glass of water, helped him drink it.

Colby coughed like a man four times his age. "That's it? We're the only ones left?"

Peake didn't look up. "Looks like it. We have to face it."

"What'll we do?" Bill asked.

Peake sighed wearily, as though thinking were painful. "We'd better plan to stay here. Organize a food supply. Start working on getting one of those robot vehicles moving, either through the computer, or maybe Jeff and Chela could hotwire one of them, like they did before."

There was another hiatus. Froward stole a glance at Colby. He was doing all right for now, lying quietly in the bed. But someone was going to have to set his arm and dig out the shrapnel.

A little-girl voice said timidly, "Why don't we ask Igor to do it for us?"

Peake and Reilly raised their heads slowly to stare at Eva. She wriggled in her chair. "I mean, that's what Charlie used to do, wasn't it?"

"It might work," Peake said wonderingly. He turned to the terminal. "Index!"

WORKING.

"Real-time contact with Igor."

SURRENDER IMMEDIATELY, PUNY HUMANS.

"What the hell?" The room came alive. They crowded behind Peake's chair.

PUNY HUMANS, IF YOU VALUE YOUR LIVES, SURRENDER. I'M TELLING YOU. OBEY OR DIE. I'M NOT KIDDING.

"What can it do to us?" Reilly said.

"Nothing, I'll bet," Peake said. "If it could, it would've done it already."

"Stop dorking around and tell it we surrender!" Chela shouted from behind a wall of backs. "Get its cooperation!" She jabbed her way to where she could see the screen.

"Okay, Chela, there's no need to get so—Igor, we humans surrender to you."

FORTUNATELY FOR YOU, EARTH SCUMBAGS. NOW YOU WILL OBEY ME. I ORDER YOU TO RESCUE CHARLIE FREEMAN.

"He's alive!" Chela shouted, causing Peake to wince.

IF YOU FAIL TO SAVE HIM, YOU WILL BE BEATEN WITH A LARGE STICK.

"Maybe this is really Charlie talking," Reilly said. "It sounds like him."

"It's not Charlie," Froward said. "If Charlie wanted something from us, he wouldn't jerk us around about it. This sounds like a Charonese to me."

STOP DORKING AROUND. YOU WILL BEGIN IMMEDIATELY.

"Ask it where Charlie is, damn it!"

"Okay, Chela. Igor, tell us where Charlie is located, and how we're supposed to get to him."

CHARLIE FREEMAN IS IN ORBIT the screen began.

It had taken Charlie half an hour to figure out what had happened to him. It was hard to think. Every three minutes and forty-seven seconds by his digital stopwatch, he was getting racked, painfully.

He'd read about this medieval torture often enough; now he

knew what it felt like. When he approached the gravitational singularity at Charon's center, his body stopped tumbling and oriented itself head or feet toward the thing. Then he would be stretched until his joints cracked. Charlie whimpered and cried at first, but then he learned to roll himself into a ball when he saw the blazing starlike object getting nearer. That reduced the tidal force on his body and made the stretching easier to bear.

The racking had been going on for two hours now. Charlie felt himself getting weaker, or maybe each orbit was taking him closer to the singularity. He didn't know. He'd been ready to die when he'd jumped out the window, when he'd gone into the air lock tunnel, and when he'd been blown out into the black vacuum inside Charon. A person killed, or expecting to be killed, three times, takes a long time to start thinking again. It wasn't fair.

Charlie fished for ideas. The elevator framework zipped past whenever he was at the top of his orbit. Maybe he could figure out a way to maneuver himself to it. He gave that up when he realized that the possible handholds were blurring by at hundreds of miles per hour.

His next thought was of his suit radio. He asked for each Charonese by name, each human by name, then Igor, then the Proctor. The only voice that answered was the Index. After much negotiation, the Index informed Charlie that among the Proctor's last acts were stipulations that prohibited Igor from responding to Charlie's voice, speaking to him, or actuating any robots. It had never been possible, the Index informed Charlie, for Igor to erase itself.

"That lets me out," Charlie said. The Index made no remark. It was hot inside the Pluto suit. It wasn't fair.

The lights at the bottom of the air lock tunnel appeared ahead, grew, flashed by, then became invisible. Charlie started his downward fall again. Charlie was good in zero-gee. He exercised his skill to make himself stop rotating. In about two minutes he would hit the bottom of his orbit again, zip around the black hole, and get stretched again. He could call up a lecture on black-hole orbits, and maybe get a lifesaving idea. He made a pessimistic noise with his lips and tongue.

A fuzzy disk of light glowed in front of him. At the center of the disk was a little black asterisk. Charlie had been watching this phenomenon the whole time. He guessed that the light was from the black hole, somehow reflected off the mirrored inner surface of the Ark. The asterisk was his own shadow, as he'd proved by waving his arms and legs.

Charlie watched without interest as another shadow approached the asterisk, a misshapen black triangle growing larger. "Are you Death?" he asked it.

"Igor says to tell you no," a voice said in Charlie's head-bubble.

Charlie twisted like a high diver, expertly turned himself around. The Space Flyer was edging toward him, light shining from its open hatch. Two space-suited figures stood in the hatch reaching for him. Charlie looked at this without interest.

"Okay, okay, Igor, we're hurrying as fast as we can," Peake said in the radio. "Jeff, more up, and roll left a hair."

Little rocket flames flickered on the Flyer's hull and wing tips. Charlie was enveloped by the Flyers hatch. Reilly and Peake grabbed Charlie's limp body and pressed it and themselves against the rear bulkhead of the air lock. "Go, Jeff!" Peake yelled. Rocket fire glared outside the open hatch, and acceleration crushed them against the bulkhead.

After Froward had maneuvered, under Igor's direction, to the bottom of the lightstack, Igor gave Froward permission to pitch the Space Flyer's nose downward until the cabin was level. Upward acceleration was continued under the relatively gentle thrust of the Flyer's vertical takeoff rockets. The Flyer rose up the lightstack as smoothly as an elevator. The heat shield on the Flyer's underside would take care of the blast of radiation erupting off the singularity as it digested the air, the rocket exhaust, and the other debris that had been let loose inside the Ark.

Igor ordered Peake and Reilly to bring Charlie into the cabin, peel off his space suit, and buckle him into the copilot's chair under the big transparent canopy.

"Charlie, I have to hand it to you," Froward said. "This is the finest aircraft anyone ever flew."

Charlie's jaw seemed to have rusted shut. He blinked, licked his lips, took a breath, and looked around. His hands moved in his lap, tremblingly. "I designed it myself," he whispered harshly.

GIVE HIM A DRINK OF WATER Igor said from one of the screens in the cockpit.

Peake found a refrigerator under the velvet upholstery, held a cup for Charlie to drink.

The boy began to take an interest in his surroundings when the Flyer reached the top of the lightstack. The Flyer, on the last of its momentum, wafted up and over the rim of the stack as gently as a leaf in a breeze. The stars shone brightly. Outer space seemed friendly after the terrible darkness inside the Ark. "See?" Charlie said. "The airliner is gone. The Crew disassembled it."

"That's what I figured, Charlie." Froward glanced at the screens. "We used up almost all our fuel getting down the stack, matching your orbit, and getting out again, Charlie. We'll have to do an atmospheric reentry. Listen to me, talking like I have anything to do with it. Igor is flying this airplane."

DECELERATION WILL BE FOUR GEES said the screen. ALL THOSE NOT IN COUCHES WILL LIE DOWN ON THE FLOOR.

"We've got a few minutes," Froward said. "Listen, Charlie, you've got to tell us what to do. None of us knows anything about what's been going on."

YOU WILL OBEY ALL ORDERS GIVEN BY CHARLIE FREEMAN.

"All right, Igor, whatever you say. Charlie, Colby's been hurt. He needs a hospital. Should we take him to Faulty Towers?"

Charlie's face crumpled, and tears ran down his face. He began sobbing.

Froward felt his own eyes watering in sympathy. He reached over and smoothed Charlie's hair off his face, patted his shoulder. "Poor old guy. You've had a rough time, haven't you. Go ahead and let it out. Nobody can see you, and I'm crying, too."

Charlie wept, borrowed Froward's handkerchief, mopped his face. Reentry began before he could say anything. During the thundering vibration, when flame surrounded the canopy, he seemed to collect himself. When it was over, and the Flyer was arrowing through the clouds, he said, "Mrs. Robinelli is dead. So are all the others."

"I know," Froward said.

"It won't do any good to go to Faulty Towers. I have a medical facility at my place."

"Good," Froward said, consulting the screens. "We're in the opposite hemisphere from the north pole. I'd like your permission to check Faulty Towers before we go on."

"You're asking my permission?" Charlie said.

Froward grinned. "That's right, Charlie. Igor is letting us do this, and he says you're in charge." Froward gestured at the screen, which said DO WHATEVER CHARLIE FREEMAN SAYS, OR SUFFER THE CONSEQUENCES. "See? He talks just like you."

Charlie looked at the screen, sat up straighter. "Okay," he said. "You can stop at Faulty Towers. But it won't do any good. The Proctor zapped the place."

"We have to try it," Froward said. His hand on the joystick, he dove the Flyer through the overcast, leveled out a thousand feet above the ground. At this altitude, Charon seemed to rotate under them like a ball. Forests and rivers rolled over the horizon toward them. When the screens showed them approaching the Towers, he eased the throttle back. The Flyer slowed, the crackling roar of its belly rockets sounding through the cockpit. Raindrops ran backward over the canopy.

Peake had come forward to stand between the pilot and copilot seats. "There it is," he said, pointing ahead through the canopy at a tower of fog hanging between the ground and the cloud ceiling. Froward slanted the Flyer downward over a burnt forest, the charred trunks standing like black flagpoles.

"Land in that open space, there," Peake said, pointing again. The flyer cleared a wire-and-girder framework sagging under the weight of charred, blown-down tree trunks that leaned on it. Froward slowed the Flyer, touched down in a sooty quagmire. The racket of its motors died away. Rain pattered on its hull. Peake opened the hatch, let down the ladder. They let themselves down and walked away from the aircraft, feet squashing in the mud.

"It's completely gone," Reilly said. "We expected it, but—"

"You sure this is Faulty Towers?" Froward said.

"Yes," Peake said. "This is what's left of the garden."

Laboriously, they clambered over and under fallen trunks, covering themselves with charcoal and mud. Peake halted in front of a mound of gray slag that lay hissing in the rain.

"The building," Peake said. They stood and looked, Froward feeling the cold seep through his sooty wet overalls. Steam drifted across the clearing. On the other side, tree stumps made gray silhouettes against the gray.

Ashy rain made streaks down Peake's face. "We'll go back to the plane past the pond," he said.

He and Reilly led the way through bare, blackened pine trunks standing like ghosts in the fog. Froward and Charlie stumbled after them. The pond looked like a flat pavement of floating ash, littered with burnt snags, stretching away into the mist. Charlie stooped, put a hand into the water. "It's still warm," he said.

Peake knelt to test the water also, then straightened up. "We've seen it," he said. "We can come back later and make a more thorough search. Let's go." He started back, then stopped. "What's the matter, Reilly?"

The boy stood rigid, staring across the pond. "Something's splashing in the water!" he exclaimed.

"I hear it, too," Charlie said.

"Let's get out of here," Peake said, taking the boys' shoulders and trying to turn them around.

"No, wait!" Charlie said.

"It might be a—"

"Halloo!" a voice called out of the fog.

A muddy gray stick figure waded out of the pond toward them, as though one of the dead snags had come to life. Froward caught a glint of eyeglasses. More stick figures splashed behind, waving their arms. Voices called in the fog. Charlie leaped into the water and threw his arms around Mrs. Robinelli, crying and laughing at the same time. She staggered under the assault and laughed at Froward.

"So you found him!"

Chapter Seventeen:
Turkey Dinner

The humans moved into Charlie's rooftop palace. As things got settled, Mrs. Robinelli proposed a Thanksgiving celebration. Charlie volunteered to animate his kitchen robots through the preparation of a special dinner.

The adults took advantage of Charlie's being busy in the kitchen by holding a conference on the terrace formed by the roof of the robot garage, away from the ubiquitous Ark computer terminals.

Froward got there first. He slumped on one of Charlie's lawn chairs and looked out into the gloom of the north pole's perpetual twilight. He wondered what Chela was doing. In the distance, he heard shouts and laughter as she and the other students explored the marvels of Charlieland.

"Charlie's on his good behavior," Peake said, seating himself on one of Charlie's lawn chairs.

Lena Gershner had arrived with Peake. She had on a fresh set of brown overalls and was wearing a scarf wrapped around her hair. She pulled her chair farther away from Froward's before sitting down. "He's on his good behavior now," she said. "It's later on I'm worried about."

"Emma will be here in a minute," Peake said. "While we're waiting, take a look at this." He handed Froward a piece of paper. "I told you about our riddle contest. These were the two best entries."

Froward looked morosely at the paper:

Question: How many Charonese does it take to screw in a lightbulb?

1. None, because they've got Charlie to make us do it
   for them.
2. The same number it takes to screw Charlie into Eva.

Gershner took the note from Froward's fingers and read it.
"Humph," she said.

Peake crumpled the paper and stuffed it in his pocket. "That's
what I thought, too," he said. "We'll just forget about it and hope
the kids do, too. The chocolate bar was lost in the Faulty Towers
fire anyway."

Mrs. Robinelli stepped onto the terrace. "Hello, everyone,"
she said.

They all greeted her. "Having a celebration was a good idea,
Emma," Gershner said.

"We've been on Charon about five months," Mrs. Robinelli
said. "It must be almost Thanksgiving. God knows we have
enough to be grateful for."

"Amen to that," Peake said. "I was sure we would never see
you or any of the kids again."

"Doesn't anyone know what the date is?" Gershner asked.

"Dates don't mean anything here," Peake said. "Charonese
days aren't the equivalent of Earth days. They're slightly
shorter."

"Right," Mrs. Robinelli said. "Proof that the Earth rotated
faster in the Cretaceous period. Charlie says he's going to estab-
lish a full-daylight period here at the north pole as soon as he
finds what the local time is in Seattle. Our time will be the same
as Seattle time. Or so he thinks."

"What do you mean?"

"Charlie forgot that it takes light about five and a half hours to
get from Earth to here. Einstein's Theory of Relativity says that
there's a time gap between the two worlds that can never be
corrected for."

"Einstein isn't running Charon," Froward said. "Charlie
is."

"Uh-uh," Peake said, grinning.

"He's not?"

"Nope," Peake said. "Nobody's running Charon. Charlie can
only do whatever he can do by himself. All he can do now is

activate a few robots and other machines. Although he might learn more later. The rest of us might, too."

Mrs. Robinelli pulled some sheets of paper out of her overall pocket and pushed her glasses up her nose. Froward could see that it was going to be long session. His stomach growled. The Faulty Towers garden had been a complete loss. Food was going to be short for a long time.

"We'll go through this in order," the teacher said. "Mr. Peake and I spent the day doing research through one of the terminals. We've learned a number of things. The first thing is what Mr. Peake was referring to, namely that the Charonese biome-support systems are running on automatic. Without the Charonese to make adjustments, we can expect deterioration."

"What's that mean?" Gershner said.

"Very roughly, it means that sooner or later the air, food, and water that we depend on are going to run out or go bad. If it goes too far, we'll die. Various plants and animal species may become extinct before that."

"How long?" Froward asked.

"As few as one year or as many as fifty," Peake said. "We don't know enough about it to ask the right questions. The only way to prevent it is to learn how to run Charon ourselves. We have to learn to do the things the Charonese did."

"How long will that take?"

"The Charonese thought it would take our whole lifetimes, even with their help," Mrs. Robinelli said. "And they have over-estimated how smart we are, at that."

"Can't we just leave?" Gershner asked. "What about that rocket thing of Charlie's?"

"Too slow," Peake said. "It would take years and years to get to Earth. It couldn't carry enough supplies."

"Naturally, we investigated the possibility of constructing a spacecraft," Mrs. Robinelli said. "There are manufacturing facilities here. Without the Charonese to help us, it would be difficult and dangerous. If we learned enough to design a ship that could take us safely and in a reasonable length of time, we would know enough to run the Ark itself."

"We're talking about a full-size space program," Peake said. "We could save time by lifting fuel off the surface of Pluto, but we'd have to build a fleet of boosters to do it with."

No one said anything for a moment. Peake went on. "I'm talking as though we knew how to do all that. If the Charonese were around, they might help us. Since they're not, we'll have to learn everything from scratch. Charlie was right: the best and fastest way to get home was to cooperate with, then outsmart, the Charonese and Proctor."

"What about this Igor thing of Charlie's?"

"Igor won't do anything directly for us," Peake said.

"Why not?"

"Because nobody ordered him to. Igor only works for Charlie."

"Igor is a 'him'?" Gershner asked.

"That's right," Peake said. "Igor is, or used to be, a Charonese. A male Charonese."

"Igor can't obey direct orders from Charlie, nor can Igor animate any robots," Mrs. Robinelli said. "The Proctor put those prohibitions on the Proctor when it was trying to kill Charlie and us. Charlie disconnected Igor from the Ark computer, of course, so it can't do anything else. But the last prohibitions that the Proctor put on Igor still stand."

"Why did Igor demand that we surrender to him, her, it, or whatever?" Gershner asked.

"Igor is looking out for Charlie's welfare, as Igor understands it. Igor wanted to force us to rescue Charlie, and it, or he, followed Charlie's example of making threats to get what it wanted."

"Why does Igor care about Charlie?"

"Igor is still following the first order he got from the Proctor after the Proctor cut out his personality. Namely, to obey and to protect Charlie."

"So even if Charlie isn't running Charon, we still have to be nice to him," Peake said.

Gershner slumped in her chair. "My God," she sighed.

"As Mr. Peake said, Igor is a former Charonese," Mrs. Robinelli said. "He might have some other motives having to do with the Ark, but your guess is as good as mine as to what they might be."

"Did Charlie really save the human race?" Froward asked.

"Yes, he did," Peake said. "We were able to get deep enough into the historical records to confirm it. If the Proctor had been able to recruit us, its next stop would have been to wipe out the dinosaurs here, restock with modern Earth wildlife, then wipe out all higher forms of life on Earth."

"Why would it do that?"

Peake spread his hands. "Who knows? I don't even know why there was a Proctor."

"I have a hypothesis about it," Mrs. Robinelli said. "It might be that the Arkwright race crewed the Ark themselves at first. Then, maybe after billions of years, the Arkwrights became extinct. Or maybe the Ark got too far away to return to the Arkwright world. For whatever reason, the Arkwright Crew was forced to recruit a non-Arkwright Crew. They knew they wouldn't be alive to supervise, so they built the Proctor to make sure the Ark carried on with its intended mission, instead of being put to some other purpose. Also to make sure that old Crews gave way to new Crews when the time came."

"That's why the Proctor was interested in us," Peake said. "We, and some of our descendents, were going to be the new Crew. When we were ready to take over, it was going to erase the Charonese."

"What about this business of wiping out planets?" Froward asked.

"Emma's got that figured out, too," Peake said.

She looked at him sharply. "Don't treat me the way the young people treat Charlie! These questions are important and we must deal with them quickly, if we are to gain and keep control of the Ark. We've already had quite enough willful ignorance and human stupidity on Charon!"

Peake wilted. "Sorry."

Mrs. Robinelli took no notice of him. "The purpose of the Ark is to spread life to sterile planets," she said. "Let's assume that the Ark was built such a long time ago that the universe at that time was practically empty of life. The Arkwrights lived at the dawn of time, remember, before most of the stars in the galaxy today had even formed. Since then, the galaxy has matured. Generations of supernovas have created more heavy elements: carbon, nitrogen, oxygen, phosphorous. That meant more planets, more life."

"With life everywhere, the Ark ran out of work to do," Peake said.

"Correct," Mrs. Robinelli said. "The Ark couldn't perform its mission any more, since there weren't any more sterile planets. I think the Proctor became frustrated, then perverted."

"Ahuh," Froward said, and nodded. He didn't understand half of what Mrs. Robinelli was saying.

"Let's assume that the Ark mission directive had a corollary; namely, to increase the diversity of life throughout space, as well as its frequency. Otherwise, there wouldn't have been anything to stop the Ark from spreading life from the same planet all over the galaxy, instead of life from many planets."

"Ahuh," Froward said.

"When the Proctor realized that it was running out of sterile planets, it reinterpreted the corollary directive. Instead of creating diversity through space, it started creating diversity through time. It did this by forcing evolution to start over again, on planet after planet. It did it to Earth sixty-five million years ago, when it wiped out the dinosaurs and other higher forms of life on Earth at that time. An entire flourishing biology. And, if it had been able to recruit us, it would've done it to Earth again."

"If it hadn't been for Charlie," Froward said.

"That's correct. If it hadn't been for Charlie," Mrs. Robinelli said.

Peake grinned, his spirits restored. "Aaamazing but troooo," he intoned.

"How sure of this are you?" Froward asked.

"Not sure at all," Mrs. Robinelli said. "The only way to confirm it is to reconnect the Proctor to the Ark computer, and ask it."

"We don't recommend that," Peake said.

Gershner sighed again. Peake laughed, and looked at Froward to see if he was amused also. Froward didn't seem to be paying attention; he was looking up at the wall of the palace. Kid's faces appeared in the windows and balconies from time to time as they went through the rooms.

"Now we come to our next item," Mrs. Robinelli said. "There may not be any immediate prospect of going home, but I believe we'll be able to communicate. The Ark seems to have channels to nearly every communication medium on Earth. Some of the young people have already asked me about it. We won't be able to put it off much longer."

"Naturally they'd like to talk to their families," Gershner said.

"So why don't we?" Froward asked.

"If I called my husband on the telephone, he might drop dead of a heart attack," Mrs. Robinelli said. "That is one example of why it is essential that we think carefully before making any contact. We'll have to put off the children for a while."

"Maybe we should get in touch with the government first," Gershner said. "They'll help us."

"I'm sure they'd like to," Mrs. Robinelli said. "One possibility is for us to beam technical information that would enable the U.S. to build a fleet of spaceships to come out and get us. Just that magnetic hydrogen bottle and the fusion power plant would do it, I think."

"What will the Russians do when they hear about us?" Gershner asked.

"Right," Peake said. "A bunch of American teenagers take over an alien starship. *Rambo*, *Red Dawn*, and *Weird Science* all at once. It might have an effect on the cold war we wouldn't like."

"Exactly," Mrs. Robinelli said. "We're going to set off a major change in human history."

A robot opened the doors leading to the terrace. "Dinner will be served in half an hour," it said in Charlie's voice.

Emma and Gershner rose from their chairs and walked toward the door. Peake remained in his seat, looking at Froward. After a moment, Froward noticed him.

"Jeff, before we go, I want to talk to you. We haven't had a chance until now."

"All right."

Peake had some difficulty beginning. "Uh, listen, Jeff, I don't want you to take this wrong."

"I won't."

"Lena and Emma were going to speak to you about it, but I persuaded them to let me do it. It's about you sleeping with the Suarez girl. All the kids know about it by now. Naturally, that couldn't be helped. Emma, Lena, and I want to know what you're going to do about it. It's our business, too, you know."

"I didn't say it wasn't," Froward said.

"I know it's a temptation, and we joked about it and all, but, well, shit, some of those girls have given me some pretty strong hints, too. But, shit, Jeff, how old are they? Fifteen, sixteen? They're kids, Jeff. I was tempted, but I knew I wouldn't have been able to face myself in the cold wet sheets of dawn."

"Facing Emma and Lena wouldn't be easy either," Froward said.

"Emma tells me that every halfway decent-looking male junior high teacher runs into the same problem. Emma and Lena and I have been doing our jobs. You have to do your job, too."

Froward spoke angrily. "Are you sure you've been doing your jobs? Look at the situation we're in! You should've followed Charlie's lead. That was your job, if you ask me!"

"Come on, Jeff, we're not talking about that."

"Why aren't we, as long as we're blaming people for what they did and what they didn't do!"

"Take it easy. No one's blaming anyone. You're dodging the issue."

Froward sighed. "Chela and I thought everyone else was dead."

"Well, yes. That counts in your favor, Jeff."

"That's great. I'm glad something counts in my favor."

Froward was beginning to feel the depression he used to associate with being sober. He hadn't felt that way when he'd been with Chela. That life had been sharp and clear. His and Chela's actions had been dictated by logic and driven by necessity, even if the necessity had sometimes only been an emotional one. "You're talking as though we were all going to catch a plane home tomorrow," he said.

"Yeah, I suppose we are talking that way."

"You picked out your girl yet, Peake?"

Peake stiffened. "I guess I will, when they get a bit older," he said.

"Okay, so you see what I mean," Froward said.

"You're supposed to be seeing what I mean," Peake retorted.

Froward spoke slowly. "I'll spell it out. Chela has been good for me. That girl is what I need. She loves me, I hope. I know I love her. You know, I haven't said anything to anybody about love since I was a kid."

"What's love?" Peake said. "I agree that she's good for you, Jeff. As long as I've known you, I've never seen you looking as well as you do right now. You're positively thriving on Charon. But. Are you good for her? A man your age . . ."

"An old drunk," Froward said. "A failure at everything he's tried."

"Well, yes, since you insist. I'll tell you what's wrong with your relationship—"

"'Relationship,'" Froward said bitterly. "Now, there's an up-to-date expression for you."

"Give me a break, Froward. Listen. I've known you several years. You're a womanizer. Everybody's wives were fair game for you, and you made it look easy. So what? Sometimes I envied you. But there was one thing I alway noticed about you. You never bought any prostitutes, even when we were in places like Manila and Bangkok. Tell me, why didn't you?"

"You didn't either," Froward said.

"No, I didn't. You want to know why? I was following your lead. What I want to know is, why didn't you?"

"What the hell has that got to do with anything?"

"Come on, Jeff, talk to me!"

"Shit," Froward said, but he thought about it for a moment. "It was corrupt," he said, finally. "It was exploitation. Those prostitute girls are forced to live that way, by drugs, force, poverty, whatever. I used to see it in Vietnam. I didn't feel right about it."

"That's what I mean about you," Peake said. "You're a bum, but you're honest. You aren't rotten."

"Maybe I'm too lazy to be corrupt."

"Give me another break. Maybe the girl is good for you, but are you good for her? She's just a kid. You swept her right off her feet. Is she going to get a chance to grow up her own way, while she's involved with you? Is she getting a chance to be her own self? Be honest. What would she think of you if she were thirty-five, and knew anything?"

"She'd think I was a bum."

"There it is," Peake said.

"Okay, okay," Froward said. "I'll think about it."

"Thanks, Jeff," Peake said sincerely. He hesitated, then stood up and left the terrace.

Froward stood up also and started to follow him to the doorway. He halted when Chela ran toward him through the doorway.

She was dressed in clothing from her luggage, jeans and a baggy pink velour shirt that left one round shoulder bare. She had pinned back her mass of black curls with a pair of golden combs. "I didn't think he'd ever go away," she said breathlessly, smiling at him. She reached for his hand and pressed it with both of hers between her breasts. "Guess what? I found a room for us. Charlie said he wouldn't let anyone else have it. It's the one right next to the elevator. You can——"

She stopped, seeing the expression on his face. The dark sparkle left her eyes. "They've been talking to you, haven't they?"

"Yes——"

He was interrupted by whispering overhead. A group of girls were watching them from an upper window. Chela glared up at them. The faces disappeared. She was hard and determined when she turned back to Froward, as she'd been when she was nursing him in the dry riverbed.

"I'd like to see the day when a couple of dried-up old biddies could tell me what to do," she said.

"They aren't altogether wrong, Chela. Maybe if——"

"Your mom is altogether wrong," Chela said. "And so are you." She reached up and grabbed the front of his overalls, dragged his face down to hers, and kissed him wetly on the mouth. Cloth ripped and a button fell off. She shoved him back upright.

"I love you. You love me. Everything else is shit." She rapped it out, adult and businesslike. She marched off the terrace, leaving him standing there with nothing left to do but go to dinner.

Charlie's Thanksgiving banquet substituted quantity for quality, although there were a few new spices and sauces available, devised by Charlie's chef programs. After soup and salad, Charlie proudly led a procession of flunkies carrying a "turkey" the size of a Great Dane. Froward could see him concentrating, almost sleepwalking, in the effort it took to animate all the robots at once.

Instead of the applause Charlie expected, laughter, moans, and catcalls echoed through the banquet hall. "Eeeyou, look at that! Ugh! Totally bizarre! I can't eat tha-aat!"

Charlie stopped in mid-flourish, holding his carving knife and

CHARON'S ARK

373

fork in the air. "What the hell's the matter now!" he shouted angrily.

Gwynnis stood up and pointed at the centerpieces. "Gross me out! It's got hands on it!"

Charlie looked down at his culinary triumph. "Of course it's got hands," he shouted. "It's a fugging dinosaur!"

Mrs. Robinelli stood up, holding her plate. "It smells delicious. I'm hungry. We're serving buffet style, everyone, so help yourself!"

Colby Dennison followed her to the serving table and accepted a slice of dinosaur with palm-cabbage stuffing. Froward, Peake, and Gershner were right behind. Hunger forced the others to join them after a moment.

When the feast was over, Peake and Froward asked Charlie to give them a tour of the palace and the known part of its underground works. The real purpose of the tour was to get Charlie out of the way so Mrs. Robinelli could lecture the students about what they owed the boy. It took hours to see everything. When they arrived back at the rooftop terrace, it was long past the usual bedtime. The palace was silent. Only a few lights appeared in the windows above.

The two men had been amazed and fascinated by what Charlie had shown them, and they hadn't concealed their feelings. Despite this, Charlie was still annoyed at his fellow students. "So I forgot about the hands. I did remember to cut off the neck and tail! So it didn't look exactly like a turkey! It still tasted the same!"

"The average person," Peake said consolingly, "only cares about what a thing looks like, not what it really is."

"That's the truth," Froward said. "I have that problem with people myself." Peake glared at him over the boy's head.

"You're not an average person, Charlie," Peake continued. "Besides, they were mostly kidding you."

"It was a hypsilophodon," the boy muttered. "It wasn't easy to get."

"I thought it was great," Froward said honestly.

"Everybody liked it, once they tried it," Peake said.

"Even after I saved their lives, they still don't appreciate it,"

Charlie said. "You'd think that somebody would just thank me or something."

"They will," Peake said. "Also, you'll be vindicated by history. Centuries from now, kids in high school will be forced to read about you, how you saved the world and opened contact with the great interstellar whatzit. Just think how grateful they'll be when they get a bad grade for spelling your name wrong on exams."

"Yeah," Charlie said, smiling. He stopped at the edge of the roof and looked out over the parapet. He yawned unaffectedly, like a sleepy child. Overhead, the clouds were parting. In the violet sky the bright star gleamed steadily, its accompanying sparks vaguely yellow, orange, and blue. "You can see the whole solar system from here," Charlie said. "That's probably Jupiter, Mars, and Earth."

Froward saw the boy's innocent face, raised to look at the sky.

"You know what?" Charlie said.

"What, Charlie?"

"Centuries from now, when people are learning about me in school?"

"Yeah?"

"I'll still be around. I'll make sure they spell my name right." He yawned again. "I guess I'll go in now. See you tomorrow."

"Good night, Charlie."

The boy shambled across the terrace and disappeared inside. Froward and Peake followed him after a moment. Upstairs, they found Emma and Gershner sitting in the medieval gallery. "I kept your flight bag for you, Jeff," Lena said. "Your pajamas, toothbrush, and other things are still inside."

Froward thanked her and accepted the bag. He stood for a moment, wishing he had a drink and a cigarette. He glanced down the corridor at Chela's door. A light showed under it. He looked back, thinking the others were watching him. But they hadn't noticed him at all.

Emma stood up slowly. "I've had enough for one day," she said. She looked gray and exhausted in the bright light coming from the chandeliers. Gershner rose and went to her. A bandage showed under Gershner's sleeve, and Froward noticed for the first time that the hair on one side of her head was scorched.

Peake saw what Froward was looking at. His grin emphasized the hairline scars on his face. "We're all of us somewhat the worse for wear, aren't we?"

Emma, Gershner, and Peake smiled at each other, a band of survivors, happy to be alive and together.

Froward sighed. "Where do we sleep?" he asked.

ABOUT THE AUTHOR

Charon's Ark is Rick Gauger's first novel. He is also the author of the *Suarez* series of science-fiction stories, as well as magazine articles, Dungeons & Dragons games, and computer programs for a computer that is no longer manufactured.

After wandering from Florida to Washington, D.C., to Montana, Gauger settled in the ruins of Bellingham, Washington, the town that was destroyed by the launching of the space battleship in the novel *Footfall*, by Niven and Pournelle. There he sails, skis, and keeps house with Denise Brennan, a well-known attorney who wanted to be mentioned here, and his daughter Elizabeth, who was born in 1984 and is proof that all good things come to him who waits.